THE PRICE OF INFAMY

THE BAD BOYS OF WALL STREET

EMBER LEIGH

Published by Ember Leigh, 2023

EmberLeighAuthor@gmail.com

Cover Model: Gil

Photographer: Wander Aguiar

Cover art: Covers by Combs

Editing: Elisabeth R. Nelson

CONTENTS

CHAPTER ONE
TRACE

"Oh my lord—she's taking her diaper off again."

My mother's exclamation—the third time in the past hour—sent me racing back into the living room. The luxury apartment I'd moved into four days ago stretched out in front of me, still a sight I hadn't quite gotten used to. Hell, I hadn't gotten used to any part of this whole situation.

Not only was I in Kentucky indefinitely, I had a year lease on an apartment in Louisville.

And the little girl I was suddenly responsible for?

Yeah, I really hadn't gotten used to that one either.

"Did she pee or anything?" I asked as I darted over to help my mom. She swatted me away as I tried to bring a new diaper her way. I'd gone from playboy bachelor to custodial guardian in the blink of an eye. Four days ago, I didn't know how to change a diaper.

Now I knew about nighttime protection and why the good diapers mattered.

"She's just uncomfortable, I guess."

Willow's little stink face as she looked up at me and my mom from the play pad in the living room made me snort with laughter. She grinned devilishly and then lifted her little dress and tore at the diaper again.

"Okay, see, you need to leave that *on*," I told Willow.

She shrieked something unintelligible and stomped away, toward a corner of toys my mother and I had quickly assembled in the day before Willow's arrival. Everything had been a disorienting whirlwind since taking sole custody of Willow—the niece I never knew I had, until my surprise half-brother went to jail and left her in my care.

Personally, I didn't think that a single businessman in Manhattan was the top choice for taking custody of a two-year-old. But if I was the best option, I sure as hell didn't want to know who my competition was.

"I think she's doing better," my mom said, watching as Willow tucked herself behind the Fisher Price food truck and crossed her arms, staring out at us through the serving window.

"Yeah," I said, not at all agreeing. These first few days had been *rough*. But then again, my entire existence had been rough for approximately the last seven months, so something like this just seemed normal now. One more exciting addition to the shit pile that my life had become.

"Willow, do you want some lunch?" my mom asked in that sweet grandma voice. I loved that she was here, offering to help in these vulnerable early days. She probably knew I had zero idea what to do with a two-year-old. More than that, she knew that her sons were in a special sort of...*helpless disintegration*. There were endless ways to describe the ramifications of having an active investigation launched by the Securities and Exchange Commission tearing apart the business I helped build from the ground up. And believe me, I'd been using every synonym available over the past seven months, trying not to let the despair and the anxiety burrow to my bone marrow.

But I had to keep my chin up and my shoulders back, all that positive bullshit people said when they weren't facing the possibility of a ten-year prison sentence and the complete destruction of their business venture and livelihood.

"What about a...bologna sandwich?" I offered, heading to the kitchen. I'd rented this place furnished, so all the kitchen essentials were ready and waiting for me upon move-in. All I had to do was supply the food and copious amounts of alcohol needed to survive my new reality.

I stared into the fridge. What the fuck did two-year-olds eat? This was only the fifth entry on my list of questions that could unfurl to create a miles-long scroll. A week ago, I had been ordering oysters on the half-shell for a pretty girl I wanted to impress at a swanky bar. Now I had a fridge stocked full of basic lunch meats that I personally hadn't eaten since I was a child myself.

My, how things could change.

Willow didn't answer. She didn't even react. She just kept her arms crossed over her chest and frowned at my mom.

"I'll make her a sandwich anyway, just in case," I announced, pulling out the ingredients. I couldn't help feeling like this whole arrangement could have been made even slightly easier if Ian, my half-brother, could have provided me with *any* details or tips about suddenly raising his daughter.

But he wasn't available. He was in jail awaiting trial for drug smuggling charges. Not exactly the family reunion I would have envisioned, but hey. My brief interactions with Ian back in New York had been guarded at best—he'd never let me in on what he was really doing or why. But the drug charges illuminated everything, and it turned out he'd been scaling up to larger clients in the area. As Willow's custodial parent, he found it fitting to hand her over to me once he was taken to jail. Apparently her mother was MIA or possibly wildly unfit—or both.

"Willow, we should play with some dolls. What do you think?" My mom's sweet, approachable demeanor never wavered. And she deserved a thousand blessings for it.

Willow was my father's granddaughter, but not my mother's.

Dad had kept his affair from my mom for twenty-four years. Short as it had been, its consequences seemed to go on to eternity.

Family drama: the gift that keeps on giving.

Personally, I'd had about e-fucking-nough.

Knock knock knock. The sudden banging at the door reminded me to check the time—eleven thirty. The social worker was right on time. I plated the plain bologna sandwich, passed it to my mom, and then hurried to open the door. An older lady with a tired smile looked in.

"Hello. You must be Trace Fairchild." She offered a hand, eyes crinkling behind wire-rimmed glasses. "I'm Bev with social services. I wanted to check in on little Willow and see how she's doing."

"Absolutely. Please, come in." I stepped aside, gesturing for Bev to come inside. She stepped carefully—noiselessly—and her head bobbed as she looked all around, taking in the apartment.

"This is a lovely place," she murmured, bringing out her clipboard to scribble some notes.

"Thank you. We're still settling in, but this is home for now." I headed for Willow, gesturing to my mother. "Bev, meet Deb, my mother. She's been helping out as we...adjust." I laughed, though I wasn't sure who it was a bigger adjustment for—me or Willow.

"Pleasure to meet you." Bev sent the same mild smile to my mother, and then bent down to peer at Willow through the serving window of the food truck. "And you, little miss? How are you?"

Willow grunted and crossed her arms. Bev nodded as I sighed.

"We've been getting a lot of that lately," I admitted.

"I'm not surprised. For her age, it's expected. Don't take it personally. Just keep trying." Bev offered me another crinkle-eyed smile. She asked for a place where we could chat, so I led her to the two-story great room with big windows overlooking downtown Louisville. A gray-brick fireplace stretched to the ceiling. As we sat down, I flicked on the remote that lit the fire. She smiled at me.

"You seem like you have things taken care of here."

"Do I? I feel pretty lost," I admitted. That might not have been the best thing to admit to a government worker who controlled whether I was fit to care for a child, and I hurried to add, "I'm making it through. But this is all new to me. I'm the CFO of a wealth management company. I'm not...a dad."

"I understand completely. It's a big shock, especially if you weren't already in her life."

"I wasn't. I only recently met my brother. He's my half-brother, actually, and I..." My gaze swept back to my mother. Her mouth had thinned, though she focused on breaking apart the bologna sandwich. The topic of my father's *other family* was still raw for her. It was still raw for all of us. Ian had only popped into our lives a few months ago when he surprised Axel, Damian, and me at our office in Manhattan, claiming to be my brother. A little investigation proved the worst: he *was* my half-brother, which proved my father had maintained a secret family for years, though he was only involved with Ian's mother romantically for a short time. Now my parents were divorcing, Ian was in jail, and suddenly I had his daughter—my niece—in my care.

Pretty much every day of my life contained a solid WTF moment.

"Regardless, you're doing as well as you can," Bev said in a reassuring tone. I'm sure she would have patted my knee if she weren't a government official. She guided me through a list of questions that she'd brought, occasionally scratching something on her sheet or nodding for a few moments before continuing. Willow stayed in her hiding spot behind the food truck the entire time. Eventually, Mom gave up on the bologna sandwich and went to tidy the kitchen. Not like it needed tidied. This place was still sparkling from move-in day, and besides, I wasn't an anal-retentive executive for nothing. I couldn't go to sleep at night with dishes in the sink.

Bev eventually went back to trying to talk to Willow, asking her questions to no avail. Finally, she stood up, looked around the place, and nodded.

"So you plan to stay here long-term?"

"As long as I need to. My lawyer has told me it may take some time to finalize the custodial details, and I'll do whatever the courts require." I'd hired a lawyer almost immediately after getting the call from Kentucky Children's Services back in New York, and she'd advised me to set up a residence here until things were settled with Willow. That included figuring out long-term custody arrangements based on what happened with Ian's charges...and what back-up plans could be depending on whether or not the SEC filed charges against *me*, as well. Depending on how all that went down, Louisville could become 'home' for a long while. Now that my brothers and I were so unstable, I had half a mind to never return to New York City. Having a Louisville outpost just made sense right now. It was my place to let the dust settle and figure out my next steps.

She smiled warmly. "Any questions for me?"

How the fuck am I supposed to make it through my days if I might go to prison and Willow won't eat the bologna sandwich?

"No." I crossed my arms, pretending to think. Only more unhelpful questions sprouted inside my head. "I'll be going back to work soon, so I'll need to figure out what to do there."

"Ah, yes. Babysitter references." Bev flipped through the pages of her clipboard and presented me with a sheet. "Actually, skip all the names on here and go straight to the last one. It's a private nanny agency—the best of the best in Louisville. You look like you can afford it." She sent me a wink before she headed for the door.

"Thank you." I skimmed over the entries, finding the agency she'd referenced. Bev waved to Mom and said her goodbyes before letting herself out. The door snicked shut behind her.

"Well that was painless," my mom commented as she came around the kitchen island. She reached for the sheet. "You plan on hiring one of her recommendations?"

"I don't see much choice. I need to get back to work ASAP, and I don't plan on asking you to become Willow's full-time grandma."

My mom sent me a look, her lips pursed. "Trace, you know I would."

"I know you'd do anything for me." I wrapped my arm around her in a side hug. "And I appreciate that. But I'm not trying to capsize your life just because I got dealt this hand. It's my responsibility. I'll handle it." Besides, I didn't want to make my mom grapple with even more than she had on her plate recently. Finding out about her husband's infidelity beginning twenty-five years ago was one thing. Now all her kids were waiting to find out if they were going to prison for financial fraud. We were more fun than a barrel of fucking monkeys.

She drew a deep breath and nodded, a few gray wisps escaping her thick braid down her back. "You're right. You will. There's nobody better for this than you, Trace."

"Aw, come on. Not even Damian or Axel?"

She snorted. "I stand by what I said."

We smiled at each other as I headed back over to Willow.

"All right, Willow. What about some screen time? I know that motivates the youth. If you have four bites of bologna, I'll give you ten minutes of Peppa Pig."

She frowned up at me and didn't budge. What a negotiator. I needed to work on my skills.

"Okay. Twenty minutes of Peppa Pig."

Her hand shot out in the direction of my mom in the kitchen, which I took to mean *give me the damn plate*. My mom's brows rose as she brought the plate over. I smirked, satisfied, as though I had any clue what I was doing.

"Maybe I have a shot at this dad thing for real," I told my mom as Willow took a tentative bite of her sandwich. I made my way to the flat screen TV near the fireplace, grabbing the remote.

"I always thought you'd make a great daddy. Your brothers too." She sighed wearily, coming down to her knees in front of the food truck as Willow nibbled at her sandwich. "Just didn't imagine things playing out quite like this."

That was the understatement of the century. Willow wasn't the only thing I hadn't envisioned playing out like this. I never expected to be back in this city after I left the last time six years ago. Back then, I'd been traveling from New York every other week courting a big-ticket client who turned into a grade A nightmare. But during all those visits, I'd fallen for his niece. Hook line and sinker. I'd been a breath away from asking her to marry me.

Until she told me to fuck off, that was.

I supposed these unpleasant flashbacks from my former life in Louisville were par for the course here. That meant I had no time to waste in writing a different reality. One that included no vestige of the former failure of my past. Time to get my present and future on track. I wasn't about to combine new parenthood with remote work investing millions of dollars an hour. At least not *yet*.

I picked up the babysitter listing again and found the number for Aurora's Nannies.

"All right. Let's see what Aurora's got for me." I dialed the number. Willow took one last bite of her sandwich and then scampered over to the couch, looking up at me expectantly. Her little face looked gaunt, like the type of face you'd expect to see peeking through a grimy window in a Charles Dickens novel. Not at all the pudgy cherub face plastered in diaper ads, which I received too many of now that my smartphone knew a toddler was in my life. I deflated a little. What had this girl lived through until now?

"Aurora's Nannies, how can we serve you?" The chipper, feminine voice on the other end of the phone snapped me back to reality. I cleared my throat.

"My name is Trace Fairchild. I'm looking for a nanny for my..." I blinked, looking at Willow. "...daughter. It's urgent. I'm new to the area and I'd need a nanny as soon as tomorrow, if you can accommodate."

The woman on the other end cooed, and then said, "Why, of course we can accommodate you hare at Aurora's. Would you be able to come to the office? That would expedite the process for sure. We can get your paperwork filled out, look at available nannies, and make our selection today."

Relief trickled through me. "Excellent. I'll be there within a half hour."

At least there was still one person in the world happy to hear from Trace Fairchild. After everything my brothers and I had been through over the past seven months, sometimes it seemed like the entire world was against us. The active SEC investigation sure didn't help the ole reputation, especially since the Fairchild brothers had been media darlings *before* the investigation was launched. Now, our names were splattered everywhere, all the time. Less of the celebrity gossip splatter and more of the rotten egg on the front door splatter.

"Mom, could you sit with Willow until I get back? I'm going to head to the nanny agency and see what I can set up." I headed to the back of the couch where she sat beside Willow, both of them seemingly entranced by the pig-like cartoon character whose head looked suspiciously like a dick and balls.

"Of course, dear." She reached up to pat my hand, not looking away from the cartoon. "I'll finish making my list of things you need, too. I remembered the newest one—those doorknob covers, so kids can't escape. Course, it makes it pretty hard for adults too, but we should be able to figure it out."

I smiled, squeezing her shoulder. "Thanks, Mom. For everything." I meant those words more than I could properly convey. "You don't have to be doing all this. I mean...I understand if it becomes too much."

"What, helping take care of my ex's secret granddaughter?" She laughed bitterly. "Life never goes as planned, Trace baby. Remember that. Even when you do everything right."

I mulled her words over as I let myself out of the apartment and headed for the underground parking garage. They were both a mantra and a wound. I lived my life striving to do everything right. Not just right, but *perfectly*. And how was I rewarded?

An estranged brother. An active SEC investigation for fraud. A fractured—crumbling—empire.

There had to be some way to turn this ship around, but I couldn't for the life of me figure out what the fuck it was.

I slipped into my Kentucky car—my S-Class Mercedes Benz, fully loaded—and crept toward the exit of the underground parking garage, my blinker ticking. Louisville still felt so familiar, despite the new development and hipster vibe that hadn't existed when I left town. I'd done my best to become a Louisville fixture as I courted Tatum Hendricks, which meant nearly every building I passed I'd visited at least once. As I cruised through town toward the agency, I spotted even more familiar sights, and nearly all of them were places Mercedes and I had frequented or loved six years ago.

Mercedes. Where are you now?

I tamped the thoughts before they could spiral. All that mattered now was making it through each day. Six years ago, I'd been on the brink of asking Mercedes Henricks to marry me. After the way she'd brutally blown me off, you'd think I'd be well on my way to never wondering about her again. In fact, at thirty-two years old, it was embarrassing to admit that I still wondered about an ex at all, especially when I'd had so many other women to distract me. So I told no one. I barely admitted it to myself.

I didn't know how many women it would take to fully erase Mercedes from my mind, but whatever number I was at wasn't enough.

It's for the best. She'd been too young then. If you'd married at age twenty-seven, everything after would have been different.

My usual rationalizations hit differently back at ground zero. I let myself toy with the memory of Mercedes just a moment longer but vowed to push all thoughts of her out of my mind for good once I eased into the parking lot of Aurora's nannies. The one-story building was a real-life version of a cutesy cartoon home, with rectangular raised beds and carefully placed paver stones leading to the front door.

I pushed into the reception area, where two women immediately smiled at me.

"Trace Fairchild." The taller brunette swept toward me, a big grin on her face. I recognized her voice from the phone. "I am so pleased to finally meet you. I'm Denise."

I shook her hand and returned the greeting, quickly taking stock of the sparse, trendy interior design. The receptionist watched me with shy curiosity. I nodded her way as Denise, the lead placement coordinator, led me back to her office.

"Let me just reiterate how much of an honor it is to have someone like you consider working with Aurora's Nannies. I follow your charitable endeavors. I'm not sure there's anyone who's done more for supporting children in need than you," Denise said in a smooth voice as she settled behind a large wooden desk. I took a seat in front of her as she turned her computer screen so that we could both see.

"Why, thank you. That's touching." And it was, given how much discord I'd felt recently.

"Let's get down to business. Here at Aurora's, we value transparency and high-level communication," she explained as she clicked through screens. "I want to be available to you at every step of the way. Even once you receive your placement—if there's ever anything you don't like, or any questions you might have—I'm your go-to."

Denise's flashy grin was typical for VIP, bend-over-backward service. I was used to it in Manhattan. For the right price, people would do nearly anything you asked of them. But I had no intention of abusing my status. I'd blazed through that phase after we made our first five hundred million. I just wanted a damn nanny and some internal peace and quiet. Hopefully finding the former would provide me with the latter.

"I appreciate that."

"So tell us a little bit more about what you're looking for." Denise leaned forward, her attention settling squarely on me.

"Well, Willow has been...a bit difficult recently." I didn't know how else to describe it. And honestly, I didn't want to get into the clusterfuck of my family situation right now. It was easier to pretend she was my daughter than to rehash why I was in this position or what had preceded it. "She's a little anxious around new people but has severe anxiety with unexpected visitors. I think we need someone a bit more adept at...special cases."

Denise nodded, tapping at her chin. "We have a few available nannies right now that fit the bill," she explained with a conspiratorial grin, pulling up a roster of head shots on the computer screen. Each nanny had a quick summary below her portrait. "You get the final call, but I'll give you a full rundown of each girl and her particular strengths and weaknesses."

"As long as she knows more about kids than I do," I told her. "And my knowledge is pretty much the bare minimum."

Denise's tinkling laughter floated through the room. "Oh, Mr. Fairchild. We'll be providing much more than that." She pulled up the first portfolio—a nanny named Yvonne. Equestrian history. Came from a large family. Trilingual. Then there was Tracy. Bilingual. Skilled in art. Certified to homeschool through sixth grade.

And then there was Mercedes.

Long, blonde hair with highlights that sparkled in the sun like spun gold. Green eyes I'd never forgotten—couldn't forget if I tried. Excellent with special needs children and histories involving trauma. Denise's summary didn't mention *the woman who cut you off six years ago and took the biggest piece of your heart with her.*

"She—" I started, but my voice failed. I wasn't sure I even had it anymore, because I suspected my bottoming-out stomach had yanked it from my throat on its way to my feet.

"Mercedes is an *excellent* choice. She's who I would have recommended myself," Denise purred, pulling out her phone to check something. Then she looked up at me with excitement on her face, lips pursed together like she was dying to spill a secret.

"She just came back from an assignment. So you can meet her now if you'd like."

CHAPTER TWO
MERCEDES

T HE AIR WAS DIFFERENT inside Aurora's Nanny Agency when I stepped inside.

I'd stepped into this building countless times in my year of work here. It was a hard-won position, so I counted my blessings every time I set foot in the building to seek out my cubicle and catch up on paperwork related to my short-term assignments.

"Mercedes, you're just in time for some excitement today!" The receptionist, Bethany, pinned me with a knowing smile as I glided through the reception area. My brows shot up—maybe this was why the air felt different. Taut. Somehow vibrating.

I didn't know how I felt it. I just did. The same way the air changed before a tornado, I supposed.

"What's happening?" I paused at the desk, hitching my tote bag higher on my shoulder. I relished any chance to linger at work. Working with children was the goal, but getting closer to my coworkers was an unexpected benefit of the job.

Getting out of my house in general was the most delicious icing on the cake.

"There's a big-ticket VIP client in the building." She enunciated each syllable with exaggerated mouth movements. I almost wanted her to repeat herself so I could see it again.

"Anyone I should ask for an autograph?" I asked. I'd met plenty of celebrities throughout my life, so I didn't truly think I'd be impressed. With a father as wealthy and connected as mine, VIPs were sort of the background fixture to my childhood. I'd met pretty much every conservative senator out there, not to mention a few movie stars who happened to be married to people in our circle.

Before Bethany could respond, Denise slipped out of her office. Her eyes lit up when she saw me. "Mercedes!" She hurried my way, her heels clicking on the tile floor. "There you are. I was just coming out to look for you. Do you have time for a chat?"

I sent a smile to Bethany and followed Denise down the hallway. She led me to my cubicle in the large back room, her eyes half-mooned with excitement as I set down my things.

"I have a very exciting opportunity I wanted to extend to you personally," she said.

"Ooh, please continue." I tucked some of my blonde hair behind my ear, the flutters of excitement in my belly reminding me just how much I loved being here. How much I loved being *challenged*. It still grated on me that my entire family wanted me to give this feeling up, to just abandon this line of work. To walk away from the fulfillment of it all.

It didn't even matter that this job wasn't even my end goal. This job was just the *compromise*. And I still felt guilty for grabbing it.

"The client I have in the office right now is VIP-level and looking for a full-time nanny placement. He's got a two-year-old girl who requires some extra love and attention. We're talking single father situation, high-powered businessman. I know you've been doing mostly part-time placements, but...do you think you could swing a full-time placement?"

I swallowed hard, trying not to burst out with a shouted "Of course!" I needed to at least *pretend* to consider it. "Well…my current placement is over, so I think the timing should work out."

Denise nodded effusively. "I was thinking the same."

"And I would really love to take a full-time client." Even though that was the *absolute last* thing my family wanted for me. But not all secrecy was meant to deceive. I was twenty-five years old and already at a crossroads in my life. Every member of my family and social circle pulled on one arm. This burgeoning career—and the promise of carving out my own future—was the tug on the other arm. I had to *try*. Even if my pre-carved life path careened in a different direction.

"I say let's give it a shot," I told her. "If you think I'm the best nanny for the job, I'm willing to take it on."

"Mercedes, you're going to *love* this client. Let's go meet him now." Denise squeezed my wrist and we headed for her office. On the way there, she called out over her shoulder, "His name is Trace Fairchild."

The name shuddered through me in the same way a bullet enters a thigh. I actually stumbled, and Denise looked back at me sharply.

"Are you okay?"

I drew a deep breath, popping on a bright grin. I couldn't let her know the black hole that had suddenly erupted in my gut, threatening to consume all my vital organs with its deathly gravitational pull. I couldn't tell her that Trace and I had a history—one that nearly broke me, until the clearly defined grooves of my family's life path enabled me to move again.

"Fine! Just fine! I, uh, tripped on the rug." I amped up the smile, certain it was nearing psychotic-grade. *Good Lord above, Trace Fairchild is in that office, and I am going to lay eyes on him for the first time in six years.*

Trace Fairchild had been both my ultimate fantasy and downfall. I'd fallen for him too fast, too hard. We'd connected instantly, in the way that grandparents always talk about after sixty years of marriage. We'd had a whirlwind romance, composed entirely of belly laughter, white-hot passion, and adventures around Louisville that made it hard to go almost anywhere or do anything for a year after things ended.

Because they didn't just end. They shattered.

My entire body vibrated with anxiety, each step closer to Denise's office feeling like a full mile. Denise reached for the doorknob. The door creaked once and then she stepped inside the office. *Thump-thump.* My heart pounded so loudly I knew that Denise could hear it.

"Mr. Fairchild, I'd love for you to meet Mercedes Hendricks." I glided through the threshold just as she said my last name.

And there he was. Filling the barrel chair facing Denise's desk, his square shoulders and immaculate Armani suit the perfect complement to the devastatingly neutral expression he wore on his handsome face. His dark tresses were tousled just the perfect amount, the exact middle ground between Ken doll and disheveled. I felt the moment his dark brown gaze alighted on me. Could almost hear the *crrrrack* as the axis my world turned on began to crumble.

"Mercedes, meet Trace Fairchild." Denise sounded so pleased with herself, her thousand-watt smile nearly blinding me as she stepped aside so I could shake Trace's hand.

I had no idea what my face was doing as I surged forward with my hand extended; I couldn't even recall my name as his big hand gripped mine. The heat from his grip activated every physical sensation I'd ever shared with him, stored inside my cells like ancestral memories. My entire body went hot, alive, buzzing. I swallowed hard, jerking my hand back and focused on breathing. *In. Out. In. Out.*

"Mercedes is absolutely the top pick for the job," Denise said, seemingly unaware of the way my soul was being sucked into the black hole vortex that the sound of Trace Fairchild's name had opened up inside me. Seeing him had doubled its pull. She slid into her desk chair, and I took a seat in a chair closer to the wall that faced both of them.

"She's the most recent addition to the staff but has fast become a favorite here at the agency," Denise said with a wink my way. "Any issues you might be having with Willow right now Mercedes can help with."

Willow. His daughter's name. I couldn't believe I was in the same room as Trace Fairchild, much less to discuss his *daughter.* The fact that he was a single father was news to me. I hadn't kept up with Trace's business out of self-preservation. My love for Trace had burned too brightly; if I'd given it even an inch after he'd ghosted me, I'd have never moved on. Especially given what our love had created together.

But maybe the heat vibrating through my body was proof that I never really had moved on.

Trace cleared his throat. "That's very reassuring." His voice was a gritty rumble as he spoke, which only sent my insides clenching and my heart racing.

"Ages two to four is her area of expertise," Denise went on, looking at me like I should add something.

"Yes," I blurted, "My favorite range. Of age. Uh, developmentally it's...fascinating." I wasn't sure if I was making sense. I could barely see past the throb of my heart.

"Now, Mr. Fairchild, can we go over some of the issues you've been having?" Denise prompted him to elaborate on the exact nature of Willow's struggles. They included anxiety around new people, trouble sleeping through the night, a seeming phobia of doors opening. I had tricks in my toolbelt to help every scenario—and backup tricks behind those.

Something about innocent and mischievous toddlers activated my most soothing, most helpful mode. Especially the ones who were determined to act out. That, and they were truly the most hilarious, most loving creatures on the planet. Professional challenge combined with personal fulfillment? Yes, please.

"I'm confident I can help with anything that might present an issue," I said, smoothing down my skirt as my cheeks flushed intensely. I wasn't sure why until I glanced up and noticed Trace's gaze sizzling on me like a slap to the cheek. "Toddlers are a challenging, hilarious, loveable gift from God."

Denise laughed softly. Trace didn't even blink.

"Do you have any questions for me or Mercedes?" Denise purred.

Trace cleared his throat, his jaw flexing as he studied something unknowable on Denise's desk. He shook his head *no*.

"Great. Well how about we set up an in-home meet-and-greet?" Denise cast a bright smile between Trace and me.

"I'd love that," I blurted.

Trace's gaze slid between Denise and me in a calculated way. Then it landed—and stayed—on Denise. "Do you have anyone with a bit more...experience?"

Denise blinked. "In what way, Mr. Fairchild?"

"I'm not sure about pulling the trigger quite yet. I'd prefer to work with someone with more of a...longstanding track record."

Disappointment shuddered through me, and I tried not to show it. I straightened my back instead. It didn't just hurt because he doubted my skills with his daughter—it hurt because he was rejecting me based on what had happened between us six years ago. The reason he ran from me, left me behind.

And I was still the only fool between us who didn't know what that reason was.

"I assure you, Mr. Fairchild," Denise barreled on, oblivious to Trace's *real* discomfort with my placement. "The fact that Mercedes is a newer hire does not work against her. Maybe I didn't explain fully—she's worked with us for over a year now. I've witnessed her prowess firsthand, and my only regret is that she didn't join us sooner."

I smiled over at Denise. "That's so sweet of you. I feel the same." I steeled myself to address Trace head on, forcing the wave of nausea rising from my stomach to stay out of my throat. A placement with Trace Fairchild was a horrible idea. I should have been *glad* that he didn't want to hire me. Caring for his daughter would be a ballistic missile in the center of my carefully crafted life.

The painstaking reassembly I underwent after Trace blew into and out of my life the first time around took me years to complete. I didn't have years to waste. Our six months together—semi-long distance, punctuated by intense bursts of one or two weeks at a time when we acted like a married couple—were the emotional equivalent of two years.

Trace didn't look convinced. "I need someone who is adaptable. Transparent. Comfortable with frequent, long-distance travel, usually on private jet. I maintain a high-stress work environment; hours may need to be extended at last-minute." He rubbed at his knuckles as he spoke, sounding casual, almost off-hand. But when his gaze snapped up to mine, it was anything but. The intensity there shook me to my core. He'd fired a warning shot so loud that every cell inside me understood the message.

He'd been my dream man in every sense of the word—tall, dark, and handsome, with a humility that contrasted well with his jet-setting lifestyle, not to mention the loyalty to his cause and his brothers that I admired so much it made my chest hurt. Our six months together had affected me so much I'd even switched majors in college to what I *actually* wanted to study—child psychology—until my family convinced me to switch it back to English a year after Trace left. It wasn't that I didn't want to study English—I loved all things literature and the spoken word—but what I *really* wanted to do was help children in a clinical setting. My parents' logic was that an English degree would better serve me in service to my family—volunteering at the church, tutoring children on the side, eventually homeschooling my children. Child psychology was all well and good, they reasoned, but it was structured to pursue a career—which I wasn't going to do, right?

My gaze fell to the ring on my middle finger. A promise ring of sorts, given to me by my boyfriend Caleb. We'd been family friends for years; it was only natural it turned into more. That's how those things worked. Safe, predictable paths that kept the family unity—and family future—stable and didn't result in ballistic missile-inspired shards buried in your heart.

If the reappearance of Trace Fairchild was some sort of a cosmic joke, then God needed to learn a thing or two about comedic timing.

He was six years too late.

"Furthermore, with my schedule and my life in general, I don't have time for waffling, passivity, or shrouded communication."

Trace cleared his throat, his gaze sliding back to Denise. "These are my only requirements."

Denise opened her mouth to respond, but I jumped in first. "Let it be known, without any ounce of waffling, that I am actively and openly committed to the health and safety of any child in my care. There's nothing shrouded or passive about it. That, you can count on."

Trace didn't appear moved by my declaration. Denise, on the other hand, looked ready to melt into the carpet of her office. It wasn't customary for potential clients to behave like Trace. Most were gracious, soft, inquisitive. Trace acted more like a brick wall with lips.

Extremely gorgeous lips that had once kissed their way across every square inch of my body. Lips that used to call me Birdie with the same softness that I'd used when I called him Bear.

Lips that would never be in the same room as me again, based on how this meet-and-greet was unfolding. Because there was no way in heck I was getting this placement.

"Thank you, Mercedes. Mr. Fairchild and I will continue our meeting. I'll let you know if we need anything else from you." She sent me a warm smile—strained but genuine—and I nodded and rose.

"It was a pleasure meeting you, Mr. Fairchild," I said, trying not to mumble the words. "Your daughter will be lucky to have any of the nannies on staff here."

I stepped out of the office, my heart pounding so hard the smart watch on my left wrist lit up to congratulate me on my sudden exertion. But this was no aerobic exercise, no intent to keep my waistline trim.

This was good old-fashioned anxiety.

I paced the hallway for a few moments, running through the conversation in my head at least fifty times. Whatever he thought I'd done to him was bad, if *that* was how our first encounter in six years went. Trace was probably disappointed in me, if he even cared enough to be disappointed. I'd taken all that guidance and inspiration from him and just let it wither into dust. Instead of being a children's psychologist, I was a part-time nanny en route to being a full-time wife, guarding this job with all I had until the velocity of my expected life path ripped even this from me.

Maybe that was why he was so sour now. I needed to reject the position. But there was no way in Heck Trace Fairchild would select me in the first place, based on how frigid he'd been, how clear it was that he detested me.

It was in my best interest to continue onward with my life as it was. Part-time nanny. Full-time daughter, and most likely full time wife-to-be soon, once Caleb popped the question I knew, without a doubt, would be coming soon.

The way my parents had been dropping hints about quitting this job made me think the question wasn't just around the corner, it was pulling into the dang driveway.

And if all that wasn't enough—if, in some alternate universe, Trace Fairchild actually wanted me to work with him, *and* I accepted—my family would never allow it while I lived under their roof.

Everything about this situation had *RUN* written all over it.

Denise's door opened, the undertones of continued conversation drifting out. I darted into the office area and hid behind the wall, my watch lighting up again: *Good job on the afternoon exercise!* Stress pacing, the newest way to reach a goal weight.

Denise's laughter floated down the hall, followed by the amused rumble from Trace. Their voices grew more distant until I sensed the opening and closing of the front door. I listened so intently that I jumped when I heard Denise's heels clicking down the hallway again. I tried to look busy and engrossed at my desk, praying that Denise couldn't somehow feel the way my heart pounded as if I'd just finished a spin workout.

"Mercedes?"

I turned so quickly my phone flew out of my hand. I twisted to get it, my cheeks flushing in the process. "Yes?"

"That was one of the more invigorating meet-and-greets I've had recently," she said with a small laugh. The way she fanned herself told me Trace Fairchild hit her in exactly the same way he hit me. Even though I wished he didn't.

"He seemed...determined," I said, which didn't even encompass a third of the things I felt about seeing him again.

"He's certainly a driven man, used to negotiations of a different sort, it seems." Denise's lips quirked into a secretive smile. "But despite how it may seem...he *is* interested in bringing you on board for a trial placement with his daughter."

My eyes went so wide I felt the muscles strain. I could barely understand her words. "He...what?"

"We made a convincing case, and he'd like you to begin your trial placement as soon as tomorrow."

The news transformed the previous black hole into a powerful vortex. An F5 tornado ripping through all the carefully seeded and tended aspects of my current life.

You shouldn't do it.

It'll only be bad news.

Whatever you think Trace felt for you was a lie, and besides, you're headed somewhere different in life.

I opened my mouth to respond, and when the words flew out, I wasn't even a smidge surprised.

"I'll do it."

CHAPTER THREE
TRACE

"OH MY GOODNESS. AGAIN?" I picked up the spoon that Willow had tossed—no, violently thrown—to the ground for the third time. I held it between us, arching one brow severely. "I don't want to keep picking this up, little lady."

She blew raspberries at me and lunged for the spoon as best she could while restrained in the high chair. Her eyes lit up as she plunged the spoon back into her cup of yogurt, which she wasn't even eating, just spreading across the high chair tray.

But this seemed to amuse her, and at eight a.m., I didn't want to argue. Besides, she was too cute in her pink and yellow jammies, her baby feet poking out at the bottom. She could spread yogurt if she wanted, especially if it meant at some point she'd be eating. I didn't like the malnourished look on anyone, least of all a toddler.

I sighed and sank into the chair beside her, checking my watch for the billionth time since Willow had woken up at seven. We'd had an easy morning together—one of the first easy mornings since she'd come into my care. I wasn't particularly eager to hand her off and start my workday.

No, I was dreading the arrival of the new nanny.

Mercedes Hendricks.

I massaged the sides of my jaw, which were sore from all the stress-clenching I'd been doing lately. If it wasn't one thing, it was another. If it wasn't a surprise toddler to look after, it was a former flame being the agency's best nanny.

I barely had the head space to dispute it. Six years after she told me to stop contacting her, I was confident I could treat her as she undoubtedly wanted to be treated. She would firmly reside in the distant and professional relationship category. This would be easy, since she'd be spending her days with Willow, not me.

There was nothing to worry about.

Nothing except this lava lamp of dread in my gut.

I helped Willow guide a spoonful of yogurt into her mouth—*success!*—and then let her play for a bit longer before plucking her out of the high chair and carrying her off to her bedroom. It was time to get dressed. I chose a long-sleeve white dress with black stretchy pants. I still didn't know what to do with her white-blonde hair, so I left it wild and free. Then I carried her to my room, where she played on my bed while I chose my own outfit. I'd be hidden away in my office while Mercedes was here, but that didn't mean I shouldn't reinforce the distant and professional relationship in any way possible.

That started with Armani.

Pressed black slacks with slate gray socks. Alligator shoes. Off-white button up. I normally didn't dress up so much for a day of work from my home office, but with Mercedes buzzing in my periphery, I needed to remind myself that she was a non-option.

That long, silky, blonde hair and cinched waist skirt from yesterday tugged at my senses in a way I wasn't happy about. She'd matured in our six years apart. She carried a seriousness with her now that I hadn't experienced our first time around.

I hated that I could still look at her and *want her*. She and I had already failed once. Somewhere along the line, I hadn't measured up. I'd faltered. She'd told me to never contact her again, and there was no do-over. Never mind that the mere sight of her had caused my insides to crumple from both regret and longing.

I had no time for those emotions. I'd never act on them anyway. Second chances were just another opportunity to fail.

It was that simple.

I strode through the living room, rolling up the sleeves of my shirt once, then twice. Willow toddled to her play corner and started tossing Duplo blocks around happily. She looked over at me, shrieked something unintelligible.

"What was that? You like my outfit? Thanks, Willow. I like yours too." We smiled at each other just as a knock sounded on the door.

"Hey, that's probably your new nanny," I told her, holding up an index finger. "Let's go see, okay?" Her curious gaze followed mine but as I neared the door she started whimpering. Badly. Fear streaked her face, and I stopped mid-stride. My gut plummeted to the earth, my protector mode kicking in.

"It's okay, Willow. There's just someone at the door." I lifted her into my arms and rubbed her back for a moment—the door could wait. Right now, I was the only person in her life she trusted. The connection between us had been almost immediate. It was odd, given how hesitant she was around everyone else. But as my mom pointed out, it probably had something to do with how similar Ian and I looked. I likely reminded her of her daddy.

"Can we try now?" I murmured softly. Willow didn't relax much, but she let me carry her to the door. As I reached for the door handle, she clung to my arm like I was readying to launch her into outer space.

"It's okay, sweetie," I murmured into her ear as I eased the door open. Two smiling faces greeted me. Denise and Mercedes.

My stomach plummeted to the core of the Earth as my gaze swept over the blonde beauty in my doorway. I couldn't even say what Denise looked like, what she was wearing. I was only capable of absorbing Mercedes's annoyingly perfect details. She wore form-fitting jeans with an oversized green sweater that matched her eyes perfectly. Her hair had been curled into soft waves and was pulled back into a high ponytail.

"Good morning." I tried to sound cheerful for Willow's sake. "Please come in." I couldn't play the hard-edged businessman in front of her, or else she'd lose the slight progress we'd made.

Deep inside, I knew I needed to be tough as steel around Mercedes, because those soft green eyes had already unraveled my life once.

"Good morning, Mr. Fairchild." Denise surveyed the apartment with bright eyes, her heels clicking over the wood floor. Mercedes echoed her greeting. "What a lovely place you have."

"Thanks." I let the door swing shut. Willow's grip had loosened slightly, but she watched the new arrivals suspiciously. "I can't take much credit for it. I just told the realtor what I wanted."

"Well, you have excellent taste." Denise cast me a bright smile. Mercedes waved at Willow as we spoke, using my body to play peek-a-boo with her. Willow didn't respond much, though she watched carefully. "I don't plan on staying long. I'll just be going over a formalized care plan with you while Mercedes and Willow get acclimated. Then I'll be out of your hair."

Mercedes stepped closer to me, no longer playing peek-a-boo. "Hello, Willow."

Willow shied away but didn't take her gaze off Mercedes for a second.

"Helloooo, Willow." Mercedes pulled a funny face, leaning closer. Willow giggled and twisted away. Mercedes was so close I caught the amber undertones of her perfume, which caused something deep inside my chest to dislodge and float away.

I'd forgotten about that scent. The sultriness infused there, the freedom we'd felt together while wrapped in those amber-laced notes of orange blossom. That scent had accompanied me the time she'd gotten her nickname *Birdie*. We'd been having a day date at the zoo, carefully contemplating a very lonely looking bear, when a bird landed on its head and seemed to give it a kiss. Of course we'd made it a metaphor for our lives. I cleared my throat.

"Let's start with a quick tour." Anything to get further away from Mercedes. I pointed out the kitchen, the kid food-stocked fridge, the great room and fully accessorized play area. I showed them the back hallway, pointed out the door to my bedroom, and then brought them into the princess paradise my mother and I had set up on the fly for Willow. Everything was soft, shades of pastel, adorned with rainbows and unicorns and adorably strange animals. While we were back there, I let them peek into the two extra bedrooms and my office. Once we were back in the main living area, I showed them the extra bathroom near the lounge area behind the fireplace, which led into the laundry room.

"I love the open floor plan," Mercedes said once we'd reconvened in the great room. I tried to react in some way to her compliment, but all I could manage was a grimace.

"Mr. Fairchild, maybe you and I could go over the procedure from here on out while Mercedes and Willow begin to interact."

"I'll try putting her down over here," I said, gesturing to the play area in the great room.

I carried Willow to the gray faux-fur rug I'd chosen for the play area. Her toys were still strewn about from that morning. She hinged her legs up as I attempted to put her on the ground.

Each time I lowered her, she hinged her legs higher. I laughed after the fourth attempt. "You don't want to get down, do you?" I carried her over to the long, trendy couches in a U formation, looking out toward the floor-to-ceiling windows. "Let's sit over here; we'll see if she warms up."

I doubted she'd warm up to Mercedes today. Maybe not even tomorrow. She'd known my mom for a week and still didn't fully care for her.

Denise took a seat in the mauve accent chair facing me. I settled Willow on my lap as Mercedes plunked herself a bit further down on the couch. I disliked the fact that she and I were *sharing a couch* at this point in my life, but I reminded myself this was all temporary. Once we got into the swing of things, I wouldn't see much of Mercedes at all.

Denise brought out a file folder from her handbag and thumbed through papers. "All placements are conditional, pending full approval from the client. So this allows you to really get a feel for how Mercedes and Willow interact with each other before giving the green light for a permanent placement."

I nodded, watching as Willow's gaze drifted back toward Mercedes, who had grabbed the squishy cartoon pillow in the shape of the most adorable snail I'd ever seen. I wasn't sure if this was the right stuff for kids her age, but all of it was eventually enjoyed by both of us, so my opinion had *some* bearing, right? Mercedes made exaggerated motions with the snail so that it kissed Willow on the nose, on the cheek, on the head.

Denise went over some of the protocols for the upcoming weeks. I half-listened for most of it, trying instead to strategize potential routines that would minimize the necessary contact between Mercedes and me. What if I paid her extra to not match her sweaters with her eyes? That seemed practical, given how many hours I'd spent lost in that gaze.

A gust of cool air around my lap alerted me that Willow had wrestled free from my grip. She approached Mercedes carefully, who beckoned her toward the play area. Denise smiled warmly at them.

"She's so good at winning them over," Denise murmured.

Well, she wouldn't win me over. That was for damn sure.

Mercedes and Willow continued playing near all the toys. Willow occasionally looked over at me, checking to make sure I was still here. Once Denise and I had finalized the care plan and we'd both signed off on the mutual agreements, she bowed out quickly, waving brightly to Mercedes and Willow before she headed for the door.

"We'll touch base in a couple weeks," Denise said with a reassuring smile. "I think you'll be pleased, but if anything arises, you know where to find me."

"I appreciate the attention. Aurora's is number one for a reason." Number one in VIP client attention, at least. Not number one in keeping clients' former flames out of their lives. I wouldn't share that with Yelp. I shut the door gently behind her, pausing as I took in the sounds of my apartment now. Mercedes's soft cooing, the cute grunts from Willow as she interacted with Mercedes. I turned to find Mercedes sitting cross-legged on the rug, pointing between stuffed animals, one of which included the incredibly cute snail. Willow snatched up the plush doll and held it to her chest. Mercedes clapped gleefully while Willow smiled.

Whatever she was doing, it was working.

I strode over to them, burying my hands in my pockets. "What would you prefer I do: stay out of your hair or hang around a bit longer?"

Mercedes tipped her head to look me in the face. The sweater-matching green eyes were a gut punch I could never fully prepare myself for, even when I knew it was coming. "It might be best if you stuck around, so she can have you in her line of sight. When you walked over to the door with Denise, she started to get a little anxious."

I nodded, jerking my gaze away from her, looking for something else to focus on. Anything else. "Great. I'll bring out my laptop and get some work done until lunch time. She normally goes down around one and naps for about an hour. Then we can try having you get her from the nap, and I'll stay in my office."

She nodded, a dimple flashing as she smiled. "Sounds like a plan."

Once again, I thought I should react somehow to the interaction, but couldn't force anything beyond a grimace. What I hated as much as the fact that Mercedes had ghosted me was that she was only in her mid-twenties and could make me feel like an awkward, lovesick fool.

I was thirty-two, goddammit. I'd ranked on the Forbes Wealthiest Under 40 list. I was supposed to be a powerful CFO.

Instead, I was still licking my wounds from the true love that wasn't while also facing down a crumbling empire and a shattered family.

I was nothing if not a perfectionist. And right now, I felt like a failure from every angle. Look up the word in the dictionary and you'd see a gilded portrait of my fucking face right there.

I headed for my office, snatched up my laptop, and got settled in the oversized armchair near the wall of windows in the great room.

I was a sucker for natural light. The penthouse I shared—used to share—with my brothers on Wall Street was practically a top floor arboretum. Light brought me clarity, even the gray-blue winter variety blanketing downtown Louisville. Even when I felt like a failure, natural light reminded me there was a future to aim for, to *hope* for.

I opened my laptop, forcing my gaze to stay fixed on the screen. But focusing on the screen only reminded me of the other failures in my life. Fairchild Enterprises was in the crosshairs of the SEC for what they suspected was financial fraud, based on an algorithm my freaky-genius brother Damian had cooked up that kinda sorta skimmed profits and dispersed them to the neediest people and the organizations doing the most good in the world. We still didn't know how they'd caught wind of it, given the fact that our clients were reaping more profit on average than any other wealth management firm was delivering. Yet still, somehow, we'd failed. *I'd* failed, by preventing this devastating outcome. And on top of that? Axel wanted me out of the family business because he still felt so betrayed that I'd kept a secret from him since I was eighteen.

A future without my brothers at my side, in life and in business, was the last thing I'd ever envisioned. I hadn't grown up with Axel and Damian my entire life, but once they entered my world at age nine via the foster care system, they'd become *my brothers,* even before my parents went through the legal adoption process three years later. I'd have torn the world apart for them if they asked it of me. I'd lived my life in service of their mission, to support the less fortunate and to act as the rising tide for the rest of the boats that needed it.

Yet Axel wanted to throw me to the curb because of that decision I'd made at age eighteen. Back when I'd accidentally found out our dad had been having an affair, I kept the information to myself, because my father had asked me to. I didn't want to rock the boat. I didn't even know how devastating the affair would become for the family. So I kept it my dirty little secret, until it came rocketing out of the vault in the form of Willow's father showing up in our lives three months ago.

Now that everything was crumbling around me, one question remained.

What glimmer of natural light-inspired hope was I going to cling to? What did it look like?

I didn't fucking know. But being here in this apartment, bathed in the daylight of Louisville, my ex playing happily with a niece I barely knew, it seemed like I needed to forget about any plans I might have had for myself.

Maybe I needed to start fresh. Start something entirely new. Without my brothers. Without anyone.

It would just be me and Willow against the world.

I drew a deep breath, working my jaw back and forth as I toyed with the idea.

Maybe it was time to say *fuck you* to Axel and Fairchild Enterprises altogether.

I existed in a pensive state of non-productivity, staring at various tabs of my browser and compulsively refreshing emails until Mercedes began preparing lunch for Willow. After Willow spent some time shrieking and tossing macaroni, Mercedes carried Willow into the bedroom. All was silent for a while. When Mercedes emerged, she looked breezy and fresh. She came over to the sitting area, leaning against the back of the other armchair. "Do you want anything for lunch?"

I snapped my gaze up to hers. "No, thank you. I'm not the one needing a nanny."

Her gaze fell and she nodded. "Just wanted to be helpful while I'm here."

"You'll be most helpful focusing on Willow only." I cleared my throat and closed the laptop. I headed for the kitchen so I could grab a sandwich and a premade protein salad, part of the daily delivery service I'd set up in advance of my arrival. I'd thought I'd need it so that I could cut down on kitchen time now that I was a full-time uncle to Willow, but it had the unintended benefit of also keeping me from using the kitchen while *Mercedes* was occupying my space, too.

"She's a sweet girl," Mercedes said, coming to the kitchen island as I tugged open the fridge. "I've noticed she doesn't speak much. She communicates in her own way, but she does seem to struggle with words."

"That's true." I twisted to look at her, realizing I wasn't sure when children even started speaking. "It's developmentally appropriate, right?"

Mercedes tipped her head from side to side. "It could be. But at two-and-a-half, I'd expect at least a few words by now. If I were you, I might see a specialist. Just to check things out. I'll know more as I spend more time with her."

I grunted, adding that to my internal to-do list. I'd have the appointment made by the end of the day. "Noted."

I stacked the wrapped sandwich and salad bowl on the counter near the fridge and let the door glide shut. Mercedes ran her palms across the top of the slate gray island countertop. "So how long have you and Willow lived here?" She gestured at some of the boxes I'd tucked away near the front hallway.

"Not long."

"I didn't realize you were back in Louisville. I'm surprised I haven't heard about it by now."

That grimace came out again. "Well, surprise. Here I am."

She offered a small smile. "It's good to have you back."

"I don't believe you really mean that." I picked up my laptop, then stacked the food on top of it. "In fact I don't believe much of what anyone in your family says. I learned my lesson long ago."

Her face fell, and she stared at her hands, picking at a cuticle. "I did mean it. And I hope you don't think that what happened between you and my uncle would ever affect my job performance. That's completely unrelated."

"It's not unrelated. In fact, it's the definition of related." I set my things down, suddenly desperate to set the record straight. Lay the train tracks, so neither of us ever strayed or deviated from the plan. "The only reason you got the job here is because I know you personally. Even though we have a less than stellar track record, I do believe you're good at this type of work and that you would never harm a child. At the end of the day, that's all I'm looking for. Somebody who isn't a secret predator and can handle the challenges that may come her way. Time will tell if I keep you on. Beyond that, I'd rather act as though you and I are strangers."

Her back straightened, and she nodded fiercely, gaze still stuck on her hands. "Understood."

I picked up my laptop and food again and strode out of the kitchen and into my office.

Those boundaries brought me one step closer to coexisting peacefully with the woman I'd thought I'd end up marrying.

So why did it feel like two steps backward?

CHAPTER FOUR
MERCEDES

Seven o'clock. The end of my first full day working with Trace Fairchild's daughter.

I'd never felt so exhausted and so energized at the same time.

I pulled through the wrought iron gates of my parents' property. They lived in a colonial-style mansion on the outskirts of Louisville, flanked by rolling green lawn and topiary displays that required so much attention it constituted the bulk of my mother's daily stress. She required perfection at all times. There was no off day for my mother or anyone in her orbit, and that included the landscaping staff.

And, of course, her children.

As I approached the white-brick garage tucked toward the back of the property, along the tree line separating their house from the neighbors behind them, I saw my brother's sparkling SUV. And Caleb's flashy new Escalade that he'd purchased last month after a sizeable promotion at his job working with a big health insurance company.

I frowned, pulling into the farthest end of the back driveway. We had Sunday dinners with family without fail, and of course Caleb always attended, as did my brother's wife and daughter. But this was a Wednesday. After the day I'd had, I wanted to head to my area of the property—a detached pool house that served as guest quarters—and sink into a bath and remember all the tiny ways that Trace had lit a fire inside me today, even though every word he'd spoken had been laced with barbed wire.

Gaining Willow's trust had been the easiest part of the day, and that had taken every last resource in my toolkit.

But these were the challenges I lived for—ex-boyfriends not included.

These were also the challenges I couldn't tell my family about.

I breezed into the side entrance of the house, drawing a deep breath before I popped on my happy face, the one that I felt compelled to show my family. The scent of dinner greeted me, onion and roast beef. From deep inside the house, I heard, "Darling, is that you?" My mother. Her intuition regarding my nearness was so accurate it needed to be studied by scientists. I hadn't even shut the door or made a noise yet.

"It's me, Mother!" I replied in a sing-song voice. I set my purse down on one of the wooden shelves lining the side hallway then roamed deeper into the house. I headed for the formal dining room, where I figured everyone would be. We ate at 7:15 p.m. without fail.

The dark wood floor hid beneath thick floral rugs. Every surface was immaculate, free of dust. Through the arches of the dining room, I saw the long dinner table, long enough for a royal family. In a sense, we were modern day royalty—it had been one of those assumed, unspoken sentiments growing up. *We are special. We are revered. We are the living embodiment of success and happiness.*

We expect our children to carry that on for generations to come.

My family milled around in the dining room. Jericho, my brother, with his smartly trimmed dark blond hair and his permanent polo shirt, poured himself a drink at the sideboard. His wife, Madison, a gorgeous brunette, who hid some type of sadness behind her warm smiles, balanced their six-month old daughter Grace on her hip. My father stood at the head of the table like the brick wall of a former football player turned hospital executive he was. My mother, her white-blonde hair in a perfect pouf around her head, tried to herd everyone to the table, but most of them weren't paying her any attention. She'd been formed by my Gramma Kay, who stood beside her with the help of a walker, my sole source of support in this family, but also the most traditional goal post of them all.

And then there was Caleb, watching me with a twinkle in his hazel eyes from across the room, a tumbler of whiskey in hand already. His big University of Kentucky class ring glinted on his finger, the one accessory he never took off.

Everyone watched me with a grin as I entered.

"Good evening, y'all," I said with a smile.

"We've been waiting for you. Come sit down." My mother ushered me into the dining room, feathering my cheek with an air kiss. While she was at my side, she flipped my long ponytail from over my shoulder. "You wore your hair like this today? You could have curled it."

"I was working," I told her.

She tutted, swatting my shoulder. "Which you don't even need to be doing. So tell me again why you didn't curl it?"

I was a living, breathing topiary to her. I brightened my smile and allowed her to shuffle me over to Caleb.

He wrapped an arm around my waist, bringing me against him. He pressed a warm kiss to my temple. "Welcome home, sweetie."

I smiled up at him, feeling the edges of my happiness straining. "I didn't realize you were coming tonight."

"It was sort of a last-minute thing," he said with a wink.

"That's sweet of you." I didn't know what else to call it, other than unwelcome. But *sweet* sounded the better of the two options. "What a nice surprise."

"Well, since Mercedes is here, I think we should eat!" My mother clapped her hands together and we all took our places at the table like marionettes responding to the puppeteer's twitch of the finger. Caleb slid into place next to me, sharing a look with my brother across the table.

"Looks good, Mom," Jericho said with a flashy grin. But it only lasted a second. His recent promotion to assistant VP of business development at the financial firm where he worked had been leaving him drained and distracted. Plus, he was making so much money now that he'd ramped his ego up a few notches. It had been sky-high to begin with, too. "Mercedes, where'd you come from so late?"

"An assignment." I spread the cloth napkin across my lap, surveying the serving dishes of food along the center of the table. They'd been waiting for me to walk through that door.

"An assignment," Jericho chuckled, looking over at Madison. She didn't seem to be listening, since Grace wriggled wildly in her arms. "What are you now, a detective? Nancy Drew?"

I sent Jericho a flat look. He always had something to say about whatever I did—whether I excelled at golf (2-time regional champion) or got voted class secretary my senior year, Jericho found a way to bring it down a notch.

"What sort of assignment, sweetie?" Gramma Kay's voice was shakier these days, her hand trembling slightly as she reached for the spoon in the green beans. But despite the signs of aging, she still wore her pearls and crisp pink blouse. "For the missions?"

"Mercedes has taken a job, Mother," my own mom said with a pursed smile. She sent me a pointed look. "Full time."

"Just to keep me occupied and productive." I avoided everyone's gaze as silverware clinked, bowls being passed around the table. I didn't bring up my job often with my family. I purposefully avoided bringing it up with my grandmother, since she had a lot on her plate already. She'd been struggling to adjust here at the house, and hadn't been happy about leaving her home and coming to live with her daughter. She knew as well as the rest of us that the move was the beginning of the end. "It's with children. I nanny for diverse clients."

"Diverse?" my father mused.

"All wealthy, VIP clients," I reassured him.

"Aren't there some similar positions open at the church?" my grandmother asked my mother.

"She won't hear it," Mom muttered. Neither of them had ever held real jobs, because there had never been any need to. They'd both been full-time mothers, housewives, domestic goddesses, moving from college straight into marriage. My mother expected me to do the same—and the fact that I'd staved off marriage and chosen employment grated on her.

"Let her work while she's young," Jericho chided our parents playfully. Beside him, Grace was getting fussier, and Madison's vestige of a smile was slowly fading. "She'll be raising kids full time soon enough."

"It isn't fair to mislead your employer," my father grumbled. I tuned out their comments the best I could. My life path had been decided since birth: trophy daughter to morph into trophy wife. Girls were meant to be seen and not heard. My parents' deepest desire for me was that I'd quit my job, give them the wedding of *their* dreams, and start popping out babies.

Work was reserved for the men. Women were expected to raise the kids and volunteer.

It had never felt quite right to me. But if I wanted to stay part of this family, I had to toe the line.

That's just how life was.

"Well it sounds like it's an experience, at least," Gramma Kay said with a wink in my direction. I sent her an appreciative smile. Gramma Kay was conservative in a lot of ways, but throughout the years she'd also tended to support me at times when no one else did. I doted on her as a result. If there was one benefit of still living at home, it was the fact that Gramma Kay and I got extra time together now.

"Did everyone get everything?" I asked.

"I'm working on it," Madison said with a little laugh. Grace wouldn't sit still long enough to let Madison do much of anything. Jericho's plate was stacked and he'd already forked a green bean into his mouth.

"Maddy, what do you want?" I knew Jericho well enough to know he wouldn't help out. I rose to grab her plate. She offered a relieved smile.

"Just a little of everything," she said softly, bouncing Grace in her arms.

Jericho sniffed, stabbing another green bean.

Our mother hissed. "We haven't said grace yet."

Jericho grumbled, setting his fork back down. "I haven't eaten since noon."

I made quick work of filling Maddy's plate with roast beef, cheesy potatoes, green beans, and a roll. I set it back down for her and winked.

"Who wants to lead in prayer tonight?" my mother asked.

"I think Jericho should," I offered.

Jericho glared across the table at me but didn't protest further. He bowed his head, all of us following suit, and said a quick prayer. Then he snapped his head up and clapped his hands. "Let's eat."

Forks clinked as the family dug in. At my side, Caleb reached for my hand under the table. He gave it a quick squeeze, his gaze lingering on mine.

"Hey, you." I lifted my shoulder at him, using my free hand to scoop some potatoes into my mouth. Everyone at the table remained oddly quiet. I glanced around to see most sets of eyes on me. Or maybe on Caleb. I finished chewing then said, "So what's the occasion? Could have sworn it was a Sunday when I pulled into the driveway this evening."

My mother tittered, sending a warm smile to my father.

"Well, I think it might be something I talked with your father about earlier today," Caleb said with a little laugh. A dimple flashed in his freshly shorn face. The man might as well have been allergic to facial hair. Sometimes I swear he shaved twice a day. "Your mother invited me to stay, and then she called over Jer and Maddy and Grace."

"I was already here, so no need to invite me," Gramma Kay mumbled.

My mother held her napkin to her mouth. It sounded like she'd swallowed a squeal. "Oh goodness, Caleb."

I furrowed my brow, looking over at my mom. "What...?"

Caleb looked between me and my mother, nervousness streaking his handsome features. He'd been in my brother's grade; I'd always noticed him as the popular older guy who would likely never want me. Every woman desired him, the natural athlete, excellent pedigree, and even better prospects. And it turned out, he'd *always* had his eye on me.

A few months after Trace ghosted me, Caleb started creeping closer. We were friends for a year, then casually dated for another year. Caleb always respected that I wanted to move slowly. He thought it was because I was virginal and scared.

He didn't know the truth: not only was I not a virgin, I'd carried another man's baby, however briefly.

After the miscarriage, it had taken me damn near two years to stop thinking about Trace every day. Caleb's slow approach was the only one that would have worked.

Caleb pushed his chair back, angling himself toward me. There was something intense and magnetic in his gaze. I let myself get lost in the hazel swirl of his eyes as he reached for my hands.

I'd known for months this was comings. I'd been anxious about it for even longer.

"Your father and I had a talk about the future, Sadie." His thumbs swiped back and forth over my knuckles as his gaze fused deep with mine. "I know you and I have talked a lot about what we want in our lives, and I think it's time for us to take the next step. You're the prettiest, kindest woman I've ever known. I came here today to formally ask your father permission to make you my wife."

Pretty. Kind. Permission to make you my wife.

I felt my eyes widen as excited gasps ricocheted around the table.

Knowing it was coming hadn't prepared me for actually hearing the words. Facing down the moment.

"I can't see myself with anyone but you, Sadie." His smile was genuine, those eyes so warm and familiar. To the rest of the world, we were the perfect story. The perfect couple. The health insurance star marrying the hospital executive's daughter. Wealth marrying wealthier. Handsome face meets pretty blonde.

It was so terribly normal. Utterly expected.

It was what I was supposed to want.

"Oh my goodness." I clamped a hand over my mouth as he freed a small ring box from his pocket. His hands trembled as he popped it open. This meant a lot to him. And that was part of the problem.

When a good man presented a—I gasped again as he revealed the ring—quite sizeable, glittering rock, what right did I have to say no?

He came from a good family. He treated me fine. Our families *loved* each other. He had a job that could sustain our future together. Handsome. Well-connected. The perfect man on paper.

It seemed wrong to say no.

Murmurs crested the table, commentary on the beautiful ring. Caleb popped it out of the box, then slid it slowly onto my ring finger, his gaze never leaving mine.

"Mercedes Faith Hendricks. Will you please make me the happiest man alive and be my wife?"

My thoughts shuddered to a stop, time and space ballooning out around me like an engorged bubble, ready to burst. In my mind's eye, I could see the scene from above. The oil portraits of family members dating back to the 1700s adorning the formal dining room walls. The excessive number of forks at each place. The Instagram-worthy details at every angle, of every person.

You have to say yes.

All I could hear inside my head was Trace's voice. Laughing at Caleb's use of the cliche words *pretty* and *kind* to describe me. His shared disdain for asking *permission* to marry a human being. We would have picked apart a proposal like this in the early hours of the morning over coffee while cuddled up on a couch.

Trace would have done it better.

And I hated myself for thinking of that, for thinking of *him*, during this momentous occasion in my life.

Mercedes, what else is out there if not this? I didn't know what life could look like if I didn't go along with the plan, which was so immutable it might as well have been carved from rock.

I needed to answer. I couldn't stay trapped in my timeless bubble forever.

"Caleb, I…" My voice stuck to my throat. I touched my chest, searching his face. Why was this so hard? "Of course I will!"

He whooped and wrapped me in a hug. My family cheered, touching forks to water glasses, celebrating the big news.

"I've been waiting for this day for twenty years," Gramma Kay said. My father appeared in the doorway holding a bottle of champagne.

"Shall we toast?" The loud *pop* sounded a moment later.

"Oh my goodness. We have to start thinking about wedding venues!" My mother fanned herself as my father poured champagne into flutes that I hadn't noticed were already placed on the table.

They'd never planned on me saying no.

Because *no* had never been an option.

Caleb pressed a warm kiss to my cheek, his arm wrapped around my shoulders.

"We gotta start thinking bachelor party destinations," Jericho said, pointing at Caleb. "Cabo. Cancun. Something like that."

"Congratulations, Mercedes," Maddy said with a big smile. Even Grace clapped and cooed along with us.

Or rather…with *them*.

I smiled down at my engagement ring. I'd often wondered what it would look like, how it would feel to receive it. It looked just like every ad in every magazine I'd ever seen. White diamonds set on a silver band. It was heavier than I'd planned. I turned it from side to side, watching it sparkle.

"Do you like it?" Caleb asked into my ear.

I watched it glitter for another moment. This ring was beautiful, but I wouldn't have chosen it. Just like I wouldn't have chosen any of the rest of my current life.

But you should be grateful. You should be grateful. You should be grateful.

"I've never seen anything like it," I told him, smiling up at him before pressing a kiss to his lips that I hoped would help erase all the doubts weighing at my heart.

I had a beautiful life with people who loved me.

What more could I want?

"Mercedes, honey, I'll start setting up appointments to look at venues." My mother's excited voice was one I didn't hear often. She was as giddy as a schoolgirl. "Do you think they'd mind terribly if you went down to part-time at work? We'll be keeping a very busy schedule, getting everything in order."

I didn't even know what to say.

This was supposed to be one of the happiest days of my life, but my gut knew the truth I didn't want to acknowledge, much less confront.

"Mom, we haven't even set a date yet," I chided with a smile. "Let us bask in the moment, at least."

She sent me a coy smile and swatted her hand in the air at me. Then she buried herself in conversation with Gramma Kay.

Caleb scooped my hand up, pressing his lips to the back of it. "Future Mrs. Randolph." His smile stretched nearly ear-to-ear. "I think I like the sound of that."

I was supposed to like the sound of that too.

Only problem was that I didn't.

CHAPTER FIVE
TRACE

THE NEXT MORNING WAS a slog.

I could have easily blamed it on Willow—the forty-five minutes early she chose to wake up were a crucial forty-five minutes for overall sleep health, as far as I was concerned. But truthfully, it had nothing to do with that. What little sleep I'd managed had been plagued by dreams about Mercedes.

I told myself, in the gray dawn light, as I changed Willow's diaper and watched her totter around the living room, even as I felt every inch a zombie, that it would get easier with time.

Being around Mercedes would eventually feel normal.

The dreams about her blonde ponytail and the way she'd pronounce "pillow" like it had an *e* in it would disappear over time. As would painfully visceral memories of how hugging her felt like finding a perfectly fitting puzzle piece. How our kisses had been made of molten lava and longing. How every time we'd made love, we'd interspersed the passion with fits of laughter or commentary on a *New York Times* article.

Six months that had felt like two years.

I was so absorbed in my quest to rationalize myself out of having emotions that I lost track of time. Mercedes knocked on the front door at 8:29 a.m. Willow and I were still playing in our jammies on the living room floor.

I briefly debated running to change first and making Mercedes wait, but when she knocked again, I opted to answer the door. Willow started to whimper so I scooped her up and hurried to pull open the door.

"Morning." I stepped aside, gesturing for Mercedes to come in. Her eyes widened slightly as she scanned me from head to toe. I wore drawstring pajama pants and nothing else. "Haven't quite had a chance to get dressed yet, but it's next on the agenda."

She offered a small smile, her gaze sliding from my bare chest up to my eyes. "No worries. Good morning to both of you." She tickled Willow's belly, which immediately prompted a shy grin. "How's my sweet girl today?"

As she chatted with Willow, I noticed something glinting on her ring finger that most certainly hadn't been there yesterday. A fucking engagement ring, judging by the hand she wore it on. I narrowed my eyes, all my focus on the ring. *Did you miss it? Is she engaged? There's no way you would have missed this yesterday.*

"...adding other trips eventually," Mercedes was finishing up.

I blinked rapidly, yanking my thoughts back to the present. "I'm sorry? I missed that."

"I was thinking about taking Willow to the playroom today, if she and I have a good morning and start the afternoon off on the right foot. Once we see how she and I interact there, we can use that as a barometer for adding other trips eventually."

The building had a common playroom, as well as a fully loaded gym and sauna. I nodded, heading deeper into the apartment. "Sounds good."

"Anything I should know about before I start the day?" Mercedes asked, pausing at the kitchen island to set down a tote bag she'd brought. "Anything strange from last night or this morning, any good or challenging examples of behavior?"

My head throbbed, unable to focus on anything other than the fucking ring on her finger. I'd been convinced she was the one I was going to marry. I'd never considered marriage before her, and certainly hadn't considered it since. But she'd cut me off. And now I was dying to know who had managed to stay close to her.

"She woke up a little earlier than normal, about forty-five minutes." My heart pounded like I'd just finished a run. I cleared my throat, hoisting Willow a little higher in my arms. She giggled, clinging to my shoulder. My gaze slid back to the ring on Mercedes's finger. "I'll be honest, I'm a little worried about that."

"What?" She looked down at herself, trying to follow my gaze.

"The little ring on your finger. I feel like it could be a hazard." Thank God Willow was the only one who knew how fast my heart raced right now. "It could snag on her clothes or scratch her. It looks kind of...pointy." *Like a cheap piece of shit,* I wanted to add.

"Oh. Right. Of course." Mercedes quickly yanked the ring off her finger and fumbled to find a place to stow it.

"You didn't have it on yesterday." It was a fact. One that I wanted her to expound upon.

She offered a tight smile. "That's right."

Silence thumped between us for a moment. "Is it an engagement ring?"

Her smile went tighter. "That's not something two people acting like strangers would really talk about, right?"

Shut down. As much as it annoyed me, I respected her ability to force me back into my lane. "Noted. Listen, have whatever you want from the fridge. She already ate breakfast. I'm going to hand her off and go get dressed, then try to sneak into the office a little earlier than yesterday. Sound good?"

"Perfect." Mercedes wore a big smile as I handed Willow over. She went willingly but reached for me as I eased myself farther away.

"I'm just going over here, sweetie," I said in a soft voice. "I'm just going to get dressed."

Willow whimpered louder the further away I walked. I paused near the doorway, watching as Mercedes bounced her in her arms.

"It's okay, sweet girl, he'll be right back," Mercedes said in a soothing voice.

"Hang tight, Willow." I offered an encouraging smile, but she reached for me even harder. It broke my heart to see her so sad, but I kept moving. Once the door shut behind me, Willow began wailing. I tore my pajama pants off and hurried to dress in whatever was most accessible—track pants and a T-shirt. As the wailing escalated, I decided socks and cologne could wait until later. I rushed back into the living room to find a red-faced, tear-streaked Willow.

Mercedes seemed unfazed and continued rocking her in her arms. As soon as Willow spotted me, she croaked out a strange noise and reached for me again.

"Let me take her," I told Mercedes, scooping Willow out of her arms. Willow immediately snuggled against my shoulder and the crying subsided. Mercedes stroked her back lightly as rocked gently from side to side. "I don't understand," I murmured. "She had such a great day yesterday."

"It's not a linear process with attachment. And she seems to be very attached to her daddy." Mercedes tilted her head. "May I ask where Willow's mother is? Does she see her often?"

I opened my mouth to respond, but realized I'd never informed the agency of the custodial situation underlying this assignment.

I wasn't sure if this would change things, but it was an integral component to understanding Willow.

"I don't know where she is. In fact, I don't even know *who* she is." As Mercedes's brows knitted deeper, I hurried to add, "Willow isn't my daughter. I have temporary custody of her through the state of Kentucky. It's a long story, but the gist of the situation is that her father is in jail and her mother is MIA. I don't have any idea of the situation she's come from, other than it seems it wasn't great."

Mercedes's mouth rounded, and then compassion softened her features. She tutted, gently patting Willow's back. "You poor thing. Who knows what you've seen or lived through?"

It was hard not to get lost in Mercedes's sweetness while she stood this close, brimming with so much empathy for Willow. Her big heart had been one of the first things I'd noticed—and fallen in love with. Which made it all the more confusing that her big heart had dropped me like spoiled meat.

"Willow is my niece," I added, once I caught myself focusing on Mercedes's pink lips and the dark curl of her lashes. "And I made an appointment with a specialist like you suggested. It's set for next week." I swallowed hard, forcing myself to add more. "Maybe you could join us, so you can stay on top of all the recommendations and medical advice."

Mercedes nodded, her green gaze sweeping up to meet mine. "I'd love to. I'm sure it will fall on a day I'm already scheduled to be here, so it won't be a problem." In a softer voice, she addressed Willow. "Do you feel so safe in Uncle Trace's arms?"

Willow jerked her head into a nod. I couldn't see her face, but judging from Mercedes's reaction, she must have looked pretty pitiful.

"He's such a good uncle. You're so lucky to have him." Mercedes offered another bright smile, stroking Willow's back again. "Do you want to go get cozy on the couch with your favorite doll?"

Willow nodded again and Mercedes looked up at me. "Will you come join us for a little bit? I think this will be a good transition."

I admired the way Mercedes made this look effortless. She had a strategy worked out, so subtle and natural that even I barely noticed. I carried Willow to the big couch and sat down. Mercedes joined us a moment later with a ratty-haired doll—the only thing Willow had shown up with, besides a trash bag full of diapers and clothes—and a plush lavender blanket.

Mercedes sat close but left a slight gap between us. I could feel her nearness like it was water on a live wire. My entire being bristled at being this close to her.

I stewed in the conflicting simmer of my emotions—hating myself for still caring six years later, upset with myself for not being able to stop the mental jumping jacks, and disappointed that after so many women in my life, this big-hearted blondie with a shitty family and a ravenous appetite for books was the one who sent my heart racing.

Not to mention a bit disgruntled with the universe overall. I was a grown man, shoved up against my former flame with only a plush lavender blanket and a toddler to separate us.

Hardly the stuff of romantic movies.

"First, we have to make a cozy nest," Mercedes said, stuffing the plush blanket between our bodies, and then out over her lap. "This is how it becomes the coziest of all." Willow watched with red-rimmed eyes, quiet but absorbing everything. "Then this is where sweet Willow girl goes. Into the cozy nest." Mercedes pointed at the slight gap between us. "With both Uncle Trace and Ms. Mercedes."

Willow blinked dully, but I helped reposition her between us. Willow allowed it, and soon she was blinking up at me from between us on the couch. Mercedes tucked her in with the blanket, and nestled the dolly into the toddler's arms.

"Now you're all cozy. All tucked in. With your favorite dolly. And we go like this—" Mercedes made a big display of taking a deep breath. She repeated it a few times, urging Willow to do the same. She eventually followed suit, ending on a smile. "That's my sweet Willow. Good job."

Mercedes knew what she was doing. She had been part-time with the nanny agency, and a new hire. But she seemed especially tuned in to children with histories of trauma. I remembered that she'd been deeply interested in pursuing a psychology degree during our time together. But I hadn't seen that on her Aurora's profile, nor had it been mentioned during the interview.

I propped my arm up on the back of the couch, above Mercedes's shoulders. Like the flash of a lightning bolt, I saw what could have been. The three of us cuddling on the couch, Willow as my daughter, and Mercedes as my wife. It seemed like such a cruel twist to find myself in this position—forced to work with the woman I clearly had never gotten over while she was set to marry someone else.

I ground my jaw through it for a few more minutes, until Mercedes softly instructed me on how to execute the retreat. I scooted further down the couch and waited. Then I moved to the armchair and waited. Then I stood in the kitchen and waited.

Finally, I blew Willow a kiss and was able to retreat to my office.

Once the door shut, I released a deep breath. Barely nine thirty and I was exhausted, mentally and emotionally.

And I hadn't even tackled the first thing on my actual to-do list.

I rolled my neck in a slow circle, surveying the contents of my makeshift office. I had what I needed. Laptop. Hard drives. Fairchild Enterprise-connected tablets, calendars, conference apps. An additional ambient light for when the virtual meetings needed to be more professional.

And then, along the back wall, a series of glass aquariums.

Full of different critters that I cared for. The most notable being the inspiration for the snail stuffie I'd selected for Willow: my very own giant snail pet.

Ferdinand was a Malaysian fire snail, a pitch-black and fire-red mollusk fascinating to behold. I'd crafted an enormous home for him, with carefully curated moss and logs throughout. His home was kept at 79% humidity, just like his native habitat. Ferdinand had been with me since a visit to Malaysia a year and a half ago. I'd been prone to collecting weird pets when I was younger, much to my brothers' chagrin, but now I had the means to support them. The other aquariums held garden-variety snails, a few leopard slugs. I was checking on the state of my pets when my cell phone vibrated against my desk.

The screen read *Kentucky.* I furrowed my brow. Was the actual state of Kentucky calling me? That didn't make sense. But I did know someone currently being held in police custody in the state of Kentucky... I sighed. It had to be Ian. I swiped the screen to answer it.

"Hello?"

"Trace? That you?" His voice sounded gritty. A thousand miles away.

"Ian. What's up? How are you?"

"Oh, I've been better." There was a commotion behind him, the sound of metal being pounded. "All good over there?"

I opened my mouth to reply but wasn't sure where to begin. "Yeah, I...I'm making it work with Willow. She's a little...skittish, I guess. To be honest, I have some questions—"

"Not too sure I can help ya," Ian said. "I haven't been a big part of her life. I've just been trying to make it work where I can. Ya know?"

I didn't know. Not even slightly. "Who was she staying with?"

"My mom, sometimes." Ian cleared his throat. "Back when Julia was in the picture, she'd take her and they'd stay at friends' houses, but when she ended up in the homeless shelter that's when I got my mom involved..."

My head was spinning, and my heart was breaking. What *had* Willow lived through? "Julia? Is she..."

"Willow's mom. Gone now, though. She OD'd a couple months back."

I blinked rapidly, trying to parse this information. So many questions sprang to life. Had Willow witnessed the overdose? How long had Willow been living in a homeless shelter? All I could tease from the confusing mix was a desperate need to make sure Willow never returned to that situation or anything similar. *She's staying with me now, possibly forever.* "And what about your mom? Why didn't she get custody?"

"My mom's...not doing well."

"Oh, is she..." I didn't want drugs to be the answer again.

"She's in a nursing home now," Ian said softly. "She's got some medical issues. It's fucked. I don't really wanna talk about it."

"I'm sorry to hear that."

"This is why I knew you'd be the best man to handle that little girl." Ian didn't even talk about her as though she was his daughter. Like she was just some person who happened to be in the family tree. "I couldn't give her shit. And now look where I am."

At least my brother was right on that front. A guard came and demanded he cut the call, so we said quick goodbyes and hung up. I stared at Ferdinand for what seemed like a half hour then, processing and trying to make sense of what I'd heard. His glistening black body was therapeutic, his sluggish movements its own type of meditation.

Willow coming into my care *was* a blessing. For her...and possibly for me, too.

I was lost in my thoughts until my phone rang again. This time, it wasn't from prison. It was Damian. I contemplated not answering it, but he'd been calling non-stop for a few days. I'd been avoiding everyone.

Maybe that needed to end. I swiped it on. "What's up?"

"Jesus, about damn time."

"I've been busy."

"I can only imagine, since you haven't told me shit about what's going on down there. Everything we know, we had to hear from Mom."

"She's been a big help." I sighed, dragging a hand down the front of my face. There were so many things to update him on, but I didn't have the energy to do it. "I'll catch you up some other time. It's just been...intense."

"Yeah. Sure. You okay?"

I opened my mouth to respond but realized I wasn't sure how to answer. "I'm not sure. My head is spinning."

Damian was quiet for a moment. "I miss you, bro."

"I miss you too."

"You made a decision?"

My gut knotted so hard I thought I could puke. I didn't want to make this decision. Not formally, anyway. It was easier to think about Axel's ultimatum, envision a fresh start in Kentucky, than to actually do anything about it.

It had been a little over a week since he'd dropped the bomb on me. We hadn't spoken since.

"Axel wants me out," I said. "I'll give him what he wants."

Damian swore under his breath. "No, Trace. That's *not* what he wants. You know how he is. He's playing hard."

"I don't have it in me to play the game anymore," I told him. "Axel's a grown man. I shouldn't have to kowtow to his fucking whims at this point in our lives. He told me he wants to buy me out of our business, and that's what I'm going to go by."

"Trace—"

"I'm really not interested in more rationalizations on Axel's behalf," I said. "He put this in motion, he's going to get what he wants. That's the best I can give him."

"That's not what I want," Damian said. "I want us to be back together. A family. How things used to be."

I raked a hand through my hair, looking at the scattered belongings from my home in Tribeca I'd scooped up and taken with me when I got the call about Willow. The freshly installed cream carpet, the lingering scent of paint in the office. These were the trappings of my life now. Tribeca felt like a distant memory.

Fairchild Enterprises was similarly growing faint, now that it was pushed to the background in favor of a sweet but traumatized two-year-old.

"What do *you* want?" Damian prompted.

I cleared my throat, opening my office door just a crack to see if I could hear or see Mercedes and Willow. Mercedes's sing-song voice narrated what she was doing: *"We're slapping this play dough, it feels so firm."*

A smile ghosted my lips briefly. "I don't know what I want any-more, Damian," I finally said. "All I know is that nothing can go back to how it used to be. The only option we have is to create something new."

But what the fuck did something new look like?

CHAPTER SIX
MERCEDES

The following Tuesday was important.

Not only did it mark *almost* a week with Trace and Willow—when Trace would decide whether he planned to keep me on—but it was also the day of Willow's first visit with the child psychiatrist.

I got to Trace's apartment about a half hour earlier than normal, so he could whisk us away in his Benz. I sat stiff and in awe in the passenger seat, trying to keep my eyes from sliding over to his powerful figure in the driver's seat. The big watch peeking out from under the sleeve of his winter coat. His calculating and studious gaze sweeping out across traffic and the dreary Louisville day. His powerfully subtle cologne, which teased as much as it soothed with its musky undertones and hints of leather.

Normally at eight a.m., I wasn't so alert and rigid. But Trace had that effect on me. Inside his huge apartment, his pheromones had a chance to diffuse and disperse. Here, they were inescapable.

"You want coffee?" He eased into the drive-through line of a coffee shop without waiting for my answer. I gaped over at him.

"I always want coffee," I told him. "But we'll be late."

"I planned for it." His satisfied smirk was the type that I saw in my dreams. From the backseat, Willow shrieked and pointed at something. I peered out my window to follow her gaze.

"Ahh, it's snowing!" Trace smiled mildly at the snowflakes hitting the windshield, then looked back at Willow. "Right? It's snowing."

Willow made a grunting sound.

"We'll say that means snow," I offered.

Trace hefted with a laugh, and I stole another glance at him. Things were almost...cordial. I didn't see much of him during the day, now that Willow had gotten used to being handed off to me in the morning. Each day with Willow helped me learn more about her, how to communicate with her.

I just wasn't sure if Trace noticed. He kept conversation to a bare minimum, and only opened up the verbal gates when it involved Willow. As any typical distant, employer-employee situation might be. But we weren't typical.

I was desperate for more from him, because I knew how much Trace usually had to say. How fascinating a man he was. His rich baritone paired well with his sharp intelligence and smart remarks.

I didn't often wish for people to open their mouths, but I could listen to Trace for the rest of my life.

"What do you want?" Trace asked off-handedly as we crept toward the ordering window.

"Don't you remember?" I teased, then immediately regretted it. *You're supposed to be treating him like a stranger.* His gaze landed on me like a whip, echoing my thoughts.

Silence thudded through the car. He squeezed the steering wheel a few times. Then he said, "Oat milk latte."

I bit back a smile and forced my gaze toward the window. "Yep." I'd opened a doorway, and I felt compelled to run through it. Who knew when I'd have another chance like this? "Are you still drinking your frighteningly strong espressos?"

I looked over at him just in time to see his resigned nod. "As a matter of fact, I am."

"Some things never change."

He didn't respond to that. And maybe it was for the better. Because the truth underneath that sentence was that our coffee orders weren't the only things that hadn't changed.

My attraction to him had not changed.

My desperation to be near him had not changed.

My mind's inability to stop imagining kissing him had not changed.

He placed our order, adding a yogurt pouch for Willow and a slice of avocado toast. Once he had started easing toward the next window, I asked, "Are you feeling peckish?"

A smile ghosted at his lips, but he didn't meet my gaze. His dark eyes remained steady on the car in front of him. "Are you reading a British book right now, by chance?"

I opened my mouth to respond but laughed instead. "How could you tell?"

"Just my telepathy, clearly." He didn't miss a beat, which forced me to smile toward the side window again.

This wasn't how strangers talked.

But it was certainly how two ex-lovers talked when forced into a car together.

As if on cue, a tiny bird coasted down from the branches of a tree and perched on the edge of the drive-through window ahead. *It's you, Birdie.* I could almost hear him say it. I turned to him to see if he saw my namesake. His eyes were on the bird, too, but he didn't say anything.

His jaw sure was flexing though.

Don't call him Bear. Don't bring it up. Just ignore the past.

I wanted so badly to keep tugging at this thread, but we'd rolled up to the next window and the barista was handing him our order. By the time he had everything safely stowed and I was sipping my latte, the opportunity for warmth and cordiality had closed.

Trace cranked the radio.

And I retreated into my own world.

We arrived at the hospital soon after, Trace effortlessly carrying Willow as we headed for the main doors. Hot air billowed over us as we stepped into the reception area. After Trace gave Willow's name, we were directed toward an office on the second floor. We approached the reception desk for the child psychiatrist, the only patients in the small, warm room.

"Appointment for Willow Erickson," Trace said brusquely.

The receptionist looked up. "Oh my lord, Mercedes!" The warm brown eyes of a college friend found me from behind the open sliding glass window. Renee and I had been good acquaintances my senior year of college, after Trace had disappeared. We'd always run into each other in the same coffee shop and chat about classes over lattes. She cocked her head, pretty as ever with lavender scrubs and pearl earrings. "What a treat to find you here!"

"Renee! I can't believe it. How are you?"

"I'm just fine. Loving the new job." She flashed me a grin, swiveling in her chair. "What's new with you? I know I haven't seen you in a while, but apparently I missed a lot." Her eyebrows bobbed, gaze sliding to Trace and Willow. "You here for her appointment? What a sweetie."

A blush warmed my cheeks. "You haven't missed much. I'm Willow's nanny. I'm just along for the ride today. My life is still as boring as ever."

Renee's mouth formed a big O, and she clicked through a few screens on her computer. "I got y'all checked in. So you're nannying now?"

Trace drifted toward the first row of plush seats in the waiting area while Renee and I finished our conversation. "I am. Full-time. I'm loving it."

"Whatever happened to the master's degree you were so excited about?" Renee asked innocently. She'd heard me talk about it, but my parents had convinced me to give it up by the time I'd gotten my first acceptance letter. Without their financial assistance, I'd been too afraid to take the plunge. And my father had waxed poetic about the pitfalls of investing so much money in a degree that would ultimately wither and turn to dust.

A bachelor's degree was one thing, they argued. That was baseline. That was *expected*.

A master's was frivolous. Unnecessary. *Not for someone like me.*

"I decided not to after all," I said, something deep inside my chest clenching. Trace had inspired me to even consider applying to grad schools. He was probably so disappointed in who I'd become. If he cared enough now to be disappointed.

"Oh, really? That's a surprise. You were so excited to get that degree and help more kids. Heck, I thought you might be working in a place like this someday," she said with a laugh.

"I'm still excited about helping children," I told her. "I just found a different way to do it."

"Well, that baby girl is a lucky one, if you're in her life." Renee's warm smile made her nose crinkle. She turned at the sound of someone's voice, and then said, "Oh! The nurse is ready to take y'all back. I'll see you on your way out, okay?"

I waved at her and joined Trace and Willow as a nurse pushed open the door and welcomed the three of us into a thickly carpeted hallway. After a sugary hello, she led us to a small but cozy room farther down the hallway. Once the door was shut behind us and we'd settled into the armchairs, she opened her laptop.

"So you two must be Mr. and Mrs. Erickson," she started, immediately typing on the computer.

"No," Trace snapped, before I could even think about opening my mouth. "I'm Willow's uncle and legal guardian. And Mercedes here is the nanny; she's simply attending for context and to be kept up to speed."

"Gotcha," she continued, typing furiously on the computer. Two moments back-to-back where we were mistaken as husband and wife. Trace had been so very quick to set the record straight, so biting, as if the mere thought of being attached to me was too heinous to bear.

I might never know what happened six years ago, why he'd ghosted me with no warning. If this was how he felt about me, I could never ask him. I hated how much it still ate away at me, like a parasite consuming its host.

The nurse asked a battery of basic questions, some of which Trace couldn't answer because of his limited time with Willow. The psychiatrist was an elderly woman with a kind face and huge blocky earrings. Willow shrank into Trace's arms, but Dr. Prenz didn't let it faze her.

"Hi, sweetie," Dr. Prenz said, keeping a respectful distance from Willow. She jiggled her earring comically. "See how crazy this is? It's huge, isn't it?"

Willow only blinked in return, and Dr. Prenz smiled at her.

"So let's get down to it," she said with a jovial tone, easing into an armchair facing the three of us. "What's little Miss Willow going through?"

Trace gave her the basic rundown of events—emergency custodial situation, worrying signs of improper care, like the matted hair she showed up with and being slightly underweight, as well as the fear of strangers and door knocks.

"She's very sweet," Trace said, absent-mindedly stroking Willow's hair as he continued. "But sometimes it seems like we're just going in circles. I don't know how else to explain it."

As Dr. Prenz nodded, I spoke up. "Willow has been exhibiting some regressive cycles over the past week. I've been keeping my eye on them and tracking them when appropriate. But, for instance, the more confidence she gains with me, the less verbal she becomes. There's a push-and-pull there that I don't quite understand yet, but it's likely linked to whatever trauma she experienced before she came into Trace's care."

"Ah, keen eye." Dr. Prenz's eyes twinkled as she looked over at me. "You're already tracking, which is typically the main thing I suggest at this stage. Have you noticed any other signs of developmental delays or symptoms of trauma?"

We chatted about Willow's communication style. Meanwhile, Willow sank deeper into Trace's arms, and he pressed a kiss to the top of her head. It was a heart-melting sight, and I struggled to keep myself fully focused on the conversation and not the tenderness unfolding at my side.

After Dr. Prenz and I had completed a deep dive into my experiences with Willow over the past week, she looked pleased. "If only all caregivers were as astute as you are, Mercedes. These types of details make my job a lot easier."

My cheeks heated at the compliment. "Thank you, Dr. Prenz. That means a lot to me."

"Willow is lucky to have her," Trace spoke up, which only sent my cheeks flaming hotter. I hadn't expected a compliment like that from *him*. I would hang onto it for dear life.

Dr. Prenz discussed her ideas for a care plan, along with some simple observation time. After a final encouraging chat, Dr. Prenz sent us on our way with a follow-up appointment date and some reading material. We each shook her hand before heading out.

"Thank you," Trace called to Renee as he strode toward the door.

I waved to Renee. "It was so good seeing you, Renee!"

She slid the window open and leaned out, smiling. "Let's get together sometime soon! Single gals are required to commiserate over wine together."

I laughed, unsure how to correct her comment. She'd asked me what was new, and I hadn't even mentioned the fact that I was *engaged* because, well, how could I? It wasn't the news I wanted to share.

"I'll get ahold of you," I promised her, just before following Trace into the hallway. Our footsteps scuffed quietly on the tile floor. Silence descended, that new vacuum of strangerhood filling the space between us.

Trace stared at the elevator doors. Willow patted at the collar of his winter coat.

"Do you regularly lie to your friends?" Trace finally bit out.

I blinked, looking up at him. "No. Why?"

"Lying by omission is still lying," Trace said. The elevator dinged and the doors slid open. Empty. We stepped inside, my heart thumping against my ribs. Even though he didn't sound pleased, this topic thrilled me. Because it meant he cared. Or at least something adjacent to caring.

"It was hardly lying by omission," I said, standing at his side as he jabbed the button for the first floor. "I was in the middle of a doctor's waiting room. It's not exactly the time to go into a whole review of one's personal life."

"The sentence 'I'm engaged' is hardly a monologue."

The doors slid shut, leaving us festering in a hot box of tension.

"She'll be brought up to speed when we get together for wine," I snipped, crossing my arms. Something inside me had cracked open just a bit, an electric wire freed from a telephone pole during a storm. "And to be perfectly honest, I find your comments to be rudely invasive, given the boundary you created."

His brow arched severely, and he turned to me. But amusement shone in his eyes as well. "A comment on something I witnessed firsthand isn't invasive. And believe me, I would have said the same to any stranger on the street, much less the woman caring for my niece."

The woman caring for my niece. I'd always just be *some woman* to him. I ground my teeth, frustrated by how titillated and trapped I felt. I wanted to stomp my foot, but I couldn't let him know how much he got to me.

"Well you don't need to be the Clarity Police."

Silence thumped around us, my own words and frustration reverberating inside me. Shame began bleeding out from the recesses of my heart where it permanently lived. But instead of a tirade following me speaking up—like it surely would have, had this conversation occurred with Jericho or my parents—Trace simply drove along.

The corner of his mouth curled up. "Noted."

The elevator slowed and the doors slid open. We walked wordlessly to the car, assuming our previous positions, returning to the apartment in a tense, charged bubble. The only thing that broke the stalemate was Willow; her coos, shrieks, and even a giggle as a snowflake landed on the tip of her nose.

Back at the apartment, Trace slunk away into his own world, and I became absorbed in mine. Willow's lunchtime flowed into naptime; afternoon sensory play turned into clean-up time. Trace had been in and out of the kitchen a few times, and since he didn't initiate any interactions, I didn't even look his way. Five o'clock rolled around, and he came into the living room, having changed into track pants and a black T-shirt.

"Thanks for your work today." He nodded my way, his quiet signal that it was time for me to leave. I tousled Willow's hair and rose from where I'd been trying to engage her with play dough.

"Always a pleasure." I scanned the great room for anything I might have forgotten to pick up or put away.

"There's something for you on the island," he called off-handedly as he lifted Willow. It helped ease the transition process. If she wasn't in his arms, she'd freak out when I opened the door. "Don't forget it."

I headed toward the kitchen island, curiosity making painful swirls inside me. With the big decision coming tomorrow—whether Trace planned to continue with me as Willow's nanny—I was afraid this would somehow convey his decision. After what happened today after Willow's appointment, I had no idea how to gauge his feelings. He'd said Willow was lucky to have me *and* essentially accused me of lying to my friends, so who knew?

Only Trace. And I'd sure as Sunday never ask him.

A few pieces of paper laid on the kitchen island. I picked them up and reached for my purse from the chair, my eyes moving across the words without really understanding what I was seeing.

Northern Kentucky University: Master's in Social Work.

Vanderbilt University: Master's of Education in Child Studies

Each page highlighted a different program at a different school. When I looked up, Trace and Willow were gone.

I gulped back a wave of emotion and slid my coat on, then tucked the pages into my purse. I hurried out of Trace's apartment, my mind spinning.

Trace did pay attention after all.

Maybe he even cared.

From Trace's apartment, I went straight to Aurora's headquarters. I needed to get some paperwork filled out in advance of Denise's check-in with Trace tomorrow. But once I parked in front of the nanny agency building, I pulled the printed sheets out of my purse.

Trace had printed these *for me*. Because he still thought I should pursue this. He could have easily not spent a portion of his workday researching this. Even if all he did was click Print, it meant something to me. After the nothing I'd received from him over the past six years, this felt like a warm embrace.

A stranger wouldn't have done this. Even my own fiancé wouldn't have done this.

But Trace...

I drew a deep breath and headed inside the building, my boots scuffing over the wet cement from the fresh snowfall. As I stepped into the empty reception area, I heard laughter and a voice I knew all too well.

"Denise, you are too kind. You truly are."

A moment later, my mother rounded the corner of the hallway, her trademark pouf of hair bobbing, Denise on her heels.

I paused mid-stride, too dumbfounded to do much beyond gape.

"Oh! Mercedes!" My mother clapped her hands together, her stage-ready smile spanning from ear-to-ear.

My brows knit together, but still the words wouldn't come.

"Your lovely mother stopped by looking for you," Denise offered. "And here you are. I told you I had a feeling she'd be back soon. She's the only one who turns her paperwork in early."

My mother reached for my hand, oozing something so sugary and cloying I could hardly stand it. Her bracelets jangled as she reached for me. "Could I convince you to skip the paperwork just once, dear?"

I blinked rapidly, finally finding my voice. "Uh...what? Why?"

"I made an appointment for us, and I don't want us to be late."

I swallowed hard. "An appointment?" After this morning's appointment for Willow, I could only think of psychiatry-related surprises. But no, my mother would never take me to a psychiatrist. This could only be wedding related. Maybe this was a surprise lobotomy so that I'd finally be excited about marrying Caleb.

"I don't want to give too much away. I've just planned a special evening for us, just us two girls." Her eyes were sparkling in the way a mother's eyes sparkled when her daughter menstruated for the first time or was getting married for the first time. Which left no room for confusion.

"That's so sweet, Mom." I tucked some hair behind my ear, looking between her and Denise. To Denise, I said, "I don't have much paperwork to do. I've been keeping up with it."

"It's perfectly fine," Denise said with a knowing smile. "You two go enjoy your girls' night. I'll see you later, Mercedes." Denise squeezed my elbow before she headed back to her office, leaving my mother grinning at me like she could burst.

"I promise, this is worth skipping out early." My mother guided me by the arm back toward the front door. "And where we're going has refreshments and charcuterie boards. I made sure of it."

"And where *are* we going?" I asked.

My mother sent me a conspiratorial smile. "Marie's."

She meant Marie's Bridal Boutique, the most famous appointment-only shop in the city for designer gowns.

The wedding dress hunt had officially begun.

I was slated to marry a perfectly decent man who'd given me a beautiful diamond ring...yet all I could think about was the man who'd given me four sheets of paper. The man who'd walked away from me six years earlier.

You're acting crazy. Don't mess this up just because Trace is too handsome.

I needed to start acting rational. Trace Fairchild was nothing but a client and a sharp mouth. Caleb was my future and the right choice.

But one question lingered uneasily in my head as I burst back out into the cold evening air with my mother on my arm.

If he's the right choice, then why do you have work so hard to convince yourself of it?

CHAPTER SEVEN
TRACE

Hot water cascaded down my back, prompting a deep sigh. As soon as I got out of bed—extra early that morning—I'd felt cold. And there was nothing better on a cold winter morning than an eternal hot shower.

The wee hours of the morning were mine. They'd always been mine. I loved skulking around my house in the cobalt-tinged dawn, catching up on reading, lingering over espresso, the quiet stretch of time that belonged to nobody but me.

Hot showers were also my thinking time.

And today? My mind was fixated on Mercedes.

I squeezed my eyes shut as I lathered shampoo through my hair, some fancy masculine shit that I actually enjoyed every time I used it. Notes of bergamot and leather.

I wondered if Mercedes would like it. Actually, I already knew the answer. She'd be delighted by it. And I could still imagine just how she'd giggle if I pulled her into the shower stall to have her sample the scent. The way my hands would glide over the dips in her waist, made slippery from the water. The easy way she'd collapse against me, our bodies two magnets that couldn't help but click together.

I sprayed water out of my mouth, reaching for the conditioner next. I was a week into this nanny gig, and I'd laid out the rules myself. So when did things start getting easier?

I didn't know how to be a stranger around her. I only knew how to engage with her, listen to her, get infinitely closer to her. And the worst part about the situation was that I sensed she wanted to get closer to me too.

It's just your previous infatuation talking. She's engaged. You have lost your fucking mind.

I scowled through the conditioner rinse, and then reached for the soap. Notes of vetiver and clove. Another thing I'd have shared with Mercedes in my former life. Another thought I needed to stop having, because Mercedes was engaged and that little waist was not for me to lay my hands on.

That gorgeous spun-gold hair was not mine to tug.

Those pink lips were not mine to consume whenever I wanted, which used to be constantly.

My soap lather journey arrived between my legs. I grunted as I found my cock almost fully hard. I gave it a soapy tug, my balls tightening immediately. Another thing Mercedes and I would have shared in a future life. No, former. There was no future with her, and there never would be.

And I had no idea how to make my heart get the message.

I let my eyes drift shut, pumping my fist over my slippery, soapy cock. My mind's eye was filled with images from my time with Mercedes. Those six months of intense lovemaking, so pure and raw that remembering that time was one of the few things that could get me off without fail. I remembered how sly and submissive she'd been with me, draped over the chaise longue waiting for me to descend upon her. Desire dripping from her eyes, her pussy lips swollen before I'd even touched her.

That was the other thing. Mercedes had always said that I was the only man who could push her to almost orgasm with hardly a touch.

Six years ago, our chemistry had been off the charts.

While I fisted myself, drawing long pulls from balls to tip, squeezing my cockhead just like I liked it, all I could see was Mercedes. The way I used to bury myself in her until she moaned my name, how she'd bounce on top of me until we were both so happy we couldn't speak.

My abs tensed and I came, spurting into the shower. The hot water washed away the evidence, and I just stared at the wall, chest heaving like I'd run a few miles.

That had to be enough. Because that was the end of the line when it came to Mercedes.

Congratulations. You're officially the creepy employer jacking off to fantasies about the nanny.

And what good timing, considering I had an appointment with Mercedes's boss later that morning to discuss her performance.

I finished rinsing and snapped off the water, toweling off quickly. By the time I was dressed—black dress slacks, a slate gray button up, standard Versace watch, black alligator shoes—Willow was stirring. I swept into the darkened princess paradise, finding her just sitting up and rubbing her eyes.

"Hey there, sweetie."

She had the cartoonish snail in her arms, and in the far corner was a new one I'd brought into the fold, a smiling earthworm. I planned to fully stock her exotic pets: stuffy edition collection. If nothing else, this would be the weird thing she shared with Uncle Trace.

"Did you sleep okay?" I held out my hands, and she reached for me. I scooped her up into my arms, her fuzzy sleeper warm from her little burrow in the crib.

She didn't reply, just rested her head on my chest. I swayed back and forth for a bit, patting her back gently. It was times like these that I wondered if she'd ever had anyone to do this for her before. Was I the first? Had Ian loved on her? I hated how many questions I had, how unlikely the answers were to come.

I slipped into the main area of the apartment, finding everything bathed in the weak rays of the winter morning. Everything had settled gray, silent, neutral. I moved slowly around the kitchen, starting the espresso machine, getting out her milk, going through the morning routine I'd come to appreciate.

By the time Willow had woken up enough to slip into her high-chair and drink a little milk, Mercedes was knocking. I booped Willow on the nose and almost left to answer the door, remembered Willow's aversion to my heading to the door without her, and scooped her up into my arms. We answered the door together.

Willow clapped her hands when she saw Mercedes.

To be honest, I would have too had I not made it clear that Mercedes and I needed to treat each other like strangers. She wore her hair in soft waves, her cheeks still rosy from the chilly morning. She slipped off her puffy, white coat, revealing a fuzzy, moss-colored sweater.

"Morning, you two." She sent us both a warm smile, but her gaze lingered on Willow. She held out her hands, and Willow leaned forward.

"She must have missed you," I said, handing her off.

"I was only gone for a little bit," Mercedes cooed, tickling Willow's belly, which prompted a little giggle. "Every morning I come back to see you. You're starting to realize."

Mercedes carried Willow toward the kitchen. Mercedes had opted for black leggings today, which showed off every curve of her ass and calves. I jerked my gaze away, heading instead for my cellphone on the kitchen counter.

"She's started breakfast but not finished. Had a normal wake-up time. We had a good morning together...I guess all in all, not much to report."

"That's good to hear." Mercedes swayed back and forth with Willow in her arms, prompting more giggles. "No news is good news."

I nodded, shoving my hands in my pockets. "I've got to run. I'll be back later."

I headed for my overcoat hanging near the front door.

I had my hand on the doorknob when Mercedes said, "Thanks for the papers yesterday."

I gripped the handle, turning back to look at her. "It was no problem. I hope they're helpful."

Mercedes's throat bobbed. "I hope so too. I'm just not sure I'm...cut out for it."

My gaze dropped to the floor. I knew she was cut out for it, but an inspirational pep talk definitely fell on the too-intimate end of the spectrum. "Well...only you can determine that."

She nodded, and I tugged open the door, stepping into the hallway before I could add anything.

My head swirled with conflict and questions during the drive to Aurora's. Part of me knew that getting Mercedes out of my house was the only way to sidestep the issue of being wildly attracted to her. But the progress she'd made with Willow in this short time was spectacular. Not to mention a relief.

I needed Mercedes as much as I needed her out of my life.

Inside Aurora's, Denise welcomed me with her familiar sugary smile and easygoing chit-chat. In her office, she offered me coffee, which I accepted out of principle, even though I was still feeling the zing from my morning espresso. As I settled into the armchair facing her desk—the same place where Mercedes had come in for the first time looking like a deer caught in headlights—she wasted no time getting down to business.

"I don't want to waste your time, Mr. Fairchild. So let's hear it. How has Mercedes been working out for Willow?"

I sipped my coffee to prevent myself from blurting out *fucking amazing.* Once I'd set the mug down, I said, "It's gone well. They've bonded. It's…great, actually."

Denise clasped her hands to her chest. "I knew she'd be a good fit."

"She's…" *A delicate flower you can't stay away from. An angel in disguise. The woman of your dreams—engaged to somebody else.* "Wonderful."

"Excellent. Excellent." Denise was all-smiles as she brought her own coffee mug to her lips and took a sip. "I take it you'd like to continue with this placement?"

I cleared my throat, thinking back to that morning's shower session. Continuing with this placement would mean a lot more of that early morning ritual. But I couldn't switch nannies on Willow now. Not after this hard-won progress. "I think it's the best choice for Willow. I see a lot of potential in their relationship. It definitely started off on the right foot."

"Great." Denise turned to her computer, the keyboard clacking as she typed a quick note. When she turned to me, her smile had fallen slightly. "I'm more than happy to continue Mercedes's assignment with your family. But there is something I'd like to share with you. This is a bit…abnormal, I must admit. I don't typically discuss things of this nature with clients, but given your VIP status, I thought you might be appreciative of the heads up."

I blinked a few times, letting her words swirl around inside me. "Okay. Let's hear it."

Denise's smile had disappeared completely, and she leaned forward, interlacing her fingers. "It's come to my attention that Mercedes's time with the agency is limited. I haven't received her formal notice yet, but it's become clear that Mercedes's upcoming wedding could mean she'll be resigning. I know you're looking for a long-term solution, which is why I mention this. Since Mercedes may not be the best long-term option, given her personal circumstances, we may want to consider other options."

It took me a few moments to comprehend what Denise was saying. Mercedes planned on quitting soon...and hadn't told me? Hadn't even though to mention it, despite the situation with Willow? Disappointment and anger threaded through me, tensing my muscles, making my jaw tick.

"Limited time," I muttered. "That's disappointing, to say the least." The fear that I wouldn't get to see Mercedes again streaked through me—similarly disappointing, but for different reasons.

"It may hurt less in the long run to consider switching nannies now," Denise said. "But this is completely your call. This is simply advance planning, let's say. I'd rather we're prepared than caught with our metaphorical pants down."

I nodded, then took another sip of my coffee. "I appreciate the heads up. It's good information to have. I'll think on it and let you know—sound good?"

Denise's confectioner's grade-smile returned. "Absolutely perfect."

Denise and I wrapped up our meeting after discussing some of the finer points of Mercedes's skill with Willow, and then I was back on the cold streets of Louisville, trying to remember what else I'd intended to do with my morning.

I couldn't remember, because all I could think about was returning to my apartment to confront Mercedes.

This was underhanded, pure and simple. She acted so righteous, so concerned, so devoted to her cause, yet planned to leave Willow high and dry? This was exactly the type of shady behavior I expected from the Hendricks family—and given how things had ended between Mercedes and me six years ago, I wasn't sure why I was surprised that a Hendricks was wrapped up in miscommunication and sneakiness yet again.

Denise's plan was solid. Switching nannies now *would* be best.

I just couldn't move forward without confronting Mercedes myself first.

I decided to wait until lunchtime to go back, so that Willow would be napping and I wouldn't have to bite my tongue or watch my tone. I wasn't afraid to let Mercedes know I was pissed. This new betrayal dredged up my anger at the first one. A dressing-down six years later wasn't too late, if she'd earned it fair and square.

After trying a new coffee shop, taking a business call, and investigating a co-working space I had no intention of renting but wanted to check out just for shits and giggles, I headed back to my apartment. As expected, Willow was already down for her nap, and Mercedes washed dishes in the kitchen sink as I came inside.

She looked up as the door shut behind me, offering a small smile. I didn't bother to remove my overcoat as I strode toward her.

"Hey," she started.

"Were you planning on telling me that you intend to quit the nanny agency?"

Her green eyes went wide as saucers, and she blinked rapidly. "What?"

"I just met with Denise. She informed me that you may no longer be the best long-term option for Willow because...what was the reason?" I rapped my knuckles on the kitchen island, pretending to think. "Ah, that's right. Apparently you're getting married, and once you've taken on the mantle of wife, your previous obligations no longer matter."

Her chin jutted out and she stared up at me, emotion swarming her eyes. "I...I...wait." She held up her palms, eyes squeezed shut. "We need to back up."

"There's no backing up. There's a simple yes or no. Do you plan to leave Willow high and dry soon? Because if the answer is yes, then we should all just do ourselves a favor and find a new situation. You can leave now, go find yourself some easy temp babysitting gigs until you change your last name, and then Willow doesn't have to suffer getting attached to you and then losing you." Mercedes still looked like she'd been slapped. The nanoseconds of silence on her end were enough to send me spiraling. "And honestly, the part that gets me is I don't even understand what happened to you. The woman I knew six years ago would not have done this."

"Done what?" she sputtered. "I haven't even *done* anything."

"She wouldn't have thrown everything away just because she got that Mrs. title. My only question is who's making you quit? Is it him? Or have you been waiting for this all along?"

Mercedes's nostrils flared and her neck flushed. She squeezed the dish sponge she'd been holding, and for a second I thought she might throw it at me.

"We are backing up," she said through gritted teeth, her gaze turning sharp as a gemstone. "First of all, I am not quitting. I never planned on it. Second of all, do you even fact check anything before you come in here as angry as a bull?"

"I got my facts from your boss," I reminded her.

"Well, she gossiped," Mercedes shot back, her voice rising. "Yes, I'm getting married, and everyone in my life wants me to quit this job. But *I* don't want to, so I'm not going to. And I don't know who could have told Denise any of this except…" Realization crested her face and she expelled a burst of air, which lifted a piece of blonde hair that had fallen in her face. "My *mother.* I ran into her at Aurora's last night, which I thought was strange. She and Denise were acting so chummy. She must have politely informed Denise of her wishes for my life, which Denise then took as fact and conveyed to you."

Her words had a calming effect on me, but I didn't soften my gaze or turn down the tension. Not when we were talking about her upcoming wedding.

"So do I need to source a replacement or not?" I bit out.

"No. I'm not leaving unless you fire me," Mercedes returned, her cheeks flushing this time. "I want this job. I want to work with Willow." She straightened her back, some of that familiar fire returning to her eyes. The flames I'd fallen in love with six years ago. "And shame on you for listening to gossip instead of coming to ask me first."

Her words landed like the slap she intended. I clenched my jaw, finally sliding my coat off. "I did come here to ask you first."

"What you just did wasn't asking. It was accusing."

She had a point. I hung my coat up, taking the few moments with my back to her as a chance to recalibrate. I didn't normally lose my cool like that, but Mercedes held a special spot in my Unhinged and Nonsensical internal filing cabinet.

"I think we need to create an addendum to this arrangement," I said before turning back to face her. "If at any time you cave to the demands of your family and decide to forego a career, I need a three-month lead time."

Her throat bobbed, but she nodded. "That's fair."

Silence hung awkward and bloated between us. We'd reached a resolution, but things didn't feel *resolved*.

Water rushed again as Mercedes started the sink. She scrubbed furiously at a dish for a few moments before she muttered, "And nothing *happened* to me. But it's good to know that you think I'm some pathetic creature who can't follow through on her promises."

"You and I don't have an excellent track record. Same goes for your family." I unbuttoned the cuffs of my shirt and began rolling them up. "I'll presume things haven't changed until it's proven otherwise."

"I thought you said we were supposed to treat each other like strangers. That sounds like the opposite of strangers. Sounds instead like a man with a chip on his shoulder." Her tone of voice was pure challenge. She'd turned the water off again, sponge still in hand. It could turn into a wet weapon at any moment, with the way I needled her. But I couldn't help myself.

"There's no chip, I assure you. Just a very detailed memory of what happened, with no desire to become entrenched again."

Her chin wobbled, and she reached for the sink again. Silence boomed between us. Instead of continuing with her rage dishwashing, she reached for a piece of jewelry sitting near the sink.

Her engagement ring.

She slipped it back on, looking away as she did. My gaze zeroed in on the ring like a laser, but with the way my heart iced over and my chest tightened, it was more of the Terminator-variety laser eyes. I swallowed a noise of disgust, despite how badly it wanted to rip out of my throat. I couldn't stand seeing the thing. My possessiveness knew no bounds, apparently. Even when I condemned Mercedes, I wanted her.

"You just really shouldn't even bother bringing that," I murmured, heading to the fridge even though I didn't want anything from it. I pulled open the door and stared at the contents, only able to focus on the insane rhythm of my heart. "I don't want Willow getting injured due to questionable workmanship."

"It'll be off before Willow wakes up," she said curtly.

I abandoned my quest for a snack and shut the refrigerator door. I turned at the same time Mercedes swiveled from the sink. We bumped into each other in the middle of the kitchen, her chest hitting my ribcage. I reached out instinctively to stop her, gripping her arms. I caught the sharp intake of her breath, the way she straightened beneath my grip, erasing even more of the distance between us. Her startled green gaze swirled with a lot more than just surprise.

I grunted, the warmth of her nearness sinking into me like a salve. Tenderness washed over me, alongside wildfire-grade heat. Something told me our chemistry hadn't fizzled a bit over the years. But that wasn't for me to prove or disprove anymore.

"Watch where you're going." My voice was gruff, but I squeezed her arms gently before releasing her and stepping away. The first few steps away from her were cold, barren. A mistake.

But the only safe place around Mercedes was out of sight.

And I really needed to fucking remember that.

CHAPTER EIGHT
MERCEDES

THE REST OF THE week passed in the same way a horse trots through mud.

With difficulty and strange suctioning noises.

The suctioning noises, of course, came from my newest vibrator—the clitoral suction kind—which I spent too much time with in the wake of Trace Fairchild gripping my arms *accidentally* in the kitchen.

Whether or not the man meant to grab me meant nothing to my lady parts. His warmth affected me now in the same way it aways had—cataclysmic need, earth-drenching desire, and plenty of other exaggerated phrases that came to me while I was in the hazy aftermath of another explosive orgasm.

It didn't matter if he disliked me. If he touched me, I could use it as masturbatory fodder. And the fact that I barely saw him from that day through the end of the week only meant I fantasized harder about him.

This does not sound like typical wedding preparation, Mercedes.

The thought wouldn't leave me as I drifted toward Sunday, the one day of the week I met face-to-face with both God and my family. Without fail, we went to church at nine a.m., took our time socializing afterward, and then meandered back to the house for a huge

Sunday lunch. Our denomination didn't include a confessional, but I sure felt like I needed one.

I was engaged to an amazing man, and I couldn't stop touching myself while thinking about a different man.

Mercedes Hendricks, what on earth is wrong with you?

There were a lot of things wrong with me. I was too forward-thinking. Too idealistic. Too romantic. Too dreamy. Too ambitious. Not submissive enough. And the worst part of all? For every trait my family thought was a fault, Trace would say it was a gift.

I was a Stretch Armstrong doll from the nineties being tugged in opposite directions by warring siblings.

"Mercedes, dear, where's your smile?" My mother's low voice at my side caused me to snap to attention, straighten my back, and curl my lips upward, regardless of the foggy storm inside me.

"I was just lost in thought," I said, as Caleb came to my side and pressed a kiss to my temple. We'd just gotten home from church, but Caleb had skipped this week due to something work-related, which still kept him glued to his phone. He blew me an additional kiss as he pointed to the phone pressed to his head and drifted down the hallway, his UK ring glinting in the light.

"The mayor's wife is joining us," my mother reminded me with a pointed look. "Please pay attention."

"I am," I reassured her, though I absolutely did not plan to.

"We want her to attend the wedding," my mother reminded me with another look.

"I know," I told her, though I did not care at all whether the mayor's wife attended or not.

Life bustled around me, far speedier than my orgasm-heavy brain could capture. I'd never pushed myself to the heights of pleasure so many times in one week. But Trace Fairchild's handsomeness demanded it.

After all, it was just a fantasy or two.

Nothing that would become real.

That's what I kept telling myself, at least, in order to feel like I wasn't derailing my life with this rekindled attraction.

"Oh my god, you have NO idea." Jericho's voice boomed across the dining room, making me wince. "No idea at all." He could be so loud, eating up attention like he'd been starving for it his entire life. But as the golden child of this family, he'd always had the spotlight, so I didn't understand why he needed *so much more* of it at this age.

The man he spoke with—someone from the mayor's office, if I remembered correctly—laughed as Jericho elaborated on some difficulty he'd had at the country club recently. Sunday lunches weren't always so bustling, but my mother had ramped up the social calendar now that Caleb and I were officially engaged.

This was thrilling to her—she'd been waiting her entire adulthood for this moment. To plan her daughter's wedding. To assist in handing me over to "the man of my dreams," though I sometimes wondered if it was more about the son-in-law of *her* dreams.

Caleb wandered back into the dining room with a bright smile, looked down at his phone again, and took another call. He stepped out again a moment later. No doubt his never-ending contact with the doctors he was trying to sell his company's new drug formula to.

The dining room buzzed with conversation, everyone dressed to kill, pearls on point, rumbles of agreement mingling with dainty laughter. My Uncle Tatum showed up next, his wide shoulders and booming voice a perfect fit for the ex-quarterback that he was. His wife, Aunt Helen, glided in after him, their two children, Mark and Greg, trailing behind. Twins in their late teens, they mostly blinked and nodded through daytime activities. According to Uncle Tatum, they were avid gamers who needed an intervention yesterday.

From the looks of it, this Sunday lunch was getting closer and closer to the attendance of the actual wedding my mother was planning.

And here I was, on the fringes, feeling like the only person looking in from outside the snow globe.

"This is a busier lunch than normal." Maddie's voice at my side caused me to gasp. She stood beside me with a wry smile, bouncing Grace on her hip.

"You scared me." I wrapped my arm around her and pressed my head to hers. I wasn't as close to her as I wanted to be, because now that Grace was here, she was essentially a single parent. Jericho barely lifted a finger for them, which ate me up inside. "I was just thinking this lunch might as well be the rehearsal dinner for my wedding."

Maddie laughed, surveying the crowd. My grandmother had just entered, followed by two of my aunts from my mother's side. The mayor's wife was in attendance today as well, though the mayor couldn't join due to a previous engagement. "You're right. This looks like the start of the guest list." She knocked my hip with hers. "You getting excited?"

I tried to conjure the appropriate response, because I knew this would be the single most asked question over the coming months. "Well, we haven't set a date yet. Once we do that, then I'll be able to start feeling all the things." I smoothed down the front of my pastel green skirt, wondering if I'd done a good job at playing the part.

"It's good to delay feeling all the feelings," Maddie said, her warm brown eyes flitting across the growing crowd of the dining room. "Because some of them aren't the best when it comes to wedding planning."

"I'm not looking forward to the stress and anxiety," I murmured.

Maddie turned to look at me, something unreadable in her expression. "Just make sure it's what you really want, okay?"

I blinked, unsure if her comment was friendly advice or a warning. "Well, of course I want to be married…" As the words left my mouth, I heard how hollow they sounded. Even though I'd been trained to say them my entire life.

Maddie hoisted Grace higher on her hip, reminding me that the poor woman probably needed a break.

"Can I take her?" I held out my hands, and Grace cooed happily as Maddie handed her over.

"Phew." Maddie rolled out her shoulders. "That little chunk really does a number on the ole spinal alignment."

I smiled down at Grace, pinching her little cheek. "I bet Willow would go crazy for you."

Maddie smiled over at us, stroking Grace's back as I cuddled her. "Willow? Is that who you're nannying?"

I nodded, running my thumb over Grace's cheek. "She's so cute, non-verbal, and dealing with some tough stuff in life. But she's a trooper, and I know she'll come through great."

Maddie's smile faded. "Won't it be hard for you to quit?"

I cleared my throat, my gaze darting around the room before I spoke, as if checking for spies. "I don't plan on quitting."

Maddie's expression went plasticized, a subtle admonishment. I could see the *are you fucking crazy* written in the gleam of her brown eyes. "That doesn't sound like it'll go over well."

I expelled a breath, deflating slightly. "I know. But I'm going to try."

"Caleb and Jericho are best friends and cut from the same cloth. I know you'll get the same rationale I got. 'I work hard enough for

the both of us—and besides, you have your job. Domestic goddess.'"
Maddie's wry grin made me laugh softly. "You'll hear it soon enough
if you haven't already."

I fingered the lacy hem of Grace's Sunday dress. She kicked her
cutesy winter baby boots, much more for display than anything else,
as I examined the design of her clothes. "Do you miss your old job?"

Maddie didn't answer right away. Her gaze went out toward the
dining room again, her pretty features wrought into a pensive expression. "I do. But I wouldn't give up what I have now either. I love
having Grace's early moments all to myself."

I nodded, bouncing Grace on my hip as she started to fuss a little.
It made sense. I knew the same fate lay ahead for me. I just needed
to accept it already.

Maddie's doing it. You can do it too.

Caleb breezed back into the dining room, his gaze landing on
me briefly. He sent me a smile, but immediately launched into
conversation with my uncle Tatum. Part of me deflated, though I
wasn't entirely sure why. I was looking for something from Caleb,
much more now than I had before. As much as I didn't want to
acknowledge it, I knew it was related to Trace.

Trace had woken something up inside me. He'd prodded the ashes
of my heart and discovered there was still a burning ember there. It
shouldn't have burned for him at this point, and I wanted to prove
that Caleb could provoke the same heat inside me.

But seeing Caleb across a crowded room inspired nothing but a
warm smile.

I knew that Trace's gaze would have sizzled on me from across this
same dining room until I spontaneously combusted. Just imagining
it had my panties damp and my breath hitching. And this was after
I'd orgasmed to Trace's image five times in the past few days.

When would it be enough?

I rubbed at my forehead, squeezing my eyes shut. These thoughts needed to leave and stay gone.

"Are you okay?" Maddie asked, taking Grace out of my arms.

"Yeah. Just a bit of a headache." I sighed, rubbing at my temples as if I could somehow cleanse my Trace-addled brain. "I wish I could go lie down." Even though I knew that would inevitably turn into a self-pleasure session, no matter how much I tried to convince myself otherwise. For being a God-fearing lady of the South, I had quite the vibrator collection, including a small curved one that slipped into its own little purple satin bag just for when I traveled. I planned on informing Caleb of this collection approximately *never*.

Some things were for a lady to keep to herself. And that included both jobs and vibrators.

"You *could*," Maddie offered.

I scoffed, gesturing to the guests. "At my wedding reception? Never." We shared a laugh, and a moment later, my father's voice boomed above the din of voices.

"Time for lunch! Let's take our seats, everyone."

Guests circled the table, which had name cards with elegant script at every place setting. Caleb and I were next to each other, of course, with my Gramma Kay to my right. Our dining room table had turned into a king's table; pitchers of water, bread baskets, and an excessive number of forks adorned the table, set against my mother's trademark ivory and purple table decorations. Smiles abounded at the table as everyone settled in and one of the caterers for the day began bringing in the first course—vegetable soup.

"This is shaping up to be a lovely lunch," my Aunt Rosie said as a waiter came around, pouring mimosas.

"You know Cassandra wouldn't have it any other way," my father rumbled.

"Well, when my one and only daughter is engaged to be married soon, why wouldn't I kick things off with a fabulous Sunday lunch?" My mother lifted a shoulder in her coquettish way, the white pouf of her hair as impeccable as always.

"Pretty sure Mom didn't throw a crazy Sunday lunch when you and I got engaged," Jericho stage whispered to Maddie, who laughed off his comment.

"Hey now. Don't upset the bride-to-be," Uncle Tatum warned, pointing a knife at Jericho. "Our Mercedes needs to have her time in the spotlight."

"I only get to give away my daughter once," my father said, looking my way, tenderness filling his face.

Caleb reached for my hand and scooped it up, bringing my knuckles to his lips. "And I only get to marry the woman of my dreams once."

The whole table said *aww*, while every organ inside my body contracted into itself.

"Y'all, I wasn't prepared for this," I said, reaching for my champagne flute full of mimosa. "You trying to make me cry?"

Laughter drifted down the table. The mayor's wife, Yvette, raised her glass. "To finding love young and keeping it forever."

Everyone at the table raised their glasses. We'd toasted to my pending nuptials within the first five minutes. I swallowed hard, absorbing all the faces around me. A taut expectancy hung in the air, a need to perform, lest someone suspect that I had impurities in my heart and another man on my mind.

"To Caleb," I added, looking over at my fiancé. He smiled back at me—genuinely—and instead of clinking my glass he leaned in for a kiss.

The warmth of his lips against mine surprised me—we so rarely kissed anymore, with how busy we both were. Our relationship was practically long-distance. Trace's face seared through my mind, the stain of anger that had flashed across his face each time he spotted my engagement ring. My eyebrows shot up when Caleb pulled away.

"That was sweet of you," I murmured to him.

"Not as sweet as you."

I pressed my hand to my chest as he rubbed my shoulder.

"When is the wedding?" Yvette asked.

"June tenth," my mother responded.

I gasped, swinging my gaze to her. "What?"

She pursed her lips and nodded. "Yes. I weaseled our way into the venue we wanted."

I blinked rapidly, trying to parse this information. Nobody had told me a date had been chosen. Nobody had told me about the venue.

"June tenth works for you, right?" Caleb murmured into my ear. "We wanted to surprise you."

My gut shrank into a painful knot. My mother *and* my fiancé were conspiring behind my back about my own wedding.

"It's fine," I said. "It's just so...soon."

"Isn't that better?" Caleb asked.

"There's so much to do," I reminded him.

"You'll get it all done," Jericho piped up. I hadn't even realized he'd been listening to our conversation. "It always gets done, with women in charge."

I knew he didn't mean that in the vaguely feminist way it sounded. "That's four months away," I reminded him. "And I pretty much
only have weekends to devote to this."

"Well there's an easy fix for that," Jericho mumbled before taking
a sip of his beer.

"Honey, we can do this, because we're a *team*." My mother's green
gaze cut into me, so intense it nearly broke skin. She looked around
the table. "And we already have the dress selected, so what else is left,
truly?"

I shrank into my seat, unwilling to comment further, as laughter
tittered around me. I hadn't selected the dress yet—not even close.
I merely had four options on stand-by at Marie's that I'd liked but
hadn't been convinced by, from our visit earlier that week. We'd had
a great time at the boutique as I tried on dresses and she cooed over
champagne. But nothing clicked for me.

As soup turned into the main course—chicken piccata and green
bean casserole—conversation turned to the goings-on in Louisville,
as they always did regardless of the head count at Sunday lunches.

"There's a special election coming up," Uncle Tatum remarked as
he cut his chicken into bite-size pieces. "Issue one. Some of those
Highland libs want to develop abandoned churches into music
venues." He hefted with disgust. "Over my dead body."

"Good lord," my Aunt Cathy murmured. "What is this world
coming to?"

"Louisville has seen some seedy influences recently, that's for
sure," my mother mused over the rim of her champagne flute.

"Tell me about it. Anybody want to take a guess who was spotted
lurking in the Highlands recently?" Jericho's mouth had taken on a
smug curve as he cut into his chicken breast.

"Do we want to know?" my father asked.

"What's the prize if we win?" Uncle Tatum joked. "Because I could use some more stocks for my portfolio."

"Funny you'd say that," Jericho said. "Because it was Trace Fairchild."

Cutlery clanked against the porcelain dish and Uncle Tatum's expression turned dour. "Son of a bitch," he muttered to himself. An awkward silence settled on the table like algae on the bottom of a lake. Mushy. Unsettling. Extremely weird to experience firsthand.

"I know that name," Yvette said, tapping the side of her face. Her husband had only been voted into office last year, so she and her family hadn't been around for all the *drama* that went down six years ago. "Somebody catch me up to speed?"

My father hefted with a humorless laugh. "The Fairchilds. What could we possibly say about them that isn't negative?"

Uncle Tatum sent Yvette a weary look. "I'll put it to you this way. I'm not a man to be swindled. But Trace Fairchild is the biggest swindler I've ever met in my life."

I swallowed hard, wondering if my cheeks were betraying me yet. I'd heard plenty of my family's diatribes over the years. The executive summary went something like this: Trace Fairchild had been recommended to my uncle for some investment advice. Trace spent several months traveling back and forth between New York and Louisville for business meetings with Uncle Tatum, during which he advised him extensively and personally handled some risky investments. It was also during this time that Trace and I met and fell in love, but those were irrelevant details now.

Somewhere along the way, the investment that Trace had pushed my uncle to go after went south, costing my uncle millions of dollars. He'd never forgiven Trace and seemed to only get louder about it as time went on. Personally, I thought something seemed odd about the whole thing, and in my gut, I didn't think Trace would behave the way Uncle Tatum said he had. But I never dared to speak those opinions in front of my family.

"So he works in investments, I take it?" Yvette asked, sounding only partially interested as she forked a green bean into her mouth.

"His whole family is a bunch of underhanded scumbags," my father muttered.

"They're being investigated by the SEC right now," Aunt Rosie spoke up. "If that tells you anything."

"I'm not surprised. What the hell was that man doing in the Highlands?" Uncle Tatum turned to look at Jericho. "You saw him yourself?"

"No, a friend of mine did and reported back." Jericho sniffed, dabbing at his mouth with a napkin. "Sounded like he was looking for office space of some kind. Like he's moving into the area."

"Oh lord above," Aunt Rosie said, eyes rolling to the heavens.

"Our city does *not* need him or any of his shady relations staining our business culture," my father said. "People like that only drag a city down." After a moment of contemplative silence, he added, "Yvette, isn't there any favor you can call in from your husband, to get that man out of the city?"

Yvette laughed nervously.

"If he can't, I might know some people," Jericho said haughtily.

I forked a piece of chicken into my mouth and chewed, glancing up in time to catch my brother's gaze. He watched me intently, and I knew why.

He'd disliked Trace from the start. At first it was because Trace was too old for me, and then it was because of Trace's lineage. Finally, once everything went down between Trace and my uncle, it was because Trace couldn't be trusted. He was a con artist, a scammer. A shady businessman that nobody wanted to be associated with.

Once I found out I was pregnant with Trace's baby, I told my mom. I was only twenty years old at the time and foolishly thought my mother would have been excited to get a head start on the grandmother thing. But she hadn't been excited. She wanted me to get an abortion or put the baby up for adoption. Then Jericho found out. Not long after that, Trace stopped calling or texting, further proving to my family that he was an unreliable con artist. He just disappeared from my life, evaporating into fog and memories with a soft *thhhwick*. Like he'd never existed.

Three months later, after my miscarriage, I swore I heard my mother's sigh of relief. My brother hadn't even pretended to be sympathetic. To them, it was just a disaster averted.

To me, it was the greatest trauma of my life.

I could still taste the tang of my brother's righteousness; he still held himself up as the smart one, the one who'd known all along.

He'd been right about Trace, in his mind.

In my heart, I knew they were all wrong. I just couldn't prove it.

Nobody at this table could ever find out that I worked for Trace Fairchild.

If I had a hope or a prayer of keeping my job and maintaining some small semblance of independence, the identity of my client needed to stay the strictest secret.

There wasn't a snowball's chance in Hell that anyone in my family would allow me to continue working for Trace Fairchild if they found out.

And what they didn't—could never—understand was that it was the only place I wanted to be.

CHAPTER NINE
TRACE

IT WAS SIX THIRTY Monday morning when I got the urge to text Mercedes.

I'd spent most of the weekend trying not to think about her, but this was a legitimate work reason, one that I'd told myself I would wait until Monday morning to address. It seemed wrong to text her over the weekend, desperate, somehow, given how much I already had to fight not to think about her.

But duty called.

I needed her to spend the night tonight. Because I had a fucking *date*.

My weekend spent canvassing the city and establishing business leads had paid off. I'd been invited to a fundraiser, and I planned to take an old friend to the event. An old friend who just happened to be incredibly sexy, single, and ready to mingle.

Sort of like me.

As I stood near the espresso machine, placated by the whoosh and sizzle of the machinery inside, I read and reread my text.

TRACE: Hope it's not too early to text. Come prepared for an overnight shift; had a last-minute engagement come up that I need to attend.

Short and to the point. I finally hit send just as my espresso was sputtering into the demitasse.

Her reply came moments later.

MERCEDES: Not too early at all. Sounds good, thank you for letting me know. See you soon.

I frowned at her message. Of course it hadn't been too early to text. We'd both been early risers back in the day, one of the many things we'd bonded over. Why would it have changed? I tossed my phone on the island and grabbed my steaming espresso.

After the accidentally sizzling encounter in my kitchen on Friday, I needed to reinforce—mostly to myself—that I was serious about staying the fuck away from Mercedes. And what better way than bringing another woman to my apartment in front of her?

Mercedes was engaged to someone else. There was no way in hell she could care about what we'd shared in the past. Still, a small voice inside me insisted she did.

I headed for the couches near the big windows overlooking the dreary, early morning city. I sank into the armchair and pulled out the magazine I'd started yesterday, ready to get lost in some reading. I needed to recalibrate in every way possible. Not just because Mercedes was on her way over, but because I was facing an ever-growing social calendar.

I was trying to start over down here. Start *fresh.* If I hoped to launch Fairchild Solutions—my offshoot investment business that I would operate independently from my brothers—then I needed to get my networking game in peak form. I needed to be rejuvenated and *ready.*

Everything would be on my shoulders. I wouldn't have Damian's tech know-how, nor Axel's cutthroat schmoozing. I had to do this shit on my own, which terrified me.

It had been so long since I'd stepped out on my own, truly independent and answering to only myself. I was out of practice. I'd let my brothers guide my way for too long.

What better way to recalibrate than with a gorgeous lady, copious alcohol, and networking in a new city?

Willow roused around eight; she was dressed and having a yogurt pouch and banana slices by eight thirty. Mercedes showed up exactly on time, never more than forty seconds after the half hour, a trait I appreciated—not that I would ever tell her so.

"Morning," she said as soon as I'd opened the door with Willow in my arms, an oversized leather handbag dangling from the crook of her arm. "I came prepared, like you said."

"Great." I stepped aside. Willow clapped happily, gurgling and reaching for Mercedes.

"Aw, hello sweet girl." Mercedes stepped closer to me and tickled Willow's belly, which caused a shrieking giggle. "Did you miss me? I missed you."

I steeled myself for the sweet gestures so close to my airspace. The six inches of distance between Mercedes and me in these brief moments was a challenge.

"OK to hand her over?" I asked.

"Of course. Let me put my things down." Mercedes headed for the small bench by the front door and set her bag down, then slipped her coat off. She pulled her long hair back into a low ponytail, fanning out the oversized gray T-shirt she had on. Each puff of her shirt sent a new wave of her perfume my way. I gritted my teeth.

"So what are the plans for tonight?" Her tone was good natured as she reached for Willow, some of her bracelets clanging.

"I'm going to a fundraiser," I told her, shoving my hands into the pockets of my gray sweatpants. "I'm not sure how long I'll be out. I don't want to give myself a time limit, if you know what I mean."

She nodded, smiling up at me like nothing at all had transpired between us. Like she hadn't just stopped talking to me one day six years ago. Like I hadn't told her to treat me like a stranger last week or attacked her for the idea of quitting because she was getting married.

All I could see was openness. Beauty. Curiosity. She was a fucking blonde angel with green gemstones for eyes that saw all the way into my soul, even when I did my best to put up the walls and keep my distance.

"We'll be leaving from here around six-thirty. Not sure when we'll be back." I wanted to add more—something that might impress upon her that I didn't think about her nearly half as much as I currently did—but nothing made it past my lips.

I headed for my office and locked myself inside. Just me and my Malaysian fire snail Ferdinand.

I went over to look at him, hoping that his slick, inky black features would help me focus on something else. Ferdinand and I stared at each other for a while, until I eventually turned to my computer and became productive for the day.

Hours melted away; emails turned into calls with local realtors, which turned into calls with some of the potential leads I'd reached out to in the past couple of weeks. Around three, my date for the night—Kirsten—began texting her excitement about the night, asking what color dress she should wear, what style suit I planned on.

I'd crafted this plan myself, yet I couldn't help but wish Kirsten would stay home so I could take someone entirely different.

My workday whizzed by, and I took a shower and got ready for the evening. Slate gray, single-breasted Armani suit paired with black, patent leather derby shoes. Classic and refined. I sprayed on my best-smelling cologne, the type that had brought plenty of women to their knees before, and made sure my dark hair was smooth and precise.

Kirsten planned to meet me here at six; after some white wine, I'd take her to the fundraiser, and if all went well, I'd not come back here at all. If I wanted to excise Mercedes from my mind like a concerning mole, boning someone else should do the trick. Since time, space, and resentment had no effect, this was my last ditch effort.

When I waltzed into the living room at a quarter till, Willow was the first to shriek. She ran over to me in her disjointed, stumbling, toddler way; I smiled down at her and picked her up effortlessly. I still caught Mercedes's raised brows and the way her gaze raked over me.

"You guys have a good day?" The question was for Mercedes, but I focused on Willow. It was easier that way.

"Great day. She seemed a little sleepy. I wonder if she's going through a developmental thing." Mercedes drifted closer to us, and I sensed some hesitancy. "Any thoughts on what I should prepare for dinner? What has she typically liked in the past?"

"Spaghetti has been a big hit. Along with sausage and eggs, even though I know it's more of a breakfast meal. Feel free to order out, too. I know this is a long-haul day."

Mercedes shrugged, sending me that angelic smile again. "It's fine. It doesn't bother me."

"Great. Kirsten will be here soon." I drifted toward the couches, easing down so Willow could cuddle on my lap. She rested her head on my shoulder once I'd relaxed back into the cushion. "Then I'll be out of your hair until tomorrow."

Mercedes stood behind the couch at the other end, curiosity swarming her expression. "Sounds great. Is Kirsten your..."

I sent her a sharp look. "That's none of your business."

Mercedes bit her bottom lip. "Sorry. Just trying to make conversation." She gnawed at the inside of her lip, looking around the living room as I focused again on Willow. The countdown to Kirsten's arrival had turned eternal.

I cuddled with Willow on the couch as Mercedes busied herself picking up the toy area. When the knock sounded on the front door, Mercedes jumped first, not Willow.

"Don't you even worry about that knock," I murmured to Willow as I came to standing with her in my arms. "It's an old friend. You'll love her." Though I was getting the feeling I couldn't say the same to Mercedes.

I kept my eye on Mercedes as I crossed to the door. She arranged her shirt then redid her ponytail, all while gnawing on the inside of her mouth.

When I pulled open the door, the first thing I noticed was Kirsten's painted red smile. Her most striking features were her generous lips and mouth—I'd experienced them firsthand plenty of times back when we used to hook up—and there was never anyone with a more eye-catching smile than Kirsten.

At least, that used to be true. There was one other smile that caught my eye more, but I wasn't supposed to notice it and I sure as hell would never admit it.

"Kirsten." I couldn't fight the huge grin as she gasped and fanned at her face. "Welcome."

"Look at you! Uncle Traaace!" She held out her arms and surged forward, embracing Willow and me at the same time. Willow recoiled, burrowing deeper into my arms. Kirsten didn't seem to notice and stepped back, making a big display of looking me over from head to toe.

"Trace Fairchild, I swear to God." She hit my shoulder as she strutted past me, making sure to knock my hip with hers. I caught the subtle shift of her tone, the heaviness of her gaze as she'd raked it over me. "The one man in the world who gets hotter on an hourly basis."

I laughed and shut the door behind her, hoisting Willow a bit further in my arms. Mercedes stood near the couch, her gaze darting between Kirsten and me.

"Oh, I didn't realize..." Kirsten stopped in her tracks, looking over at Mercedes.

"Kirsten, this is Mercedes. Willow's nanny."

Mercedes waved, revealing the one smile I preferred above all others. "It's a pleasure to meet you. Your dress is spectacular. Where did you get it?"

Kirsten fingered the ribbed purple fabric, blinking while she thought. "Just a little something I picked up at Saks."

Willow wriggled in my arms, reaching for Mercedes. She'd been watching Kirsten like she might lash out at any second, so I handed her over.

"It looks so good on you," Mercedes said, hoisting Willow on her hip. I couldn't stand how genuinely she said it. Kirsten tilted her head, her eyes sparkling.

"You're such a sweetie." Kirsten turned to look at me. "Your nanny is a sweetheart."

I nodded tersely but didn't say anything. Instead, I guided Kirsten by the dip of her waist toward the kitchen. "Listen, I got us a reserve chardonnay that I'm dying to try. I'll pour us some."

"You smart man. Soften me up early so you can just have your way with me." She swatted at my chest as we came to the wine fridge tucked into the corner of the kitchen.

"Oh, come on. You know my intentions are pure." It wasn't true, of course—she just didn't realize my intentions were laced with provocation as well. If Mercedes had any hint of feeling left for me, I planned to confirm it.

Kirsten laughed raucously as I popped the cork and poured us generous glasses of chardonnay. Past her shoulder, I could see Mercedes carrying Willow, her gaze sizzling on us.

"To wonderful evenings," I said, lifting my glass. Kirsten clinked it with a grin.

"And to many more," she added.

Hours later, I was drunk. No scratch that. I was drunk *and* I was ravenously horny.

And I was trapped at the fundraiser with a woman I didn't want to have to sex with.

The evening had been lovely. Exactly what I'd been looking for. Beautiful and important people gathered in one area, the influential and the wealthy rubbing elbows, giving me this much-needed entry point into the Louisville business world.

I had too many business cards to count inside my breast pocket. I'd shaken countless hands. And now, sitting drunk and warm at the big eight-person table, unoccupied except for me and an investment manager who'd shot the shit with me for a full hour over dinner, I could think of nothing else to do but bug Mercedes. All the women had fled to the bathroom or the dance floor.

Kirsten had done a great job of distracting me for the evening, as had all the other people I'd met and schmoozed, but there was no way to truly erase Mercedes from the back of my mind.

I was only human. My willpower had limits. And I'd reached mine.

I pulled my phone out of my pocket, tapping out a quick text.

TRACE: How's it going?

Mercedes replied nearly instantly. I checked the time; it was after nine.

MERCEDES: Great. Just got Willow down for the night. She was extra tired and fussed a lot at bedtime.

TRACE: Maybe because I wasn't there? What are you doing now?

There was a pause before she responded, and I noticed I was now totally alone at the table. I spotted Kirsten across the room, her electric smile on display as she regaled a small group with some anecdote or other.

MERCEDES: Just sitting here reading.

TRACE: You should finish the wine I left. Don't let it go to waste.

MERCEDES: Are you sure?

TRACE: Positive. It was excellent. You'll enjoy it.

I set my phone down, propping my elbows on the table as I massaged my face. I didn't know what I was doing, only that I needed to get back into Mercedes's head and heart more than I needed air. I was drunk enough to find a way, too. Drunk enough to ignore the repercussions and all the reasons this was a fucking horrible idea.

Why try to reopen the door with an ex? Especially when she *left you? And who's engaged!*

Nothing made sense. I was driven by this base impulse to get closer to Mercedes, like an overly excited bonobo who could just not stay away from the female with the plumpest rump. I was propelled closer to Mercedes, desperate for something from her that I didn't fully understand.

Maybe it was closure.

Maybe I just wanted one last kiss.

I didn't fucking know.

Kirsten returned then, sliding back into her chair, reminding me I needed to focus on the present. I needed to focus on *this* gorgeous woman who would happily take my cock down her throat as soon as I told her I was ready.

She ran a hand over my back, concern etched across her face. "You okay?"

I opened my mouth to respond but found that I couldn't give her the breezy answer I'd planned. "It's been a rough few months."

The corners of her mouth turned down. "Are you getting drunk and sad, boo?"

I hefted with a laugh. "Maybe a little. It's weird being here without my brothers. But that's life, I guess. Things don't always go as planned."

The hand on my back slipped upwards. Her fingers were cool as she stroked the back of my neck. "That's why you need someone to take your mind off things."

I held her gaze for a moment, understanding the meaning behind her words. She cocked her head, leaning in closer.

"Can I make you feel good, Trace baby?" Her breath hit my lips, her free hand sliding to my thigh. My phone vibrated on the table, begging me to look at it. It had to be Mercedes. But Kirsten was all but mounting me, though we didn't look out of place. We looked drunk and happy.

Someone approached the table, calling Kirsten's name. She swiveled away from me, and I swiped my phone on.

MERCEDES: Oh my goodness you weren't lying. This is phenomenal. I feel drunk off a third of a glass.

TRACE: You don't drink enough wine apparently. Guess we need to change that.

MERCEDES: Drunk caretaking isn't mentioned in the 5-star reviews of Aurora's Nannies on Yelp. <laugh emoji>

TRACE: After hours is fair game. And hopefully you'd recommend me as an employer simply due to my exquisite taste in fine wine.

I swiped through my photos folder and sent along a picture I'd taken that evening of Kirsten and me holding up wine glasses. We looked amazing, the venue sparkled behind us, and it was a fundraiser's social-media dream.

It related to wine. But it also reminded Mercedes who I was here with.

MERCEDES: Hope you're having a good time. But you don't need to flaunt your date.

TRACE: Interesting choice of words. And if I know you, they weren't a mistake.

I ran my tongue over my teeth, assessing the party for a moment before I decided on my next response.

MERCEDES: You aren't supposed to know me remember?

TRACE: After hours rules apply here too. This was about the wine, but apparently you've forgotten all those times you've flaunted that little ring in front of me.

My heart was pounding by the time I hit Send. I put the phone down, rubbing my jawline, dissolving from anticipation of how she'd respond.

Shots had been fired.

And I was fucking desperate to enter the fray.

MERCEDES: You always call it little. How could I flaunt something so tiny?

TRACE: You seem to find a way.

MERCEDES: Should I go ask Caleb for a bigger one?

I frowned down at my phone. So his name was Caleb. He already sounded like a puny, worthless douche.

TRACE: If you have to ask for an improvement to an engagement ring, then you're marrying the wrong man.

MERCEDES: You're just a barrel of wisdom. Any idea where the right man is?

I pinched my eyes shut, willing myself not to take this too far.

TRACE: Haven't seen him. Sorry.

MERCEDES: If only a good marriage depended solely on the size of the ring. Life would be so much simpler.

TRACE: You're lucky it doesn't.

MERCEDES: I'll be curious to see what sort of ring you give Kirsten someday.

TRACE: I'll be sure to flaunt it when I do. Unfortunately for you, if you'd stuck around for the right man, you could have seen for yourself.

I pocketed my phone then, intent on not engaging in that conversation even a second longer. I was drunk. Too drunk, I now realized.

Dangerously drunk.

I'd blasted open the one door I'd vowed to keep shut tight.

Kirsten wandered back my way, dipping down to put her mouth near my ear. "Should we get out of here?"

I pinched the bridge of my nose, prepping myself to give her my answer. She wasn't going to like it. And neither was my cock.

"Don't hate me," I started.

She swatted me with her handbag. "Oh come on."

"Something I ate tonight isn't agreeing with me." *Lies.* I was just mildly obsessed with my niece's nanny, that was all. "Rain check?"

She narrowed her eyes, propping her hands on her hips. "I'd be pissed at you if you weren't so handsome."

I flashed her a grin. "And even if you were pissed, you wouldn't stay pissed for long."

"You know me too well." She gave me an exaggerated pout. "But I'm sad. Don't make me wait long, okay? Now that you're back in my neck of the woods, I want to see more of you."

I came to standing, bringing my lips to her forehead. "Promise."

That was the most she'd get out of me. The most I could give her: lies.

When Mercedes was alone and half-drunk in my apartment, there was only one place I could continue existing: *with her.*

I parted ways with Kirsten—she said she'd grab a rideshare home after she bar hopped a bit more—and hurried to the parking lot. I pulled into the underground parking garage at my building fifteen minutes later. I was at the front door by ten thirty.

If I had any brain cells left to focus on anything that wasn't related to seeing Mercedes, I would have realized how pitifully early it was. Especially for a night I was supposed to be out on the town.

I pushed open the door. My gaze landed on Mercedes, curled up in an armchair near the big windows. She clutched at her chest.

"Lord above, you scared the *piss* out of me!"

I shed my coat at the front door and tossed my car keys into the small bowl near the door. "Sorry. Didn't mean to. Should I get the upholstery cleaner?"

Mercedes still clutched her chest. She'd curled up with a book, a fuzzy gray blanket draped over her lap. "I didn't actually *pee*. Why are you here?"

I laughed, picking up the bottle of wine and another glass, on my way over to her. "Because I live here. Any other questions?"

She blinked rapidly, looking past me at the front door. "I just...didn't think you'd be coming back tonight." Her gaze darted between me and the door. "Where's your date?"

"Why are you so eager to know?" I plopped down in the armchair facing her, pouring more wine in her emptied glass, and then mine. I lifted my glass, encouraging her to do the same. Her throat bobbed and she reached for the glass I'd filled.

"Just wondering if I should have brought ear plugs or not," she murmured as she clinked her glass to mine.

I sipped my wine, then set it down on the end table between us. "Oh please. You think I'd rent an apartment with such inferior construction?" She sipped demurely at her wine, her gaze heavy on me but didn't reply. "Though I'm honored you remember how loud I used to make you moan back in the day."

Her cheeks flushed, and she set the glass down gingerly. "I remember a lot of things from back in the day. Do you?"

The question sent me slightly off balance, but I didn't let it show. "Of course I do. I remember you swearing you'd buck your parents' expectations of you."

Her chin dipped but she didn't say anything.

"I remember you switching your major to psychology."

"It ended up not working out," she said softly.

"And I remember our favorite little coffee shop in NuLu—what was it called? Ah, Coffee Thyme. With the herb-infused blends."

She smiled, but it looked sad. Her gaze drifted across the room. "What a great play on words."

I downed the rest of my glass and stood. "Yeah. Speaking of words. I've said enough of them. And you should get back to yours."

Her eyes widened and she looked panicked. "Wait."

"What is it? Do you want to walk further down memory lane?"

She tucked some hair behind her ear. "Do you want me to leave?"

I jerked my head. "No. You can stay. I was talking about your book. You've had a drink or two. Wouldn't it be easier to stay?" When she nodded, I added, "Though I'd hate to disappoint Caleb. Maybe you should take your little ring back to him so he knows it's safe."

Her lips formed a thin line. "He won't be disappointed. He won't even know. We don't live together."

"Wow. So you're going to marry a man you've never lived with? I can't tell if that's bold or just the stupidest idea I've ever heard."

She expelled a loud sigh. "Okay, Trace. I get it. You don't like Caleb."

I held up my palms. "Hey. I never said that." I couldn't stop myself. I was careening into outer space, an asteroid on a collision course.

Mercedes sat up, pushing the blanket aside, setting her book on the end table. "Why do you even care? This is what I don't understand. How could you possibly care after you up and left me?"

Her words formed a logjam inside my head. I couldn't even comprehend what she was saying. I blinked a few times. "That's a fascinating summary of events."

"Is it? You had your chance Trace, and you left me behind."

I set my wine glass down on the kitchen island, along with the drained bottle. I propped my hands on my hips as I looked across the room at her. Where to begin? And more importantly, *why* begin when I wasn't supposed to be *going there* with her?

I huffed and shook my head. "Honestly, at this point, I shouldn't be surprised. The Hendricks are known for their questionable takes on the truth. It sounds a lot like something your uncle would say. A lie disguised as a world view."

She didn't say anything, so I strode toward the back of the apartment.

"I'm going to bed," I spat out. I'd gone from fixated to drunk to horny to deflated.

I don't know what I'd been searching for with Mercedes. But whatever it was, after tonight, I was certain I'd never get it.

CHAPTER TEN
MERCEDES

Whatever progress Trace and I had made as amicable colleagues evaporated after his night at the fundraiser.

Two steps forward. Fifty steps back.

For the rest of the week, he barely spoke to me, which was as much a necessity as it was torturous. We'd opened a can—no, a Costco-sized jar—of worms, and now we had to sift through the awkward carnage. Trace's method of avoid-and-ignore worked by default, because I barely glimpsed him outside of handing over Willow each day.

But being so physically close yet so emotionally far away from him was awful. It was the *worst*. Because that super-sized glass jar of worms demanded answers. And I wanted to get them.

I thought back to our charged conversation daily. The text messages that betrayed so much more than just a friendly offer to drink some wine.

Trace didn't like Caleb. And more than that, he didn't like being reminded that I was with him.

Trace still cares about you. If this wasn't the most thrilling news of the century, I didn't know what was.

But what was I supposed to do with it?

Come the weekend, my entire family became laser-focused on wedding prep. Now that we'd set the obscenely early wedding date—*four months from now, lord save me*—we were perpetually behind on the to-do list. Which meant that on Saturday, my mother had a schedule for me that started at seven a.m. and ended at ten p.m.

Even the breakneck wedding prep couldn't keep my mind off Trace. My mother and Maddie and I were the wedding prep trio today, since Maddie's mother had volunteered to watch the baby for the first time. We were three women loose in Louisville, but this was a far cry from a bachelorette party.

We started at Marie's boutique for another fitting of the final dresses in the hopes that one would finally become the winner. As I tried them on again, I decided I'd make it simple—I chose the best one of the four, even though I knew it wasn't *the one.* Sleeveless, beaded V-neck, princess cut lace details, long A-line skirt. Maddie teared up when she saw me in it.

"Caleb's going to die when he sees you in this," Maddie promised, which served as a reminder that I was marrying Caleb. Caleb. Caleb.

Trace was not a part of my life.

Even though he'd insinuated that he would have asked to marry me. *Stop it, Mercedes. Stop thinking about that. For the love of everything heavenly, stop thinking about it!*

Easier thought than done.

Lunch was spent at a catering company trying potential entrees. Caleb and Jericho joined us, and we had a fun time nailing down the menu. But my choices—lobster bisque, lump crab cakes, bourbon smoked pork chop, with a live Asian stir fry station —were all vetoed. My mother and Caleb opted instead for a more classic menu: charcuterie boards, filet mignon, brisket.

Trace would have chosen lobster bisque and lump crab cakes with me.

Not a helpful thought, but one that ran through my head like a title on a marquee anyway.

Once our menu was set, we split up to tackle different tasks. My mother, Caleb, and I visited the venue, while Maddie and Jericho went to oversee some of the details for out-of-town visitors at a local hotel.

The venue was Acrewood, a wildly popular and exclusive event venue that typically booked up years in advance. How my mother had booked it so quickly—practically effortlessly—was a question I wasn't prepared to ask. Part of me wondered if she'd reserved it years ago and never told me. Maybe she'd even arranged for the untimely demise of another bride and we were simply occupying the sudden vacancy. The thought made me laugh to myself with its ridiculousness. My fingers twitched, wanting to share the idea with Trace.

But no. There'd be none of that.

The grounds were a social media influencer's dream, with the pillars and rough-hewn wood accents and all the cobblestone paths. As we met with Sherri the wedding planner—the *official* one, not just my mother—and walked the grounds, she pointed out all the different details that would delight us come June. The currently dormant weeping willows. The pond and burbling brook. The miles of manicured grass that would provide the perfect backdrop for the ceremony.

"This is gorgeous," Caleb said with a smile as he looked around, rubbing my back over my thick winter coat.

"So beautiful," I agreed. Because it was.

It just wasn't what I would have picked.

"We're blessed to have a venue like this for our special day," Caleb added, which only drilled the nail of guilt deeper into my heart. We *were* blessed. I needed to be grateful—to strike the devil of longing and comparison from my heart.

"We have an expert floral team on staff as well," Sherri said once we'd come back into the event space, which stretched stately and silent around us. "So whatever vision you have for the wedding, we can make it come to life."

"That sounds great," Caleb agreed.

"I want peonies," I said.

"We'll do a rose feature," my mother said at the same time.

I looked over at her. "Peonies *and* roses, then."

"Honey, peonies?" My mother grimaced, glancing at Sherri, embarrassed, like I'd suggested we use dead flowers. "Are you sure?"

"They're my favorite," I said. "Specifically the Command Performance variety."

"Command Performance," Sherri murmured. "I don't know about that exact one but we can definitely get peonies..."

"Honey," my mother started, stepping closer and lowering her voice a notch. "Instead of demanding some obscure variety even Sherri hasn't heard of, why don't we stick with something more timeless? More elegant. More..."

"Romantic," Caleb offered.

"Peonies are romantic," I reminded her.

My mother grimaced again—a sign of my faux pas. She turned to Sherri. "How about we come back to this? We don't have to decide now. Then my daughter and I can get on the same page."

"Of course. There's no need to decide today. But if we have the theme ready by next week, then we can move forward with the other parts while you two hammer out the floral details."

My mother sent Sherri a big smile which immediately dropped as soon as she looked my way. She wasn't pleased with me speaking up about the variety of peony—I'd hear about this later for sure.

She's footing the bill. I shouldn't have said anything. How could you be so ungrateful?

Not only was I coveting a man who wasn't my fiancé, I was upset about the beautiful designs that someone wanted to gift me for my wedding. This understanding sizzled inside me, lacerating me with its shame. I had no right to speak up, no right to steer the course when all that was required of me was some damn gratitude.

I vowed to keep quiet for the rest of the visit, and once we'd been fully wowed by everything Acrewood had to offer, it was almost time for our dinner date: meeting the rest of the family at the country club for dinner.

"This is going to be the event of the century," my mother oozed as we headed for the car.

Caleb strutted at my side, casting an easygoing smile to my mother as he turned his ring on his finger. "With you planning it, people's grandkids will hear how amazing this wedding was."

My mother laughed and swatted at his arm. "Oh, stop. You're just saying that because you want to butter up your future mother-in-law." She checked her wristwatch, then looked at me. "Are you ready to butter up *your* future in-laws? It's almost time for the reservation at Harrods Country Club."

My father planned to meet us there, along with Caleb's parents, Caleb's younger sister, and Jericho, Maddie, and Grace. My parents were lifelong members of the country club, and Jericho and I had grown up at their socials and alongside the pool. As a result, we could both golf proficiently, a skill our parents insisted we master—even though I'd disliked every moment of gaining the skill.

"I'll meet you ladies there," Caleb said, pressing a kiss to my cheek before heading toward his car. "Can't wait for some French onion soup."

"Ooh, that's my favorite," my mother cooed, before sliding into the passenger seat of my Lexus. Once we'd pulled the doors shut and a moment of silence passed between us, my mother murmured, "You know, honey..."

Just those three little words sent me into an exasperation spiral. I deflated, slumping into the driver's seat as I joined the stream of traffic behind Caleb.

"What?" I asked.

"You're going to have a better shot at getting into the bridal magazines if you keep things classic."

If I could have, I would have pinched my eyes shut and shaken my head so hard I couldn't see straight. But that wasn't exactly recommended for the driver.

"Mother..." I began, schooling the annoyance out of my voice. "I get that you're trying to hit all the big magazines and social outlets. I want my wedding day to be featured just as much as the next girl. But I don't think that one variety of peony—"

"The editor of *Bridal Scene* doesn't prefer peonies anymore," my mother snapped in the voice that had always meant business. I'd learned as early as four to shut my mouth if I heard that tone. "She's not going to select your wedding day as the feature if you insist on them. She's publicly shared that she considers it a worn-out trend. Do you get it now?"

I clamped my mouth shut. I didn't care about the editor; I didn't care about the magazine. I just liked peonies. And this was supposed to be *my* wedding day.

Clearly it was anything but.

"I get it," I finally said in a small voice, once the silence in the car had become unbearable.

"We can do a mix," my mother said on the heels of a sigh, as if this was the greatest concession she'd ever made. "But the bouquet should be primarily roses. We're flirting with danger if we do too many other flowers. This is for *you*. I'm telling you this because I want what's best for *you*."

I swallowed hard, staring hard at the taillights of Caleb's car ahead of me as I followed him through Louisville traffic. The stoniness spreading through my veins was something so familiar, but it was still just as unpleasant as when I'd first begun to notice it, back in the earliest days of my childhood.

"Roses are fine," I told her. "Roses are beautiful too."

The country club was bustling as my family gathered for our dinner reservation under brightly lit chandeliers. So many familiar faces, acquaintances and business partners that I'd been seeing in our social circle for decades. It was always a social affair—so many pauses, clapped shoulders, shared guffaws as someone stopped to chat at our table.

This routine was the status quo. Smiling, nodding along, getting swept up in the social stream like an inert and pretty piece of driftwood.

The volume of the chatter in the dining room was higher than normal tonight. My father let us know, as we all took our respective places around the ten-person table, that there was a networking event going on that night, some sort of city-wide initiative to highlight local businesses and foster new connections around town.

It didn't bother me. I was content to sink into my own world and wait for a chance to order lobster bisque. My own wedding might not feature the soup, but gosh darn it, I was going to savor the world's best crustacean concoction on my own tonight.

Caleb sank into the seat next to me, casting me an easygoing smile before he was summoned by my father for some very important hospital-focused conversation. Across the table, my mother debriefed Maddie while she bounced Grace on her lap. Jericho roamed the dining room, weaving between conversations, the family-dodging social butterfly that he was.

Caleb's sister plopped into the chair beside me, patting my knee.

"There you are, pretty girl." Leah's red-lipped smile was a mile wide. She was the epitome of a southern belle—perfect blonde curls framing her face, a baby blue dress that every doll from my childhood wore; a perma-smile that accompanied her calculating gaze. She shimmied her hips into place on the seat, keeping her chin held high as she scanned the room. "How was the venue visit? Is this going to be the wedding of the century?"

"Of course it is, with my mother behind it," I told her, squeezing her hand. She'd been like a sister to me for years, one that I never connected with fully, but who was family all the same. "With our families' combined networking skills, I'll be surprised if the President of the United States doesn't show up."

She snorted, then lowered her chin as she spotted someone across the room. "Oh, look who's here tonight." Leah was single but never divulged too much about her love life. She seemed to have a revolving door of guys, but hadn't settled down with anyone since one serious boyfriend her sophomore year of college.

I followed her gaze across the room, not recognizing whoever it was she looked at. "Clue me in?"

"Franco Bertolini," she murmured, leaning in closer as she jerked her chin in his direction. "Hedge fund guy. He was in the news last week for something. I can't even remember now." She sighed dramatically. "Pretty abysmal turnout tonight. Not a single potential Prince Charming."

I snickered, swatting at her arm. "He'll show up."

"I'm a college graduate with no prospects," she mused, twisting her lips. "I'm practically a spinster."

"You're twenty-five. You're just starting."

"Tell that to my parents!" She let out a quick, sharp laugh, then flipped her hair over her shoulder. "It's okay, I'll be a seasoned veteran for whenever I end up tying the knot. Even if it doesn't happen until you and Caleb have grandkids."

I laughed, something deep inside me wrenching tight. A lightbulb went off inside my head. *Every time I see her, we talk about how she isn't married yet.*

It was the focal point of her world.

And here I was, wanting to focus on *anything* else, battling misery when it was supposed to be the whole point of existence for a woman my age. This was supposed to be *it*. The most exciting time. The most wonderful era.

Leah was dying to be in my position, and that just made everything feel so much more shameful.

Be grateful. Be grateful.

Leah and Caleb's parents arrived next, a flurry of *hellos* distracting me from Leah's plight as a poor, single woman of marriageable age. Throughout all of it, I couldn't stop thinking of Trace—*of course,* since that was all my Fairchild-addled brain could focus on these days—or the book I'd started reading the night before, which was a historical romance that reminded me a little bit too much of Leah's complaints. That was the only similarity, since the unexpected threesome between the duchess heroine and two of her stable boys in the middle of the book probably didn't compare to Leah's life—and if it did, I'd never know. And didn't want to.

My gaze wandered around the dining room as I pondered Leah's potential stable boy situation, taking in the scene without really noticing the details. Clusters of businessmen. Clinking silverware. The scent of ham.

Until my gaze landed on *him.*

Trace Fairchild.

Standing across the room.

His back was to me, but I knew it was him because I knew every inch of the man. I knew the width of his shoulders and the way he filled out his suits because I'd devoted countless hours to absorbing every detail about him. I knew the way he walked, held himself—cocksure, just this side of haughty, but with an approachability that convinced you to let down your guard.

I almost gasped—but caught myself. Excitement swelled inside me, the exact same kind that had overtaken my body in high school when any of my crushes came into view. But I wasn't a teenager anymore, and I was seated next to my fiancé. This wasn't the time or place to react to Trace Fairchild. I schooled the swelling curiosity from my face and tried to continue existing normally. As though the man of my dreams weren't across the room; the man I wasn't supposed to want, or think about, or care about.

But keeping my attention off him was hopeless. He spoke animatedly with two men I didn't recognize, clearly on the networking event side of the dining room. My and Caleb's families were deep into loud and lively conversation all around me, but that didn't mean they wouldn't quickly spot the new man in town.

Besides, what if he spotted me and tried to swing by and make small talk? What if he mentioned Willow or Aurora's Nannies or any other detail that might alert my family to my position with him?

The entire house of cards would come crumbling down. I'd be cast out for willingly associating with a Fairchild after what went down between Trace and my uncle; my father might not speak to me ever again. The bad blood ran deep, thick, clotting. Whatever my uncle said was gospel in this family. He was the richest, the most successful, the most powerful Hendricks, and my father deferred to his older brother *always*.

Association with Trace Fairchild was a no-go.

Panic flared to life, sizzling through my veins. I needed to warn Trace. Not just that I was here, wearing my *puny ring* around him, but that my family was in attendance. People who disliked him. People who could not find out that I worked for Trace if he wanted to keep me as Willow's nanny.

Precarious. Precarious. The word stamped itself through my mind as I pulled out my phone from my handbag and fired off a quick text to Trace.

MERCEDES: I'm here at Harrods with my family and I see you. Can we chat in private?

I watched as Trace continued talking with the men. A moment later, he reached into his pocket and pulled out his phone. His chin dipped and I watched as he read the text. He twisted, scanning the room, but his gaze didn't find me.

He tapped out something into his phone.

TRACE: Sorta busy here. What's this about?

MERCEDES: Please Trace. Just a minute. Somewhere discreet.

I watched him rub the back of his neck, looking down at his phone. He looked back up at the men, chatted with them for a moment, and then swung his head from left to right.

TRACE: There's a hallway at the back of the dining room. Meet there?

MERCEDES: Ok. Two minutes.

I slipped my phone back into my handbag and eased to standing. "I'm going to head to the ladies room," I announced to whoever was listening. Caleb nodded my way. Maddie smiled in my direction.

I was free to go.

I hurried off in the direction of the bathroom, then hooked a left and got lost in the crowd of networkers. I slipped between businesspeople, weaving toward the back hallway Trace had pointed out. My heart throbbed with every step, the illicit thrill of getting Trace alone, with my family mere feet away, both delicious and terrifying.

One thing was certain. If anything interfered with this job with Trace, I would die.

I couldn't lose it. I couldn't lose Willow or Trace.

I slipped into the back hallway, the sounds of the dining room dull and distant. The walls were adorned with past presidents of the country club, some sort of memorial corridor that led to administrative offices. Trace stepped into the hallway a moment later, and all the air in my lungs evaporated.

Him.

He walked toward me, broad-shouldered and cocksure, a tumbler in one hand and a smirk tugging at his lips. I swallowed hard, my tongue finding the roof of my mouth dry, as I took him in. I fiddled with the zipper of my handbag, suddenly unsure what I'd come here for. What I'd planned to say. How I was even supposed to act in this situation.

The rulebook had been thrown out. We were meeting as adults, in a neutral space with danger around the corner.

As he approached, I could feel his gaze sliding over me, from top to bottom. I physically *felt* the moment his gaze landed on my engagement ring in the way that my throat tightened and the air grew taut.

He stepped a little too close. And I didn't give him the room I might normally allow.

We were nearly chest-to-chest, and the urge to step closer and tilt my head up to his was greater than ever. Why was it still second-nature to seek that kiss from his lips? We hadn't kissed in six years. This was madness.

"Mercedes." His voice came out low, gritty. "How's the subpar fiancé you don't even live with?"

I squeezed my eyes shut, wondering if he could feel that pulsing desire to brush our lips together. I straightened my back and forced myself to meet his gaze. "Where's Willow?"

The smirk returned. "Is that what this was about? She's safe at home with my mother."

"I was just curious," I whispered, my gaze wandering over the details of his business-casual attire. The cream button down, undone enough to allow a few curls of chest hair to poke out, and matte navy slacks, topped off with derby shoes. This man forever made something clench deep inside me, dizzy with need. Caleb could have worn the exact same outfit and it wouldn't have affected me half as much.

There was just something about Trace, his powerful frame, the fire that swirled in his eyes. The way he could penetrate me instantly, see me in a way that nobody else could. Sometimes he used that talent as a salve, other times as a weapon.

I got the feeling he'd be using it as a weapon tonight.

He sipped from his tumbler, a challenge lighting up his gaze. "Anything else?"

"I'm here with my family," I said in a low voice. I gnawed at the inside of my lip as I looked over his shoulder, toward the entryway of the hall, to make sure nobody had followed us. "This a warning and a request. Will you promise me you won't come over to our table?"

Confusion knit his brows together. "A warning? You just really can't stand to be associated with me in public, huh?"

"It's not that." I swallowed hard, steeling myself against the sudden wash of his scent—vetiver and leather and that untouchable hint of working man. "They can't know I work for you. I just want to make sure we avoid any interaction, because I value my job."

"Avoid interaction."

"Yes."

His gaze was heavy on me. "So they don't know you work for me?"

"Right. And I don't want them to get in the way or make trouble. It'll just be easier if they remain in the dark."

Trace's jaw ticked and he nodded slowly. "Fair enough. Request accepted."

I sighed with relief, my shoulders slumping. "Thank you."

"Though I can't imagine you'd really think I'd have anything to say to your family." Trace hefted with a laugh. "Maybe to Caleb.

About you-know-what." He jerked his chin in the direction of my ring before sipping from his tumbler again.

I covered my ring finger with my handbag. "Now would be the time to mention it. We've been prepping for the wedding all day. Though I should say *they* have, not me."

Trace's brow lifted. "What's that mean?"

Frustration burbled up inside me, bursting past my lips before I could think better of it. This wasn't the place—or the audience—for my grievances. But I couldn't stop it. "They're planning it all as though I'm not even part of it. My ideas and preferences don't matter in the slightest."

Trace studied me for a moment. "Where will the reception be? So I can come crash it with all the things you would have preferred."

I smiled but it faded quickly. "Acrewood."

Trace grimaced, swirling the liquid in his tumbler, ice clinking. "That's about as stiff as I expected. I thought you would have picked that winery out toward Lexington. The one with the barn and the gardens and trellises. What was it called?"

I almost couldn't answer him, the way my throat seized up. Of course he'd known with hardly a moment's thought the best place to exchange vows. One of our favorite places, a little family-run winery that had wowed me with its quaintness, its cuteness, its humility. Our date there had been one of our best days together. The memory was wrapped up in so much warmth, laughter, tenderness.

I needed to get a grip. We were in the back of this hallway with the clock ticking.

"You would have loved to have it there, wouldn't you?" Trace stepped closer, eliminating the distance between us. I sucked in sharply, goosepimples flaring on my forearms.

"That would have been the perfect place," I said softly, hoping he didn't catch the waver in my voice. "For *us.*"

He rumbled low, dipping his chin, our faces growing even closer than before.

"Trace..."

All I could see, hear, or smell was him. Each passing second sent me into a deeper tailspin. I'd come here to make sure I could preserve the status quo, but if we were discovered, everything would be ruined. I needed to get out of here.

I couldn't pull myself away.

"What, Mercedes?" I could hear the jauntiness in his tone, the clear challenge. The smile tugging at his lips only proved it. "Why are you breathing so quickly?"

"You need to stay back," I bit out. "I need to act right, and I...I can't, when you're..."

"When I'm what?" This time, he slipped the fingers of his free hand along my jawline, bringing my gaze to meet his. Whatever distance remained between us disappeared. Each inhale brought my breasts flush against his chest. I looked up into his eyes because I had to. Because he demanded it. Because I had never been able to fucking look away.

I swallowed hard, shaking my head. But it was a display. I was only acting like I needed to get away. Really, *here* was the only place I wanted to be.

"We're too close," I said on a whisper. "And I don't want to walk away."

The smirk on his lips blossomed into a full-blown smile. "But *shouldn't* you want to? Seeing that you're engaged and all."

I clenched my teeth, forcing myself to look away from his captivating dark gaze. "I do want to. Except when you're this close. I don't

want to hurt anybody, Trace. I just want things to stay…amicable."
Deep inside, something began laughing raucously. "Okay? Can we
do that? I don't want to act improperly."

A low laugh rumbled out of him, and he dragged his thumb so
gently across my lips I thought I imagined it. I squeezed my thighs
together, that nearly imperceptible movement heading straight for
my clit. Then he straightened, stuffing his hand into his pocket.

"I would never want anything improper to happen," he said,
backing away slowly. His gaze raked over me, igniting small fires
wherever he looked. "At least not *here*," he added, before turning to
walk away.

I watched the hallway entrance for what felt like an eternity after
he left, chest heaving as I replayed what had just happened.

Illicit encounter? Check. Sexually charged exchange? Double
check. A definitely-not-employer-appropriate caress of my lips? One
thousand checks.

Houston, we had a problem.

And it smelled a lot like the brewing storm of infidelity.

The thought jostled clarity—and fear—into me. I shook off the
encounter, reminding myself that nothing happened technically. I'd
drawn a line in the sand. Everything was fine.

Everything is fine. You hear that?

I strode back into the dining room. The wall of sound hit me first,
the crush of competing conversations, and I wove back through the
crowds, heading for my family's table. I sank into my seat, carefully
studying those around me to see if they noticed me. To see if anyone
suspected my transgression in the back hall.

But hardly anybody noticed I'd even returned. Everyone sat tense,
listening, as Jericho finished addressing the table.

"...total scum," he said, his gaze flicking my way. "Sadie, in case you didn't hear, we had a Fairchild spotting. Be warned."

"Ohhh boy." My voice came out shaky, hollow. All I could think of was the way Trace's thumb had glanced over my lips. A ghostly reminder of the way he'd touched them in the past. He used to rub his thumb back and forth over my lips, like mapping the terrain. It was one of the many ways in which he'd claimed me.

Trace hadn't just been my lover. He'd dominated my heart, my head, and my body.

"Why on earth is he back?" my mother lamented.

"Who knows?" Jericho scoffed. "Must have been run out of Wall Street finally."

"Somebody needs to take care of them," my father rumbled. "Get them out of our town. Get them out of our circle. They're not welcome here."

"I agree," Caleb said, crossing his arms, nodding over at my dad. "No room for them here. Not welcome at all."

Jericho smirked, his gaze darting my way before landing on our father. "If only there was someone who could make that happen."

My gut cinched into a tight knot as the conversation turned to full-blown shit-talking about Trace and his brothers. This wasn't the first time the family dinner conversation focused on the Fairchilds, and I knew it wouldn't be the last, not while Trace was in town.

Caleb was the one my family wanted for me.

But Trace was the one *I* wanted.

The one they'd never accept, not in a million years.

CHAPTER ELEVEN
TRACE

I wasn't a huge fiction reader. At least I hadn't been until I met Mercedes. One of the books she'd gotten me to read for fun years ago was *The Great Gatsby*, which I picked up again after our back-hallway encounter at the country club. Back then, I'd said my life with my brothers was sort of like Jay Gatsby if it had been rewritten without all the directionless glitz, infidelity drama, and murder-suicides. I'd thought I was being cheeky, but Mercedes, the true bookworm, admonished me for my incomplete understanding of the book. *"Jay isn't a great person,"* she'd insisted then. *"But you are. He's a fraud who made his money through criminal means, but you're the purest, most whole-hearted man, doing the most for everyone you meet. You couldn't be more different."*

Re-reading the book made me feel close to her...made me wonder if she still believed those things about me, especially now that I was actually under investigation for fraud. Maybe my assessment had been correct—maybe *she'd* been the wrong one. It was a conversation I'd never have with her. And despite all the reasons getting close to Mercedes was a pitiful and awful idea, I wanted to do it anyway. Weird how six years apart suddenly made me feel a lot more similar to Jay Gatsby—fraud included—and his obsessive quest to rekindle love with Daisy Buchanan.

I charged through the pages of *The Great Gatsby* like a man on a mission, though I wasn't entirely sure what I was searching for. One passage made me pause:

"The loneliest moment in someone's life is when they are watching their whole world fall apart, and all they can do is stare blankly."

Jesus Christ I *was* living in the Great Gatsby. Though I still hoped my version wouldn't include the murder-suicides.

But at this point, who knew? The SEC was after my business—and my future—and here I was, floating around Louisville trying to start a new business, acting like everything wasn't coming apart at the seams. Staring blankly into the abyss.

When Monday came, I handed off Willow with barely a glance at Mercedes. I needed to double down on my focus because *that* was the ticket out of this. If I focused harder, I could ignore the engaged ex-love of my life. If I focused harder, I could create a successful sequel to Fairchild Enterprises.

I would accept nothing less.

The book echoed what I believed in my heart: it never worked out a second time. My brothers had been the exceptions to the rule. They hadn't fucked up as much as I had. They hadn't made as many poor decisions.

I don't know what I'd been thinking brushing my thumb over her lips in the back hallway at the country club, but it had something to do with the whiskey I'd been downing that evening. Just like when I'd come back from the fundraiser.

Alcohol was to be avoided when Mercedes was within arm's reach.

Lesson learned.

Time for the future, which didn't include Mercedes in any context but *nanny*.

I clung to this resolution as I went about my Monday: answering emails, one conference call, and then downtown for a Chamber of Commerce luncheon. I'd been cramming my schedule with networking events in my attempt to rub elbows with literally everyone in Louisville, regardless of industry, age, or personal interest. Today's luncheon promised a fair amount of boredom, but my success in Louisville rested on my *being seen*. Participating in the city. Becoming involved in the circles.

The luncheon was a buffet held in the banquet room of a popular steak and chophouse. It was yet another white-linen affair, with dozens of circular tables filling the room, decked with simple floral arrangements and numerous businesspeople milling around. Everyone scratched out their own nametag upon arrival, which meant you wouldn't be able to read at least half the names of people in attendance given the sheer number of doctors that seemed to be here today. That's when I spotted the theme: *Healthcare at the Forefront.* Great. I drew in a breath, prepping myself for even more mind-numbing socialization.

At times like these, I *did* miss Axel. For his gregariousness, at least. Not so much for the grudge-holding.

I tried not to think about it too much. It was easier to ignore the ache of emptiness he'd left behind than to try to heal or address it. He'd started this rift. We were going on four weeks no-contact. Damian and I spoke at least a few times a week, though most of it was him checking in on me, asking me to reconsider.

I hadn't mentioned my plans yet. I didn't want to ruin things before they'd taken off. I needed to have a solid base in Louisville before I shared a single detail with my brothers.

I roamed the dining room, peering at the trays of food on the tables—Caesar salad, fried shrimp, thick cuts of sirloin and ribeye under heating lamps. Servers brought out fresh additions nearly constantly as attendees scooped up their helpings and wandered away. I smiled at an attendee as he approached the buffet line. I didn't know him, but I figured I might as well try to know him, along with everyone else in this room I didn't recognize.

"Hey there." I held out a hand, scanning his name tag. Dr Somer-something. The handwriting faded to chicken scratch. "I'm Trace Fairchild, it's a pleasure to meet you."

He shook my hand reluctantly, offering me an awkward grimace. "Thank you. Uh, yes, I've heard of you...I...oh, let me grab my plate..." He stepped away, scurrying ahead in line. I shoved my hands into my pockets, staring after him.

Socialization—1, Trace—0.

I wouldn't let that weird encounter ruin my day. Doctors could be strange. Maybe he forgot how to speak to people outside of the exam room. I mulled this over as I advanced in line and picked up my own plate. I heaped sautéed mushrooms, steamed greens, and the least-overcooked piece of meat I could find onto my plate, and then scanned the dining room.

I knew essentially no one here, which meant that any table with an opening was fair game.

Something cold shivered through me, and I scanned the room again. This time, I realized I was wrong.

I *did* know somebody here.

Across the room stood Jericho and Gunther Hendricks.

My stomach twisted into a razor-edged knot, and I veered away from the table they stood in front of. I'd never known Mercedes's brother very well, but I'd schmoozed her father plenty in the meetings leading up to her uncle's investments. Neither of them liked me. Hell, I assumed they hated me—possibly until their dying days—based on the way Mercedes's uncle spun that failed investment. He'd been committed to his fallacy, making sure to paint me as the absolute scumbaggiest of scumbags, the irresponsible fraudster, the white trash posing as a banker.

The memories grated at me still. I hated when people were so wrong about me, especially when I made it my life's mission to succeed and help my clients succeed. They said success was the best revenge, but that didn't take into account the bellowing of the haters or the disparaging word-of-mouth from sociopaths.

What if the strange doctor was a friend of Mercedes's Uncle Tatum? Maybe his bellowing *would* ruin my chances in this city. The thought hung awkwardly in the back of my mind as I selected a table with two open seats. I smiled down the unfamiliar faces as I settled in.

"Hope you guys don't mind I join you," I said, smoothing my tie. Two women and three men at the table offered smiles with varying levels of distant interest. Everyone introduced themselves. I caught a few names; one conversation rumbled to life about our industries. When two of my tablemates started trading comments about different marketing tactics for healthcare-adjacent companies, I tuned out.

It was official: I didn't want to be here.

Just eat your steak, trade some business cards, and go.

One more attendee swooped into the empty seat at my table just before the Chamber of Commerce secretary began her opening remarks. I glanced to my side to offer a placid smile, and all the hairs on the back of my neck stood up.

It was Caleb.

Mercedes's fucking fiancé.

Right next to me.

I swallowed the grunt that threatened to escape, my intended smile coming out more like a grimace. I wasn't supposed to know who he was—Mercedes had been very clear about my position relative to her family—so I couldn't let him think I had any inkling, or judgment, or very serious thoughts about the size of the ring that he deigned to gift his fiancé.

No. I could have none of that.

I forced myself to focus on the speaker while dark curiosity thrummed inside me. He had to know who I was, simply because he was part of Jericho and Gunther's orbit, right?

Or maybe he had no idea at all.

Maybe this was a funny *ha-ha* from the universe.

The meeting dragged on to the soundtrack of forks scraping and people sipping their drinks. Two speakers presented about different aspects of the healthcare industry—one of whom was Mercedes's father, much to my overwhelming chagrin—and then there was a Q&A session with the city's healthcare task force.

Once plates were cleared, people began table hopping, and I forced myself into social mode. Time to distribute my stack of cards and be gone. I'd created a bare bones business card for my new venture, Fairchild Solutions, that included a basic email address and landing page I'd whipped up in under half an hour. It was simply to give legitimacy to this burgeoning chapter as I figured out what the hell I was even doing with my life.

I pulled some of the business cards from my inner coat pocket, side-eyeing Caleb as he polished off his beer.

God, he looked underwhelming. Completely normal. The most average human being ever conceived. He looked like a cardboard cutout of a stock model, with the kind of features that everyone could agree were *human* or *attractive* without stirring even an iota of emotional response or interest.

"Well, now that *that's* over," Caleb stated loudly, to no one in particular. He cast a smile out at the table, swinging his head around to look at everyone. His gaze landed on me. "Enjoy the presentations?"

I flexed my jaw, not exactly wanting to be friendly with this guy. But according to him, I didn't know who he was. So I had to play the part, however much it hurt.

"Illuminating." I cleared my throat. "I didn't catch your name, since you sat down late."

"Caleb Randolph." He stuck out his hand, something hard in his gaze. He searched my face like he was hunting for evidence. "And you are...?"

"Trace Fairchild." I gripped his hand as hard as I could in a handshake. Energy surged between us, and I knew in a heartbeat that Caleb *did* know who I was.

He pursed his lips and nodded, crossing his arms, as our tablemates stood and filtered away, leaving just us. He wore a class ring on his fourth finger, one that glinted even brighter and bigger than the diamond he'd given Mercedes. What a loser.

"Right, right. That name sounds familiar..."

"Wealth management," I offered, scanning the room. I figured Jericho and Gunther couldn't be far off. Hell, Caleb probably picked this table for one of two reasons: either to get that front-row seat to his future father-in-law's presentation, or to intentionally fuck with me.

"Do you have a card...?" The note of condescension was subtle, but it was there.

I bristled but offered him one from my stack. "Here you go."

He flipped it back and forth between his fingers, his gaze landing on the card briefly before returning to my face. "You know what, I *have* heard of you."

"Have you?"

He cocked a smirk before setting my business card on the table. "You're infamous."

"I'd love to know in what way."

Caleb shrugged, looking down at my business card again. "From what I understand, your wealth management skills could use some work."

I chuckled and crossed my leg over my knee, making sure I didn't flinch or look away from him. "And why's that?"

"Based on the experiences of some people close to me."

I knew he was referencing Mercedes's family. I leaned closer. "I've led thousands of people to the upper reaches of wealth, and I've got the earnings reports to prove it."

Caleb grimaced, flipping the business card back and forth across his fingertips. "That must be a great comfort when your reputation is shot. Especially in Louisville."

I narrowed my eyes and tilted my head. "What's your point, other than you listen to gossip?"

Caleb met my gaze. He didn't look as confident now, but he certainly hadn't backed down either. "This might not be the place for you and your kind."

"My kind?"

"Yeah."

"What are we, a sub-species of raccoon?" I laughed, though it wasn't funny. I leaned forward, speaking in a low tone. "Who the hell are you even? Are you the fucking mayor of this place? I don't think so."

Caleb's throat bobbed and his gaze flipped to somewhere beyond me, then returned to me. "I'm not the mayor, but I've sure got the mayor on my side. Louisville just might not be the place for you."

"And how would you know?"

"Because I'm connected. I was born and raised here. If I tell my network to stay away from you, you won't be able to make a living."

I sent him my fakest smile. "I'll take my chances. Louisville doesn't scare me, no matter how big you think your fucking britches are."

Caleb flipped my business card one last time, letting it flutter to the ground. "Great talking to you, Trace. I'll be seeing you around."

"Oh, one more thing." I snapped my fingers, feigning confusion. "Carter was it?"

Caleb's eyes narrowed, but he didn't correct me.

"No, no. Sorry. Colton. Whatever it is, it doesn't matter. Because if you were anyone that I should be listening to, I'd know by now. You're nobody. You're C-name with a bad haircut. I bet you're single, sad, and alone, aren't you? Just running around the Chamber events, talking shit to the newcomers like you think you're still the big man on campus. And if you did somehow manage to have a girlfriend, I'd bet you'd buy her the most embarrassing engagement ring, thinking you were really knocking it out of the park. That's the worst type of embarrassment, isn't it? When you find out your best is another man's pitiful."

Caleb surged to his feet, looking down at me like he could spit nails. "Watch your fucking mouth. You're going to regret coming here." He strode off without another word. I assessed the empty table for a moment, weighing my options. I could follow Caleb to the nearest secluded area and put my fist into his mouth. But that wasn't a smart way to wrap up a Chamber function.

I stayed in my seat, drawing deep breaths to calm my temper. I had half a mind to follow Caleb and shout out the other thirteen other things I'd thought of in the seconds after he'd left, but I talked myself out of it. I wasn't Axel, after all. I was Trace. The mostly levelheaded one.

But Axel would have been proud of me. That thought stung as much as it delighted me.

After a good five minutes stewing in my chair, I decided I'd jump ship. The chamber function was officially a bust, and I needed to head to the gym to burn off some energy. Mercedes must have known how much her entire family despised me. She'd done me a favor by warning me away from them over the weekend, even though I never would have dared approach her family's table. Her aim had been to protect her job, not me. But I understood the full picture now.

Anyone associated with the Hendricks was a no-go.

Still, despite Caleb's lackluster warning—exactly the same caret weight as the ring he'd gotten Mercedes—I took his threat as pure bluster. He was a twenty-something with a rich daddy and an even richer future daddy-in-law. He had no idea what he was doing.

Caleb was a joke. And the funniest part about it was that to his crew, *I* was the joke.

It was time to leave. I drew a deep breath of cold air when I reached the sidewalk outside the front doors. *Free at last.* I stormed toward my car, more frustrated than I'd felt in a long time. I needed the gym or I needed to jack off. Preferably both.

More than that, I was tired of this limbo, existing with Mercedes just beyond reach.

Mercedes needed to be mine or be gone.

There were no other options.

CHAPTER TWELVE
MERCEDES

"ALL RIGHT, SWEET GIRL. Here we are! Home at last." I cooed reassuringly into Willow's ear as I maneuvered us into the apartment. We'd had a busy morning trying new things—the library, as well as a visit to a different play area in a different mall. But by the end of the mall-library combo, Willow had dissolved into meltdown mode.

And I'd been soothing and holding her ever since.

"Look. Familiar setting. Our nice living room. Uncle Trace is nearby...I think." I patted her back as I drifted through the house, looking for signs of Trace. I checked my watch—it was past her naptime. That was probably part of the meltdown mode.

"Ready to go sleepy?" I gently tugged her puffy coat off, draping it over a tall chair at the island before slipping my own coat off. As I headed toward the back of the house, I heard a peculiar rushing noise—something between a waterfall and a hum. I would check it out once she was down. I stepped into her darkened bedroom and got her snuggly in her crib. Her breath hitched, a lasting effect of the serious scream-a-thon she'd had in the middle of the Parkland Mall. I winced at the memory as I patted her back.

This was par for the course with a toddler. But that didn't make it any easier.

Willow rolled onto one side and clutched at the bizarre snail stuffie in her crib. I'd always wondered why there were so many snail things in her room, but that was just one more question for the list of things to never be answered by Trace, because I wasn't allowed to engage with him *at all* beyond the realm of being Willow's nanny.

The man ran hot enough to melt metal, and then cold enough to freeze. All his alcohol-fueled slips had left me desperate with desire, but there was no way I could act on them when I was engaged to Caleb.

No way, no how.

I didn't cheat, which meant that all this unresolved, unexpressed passion for the one man I couldn't have would have to stay bottled up inside.

Just great. You have a lifetime of this ahead of you. This will be fun.

Once Willow had drifted off, I slipped out of her bedroom, hearing the same *rushhhh* from before. I followed the sound, unsure if I was hearing the regular sounds of a shower or perhaps some sort of unacknowledged plumbing issue that needed my attention. I drifted down the hallway, the sound growing louder the closer I got to Trace's bedroom. I'd never gone inside before, only peeked in when I knew he wasn't home.

But was he home now? I still wasn't sure. I'd never heard the sound of his shower before, and though it was the likely explanation, I needed to make sure.

This is your due diligence as the nanny and person-in-charge. The bedroom door was ajar so I pushed at it. *What if there's a water main leak? Even though you aren't entirely sure what that means, it could be happening.* Across the room, the bathroom door hung open, and the sound of rushing water grew even louder. *What if a pipe burst?* I stepped closer.

This was the moment that I knew Trace was in the shower. There was no burst pipe, no water damage threat.

It was also the moment I convinced myself I needed to continue investigating.

I just need to make sure. I wet my bottom lip and tiptoed through the quiet bedroom, decked in shades of gray and blue, masculine and soothing at the same time. His king-size bed looked impossibly comfortable—a fact I'd never be able to test, because *you are engaged to someone else, Mercedes, do you understand that*—and approached the bathroom door.

I pushed it with my palm and it opened soundlessly. And thank God, because even the slightest creak would have alerted Trace that he had a peeping Thomasina in his home.

Trace had glass doors on his shower. They allowed for a wonderful view of what was happening inside. His powerful back faced me, broad shoulders flexing and glistening under the water. His ass cheeks were two big melons, dark hair sprinkled down his powerful legs. Everything inside me went taut. Expectant. Ravenous.

Beneath the sound of the running water I heard something else.

Grunting. The soft, barely-there sound of sloshing.

A moment later, Trace groaned. His head tipped back, the water hitting his cheek. The muscles in his back flexed rhythmically. Like he was making some repetitive motion…

Trace was jacking off.

"Mmmmm."

The sound of his low moan sent electricity streaking through me. My panties were instantly wet and my mouth parted. I wanted to leave—*knew* I should leave—but I couldn't. I was rooted to my spot. I couldn't look away from this paragon of masculinity fisting himself in the shower. My thighs clenched together against my aching core. Had there been anything hotter than this in recorded history?

I couldn't fathom it.

"Oh, fuck." Trace grunted again and twisted.

The movement activated my fear of being caught, and I bolted away from the bathroom on instinct. My jelly legs carried me back to the living room, where I stood panting, staring blankly out the window, clutching my chest.

Oh my god, Oh My God, OH MY GOD.

My eyes fluttered shut. All I could see in my mind's eye were the rippling muscles of his back. I could still hear the guttural noise he'd made, which scraped through my memories, lighting wildfires in its path. I swallowed hard, squeezing my legs together again.

This wasn't just bad news. This was nearly fatal.

How on earth was I supposed to continue working with Trace when I couldn't ignore how much I still wanted him? I buried my face in my hands, whispering "please forget, please forget" over and over to myself.

That would be the only way to continue forward with my life. To forget entirely about Trace and his iron grip on my heart. So what I really needed was a *lobotomy.*

The sound of his bedroom door shutting snapped me to alertness. I bit my knuckle, wondering what I could do to look productive, unaffected, *normal.* I drew a deep breath and busied myself with arranging pillows on the couch. I would arrange these pillows until my mind cleared and I could resume functioning like a normal human being. *Excellent plan.*

I picked up the mustard tasseled accent pillows, stacking them one way, and then a different way. I was very intent on getting them precisely positioned when Trace's voice cut through my focus.

"When did you get here?"

I gasped and turned around so fast that I stumbled. My eyes widened as I tripped on the rug and fell gracelessly toward the armchair. My hip hit the armrest of the sofa on my way down, and I landed awkwardly in the lap of the chair.

I clamped my mouth shut and offered a tight smile. "Hi there."

He narrowed his eyes at me. "Are you okay?"

"Yep." My voice was an unnatural squeak. I cleared my throat, smoothing my shirt as I struggled to convert my awkward fall into a casual seated position. "I'm great. H-how are you?"

Trace blinked a few times. It was hard to look at him for too long. He was freshly showered, his hair still tousled and damp. He wore a simple black t-shirt with gray sweatpants. I forced myself to not look below his waist, though in my heart, I was desperate for any glimpse of his dick, even the slightest outline through sweats.

"So when did you get here?"

"Just now," I said, rearranging myself for the third time in the chair. I patted the armrest, inspecting the fibers there. "Willow's asleep. She's uh...perfectly asleep."

He nodded slowly. Maybe suspiciously.

"Are you feeling refreshed?" As soon as the words left my mouth, I felt my cheeks heat up. *CRAP.* I stood and busied myself with arranging the pillows again, just so I could look at and focus on something that wasn't Trace's post-orgasm perfection.

He blinked again. "Why do you ask?"

"You look wet. I mean—" I swallowed hard, willing myself to calm down, to stop acting like a spazz. "You know. *Damp.* Like you, uh—"

"I just took a shower. I was at the gym before you got back." He watched me a moment longer, then reached into the pocket of his sweatpants and revealed his phone, vibrating in his hand. He frowned as he looked at the screen, then answered it a moment later.

"Hello?"

I wilted with relief at the distraction. *Thank everything holy!* I drew a deep breath, willing my cheeks to cool down, while I listened in to Trace's conversation.

"No," he snapped a moment later. "That's ridiculous. I—"

A heavy pause stretched through the apartment. He ran a hand through his tousled hair, heading for the big windows overlooking the city. He paused in front of them, staring outside.

"So you think I should just drop everything and come when he calls?" Trace said, laughing bitterly. More silence, until he added, "You know what? I'm sick of his shit, so I *will* give him what he wants. This last time."

I moved my living room tidying closer to Trace, wishing I could hear the other end of the conversation. I knew something about what Trace was going through, just from my own internet research since taking the job. As a rule, I'd stayed away from knowing anything about Trace after he'd stopped talking to me. The mere notion of seeing evidence of him moving on with his life had been too painful to endure, so I forbid myself from indulging that curiosity.

But now? Knowing about Trace was part of my job. So I learned a lot about what he and his brothers had been going through during my deep dives on the internet. Including the recent hostile takeover his younger brother Axel had executed of a business called Margulis Realty, the company his now-girlfriend had been poised to assume control of.

And like any good internet sleuth, I'd made sure to conduct my research in incognito mode, since I didn't want anyone looking at my browser or phone history and linking me to Trace.

So I had an inkling, based on his tone and overall demeanor—tense but informal—that he was talking to one of his brothers. I figured it had something to do with the SEC investigation hanging over their heads.

"Fine," Trace bit out. "But I'll warn you, if I do this, I'm not going to play the happy family part. I'll see him in a business context only. I don't want him setting foot near me outside the office. Make sure he knows that."

I rolled my lips in, mind racing as I forecast what this meant for him. For me. Would he be leaving? What would Willow and I do? When would this happen?

"I'll let you know later," Trace said quietly. And then he hung up his phone without another word.

He stayed at the window a few moments longer, staring out at the city with his hands propped on his hips. The tension rolled off him, his whole body looking rigid. I fought the urge to go to him, to help ease his mind or at least give him a back massage. But no. That wasn't my role here, even though I desperately wanted it to be.

Trace heaved a sigh and turned on his heel, heading out of the living room. He disappeared down the hallway, and I drifted to the kitchen, ready to make myself a snack. I brought out carrots and celery, washed the veggies, and then found my favorite little ramekin for the dill dip I included in Trace's weekly grocery list. I smiled down at the celery as I chopped it, glancing up only when I heard Trace sigh again.

He'd wandered back into the living room, his hands clasped behind his head, back to the window to stare out at the city. I could tell he was mulling over something big. I watched him for a moment, then refocused on my celery stalks. The sound of the knife against the cutting board was the only thing to break the thick silence of the living room.

Trace paced in front of the window for a few moments, then he strode my way. He paused at the kitchen island, his gaze dropping to my veggies.

"We need to go to New York."

My eyes widened and I looked up at him, stilling my knife. "Okay. When?"

He dragged his gaze up to mine. There was deep conflict swimming his brown eyes. "Now."

I opened my mouth to respond but nothing came out. "Oh boy. I, uh…"

"I need you to come with me so you can be with Willow during the day. It'll be two days, tops."

I cleared my throat, excitement burbling to life. I couldn't deny I was thrilled to get out of Louisville. And with *Trace*, no less. This was almost my secret fantasy coming to life. If I could just somehow arrange for healing our hearts and explaining all the unanswered questions of the past, and top it off with some reconciliatory sex, then life would be perfect.

You are engaged to be married for GOD'S SAKE, MERCEDES.

"Sure," I said, as casually as I could muster. "I don't have my things, is all. I'd like to stop by my house and pack a quick bag."

"We can get whatever you need in the city," Trace said.

"There's just…some things I'd rather bring." I didn't want to tell him that one of those things was my travel-sized vibrator. After what I witnessed in his bathroom, there was no way I could survive a two-day trip to NYC *without* it. Being near Trace was a pressure cooker of relentless desire, and my vibrator was the only way I could deal with it until I figured out a better solution.

And probably the only solution will be quitting your job. But what about Willow?

This whole situation felt like it was spiraling out of control, but I amped up my smile, praying he couldn't hear how hard my heart thumped behind my ribs.

"And," I added, "we should really wait until Willow wakes up. She was so tired after our playdate. I'd hate to wake her early and have her spend the rest of the day cranky."

Trace nodded, rapping his knuckles on the island. "Yeah, that's a good point. You can make it quick at your house then?"

"Of course. It won't take me long."

"We'll swing by on our way to the airport. I'll get things set with the pilot."

I nodded, excitement swelling inside me. "The pilot...?"

"Private jet." He said it casually, like it was a peripheral detail. "You'll be compensated appropriately, too, if that's any concern. I know this is last minute."

"Whatever this is must be important." I watched him for a moment, hoping he'd offer up details.

His jaw flexed as he dragged his gaze up to meet mine. We watched each other for a moment. Then he said, "There's some business I have to wrap up with my brothers. That's all. I need it to be done ASAP."

"Of course. I'm happy to do whatever is helpful." I chopped another carrot stick. "Where will we stay?"

"My apartment in Tribeca." He drew a deep breath. "There are enough rooms for everyone. Plenty of space."

"Oh," I said quietly, chopping up the last of my snack. I wasn't hungry anymore, not by a long shot. All I wanted to do was run around the room and leap for joy. "I'm sure there is. Should I start packing some toys?"

"Sure. I'll go get a bag. And then whatever we're missing..." He shrugged. "We can order when we get there."

I nodded eagerly, swallowing another squeal that threatened to escape. This felt like a vacation, even though it was the opposite of one. Instead of escaping work, I'd have a respite from my family and my upcoming wedding.

Trace couldn't have known how badly I needed this getaway. If he did, he might not have suggested it. After all, I was *engaged*—the reminder he'd issued to me in the back hallway over the weekend still rang through my mind at the worst moments. As well as memories of his thumb brushing over my lips.

I squeezed my eyes shut, grateful that Trace had wandered off to hunt down the luggage. I needed to get a grip. No, I needed to use my vibrator. *Then* I could get a grip. I was just caught in the throes of desire, lost in the hormonal surges. If this had been the 1800s, they would have given me cocaine for my humors and sent me to sit by the sea for four weeks. Thank God I had a vibrator waiting at home for me.

Thankful for a distracting task, I busied myself getting things ready for the trip. I packed up Willow's favorite toys, then snuck into her bedroom to snag her outfits, diapers, and extra blankies, zipping it all into a bag in the spare room. Once I had her things ready, I headed for the kitchen to stuff the cooler bag with milk, juice, and snacks. The clicking of wheels over the tiled floor a moment later alerted me that Trace was approaching. He entered the kitchen a moment later, his rolling luggage behind him.

"All ready?" He worked at buttoning the sleeves of the dress shirt he'd put on. His gray sweatpants had been traded for navy slacks, and his black shirt traded for a long-sleeve white button up. Just like that, he'd gone from sexy, sporty lounger to cutthroat businessman. *Trace*

Fairchild, I love every side of you. I rubbed my forehead, pretending to study the contents of the cooler.

"Just grabbing a few more things. But once she's up, we can leave right away."

"Great." He surveyed the kitchen, his hands on his hips. Silence settled between us, and of course the only thing I could think to bring up was what had happened in the back hallway over the weekend. Every part of me wanted to ask *If you won't be improper there, where do you intend to be improper with me?*

"Do you want any snacks?" I finally blurted.

Trace worked his jaw back and forth, watching me like he hadn't understood the question. Then he cleared his throat and shook his head. "No. I had a late lunch downtown." He looked like he was going to add more then he turned. "Let me know when Willow's awake."

He disappeared down the hallway again, and I set to work making some peanut butter and jelly sandwiches, and then some cold cut sandwiches too, just in case Trace changed his mind. Sure, we were going on a private jet, but I didn't want to make any assumptions about what snacks to expect.

Maybe the only options would be terribly fancy seafood items that Willow wouldn't eat. What if there was only alcohol on board? What if the alcohol-only flight led to both Trace and me becoming drunk in the tiny space of the private jet and continuing the conversation about being improper forty thousand feet in the air? And more importantly, if impropriety occurred that high in the air, did it really count?

Willow might witness it and remember. It could form a core memory—and that didn't seem very good.

I tortured myself with thoughts like these as I lingered over sandwiches, cutting them into precise fourths, bagging them up with excessive care. It was the only way I could force myself not to follow Trace and throw myself at his feet.

Willow eventually awoke; Trace emerged from her room with her nestled in his arms and rubbing her eyes. The sight was just one more devastating blow to my uterus, which practically clenched with need every time I looked at Trace. We readied ourselves, slid on winter coats, and headed for the Benz in the parking garage.

Once we were all settled in the car and he was pulling into the gray afternoon, I blurted, "Just make sure you don't park in the driveway, okay?"

Trace looked over at me, brows furrowed. "What?"

"At my house. I'll give you the address, but I want you to park at the next house over."

Understanding crested his face. "Right."

"And it's not because I don't want to be seen with you," I hurried to add, gesturing in a way that made my fingers brush his. Heat flared inside me again, and I just knew this whole trip was doomed.

I couldn't even chop carrots without imagining him kissing my face off. I was so very screwed.

Trace's gaze flitted to my fingers, then back to the road. "I remember."

"Well, I wanted to make sure. You seemed drunk that night."

His jaw flexed. "I was tipsy. Not trashed."

"So you remember..." I trailed off, unsure what I was getting at. I just wanted him to touch my lips again. I *needed* it, even when it was the last thing I should care about.

"That your family despises me and you can't be seen with me in any setting, under any circumstances?" He flashed me the fakest of smiles. "Yes. I remember very well, Mercedes. Your dirty little secret is safe with me."

I folded my hands in my lap, rolling my lips inward. That hadn't been quite what I was getting at, but it would do. I held so many dirty little secrets inside my heart.

The main secret? For about four months, I thought he and I would become parents, until the miscarriage had stolen that future from me. But that wasn't the dirtiest secret I kept from him.

It would be the challenge of a lifetime to keep this dirtiest of secrets to myself during the next few days: *I think about running away from everything just for the chance to be with you one more time.*

None of it made sense, which was why I'd work overtime to ensure it stayed where it belonged: locked up inside my heart.

CHAPTER THIRTEEN
TRACE

I RUBBED MY PALMS back and forth slowly, observing the heat between my hands. I paused to inspect the lines of my palm next and wondered what fortunes they held. What might a mystic see in my clusterfuck future.

At this point, I would take anything to distract myself. Mercedes sat just a few feet across from me, our leather, overstuffed seats facing each other. Willow was slumped into a peaceful nap in her arms, despite her earlier nap. The comforting hum of the airplane noises might have lulled me to sleep too, if I wasn't staring down the one woman who made my heart race.

Fuck. I cracked my knuckles, moving my gaze back to the window. Mercedes hummed softly, rocking Willow ever-so-gently in her arms.

"You know," she said, "I remember being incredibly upset when I first flew and found out the Care Bears *weren't* up here living in their cloud cities."

I cracked a smile despite my best efforts. Her quirky comments made it difficult to remain stony around her. "They're up here. You just have to know where to look."

"I've been looking for years, and no luck." She clucked her tongue. "So you've seen them?"

"Seen them?" I cocked my head. "I've partied with them."

She snorted, her shoulders shaking with silent laughter. The smile she sent my way was so pure, so beautiful, that it caused that same deep-seated wrenching feeling. The blonde wisps framing her face, escaped from her loose and low ponytail, only made me softer.

"I'm dying to know what the Care Bears are into, behind the scenes," she mused.

"The usual," I said. "Cocaine, hookers, expensive cocktails. That whole purity thing is a front."

She burst out laughing and this time, I joined her. So I could still engage with someone, even when living most of my life in a bad mood. It was just the last person I needed to be engaging.

"You have a lot of insider knowledge about the downfall of the Care Bears," she added. "Are you responsible for their moral decline?"

"It would be easier to blame someone with a reputation like mine, but unfortunately, I can't take the blame." I cracked a smile.

"So you aren't personally familiar with hookers and drugs?" She asked it like a joke, but I saw a glimmer of real curiosity in her words.

I shook my head. "That's not on-brand for the Fairchilds. Expensive cocktails, yes. But the rest, not so much."

She sighed happily, gaze moving toward the window. "Do you think it's snowing in New York?"

"Clear skies when I last checked."

"Maybe it *will* snow, then?"

I narrowed my eyes. "Are you hoping for a snowstorm or something?"

"It would be lovely, you know?" Her eyes shone with excitement as she looked back at me, and I could feel the giddiness radiating off her. It was contagious. "Like from a movie. A snow day in New York City."

"I take it you don't go to New York often."

She shook her head. "I don't go *anywhere* often."

"Why's that?"

Her face softened as she thought. "I don't know...just the annual family vacation, and whatever..." She licked her lips, looking at me guiltily. "Whatever Caleb decides to surprise me with."

I clenched my jaw, running my thumb back and forth over my knuckles. Just the mention of his name had me eager to follow through on that meet-and-greet between my fist and Caleb's mouth.

"Should I not say his name now?" Mercedes asked softly.

I cleared my throat. Maybe I was being too visibly annoyed by the mention. But I had good reason now. "I met him today."

Mercedes's eyes went as round as saucers. "You *what*?"

"I didn't mention you or your employment with me." I leaned back in my seat, drawing a deep breath. "Don't worry."

"But why...how..."

"I ran into him at a luncheon put on by the Chamber of Commerce. Your father and brother were there as well."

She dragged a hand down the side of her face , looking aghast. "Did they...say anything?" she forced out.

"Caleb did. He actually sat next to me." I laughed sardonically. "He criticized my business and warned me that I shouldn't stay in Louisville. Sweet guy."

Mercedes pinched her eyes shut, tilting her head up to the ceiling. "Yes. Lovely man."

"I know I'm not a fan favorite with the Hendricks crowd. They sent Caleb the attack dog, but too bad for him, his bark doesn't scare me."

"I'm sorry," Mercedes said.

"You don't have to be. You had nothing to do with it. So where does this lovely man of yours tend to take you on vacation?"

She rolled her lips inward, looking at me heavily. Her throat bobbed. "We've been to California."

"Yeah?"

"Texas," she added.

"Fascinating."

"Florida," she said.

"Mmm. His choices or yours?"

"His."

"So he's afraid of flying internationally." I crossed an ankle over my knee. "Tell me, where would *you* go? Without your *fiancé.*"

She winced at the word, which wasn't the first time. Or maybe it was just the way I pronounced it. It did come out with a bit of a slap each time. Her lips parted, gaze drifting off as she thought.

"Well..." she started, looking out the window again. "I think I'd go somewhere exotic. But not like Instagram exotic. I mean...deep mountains. No cell signal. Um...snowfall. Tons of it. And there'd be an infinity hot tub and a fully stocked bookcase. And just...not a single soul asking me to do something I didn't want to do. Or planning my day for me. Just blissful silence."

Our gazes locked, her words settling inside me like a challenge. No, a promise. Because she had to know that now that she'd said it, I planned to deliver it to her.

But only if she was mine.

"So, a solo read-cation," I summarized.

"Yeah. Absolutely." That soft smile returned to her face, equal parts girlish and wise. "Where would you like to go?"

I opened my mouth to respond but nothing came out. I rubbed at the side of my jaw as I thought. "I can go anywhere I want, whenever

I want. And I often do. But the one place I'd like to go, I can't. And that's back to happier times."

Mercedes tilted her head. "When were your happiest times?"

With you. I averted my gaze, lest she read the truth there. "Before the SEC investigation, that's for sure."

She watched me intensely for a moment. "Were you happy when we were together?"

The question was a slap in the face. My insides seized up. Everything inside me wanted to avoid answering this question, because honesty would push me down a forbidden path. "Why does it matter?"

"I'm just curious."

"The answer to that question has no bearing on the present day."

"Were you?"

I clenched my jaw, moving my gaze to the window. The plane decelerated slightly. "We're almost there. We should wake up Willow."

"You didn't answer me."

Something inside me snapped. My gaze returned to her like a whip cracking against flesh. "You won't get the answer. Not when you're engaged to somebody else."

Her lips thinned. "You didn't seem to care about that on Saturday."

"It was the alcohol talking."

She sent me a flat look before whispering in Willow's ear. She stirred, her big blue eyes opening to look at me. I couldn't help but smile.

"Hey, pretty girl." I held out my hands and she moved toward me. I scooped her up into my arms, settling her on my lap. She blinked sleepily, gaze landing on the window and the world beyond. Mercedes's gaze smoldered on me, discontent seeping out of her.

I knew the feeling all too well. And I was determined to rid it from my life.

She needs to be mine or be gone.

The pressure had ratcheted up, and not just because we were 40,000 feet in the air. This dance we did around her engagement to Caleb was one I didn't plan to continue much longer. A decision needed to be made. And while rationality told me that Mercedes should be *gone*, every last bit of me wanted her to be *mine*. I was as tired of not having her as I was of flip-flopping between the two options.

The plane descended, and before long we were taxing at the airport. We stepped off the jet to a damp runway but no snow, the city skyline looming in the distance. I ushered Willow and Mercedes into the backseat of the waiting SUV. Damian's driver, Legs, awaited us with a big grin.

"Long time no see, boss."

"Kentucky's got me in its clutches. I'd like you to meet Mercedes and Willow. Ladies, meet Legs."

"Hi, there." Mercedes waved.

"Two new ladies in your life, huh?" Legs winked at me through the rearview mirror as he pulled away.

"You could say that," I conceded. It was more effort to correct him. And he wasn't technically wrong. He just didn't know that both were on loan, and that was the biggest problem of all.

Willow sat quietly between Mercedes and me while we chatted about nothing and everything with Legs—how the winter had been going in New York, what I thought about the most recent stock turns, whether or not Willow would go to New York schools once she was of age. Once we made it to my apartment, something deep inside loosened. Louisville, with all its recent stressors, hadn't felt completely like home. But now, we were on my turf. Legs helped me unload our bags just around the corner from the penthouse, per my request. I waved him off when he offered to help me take them up to the condo. Mercedes and Willow were both red-cheeked and smiling as we made our way through the brisk New York air to the building that I called home.

Mercedes gasped as we neared, pointing at the bright signage and glass walls that had come into view as we rounded a corner. This had been by design. I didn't want Legs to pull up in front and ruin my surprise. "You...you live here?" Her gaze cascaded over the endless rows of books visible through the street-level walls. "In a Barnes & Noble?"

I looked up at the thirty-five-story building. It was mixed-use, and the ground floor was currently rented to the bookseller. "That's right. I live in the penthouse, though."

"The penthouse of a Barnes & Noble." Her eyes fluttered and she pressed a hand to her chest. "I didn't even realize there could be such a delightful thing. Well, if you ever can't find me, you know where to look."

I bit back a grin, guiding her to the main entrance for the condos just off to the side of the book store. "Noted."

"Why didn't you warn me?"

"I didn't want you to drop everything and move to Tribeca. You have a whole life. Caleb would be devastated."

She sighed testily. "Trace."

"Just my way of keeping you on your toes. You never know what I'll surprise you with next." I flashed her an evil grin as I swiped the key fob that opened the main door to the reception foyer. Our footsteps scuffed softly on the gleaming, tiled floor as I led the way to the elevators, our luggage clicking behind me. Willow shrank into Mercedes's embrace as we neared the elevator.

"It's okay, sweetie." I patted her back as she buried her head in Mercedes's shoulder. After a moment, she twisted and reached for me. I lifted her into my arms and she nuzzled as deep as she could.

The elevator doors dinged softly. When Mercedes tried to help with the luggage, I batted her hand away and maneuvered it on one-handed. Mercedes sent me flat look, but amusement curled the edges of her lips.

We soared upward. This condo wasn't as grand or awe-inspiring as the one I shared with my brothers on Wall Street, but it was my own cozy nook in Manhattan. Mercedes let out a low hum of appreciation as soon as we stepped inside the foyer, her *oohs* and *aahs* growing louder the deeper we wound into the condo. We paused at the great room, where the floor-to-ceiling windows offered a panoramic skyline view of the city as dusk approached. The sunset promised to be a good one, based on the artist's palate of reds and oranges coalescing on the horizon. I turned on the fireplace via my smartphone, the crackling warmth a welcome addition to the homecoming.

"What's that river?" she asked.

"Hudson. And over there is Rockefeller Park." I pointed it out. Willow shifted in my arms, lifting her head. She pointed toward the window and made a noise that sounded like "Da!"

I nodded, agreeing with her. "You nailed it, sweetie." I checked my watch. "I ordered some things to be delivered for Willow, which should be arriving soon."

Mercedes stayed at the window, tilting her head back and forth as she examined the view. She sighed, crossing her arms. A few moments later, she sighed again.

I was content watching her. With Willow in my arms, the fireplace heating the room, the two of us cozy and complete here with Mercedes.

Complete.

I hated how natural it felt to have these two in my life. None of it was permanent. None of it was truly meant for me. Mercedes was destined to continue her path with her fiancé, because that's what made sense for her. And Willow might return to Ian someday, undoing all this progress we'd made.

Enjoy it while you can, because this isn't going to last.

Fuck, I hated being such a pragmatist sometimes.

Mercedes sighed again, cocking her hip. "It's just so...fascinating. So consuming. A never-ending spiral of humanity."

"Well said."

She looked over her shoulder at me. "How do you get any work done here? I could stare at this for hours."

"Maybe I've gotten a little used to it." I cracked a smile. "Or I head to the office on Wall Street. The views there are tempered by the staff reminding me I have work to do."

She laughed. "Can I see your office building?"

My chest grew tight. I didn't know why, but the request felt intimate. "It won't be mine for much longer."

"What do you mean?"

There I went again, inviting the dark cloud into my consciousness. I bounced Willow on my knee, choosing to focus on her big blue eyes, and the innocence in her tiny, perfect face. "If all goes according to plan while I'm here, I'll be writing myself out of Fairchild Enterprises."

Mercedes tutted, drifting closer to me. The concern etched into her features was a gut punch I hadn't expected. "Trace, I'm so sorry to hear that. What happened?"

I sighed, shaking my head. "It's a lot. Maybe some other time."

She lifted a brow. "Once you've had a drink? That seems to get you to open up."

I tried to hide the wry grin that threatened to overtake my face. "Is that how you always talk to your employer?"

She pursed her lips. "Of course not. But thankfully you aren't my employer. Aurora's is." She sashayed past me, and I reached for her to swat her, only realizing once my arm was through the air that yes, I was aiming to slap her ass. *Fuck.* Old habits died hard. She giggled and hurried past my reach.

The doorway to informality had been opened once more. And it wasn't the first time today. I had a feeling it was only going to grow harder to keep this door shut.

Thud thud thud.

The knock on the penthouse door jolted me, which in turn sent Willow whimpering and clinging to me like a koala. I shushed her, patting her back.

"It's probably the delivery," I said, surging to my feet. "I'll get it."

Mercedes stayed behind as I headed for the door, tugging it open. I was prepared for the unfamiliar face of a delivery person, possibly with several boxes or bags in tow.

I was not prepared to see my brother Damian and his girlfriend Jessa beaming at me.

"Fuck," I blurted.

Jessa upped the wattage on her smile while Damian just shook his head and stepped inside. "That's what you call a greeting, huh? You gonna let us in?"

"Come in," I said with a little laugh. "Sorry, I just...I was expecting someone, but it wasn't *you two*."

"Surprise!" Jessa laughed, her gaze darting between me, Willow, and just over my shoulder. "Now it's a party!"

A party I hadn't been counting on. I loved my brother...I loved Jessa...but I hadn't properly caught him up on the developments in Louisville. I hadn't even told him that Mercedes was the nanny. I'd planned on updating him over the phone tonight, but apparently he'd had other plans. Honestly, after so much strife and disconnection, part of me was glad for it.

This was what it felt like to have a brother. I'd missed it.

Damian leaned closer, peering past my shoulder to look at Willow. "Hello, miss. Are you my new niece?"

Willow burrowed deeper into my shoulder and turned her head from him.

"Sorry, guys. Let me make introductions." I pushed the door shut behind them and hoisted Willow higher into my arms. "This here is Willow, the newest member of the Fairchild family. And over there is Mercedes." I paused, remembering I should probably clarify. "Willow's nanny."

"Hi, y'all." Mercedes offered a little wave, her sweet smile taking the edge off the surprise encounter. "It's a pleasure."

"You are a doll," Jessa gushed, rushing forward to shake Mercedes's hand. "It's so nice to meet you."

Damian propped his hands on his hips, looking over at Mercedes. "Wait a second..."

I groaned internally, heading for the great room. I knew what was coming.

"I know you," Damian followed up. He, Jessa, and Mercedes followed me, and we all assembled around the couches and fireplace.

He studied her for a moment, narrowing his eyes. "Shit, I can't remember where from."

"The Governor's Ball," I filled in for him. He'd been in attendance the night Mercedes and I first met.

He snapped his fingers. "That's it. It's been a while, huh?"

Mercedes nodded. "I didn't think you'd remember me. It's good to see you again."

I didn't want him filling in more of the blanks, not while both Jess and Mercedes were present. "How the hell did you know we were here already? We only just got here."

"You underestimate me, brother." Damian clapped my shoulder, giving me a mischievous grin. There was a reason he was the Chief Technology Officer of our business. He had creepily good tech skills. "Have you forgotten so quickly now that you're back in Kentucky? I knew the second your jet landed."

"Did you hack my location services again? I turned that shit off for a reason."

Damian's gaze flitted over to Mercedes, whose eyes were slowly growing wider. "Actually, Legs told me when your plane landed. I didn't hack you or anything like that, I just used good old-fashioned person-to-person communication. Like a completely normal human. Let's not scare Mercedes right off the bat, okay?"

"At least he gave you guys time to get your things inside the house," Jessa added wryly. "I told him he needed to give you a second to use the bathroom, for cryin' out loud."

Damian shrugged. "I didn't want to wait. We don't have much time together. And with a new member of the family, I want to suck up every second possible."

"Aww. Look at that, Willow." I hugged her tighter. "The best uncle around. After me, of course."

"I intend on keeping that title," Damian said. "You're the best Dad-Uncle. I'm the best Regular Uncle."

I laughed. "This is what we get for having such a dysfunctional family."

"We put the fun in dysfunctional," Damian quipped. That earned a round of laughter from everyone.

"Used to, I guess. Now it's just...fucked," I muttered.

"That word isn't part of dysfunctional so you can't claim it," Damian corrected me. "Besides, Jessa and I want to bring the fun part back. Can we take you guys out to dinner?"

"Pretty please?" Jessa said, her gaze darting between Mercedes and me.

Mercedes's eyes lit up. She gasped, too.

"I don't know about that," I started.

"Are you sure, Trace?" Damian asked, his gaze sliding over to Mercedes. "Mercedes, you really seem like you'd like to go out for dinner somewhere in Manhattan. Tell your grumpy old boss it's part of your requirements."

Mercedes laughed, pressing a hand to her mouth. To me, she said, "Oh, I would *love* a night out on the town in Manhattan. And so would Willow! It sounds like a dream come true."

Damian watched me with a shit-eating grin. "See? And Willow would love it too." I could practically hear his unspoken words. *I got ya.*

CHAPTER FOURTEEN
TRACE

TRACE"Just look at this." Jessa tilted her head, guiding Mercedes toward a different part of the dining room. I watched the two of them drift off, captivated by the lines and curves of Mercedes's body beneath her cream sweater and dark pants.

"Mercedes seems to love the city," Damian remarked, leaning back in his seat. We were at one of the most popular restaurants in Manhattan, known for its view from approximately eleven thousand stories in the sky. This skyscraper was so tall I swore I could feel the restaurant sway in the wind. We'd just ordered dinner, and Willow sat happily in my lap, making my hands clap and smiling each time they went *slap*. She'd opened up a little but still wouldn't look Damian in the eye.

"I didn't realize how much she loved New York." I kept an eye on Mercedes as Jessa led her to the wall of windows at the far edge of the dining room.

"Why would you know that about your nanny?" Damian asked.

I opened my mouth to respond, but nothing came out. He had a point. It was a damning confirmation of my feelings for Mercedes. When I looked over at him, he wore that same brotherly shit-eating grin.

"You are too much," I muttered.

"Have you been in love with her since the ball?" he asked.

I sighed tersely, looking down at Willow. "It doesn't matter."

"What?"

"I said it doesn't matter." I looked up at him, enunciating my words. "She's engaged. I'm heading to prison. What's the point?"

Damian rolled his eyes. "That sounds familiar."

"The prison part, maybe. Not the engaged part." I tilted my head toward the women across the room. "Jessa was not engaged."

"Fine. You win on that point. But Mercedes does not see you solely as her employer."

"How can you tell?" I reached for my glass of wine and took a sip.

"I don't know. The way she looks at you. It's...like there's sparkles in her eyes or something."

"Sparkles?"

Damian narrowed his eyes at me. "You know what I mean."

"Whatever. It doesn't matter. She'll be Mrs. Somebody Else in a few months." I took another sip of my wine, then set it back down on the table. Willow reached for my palm again and continued clapping it against my other hand. "She made that choice. She's the one who told me to fuck off six years ago. I'm sure she had sparkles in her eyes back then too."

Damian nodded, looking thoughtful as his gaze drifted out over the bustling dining room. "Yeah. Maybe you're right."

"I am." I pressed a kiss to the top of Willow's head just as my phone began vibrating in my pants pocket. I pulled it out, finding a strange number on the screen. "I know I am."

"You sound a little doubtful," Damian said, rolling his eyes in case his sarcastic tone wasn't clear.

"Just preparing for the meeting tomorrow," I told him. I silenced the call. "Meeting with our brother requires a certain degree of bullheadedness and I'm getting my reps in now."

Damian rubbed his forehead, studying the white linen tablecloth as if it held the answers we all needed. When he finally spoke, he said, "Listen, Axel claims he wants a decision tomorrow, but I think he's bluffing."

"It doesn't matter," I told him. "I'll give it to him."

Damian's face fell. "What does that mean?"

"He says he wants me out of the business, and I am readier than ever to give it to him. I'm out. I've got things set up in Louisville already." My phone started ringing again, vibrating harshly against the table. It was the same number, and I silenced it again. "It's the perfect time to exit."

Any trace of Damian's jovial mood fell to the floor like deadweight. Suddenly, he just looked exhausted. "Trace. It doesn't have to be like this."

"What did Mom always say?" I drained my wine glass. "Life never goes as planned, even when you do everything right. This is me rolling with the punches. Why stay in a business where I'm not welcome?"

"You are still welcome," Damian said.

"Bullshit. Axel seems content to overlook the fact that I was an integral part in creating and growing that business to the staggering success we've achieved. Not including the SEC investigation in the staggering part," I added.

"Yeah, I had more to do with the SEC part than you," Damian muttered.

"It doesn't matter. I'll be blunt. Our brother is an asshole. And now I'm the target of his everlasting grudge." I signaled for a waiter. "Lucky me."

Damian's shoulders heaved with a deep sigh. He watched me for a moment. "It's my turn to be blunt. I can't do Fairchild Enterprises without you."

I shrugged. "I can't do it if a third of it wants me out."

Damian's throat bobbed, and he studied his knuckles for a moment. "We can still make this work."

"You're wrong. You and I could still make this work. You and I *plus Axel* cannot."

Damian mulled over my words while I focused on Willow again, clapping her hands together for a change and bouncing her on my knee. My phone vibrated for a third time from the same number. I scowled down at the screen and snapped it up, answering quickly.

"Hello?"

Silence flooded the line, but the connection was there. I could tell *someone* was on the other end. After a moment, a male voice rasped out, "Trace Fairchild."

My stomach twisted. "Who is this?"

No response. I ended the call and immediately blocked the number. Damian looked at me expectantly. "Everything okay?"

"I dunno. Seemed like a spam call." I shook it off. I spotted the server as he approached with some of our plates—filet mignon, braised scallops, the most lavish polenta and octopus dish I'd ever seen. Damian waved down Jessa and Mercedes, who quickly returned to the table.

"Wow, look at this spread." Mercedes's eyes were wide as saucers as she eased back into her seat. I popped Willow into the highchair between Mercedes and me as the server continued setting down plates of food. Mercedes got to work cutting up the chargrilled chicken breast I'd ordered for Willow while I fed her small bites of gourmet mac and cheese.

"You guys have the rhythm down," Jessa noted with a smile, before she dug into her polenta. "It's like you've been doing this for ages."

"Well, I've been working with children for ages," Mercedes said with a little laugh.

"What she means to say is that I'm the deadweight," I added with a wry smile. "She makes it look like I know what I'm doing."

Mercedes swatted my arm. "You've done extremely well. Don't sell yourself short."

"That's being generous, and we both know it." I cut off a bite of steak.

Damian leaned my way and said in a low voice, "*Sparkles.*"

I sent him the most lethal look I could muster.

"Mercedes, how old are you?" Jessa asked.

"I'm twenty-five." She reached for her wine glass, which held only water. "Why do you ask?"

"I wondered if maybe we were in the same grade in school. But I'm older than you," Jessa said with a laugh.

"And Trace is older still," Damian said.

I turned to him so I could deliver a pointed look. "Thank you for that."

"Did you go to college?" Damian asked Mercedes.

"I did. I went to University of Kentucky, graduated the top of my class." Her throat bobbed before taking another big gulp of water.

"Mercedes was on track to become a child psychologist," I offered, looking over at her.

Jessa gasped, covering her mouth with her hand. "Are you serious?"

"That's awesome," Damian said.

Mercedes's cheeks immediately went pink, which told me my subterfuge had landed as intended. "It's...an interest of mine. I haven't taken the steps to start my master's degree."

"Oh, you should! I can already tell you'd be so great at that," Jessa encouraged before taking another bite of her food.

"I'm uh...I'm not really sure if..." Mercedes trailed off.

"Grad school isn't that daunting," Damian said. "Trace and I both got our MBAs, and we survived. I bet you'd smash a counseling degree."

Mercedes looked doubtful, and part of me enjoyed seeing her so uncomfortable. I suspected her resistance was only based on her family's disapproval. She was expected to become *Caleb's Wife* and nothing else. Well fuck that. If nothing else, I'd remind her that she had a life beyond what they expected from her, which I'm sure revolved around her uterus and continuing the family gene pool.

"I've been looking into it," she said at last, before taking a bite of scallop.

"There are some awesome schools around the country, and of course some great ones here in New York," I said.

"You could have that skyline all year round," Jessa said brightly.

Mercedes laughed softly and shook her head. I could hear the excuses piling up inside of her, but she didn't shoot down their optimism. She didn't even mention that she was engaged or returning to Louisville because she had a whole life there waiting for her, omissions I found interesting. Even more interesting than when she'd failed to tell her old college friend about her engagement at the specialist's office, too.

Dinner churned on, delicious and engaging. Damian and Jessa and I barreled through another bottle of wine, though Mercedes repeatedly refused invitations to join. Once we'd had our fill of dining, wining, and laughter, Damian and Jessa said their goodbyes, and Mercedes and I headed back with Willow to wind down at my Barnes & Noble penthouse.

Willow nodded off in the stroller as soon as we boarded the elevator. As the doors closed, I tried to ignore the thrum of alcohol in my veins, urging me to resume teasing Mercedes the way I always did when I was tipsy.

I absolutely should not pull at that thread.

"So why didn't you have any wine tonight?" I asked, once the elevator doors slid shut.

She sent me a surprised look. "I'm on the clock."

"You can have a glass during dinner. It's not illegal."

She shrugged. "It just seemed...inappropriate. You brought me here to take care of Willow, and that's what I'll be doing."

I tilted my head. "But would you have *liked* a drink?"

Mercedes cracked a smile. "This seems like a trap."

"You have to be off the clock at some point. It's illegal to make you work 24/7 and I'm nothing if not a law-abiding...client." Because I wasn't her employer. She caught the reference and laughed.

"I wouldn't mind a glass once I put Willow down."

The elevator doors slid open, revealing the front door of my penthouse. "Consider it done."

While Mercedes took Willow into the spare room, I headed to the wine rack in the corner of the kitchen to select that evening's wine. I'd had a couple glasses at dinner already—I knew what more wine would lead to.

But this was the eternal struggle with Mercedes.

She needs to be yours or be gone.

The tension ratcheted up every extra moment we spent together. I chose a Chilean Petit Verdot, simply because we'd shared one together during a wine-tasting event in downtown Louisville. Maybe she wouldn't remember. But apparently these small touches were my way of inching me closer to my decision.

She's yours.

I popped the cork just as Mercedes came into the kitchen, smiling brightly at me.

"Perfect timing," she said, leaning against the countertop as she watched me pour two generous glasses. "What's the grape of the night?"

"Petit Verdot," I told her as I corked the bottle and set it aside. I lifted my glass, and she did the same. "Do you remember the last time we shared a Petit Verdot?"

Her smile didn't waver. "At the wine crawl in downtown Louisville."

The response touched me more than I wanted to admit. "It was one of the last nights we spent together before…"

She sipped her wine. The unspoken words hung heavily in the air. When our eyes locked, electricity sizzled there.

"Are you going to derail our wine experience so quickly?" Mercedes asked. "I wanted to at least enjoy a few sips before we did something to dredge up the past and make it uncomfortable between us."

I fought a grin. "I admire your bluntness. I'll allow us another five minutes before the Past Dredging schedule begins."

A laugh popped out of her, and she took a deep inhale over the wine glass. "Gosh, this smells great. I love Petit Verdot."

"Me too." I swirled the burgundy liquid in my glass, watching the legs dribble down the sides of the cup. "Maybe we should take a trip to some wineries in Chile."

Her eyes shone with excitement as she looked over at me. "That sounds fun. When should we go?"

"We could go as soon as next month. It's summer down there, you know. Perfect time to visit." I took another mouthful.

She sighed happily. "That sounds like a dream. A wine tour in Chile."

"Of course we'd have to go for two weeks, minimum. You think your beloved fiancé could survive without you for that long?"

She quirked her lips and drank instead of answering. When the glass touched the countertop, she said softly, "I think he'll have to start getting used to it."

Something in her tone felt serious. Like a confession. I tipped my head toward the couches and fireplace. "Let's go sit down. When we start dredging up the past, we're going to want to be seated."

She laughed and drifted behind me through the kitchen and into the great room. I eased onto the couch closest to the fireplace, setting my wine glass down on the marble end table. When she turned toward the couch opposite me, I shook my head.

"Sit here." I patted the space next to me. "I won't be able to hear you all the way over there."

"Have you gone deaf without letting me know?"

"Don't be a brat." I watched as she set her wine glass down on the table at the other end of the couch. "I'm just trying to be a good host and follow all the rules of social decorum." She plopped onto the couch next to me, a pleasant waft of her perfume hitting me. My belly clenched, and I felt the desire licking through my veins.

She's yours.

"Social decorum, huh?" She looked over at me with such a genuinely amused smile that it prompted an equal smile from me. "That's what you say to all your engaged nannies, isn't it?"

This time, the laughter popped out of me. "Touché. So I take it you're ready for the past dredging now?"

In the soft lighting of the room, the expanse of Manhattan visible through the big windows while the fire crackled behind me, every-thing felt so right. I wanted this to continue forever.

"Not excited for it, but as prepared as I'll ever be." She lifted her glass in a sarcastic toast, and we smiled as we clinked glasses.

Somehow, we'd managed to turn this awk-ward-and-painful-as-hell situation into something we could laugh about and bond over together. I wasn't sure if it was a sign of our compatibility or a sign that we were both a little fucked up.

It didn't matter. As conflicted as I was about whether Mercedes and I should ever be an item again, my cock didn't give a fuck. My cock still wanted her, just as much as ever. And with each sip of wine, it was harder to care about whether I *should* go after her.

I set my glass down and reached out for her hand resting on the couch. I ran my thumb over her palm, turning it face-up.

"Did you bring your ring?"

Her throat bobbed, and she shook her head, her gaze glued to our hands.

"Why didn't you tell Damian and Jessa about Caleb tonight?" I asked, watching her expression closely. "Or about the fact that you're planning a wedding or anything about what's supposed to be the biggest moment of your life?"

Her eyes fluttered shut and her head dropped to the back of the couch. "There's the past dredging."

"As promised."

"I didn't want to get into it," she finally said, opening her eyes and searing me with a look that nearly ripped me in two. "I never want to get into it. Because I...I hate it."

Alarm bells were going off inside me now. This was big. And *thrilling*. "You hate it?"

A loud sigh escaped her, and she buried her face in her hands. "No, that's not the right word. I mean, yes, I hate the wedding planning process and everyone's expectations of me and the way I have almost no say in my own wedding..." Another sigh ripped out of her as she shook her head. "This trip was a chance to get away from all that. So I didn't want to bring it up. Make sense?"

"Of course." I resumed massaging her hand, pressing my thumb into her pressure points. Her eyes fluttered shut again.

"Mmm."

"You like that?"

"It feels so nice."

"You want me to massage the rest of your body?"

She laughed. "That sounds like a trap too."

"I promise it'll stay PG. Just like the massage you pay for at the spa." These were lies, but I was too hungry for her. I wanted her as much as I knew she wanted me. We just needed to get rid of the blockade between us: her engagement. And until that happened, I was helpless to resist my attraction to her. As much as I knew I needed to stay away from her while she was engaged to Caleb, I couldn't fucking stick to it.

"I don't buy that for a second." Her eyes twinkled as she took another drink of wine.

"You're smart. At least let me give you a neck massage."

"I can agree to that." She moved to the floor between my legs when I prompted her, sitting with her back against the couch. I rubbed my hands together briskly, then started with a firm but methodical touch on the ridge of her shoulders. Her head lolled forward and she moaned.

"Trace, that feels so goooood."

I loved hearing her say my name; especially like *that*. My cock twitched and I reminded myself to focus on the task at hand. Her skin was smooth and soft beneath my fingers. Every bit of friction reminded me of all the rest of her skin there was to discover. The unending wonderland beneath her clothes that I had been dreaming of for years.

I worked on her neck until her breathy moans were too much to handle, each one sending my cock spasming. I gritted my teeth, moving my hands to the sides of her arms for a quick squeeze. This needed to stop. *Now.* I'd indulged too much.

"That's enough," I said, my voice sounding rough.

"Nooo," she moaned, tipping her head to one side. "Please, Trace, I need more."

I laughed ruefully. I'd taken myself into dangerous territory, and I wasn't entirely sure I could navigate myself out of it. One wrong move and I'd be a goner. The lust was way stronger than the alcohol—I knew that. And I suspected she knew that too.

I leaned down to speak into her ear. "Mercedes, I can't. Not unless you want to unleash a part of me that does very inappropriate things with engaged women."

I saw the goosebumps flare on her neck. She turned to look up at me.

"Things like what?"

I narrowed my eyes at her. "I'm not going to elaborate. Stand up."

"Are these the improper things you promised me in the back hallway at the country club?" I caught a note of giddiness in her voice. "Because I've been so curious about them."

"You don't actually care about your fiancé, do you?" I challenged.

"I never said that," she said in a shaky voice.

"Then what? Are you suggesting we start an affair?"

Her throat bobbed and her gaze dropped to the floor. "No, of course not. I just...I don't get it."

I laughed in spite of the situation, rubbing at my face. "I don't get it either. Trust me, Mercedes, I'd happily fuck an engaged woman until the sun comes up. *Especially* you. But I think we both know that's not what either of us wants in the long run."

Her gaze darkened and she pushed to standing, propping her hands on her hips. "Then why did you tell me to sit on the couch with you? Or offer to give me a massage? Why any of it, when you don't want it in the long run?"

The frustration bubbled over. "Because I do want it! I'm never going to not want you, Mercedes." My voice came out a gruff bark, louder than even I'd intended. "And I wish I could fucking control it, but I can't. Even when you're engaged to somebody else. It's going to keep happening. Yes, it comes out quicker when I drink. But it's there when I don't, too."

Mercedes cocked a hip, staring at me so intensely I thought she'd burn a hole through my forehead. I could see the struggle in her. The gears and the math equations happening inside her brain, trying to make sense of it all. Because it was a tough one. We had clear chemistry, unresolved history, and simmering resentment, stacked on top of an unyielding compatibility and respect for one another.

How did we move forward from here?

"Clearly you feel it too," I went on, my heart hammering at my ribs. "Which makes me wonder how the fuck you can even stay with him."

"Because I made a commitment," she spat out, her voice low and wavering. "I made a promise. Caleb was there for me after you detonated my entire life. He's been Jericho's best friend since *forever*, I can't just—"

"Leave him? Look for someone that you actually give a fuck about? Go to fucking grad school like you've been wanting since you were nineteen?"

Mercedes's face turned to stone, and she surged toward me. I looked away.

"Fuck you, Trace."

I shook my head, schooling my reaction to her use of a swear word. "Don't we both wish?"

"You are acting like an asshole, and I am going to bed. Personally, I don't want to hate myself for the rest of my life because I cheated on someone who didn't deserve it. Whatever you think about Caleb, he doesn't deserve to be treated like that. And I don't intend to disrespect him like that. I am not that woman."

"Probably for the best," I told her, examining my knuckles, forcing myself to keep my eyes on anything but her. "And you should start brainstorming."

"About what?"

"How to keep this from happening every time it's ten p.m. and we're alone together." I dared myself to look at her, finding the rawest, most vulnerable look on her face. "Because when I think of what a possible solution could be...well, you wouldn't like the idea."

She straightened her back, crossing her arms. "Goodnight, Trace." She spun on her heel and stormed off to the recesses of the penthouse, leaving me in a thick, choking cloud of my own conflict.

I needed her as much as I wanted her gone.

There was no middle ground with Mercedes.

I needed either all of her or nothing at all. And I had a feeling that by the end of this trip, we'd find a solution to this conundrum...whether we liked it or not.

CHAPTER FIFTEEN
MERCEDES

My bare footsteps along the floor were the only sound in the early morning. The penthouse lay still, sepulchral even, at this hour.

It was far too early to be up, but I had barely slept, thanks to the frustrating yet titillating encounter Trace and I shared right before bed. So what else was there to do at five thirty other than get up and start the day?

I tugged the soft blanket tighter around my shoulders, my current read—Nightingale by Kristin Hannah—tucked beneath my arm. I stopped by Willow's room to check on her—snoring softly—then headed for the great room, where the view and the fireplace awaited me. I'd been fantasizing about this since setting foot in the penthouse—reading, all by myself, Manhattan as my backdrop. Utter perfection. And nearly mine.

I stopped in the kitchen to brew a quick cup of coffee. While the machine whirred to life, I drifted closer to the wall of windows. Tiny snowflakes drifted through the dark morning air. Dawn barely strained at the edges of the city. I shivered into my blanket, smiling into the soft fibers.

Snowflakes seemed promising—perhaps a snowstorm was heading this way next. I could only hope.

Once my coffee had brewed, I poured my cup and added oat milk and a half spoonful of sugar, stirred, then heading for the big couch where Trace had given me the most amazing neck massage of my life. I snuggled into place, trying not to fantasize about what might have happened had either of us decided enough was enough. I'd only tortured myself with those thoughts for hours last night. I didn't need them to steal more of my waking hours today.

Read. It was time to read. That's what I was here to do. I drew a deep breath, ready to reset my mind and my day. It was already off to a great start, with the snowfall and the coffee and the pre-dawn solitude, as long as I overlooked the lukewarm feelings about my fiancé and the white-hot feelings about the one man I couldn't touch.

"Time to read," I murmured to myself. A reminder. I opened my book.

I sank easily into my fictional world—a blessing—and lost track of time as I always did. When I looked up next, it was only because the burbling of the coffee maker snagged my attention.

And immediately after that, Trace's broad, naked chest.

I blinked rapidly. The air in my lungs evaporated. He hadn't spotted me yet, so I shrank deeper into my blanket.

Trace was the broad-shouldered man of my dreams. Dark hair, perfectly tousled, with a brown gaze that could both see into my soul and set me on fire. He was strong, collected, and kind, even when dealing with so many difficult things at once.

Why couldn't things have worked out the first time around? This question still burned inside my heart, far brighter than I cared to admit. I should have been ecstatic to find a man like Caleb, but all I could think of was Trace.

Trace's bare feet scuffed over the wood floors next, headed this way. I nibbled my bottom lip, noticing the book tucked beneath his arm. He was heading to the same spot to do this same thing. How absolutely heartwarming—and not at all helpful in my quest to keep myself away from the man.

He neared, his gaze landing on me. He blew at the top of his coffee as he slowed.

"Morning," he said.

"Morning." I reached for my coffee and took a sip.

He settled into the couch opposite me. Our gazes met briefly before I yanked my eyes back to my open book. I so desperately wanted to ask what he was reading, what he thought about it, what he might be reading next—only to follow up with questions like whether he slept at all last night, if he'd imagined fucking me until the sun came up like he'd said, what position he might try first.

But I kept my mouth clamped shut and focused on my own book. Trace set his coffee down; after a few moments, he revealed a highlighter. The tip squeaked against the pages of his book.

The sun crept into the sky, illuminating the city in wide swaths of clarity. The snow continued to fall, casting a beautiful glimmer to everything. After a while, Willow cried, and I set my book aside so I could go to her. I found her red-cheeked and bleary-eyed, so I scooped her into my arms and shushed her until she calmed. I carried her into the living room to join us, the quiet family of three.

"Morning, pretty girl." Trace set his book on the end table as I neared with Willow. She reached for him, and he received her into his arms. Willow rested her head on his shoulder and settled into place against his chest. It was the warmest, best place to be—and I, too, wanted to nuzzle there, but for different reasons.

Trace resumed reading his book around Willow's resting body. I tried to focus on the words in my book, but I kept getting distracted by the sweet scene in front of me. It was so warm, so familiar. It felt like we were a family—like we'd been doing this for years, instead of weeks. Even more so now that we were in Tribeca.

Around eight, Willow was ready to truly start her day. I set aside my book and brewed more coffee for both Trace and me, while he set Willow in the highchair near the kitchen island and excused himself to get dressed. I got out a yogurt and banana for Willow, and by the time Trace came back out, he'd transformed into the high-profile-businessman version of himself. Perfectly crisp button-up, dark pressed slacks, derby shoes that gleamed. He was adjusting the watch on his wrist as he came out, the scent of his spice-and-leather cologne reaching me like a punch to the gut.

"I'll be gone most of the day," he told me. "But there's plenty for you and Willow to do. This building alone has—"

"Barnes & Noble," I finished for him with a bright smile. "That's all we need."

He cracked a smile. "Right. I'll text you some other options, if you want to get more out of the house. Rockefeller Park isn't far, but..." His gaze traveled to the big windows overlooking the city. "That snow doesn't look like it's going to let up anytime soon."

"We'll be fine," I assured him. "If I need to research any activities, I'll let you know. But I think we'll play here for a bit, head to the bookstore, and then make lunch."

Trace nodded and pressed a kiss to the top of Willow's head as she forked a slice of banana. "I'll be back around five, if not earlier. Just keep in touch if you need anything, okay? Anything at all."

I nodded, resisting the urge to lean in for the same kiss from him. "Promise. Have a good day at work."

Trace sent me a small smile and headed out. Once the door shut behind him, I assessed the relative quiet of the penthouse. This whole trip felt surreal—both magical yet somehow cursed, with the promise of a new future on the horizon. None of it made sense. Still, I was sitting in the penthouse suite above a Barnes & Noble. Practically a bookstore princess. My dream had come true, and Trace knew it.

I helped Willow finish her breakfast while I sipped my second cup of coffee. Around nine, my phone rang. Caleb.

"Hey there." I wedged the phone between my ear and shoulder as I leaned against the countertop. "Good morning."

"Good morning to you, too." Caleb's voice sent my gut into a knot. "How's New York?"

"A little snowy, which I love."

"Sounds like a nightmare." Caleb laughed. "The snow in the city must just turn to urine slush. Life in the Big Apple, huh?"

I grimaced, running my finger along the edge of the countertop. "It has its beauty, too."

"Maybe for ten seconds." He sighed heavily. "When are you coming back?"

"Tomorrow, I think." I nibbled my bottom lip, already dreading it. "I'll have to double check if that's still the plan. The family is here on business."

"Right. The family." Caleb sighed again. "Not *our* family. I can't wait until we can leave this behind, you know?"

"Leave what behind?"

"All this unnecessary travel. You running off to take care of someone else's kids. You should be taking care of *our* kids. Here."

My chest tightened, my gaze sliding to Willow in the highchair, where she tapped her plastic spoon against the edge. "Well...maybe someday."

"Maybe someday." Caleb laughed bitterly. "That's the enthusiasm I like to hear before our wedding day."

I rubbed the space between my eyebrows. He got testy like this when he was stressed, so I went into damage control mode. "Is work stressing you out, Caleb? You're sounding kind of angry."

He sighed again. "I *am* stressed. There's just so much left to figure out. The wedding's in three months and we don't even have an offer in on a house. I'll send you some links to places I found. Maybe you can check them out while you and the kid watch cartoons."

"That sounds good," I said, wondering if he could hear how hollow my voice sounded.

"I had my assistant write up a draft of the engagement announcement. I'll send that over too—let me know what you think. It should have been published last week, so this needs to fly out today."

I squeezed my eyes shut. Willow banged the spoon more loudly now, interspersing the noise with squeals. "Okay."

"There's a whole slew of magazines I'll send it to when its ready. Your mom sent me the master list, of course."

"Great." Dread coated my insides. "Along with the picture?"

"Yes, the one you picked out. Hey, one of these houses has an opening to view it on Thursday. I'll make the appointment so we can visit it."

Heaviness pooled in my limbs. That was two days away. "Are you sure we should be trying to finalize wedding planning and house hunting at the same time? Honestly, Caleb, we might be setting ourselves up for too much. You're already so stressed. I am too. Why don't we—"

"No, Mercedes, this needs to be done. We can't be newlyweds spending the night in your parents' pool house. When we get back from the honeymoon, I want us to have our own place to call home. We'll make it work."

My gut cinched tighter. "And where's the honeymoon? Did you decide?"

"Montana."

I nibbled on my bottom lip again. There was nothing wrong with that idea. I knew it would be lovely…beautiful…amazing, if we made it so.

But it was yet another decision that erased my wishes from the drawing board.

"Don't you ever just wish we could…pause all this?" I blurted.

"What?"

I sighed, going over to the highchair. I pulled Willow out and let her down to the ground. She toddled over to the toys in the great room. "It's just so much. And there's not enough time. We're doing this all at a breakneck pace—"

"Which is fine," Caleb said. "People put weddings together in less time. And we have all the best help. Like your mother, for starters. What's the issue?"

I stared out at the glinting steel towers of Manhattan, realizing in that instant that given the choice, I wouldn't return to Kentucky. Not now. Possibly not even in months. *I don't want to go through with this.* "It's just so much. It's so stressful."

"That's wedding planning for ya." Caleb laughed. "Listen, I gotta run. Look at the emails I just sent over. I'm heading into a meeting then we can get the announcement sent out later today."

I nodded, though he couldn't see me. "Bye."

The line went dead.

Willow shrieked and clapped as soon as I hung up, looking over at me with a big grin. I drifted her way. "What is it, sweet girl?"

She held up a picture book proudly. I knelt down to look at it. She pointed at the kitty.

"Do you love kitties?"

She said something jumbled, and then made the K noise. My eyes widened.

"Are you trying to say kitty?"

She made the noise again, looking up at me. Finally she settled on what sounded like "Kee."

"Oh my goodness." I clamped a hand to my mouth, tears swarming my eyes. "Sweetie, are you saying kitty?" I was nearly trembling with excitement. She pointed at the book again, and I laughed, repeating the word for her.

"Oh this is so exciting!" I sat down with her and reached for my phone. I had to text Trace.

MERCEDES: Big news!!! Willow just said kitty.

TRACE: You're kidding! That's amazing. Video?

MERCEDES: I'll try. It's so cute. You're going to cry—I nearly did.

TRACE: Proud of her. This is a welcome perk today.

I knew today was rough for Trace, even though I didn't know all the details. I wished he'd tell me. I wanted to be there for him, even if I shouldn't.

Before I put my phone away, my email app lit up with some new arrivals. Caleb had sent an email with four listings in it. I drew a deep breath and opened it up as Willow toddled off to hunt down a dolly.

The real estate listings were almost all the same. Grand, stately old homes, with wooden double doors and immaculately maintained landscaping. Each house toward the two or three million mark. Lush lawns, pillars, gardens that stretched and rolled.

Exactly like my parents' house.

My stomach twisted as I reached the end of the photos for the last listing. I didn't want to live in any of these houses. *But they're perfectly fine. They're beautiful. They're what other people dream of.*

But not what I dreamt of.

I opened up a text message to Caleb and started sending some of my thoughts. I needed to now, before I lost my nerve. Because the acid knot in my gut wouldn't let me say nothing this time.

MERCEDES: The houses are beautiful but they're all so enormous. They're like three houses in one. Did you want something so big?

CALEB: ....I thought you wanted a growing family?

MERCEDES: We can have a growing family with something a little cozier, right?

CALEB: So that's it, just too big? What else is wrong with them?

I gnawed on my lip, trying to figure out how to communicate "They look like we're trying to become my parents" without saying those words. Like a very un-fun version of the game *Taboo*.

MERCEDES: I was hoping for something a little more modern. Cozier. Less Mr. & Mrs. Hendricks.

CALEB: LOL these are literally some of the best houses of Louisville and somehow not good enough.

MERCEDES: They are lovely, I just...don't see myself living in them?

CALEB: Seems like nothing pleases you these days.

I pushed my phone away, my gut squeezing so hard I thought my coffee might start weaseling its way out of my stomach. I shouldn't have said anything—that much was certain. And really, who was I to course correct a decision like this? Sure, I'd be living there, but it was Caleb's money. He had more of a say than I did.

You're being too selfish. Selfish selfish selfish. I could hear my mother's voice in my head, and I needed to prove to myself that I wasn't that way. I needed to prove to myself that I could do this, I could get on board with this vision for my future that everyone else seemed to agree with except for me.

This should have been enough. This marriage, these houses, this whole plan was exactly what so many people dreamed of.

I pulled out my tablet and opened my email to review the draft for the engagement announcement Caleb had also sent over. I attached the Bluetooth keyboard to the front and sat at the kitchen island, rolling my shoulders. I could do this—I'd make a few punctuation corrections, give it a resounding thumbs up and enthusiastically tell him how great it sounded and how much I couldn't wait to become his wife.

I loved this man. This marriage made sense.

So why did every inch of my body vibrate with unease?

I swallowed hard as I read through the announcement, each new word sending my heart pitching lower toward the ground.

Gunther and Cassandra Hendricks along with David and Annie Randolph are pleased to announce the engagement of Caleb Randolph and Mercedes Hendricks. Both are graduates of University of Kentucky. Caleb is employed with PharmaFutures. A June wedding is planned at Acrewood.

Stale. Lifeless.

Abysmally normal.

I blinked rapidly, my alternate engagement announcement flitting through my mind and out my fingertips before I could stop it. What I really wanted it to say was this:

Absolutely nobody is pleased to announce the engagement of Trace Fairchild and Mercedes Hendricks, except for the couple themselves. Both are graduates of trying to do the right thing and failing. Trace is under investigation by the SEC and Mercedes has disappointed her family in every way possible. A wedding is planned at the one winery the couple loved equally, and they plan to invite no one. Except for Willow. And Damian and Jessa.

That seemed a little snarky. But just imagining it sent peals of laughter vibrating through my chest. I knew Trace would have found it funny, in the alternate universe where I'd told him that I actually wanted to be with him and not Caleb.

Willow looked over at me, clapping her hands together and joining in with some squeals.

"You like that idea, huh, Willow?" Of course she had no idea what she was agreeing to, but it made me smile to feel like I had *someone* on my side.

Because the future that the darkest parts of my heart yearned for was a future that no one would support.

It would involve casting aside damn near everyone I knew. Pissing off literally everyone and their brother.

It would require burning every bridge I'd spent the past twenty-five years building.

All these consequences and outcomes had always been enough to scare me. But sitting in Trace's kitchen, staring down the wild words of my dream engagement announcement, I realized that today, they scared me slightly less than before.

And maybe that was what I needed to focus on. I closed the email without replying to it.

Get used to it. Because you can't continue pretending much longer.

CHAPTER SIXTEEN
TRACE

Here I was again.

Inside the glass bowl of our conference room on the 20th floor of the Fairchild Building. Sitting at the long table like nothing had changed, leaning back in the leather chair and facing down my brothers.

Except we weren't collaborating anymore. We were here to negotiate. To figure out how to end this arrangement.

Axel's chair creaked as he leaned forward. He'd barely looked at me, but every time I looked away, I could feel his gaze boring into me.

"That espresso coming?" I asked Damian, looking through the glass walls for one of the receptionists. Curious glances flitted our way as employees passed by. I'd felt the inquisitiveness tighten in the air the second I stepped onto the floor. I hadn't been here in weeks. And prior to that, I'd been in Bali for weeks, riding out the fallout from Ian showing up and exploding our lives.

"Should be coming." Damian twisted around to look into the hallway. Axel sighed, clicking the top of his pen.

By all accounts, I was already the absent third of the business. The thought made me feel worse. I'd never wanted to become the ghost of Fairchild Enterprises. This was as much my baby as it was my brothers'. Yet here we were. And I was caught in limbo. Leaving didn't feel right, but staying sure as fuck didn't seem to be an option either.

So I'd be strong-armed into the decision I wouldn't have made on my own.

"Can we get started?" Axel asked.

"Sure." I crossed my arms. "Go for it."

Axel looked up at me, his gray-blue eyes sending a chill through me. I'd been dreading this showdown. What would Axel use to lash out at me? He'd had all this time to refine his grudge, to get angrier about the way things went down with Ian. He didn't know how tired I was of it all. I was out of the proverbial fucks to give. My fuck garden was barren. My fuck well, dry.

"What do you plan on doing?" Axel, too, sounded tired. "Let's just hear it."

"I plan on giving you what you want. I'll leave."

Axel's jaw flexed a few times, tilting his head to look even deeper into my soul. "Are you fucking kidding me?"

I hefted with a humorless laugh. "Isn't that what you wanted? You told me you wanted to buy me out. So make an offer."

Axel sighed testily, shaking his head. "You're not even going to fight for the business?"

"Oh my god." I rubbed my face with my hands, suddenly too exhausted to continue. "I cannot even respond to that."

"Typical," Axel muttered.

"I can't do anything right!" I shouted, the anger surging out of me. "Not since you made it your goal to hold this grudge against me through the end of time. Enough is enough, Axel. Look at yourself. Look at what you've been doing." Axel remained stony-faced, which only prompted me to barrel onward. "I find out I have a brother and try to get to know a blood relative: wrong. I step up to help a defenseless child who has no other reliable relative in her life: also wrong. And now I'm actually trying to give you what you yourself told me you wanted from me? Also wrong." I shook my head, frustration boiling over. "What do you fucking want from me, Axel?"

Felicia from the front desk approached the conference room then, carrying a tray of espresso cups.

She pulled the door open just as Axel shouted, "I want you to be transparent! Trustworthy!" He clamped his mouth shut when he noticed Felicia. The shouting match fell silent as she approached the table, the little cups clinking as she set the tray down.

"Here's the espresso," she said softly, grimacing as she dispersed the cups. "I didn't mean to interrupt."

I massaged my face. "It's fine. We're just…"

"Arguing," Damian offered.

Felicia offered an apologetic smile and scurried out. Once she door was shut behind her, I leaned forward to stare at Axel across the table.

"Axel, here's the bottom line. I've had it. I can't do anything right, and I'm done trying. Keep the business. Keep the clients. I don't give a fuck anymore. I just want to be away from this stress and this animosity. The press has been begging for us to shatter into pieces, so let's give them what they want and go our separate, fragmented ways."

My words fell like sludge in the room. An uncomfortable silence stretched through the rift between us.

Axel's gaze dropped to the table. That was the first sign something was amiss. Normally, he'd have his cutting reply at the ready, wielded like a knife. But he just massaged the bridge of his nose and said nothing.

"I'll be waiting for the paperwork." My own voice breaking the thick silence startled even me. I cleared my throat, looking between Axel and Damian. "Though I'm surprised you don't have it ready to shove down my throat. Or is that coming next?"

"Knock it off, Trace," Axel finally spit out. "You'll get what you want. By the end of the day. *Promise.*"

"What *you* want, you mean." Frustration had reached a boil in my veins. "This was your idea. And the longer you treat me like an outsider, the more you give me the cold shoulder, the farther away I'll run until you won't have to worry about ever seeing me again. And since I know your MO, I'll start cleaning out my office. I'll stay until close of business, but after that, you can mail whatever you need to my Tribeca apartment."

Axel regarded me with distaste, his mouth a thin line.

I sighed. "You act like this was my doing, but it's *yours*. I wanted to stay a part of the business. A part of the family. You pushed me out. So enjoy the consequences." As I stood, Damian surged to his feet.

"Wait." He held up a hand in my direction. "Don't go yet."

"Damian, I'm sorry negotiations weren't successful, but you saw what I was working with."

Damian licked his lips, looking between Axel and me. "If Trace leaves, I'm leaving too."

Axel paled and recoiled slightly. "Excuse me?"

"I don't agree with this split. Not even a little. And I don't want to see Fairchild Enterprises torn to pieces like this. So if Trace leaves, the whole thing needs to go. I'm not going to stick around to see it become a shell of what it once was."

I blinked a few times, more shocked than I could express. Silence throbbed through the conference room as we grappled with the implications. I hadn't seen that one coming, but I was touched by Damian's resolve.

And judging by the consternation etched into Axel's face, he hadn't seen it coming either.

"I guess this leaves the ball in your court, Axel," I said softly, pocketing my phone. I squeezed Damian's shoulder before I walked out of the conference room.

I glanced over my shoulder once I was in the hallway. Damian and Axel were continuing the conversation, but I could have no part in it. An ember of hope flickered deep inside my chest. Knowing that Damian had my back was a bolster I hadn't realized I'd needed. And part of me wondered if it would be the wake-up call Axel would need to come out of his selfish funk.

I could only try so many times, so many different ways. Ultimately, this was Axel's decision. And he'd allowed it to get to the point where one more step along this path would irreparably damage our relationship.

I headed to my office to cool down and start packing. Once I was back in the familiar confines of my corner office, the stretch of Manhattan beneath me and the mahogany and slate tones of my office to soothe me, I checked my phone. A text from Mercedes had just arrived: Willow had said *kitty*.

After letting the happiness wash over me, I texted Mercedes to ask for a video. I missed them both immensely, after so little time away. Leaving Tribeca to come to Wall Street might as well have been across the world, for how far away I felt.

Mercedes sent a picture, a selfie she'd taken that focused primarily on Willow and her half-smile. Mercedes occupied the bottom left corner of the picture, part of her forehead and ponytail visible. I smiled, the warm fuzzies spreading through my body.

How could it be that while my foundation—my brothers—crumbled, I had this pseudo-family forming right before my eyes?

I didn't enjoy the irony of it. Not at all.

I got to work in the office, taking the time to catch up on email while also beginning to pack things away. I didn't think Axel would come around. He'd spent the past couple months being an unyielding twat, so why would that change now?

A phone call interrupted me just before lunch. The Kentucky area code caught my attention, though it wasn't a number I recognized. I answered on the second ring.

"Hello?"

"Trace...that you?" It took me a moment to recognize the tired rumble of the voice on the other end of the phone.

"Ian. What a surprise. How are you?"

He laughed humorlessly. "I've been better. This place is a fucking trip."

I squeezed my hands into fists, wondering where to begin. We hadn't spoken since he'd first gone to jail, which felt like years instead of weeks.

"Everything going okay?"

"No. Every day is a little worse than the last." He heaved a sigh, and it sounded rattly. "Just imagine if you were in jail."

"I might know what it's like sooner rather than later." I pinched the bridge of my nose, trying to stuff those thoughts into the recesses of my mind. I knew they'd blossom later as an unsightly psychological issue. But for now, I needed to focus on literally anything else.

"These people here are heathens," he went on, punctuating his sentence with a cough. "They're ganging up on me, spreading rumors and shit. It's ridiculous but I can't do anything about it."

"What kind of rumors?"

"About why I'm in here. You know it's cuz of drugs, but some of these idiots are saying I'm in for child molestation and shit. And they treat you different if that's why you're in."

I rubbed my knuckles together slowly. "Okay. So what does this mean for you?"

"I'm getting my ass whooped. *Extra*." He heaved another sigh. "But they say I can make it stop if I pay them."

"Pay them?"

"Yeah. Like bribe money." Something rattled in the background, like handcuffs.

"You think that'll stop them?" Dread filled my gut. I didn't want Ian to get beat up for nothing, but more than that, this reminded me of what lay ahead if the SEC decided to convict. Was prison the inevitable future for the Fairchild brothers? I squeezed my eyes shut.

"It's about the only choice I have."

I cleared my throat. I wanted to wash my hands of the entire situation. I didn't even care if he was lying to me. "How much you need?"

"A few thousand should do it."

I studied my knuckles, mulling over the request. A few thousand was nothing to me, yet it could be everything to him. I had no problem doing it this once, either, and seeing what came of it.

"Hey, I gotta run," Ian blurted. "Just think about it, okay?"

"I'll send the money," I told him, and then the line went dead. I set my phone on my desk, an unsettled feeling spreading through my limbs. I needed to help Willow's dad, because I had the means to do so...

But what about when Willow's dad didn't even ask about Willow?

I didn't like that revelation even one bit.

I'd help Willow's dad if I had to...but I needed to protect Willow even more. There was no way she could go back to a guy who didn't ask about her once. Ian knew she was with me, but that was no reason to assume everything was just fine.

Even with the limited time for phone calls he'd had...he couldn't have even asked "How's my baby?"

Honestly, Ian's whole relationship with Willow was probably why she startled so easily around strangers, around knocks on the door, around anything that presented as the mildest of threats.

I didn't know how long Ian would languish in jail, but one thing was becoming clear: I had no intention of giving Willow back. Not if I could help it. That girl needed stability and love. I might not be a shining beacon of normalcy and integrity, but I'd give that girl stability and love while I could.

Until you join her father in jail.

I expelled a deep breath of air and stood, heading for the wall of windows overlooking the city. Times like these, I couldn't even remember how I'd gotten here, overlooking the sprawling city from the top of the world, while feeling like I was stuck under New York's dirty boot heel.

I'd tried to do everything right. For as long as I could remember. I was an incorrigible perfectionist. I'd graduated in the top 5% of my high school class, I'd been advising investments for friends' parents since age seventeen, and I'd graduated from college summa cum laude.

Yet that hadn't prevented my life from imploding. I'd driven away my first love, Mercedes, for unknown reasons. My business was crumbling. And now the rift between Axel and me was so large it needed its own zip code.

What was the use of striving for perfection when it was a fucking myth?

Fuck it all. I was ready to be the ex-con single dad. Why not? At this point, with my life crumbling around me, it felt like all bets were off.

I'd leave Fairchild Enterprises.

I'd figure out some way to adopt Willow.

And as for Mercedes...

I worked my jaw back and forth as I assessed the light snowfall coating the city.

I was finally ready to steal a man's fiancée.

CHAPTER SEVENTEEN
MERCEDES

THE SNOW FELL HARDER after our mid-morning Barnes & Noble visit, which sent me deeper into nesting mode. I was in the coziest of apartments, in front of a warm fireplace, with the sweetest baby girl and the comfiest couches. While Willow took her nap, I burrowed as deeply into the blankets as I could and started my new book, glancing up at the chapter breaks to watch the snow for a few moments. This was heaven, pure and simple.

You could live here happily forever. The thought resonated pleasantly through me, which added more gasoline to the flames of my internal conflict. It seemed like every passing hour in Tribeca pushed me closer to the point of no return.

I needed to end things with Caleb.

Whether or not I had a future with Trace was irrelevant. I was no longer convinced that I could survive marrying Caleb, much less spend the rest of my life with him.

I didn't want any of those houses. I didn't like the engagement announcement. I didn't like anything about this wedding being planned.

I wanted out, which was the scariest thing I'd ever admitted to myself.

I practiced lots of deep breathing through the rest of the day as I grappled with this truth. I needed to make a move, but I didn't know when or how. Still, just recognizing that I needed to—*was going to*—pump the brakes was step one.

The rest of the steps would follow. Somehow.

Willow woke up and we did some finger painting in the dining room before snack time. As five o'clock crept closer and Willow and I transitioned to playtime in the great room, I contemplated one more visit to Barnes & Noble. But then I wondered if we should wait for Trace, I knew he'd enjoy sharing that with us. With *me*.

Warmth spread through my limbs. It was almost embarrassing how much I looked forward to him coming back from work. To showing him my selection from the bookstore—Emily Henry and David Sedaris were next to grace my collection—and so that I could revel in the advancement of Willow with him.

A sharp buzz sounded from the front entryway. It was the intercom. I glided that way and pressed the button. "Yes?"

"There's a visitor down here, Ms. Margulis." The doorman's voice was all-business. "She's on the approved list but just wanted you to know she's on her way up." The intercom went dead.

Knock knock knock.

The noise at the front door came quicker than I'd expected. I flipped on the video monitor, and a brunette woman filled the screen. I blinked a few times, unable to believe I was actually seeing *Ms. Margulis.* Trace hadn't warned me to expect anyone.

Yet I was staring at Cora Margulis. She shifted in front of the door, pressing her handbag to the front of her long velvet-trimmed coat. Nervousness wound through me. I wasn't prepared for this. I'd been following Cora for longer than I wanted to admit, and suddenly she was at the door? I had juice stains on my shirt—she wore pristine Chanel. I assessed myself quickly, arranged my hair, brushed off some stray fibers from my leggings. And then I pulled open the door with a bright smile.

"Hi there," I said. "Can I help you?"

"You absolutely can." Cora flashed me a dazzling smile, dipping her chin. Her green eyes shone like gem stones, and I was immediately lost in the undertow of her beauty. "You're Mercedes, right?"

I nodded, my voice withering as she stepped closer and held out her hand to shake. I offered my own, my hand meeting her cool skin, and felt myself shrink in her presence.

"I'm Cora Margulis. Axel's fiancée." She released my hand with a sweet smile, and when she tilted her head, as though waiting for a response, it reminded me that I had to react. To *do something*.

"It's such a pleasure to meet you," I blurted, stepping back and gesturing for her to come in. I pushed the door shut behind her, watching her red-heeled Louboutin's click over the tile floor of the foyer. She started to slide off her long coat when I remembered that Willow was alone in the great room. Anxiety pooled in my gut—I didn't want to ruin the huge progress we'd made today. "But...stay in here for a moment, if you can?"

"Of course." Cora smiled and shrugged her coat off as I hurried past her. I found Willow still playing with the stuffed animals, seemingly unaware that someone new had arrived. I scooped her into my arms and held her close as I headed back to the foyer.

"All right. You can come in now. I just needed to get Willow into my arms since she has some anxiety around new people."

Cora hung her coat in the foyer and smoothed down a cream blouse tucked into high-waisted slacks. She clutched at her chest as she beheld Willow.

"Look at her. She's so precious. I've been dying to meet her." She reached out as though she planned to stroke Willow and then stilled her hand. "Should I not touch her?"

"It's probably better to wait," I said with a little laugh as Willow clung to me even tighter. She had her head burrowed into my shoulder, facing away from Cora. "She does have anxiety around new people, and it can be a challenge to win her over."

"But Trace hasn't had any problems with that?"

"I think he's the only man in the world she feels comfortable around," I admitted as I led her into the great room. I guided her around the toys that Willow and I had been playing with and headed for the big couches near the fireplace. "She feels most comfortable in this room, so let's chat out here and see if she loosens up at all."

Cora sat on the couch opposite us, offering a big smile. It was hard to look directly at her—it was like looking into the sun or seeing a celebrity for the first time. She was famous in the way Paris Hilton was famous, except without the reality TV show and weird obsession with baby voices. Everyone knew the Margulis family. The name was plastered across America, it seemed like, and if you hadn't seen a building with their name on it in some big city, then you'd certainly seen them in the news once or twice.

And with what the brothers had gone through over the past six months, I'd encountered Cora's name plenty during my research into the Fairchilds. In fact, it was a little unsettling to realize how much I knew about Cora while she knew...absolutely nothing about me.

"I hope you don't mind if I visit for a while," Cora said, folding her hands in her lap. "To be honest, I've been dying to meet Willow, and I wasn't sure I'd get another opportunity. I'm also hoping to intercept Trace when he gets home, which"—she looked at her silver wristwatch—"I'm thinking should be soon."

"I think he'll be back soon," I said with a small laugh. "To be honest, I'm not too sure. He doesn't usually give me tons of details."

"Oh?" Cora's brows drew together, and she tilted her head toward me. "I thought you two were...?"

I blinked a few times as her meaning hit me. "Together?" My voice came out a squeak and my cheeks immediately grew warm. "No. No, no, no, not at all. I'm just the nanny."

She pressed her hand to her chest. "I'm so sorry. I just assumed—that was my mistake."

"Don't worry about it." I tried to wave it off and appear even remotely nonchalant about it, but my heart slammed against my ribs with my secret truth. If only Cora knew how much I wanted Trace. How much I still loved him. "I was brought on to help with Willow."

"I think I heard about some prior connection between you and Trace and...made my own assumptions," she said with a small laugh, toying with some of the bangles on her wrist. "Is there anything I can help with while we wait for Trace to get back? I'd love to be of service."

"To be honest, the only thing I had planned for this evening was to make muffins. Or possibly visit Barnes & Noble again, but since we've already done that once, I thought muffins might be the better option."

"I'd love to help," Cora gushed. "If you don't mind, that is?"

"Of course not." My head was spinning. Cora Margulis wanted to help me make muffins? This was surreal, and I had approximately no one in my life that I could share this development with. "That would be so nice, isn't that right sweet girl?" I tickled Willow's belly and she stirred in my arms, offering a little smile. "I doubt she'll let me put her down too much, so your help in the kitchen will be very welcome."

Cora and I headed for the big kitchen, where gleaming appliances and a totally spotless oven awaited us. I set Willow down on the island and kept an arm around her as I searched my phone for the recipe.

"We're going to make zucchini muffins," I said conspiratorially. "So you get your veggies when you don't even know it!" I tickled her again, which elicited another giggle.

"Has she been doing well since you started with her?" Cora asked.

"She has. I think the transition to living with Trace was rough for her, but she's pulled through. And every day is a little better than the last." I smiled and booped her nose gently. She buried her face in my shoulder again. "Trace is definitely her favorite. If she hadn't bonded with him, it would have been much harder."

"He's always been a daddy in waiting," Cora said with a small laugh. Of course she had no idea that at one time, Trace *had* been a daddy in waiting—during my own pregnancy with his child. "When they were younger, Trace was kind of the daddy to Axel and Damian at times too."

"Did you grow up with them?"

"Not through childhood; I met Axel in college and saw Damian and Trace pretty much constantly until I left for grad school on the West Coast." She seemed like she would add more, but she stopped. I pulled open a cupboard, selecting the necessary ingredients. Cora got busy hunting down some mixing bowls.

Once everything was out on the countertop, I said, "But you and Axel weren't together again until recently, right?"

"That's right. We were apart for eight years until he came barreling into my father's boardroom under a false name." Cora laughed softly.

"I thought I'd seen something about you being married...." I clamped my mouth shut when I realized I'd admitted that out loud. Embarrassment heated my cheeks once more. "Goodness, that's so strange for me to say. We just met. I-I...I'm sorry."

Cora's warm smile took the edge off my anxiety. "Well, my separation from my ex has only been hashed and rehashed in the news about a million times. I'd be surprised if you *didn't* know about it. Don't feel bad."

"I feel less awkward now, so thank you for that." I covered my face with my hands and laughed. "I just don't want to overstep. I'm just here to be Willow's nanny, not the creepy nanny who's read too many articles."

"It's impossible to avoid the news about these men," Cora mused, drumming her fingertips on the island countertop. "They're everywhere. America loves them but is also fascinated by what's happening to them."

I didn't think about that part enough. How many millions of people right now knew about Trace, about the investigation, about any fragment of what he was living? It was mind-boggling.

"Tell me the first step for the muffins," Cora said. "I've been baking more since I switched careers to managing a non-profit youth LGBTQ theater, and let me tell you, I'm positively a pro in the kitchen now."

I read the recipe to her, and she worked at finding the remaining items in Trace's enormous, immaculate kitchen. Once we'd assembled all the measuring cups and spoons we needed, Willow had gathered enough confidence to begin tinkering with a spoon and a mixing bowl.

Looking out over the island full of ingredients, Cora lifted a hand for a high five. I met her palm over the middle. "Teamwork!" she said.

Willow twisted to look at Cora, then she looked up at me. She lifted her palm a moment later and I high-fived her, beaming ear-to-ear.

"That's teamwork, isn't it, sweet girl?" I kissed her cheek and shared an encouraging look with Cora. "She opens up more and more each day."

"I'm so happy to hear it. Maybe a visit to Aunt Cora's house won't be too far off then." She offered a big grin to Willow, who shyly watched. "Now that I'm an aunt, I don't intend to waste this opportunity."

"That sounds like it would be so fun." I rubbed Willow's back as she banged the rubber spatula against the mixing bowl. Cora and I proceeded with our recipe in tandem—me reading off the steps while she dutifully followed the instructions—with Willow overseeing.

Willow helped drop scoops of batter into the waiting muffin cups with minimal mess. Her eyes lit up every time a fat dollop of batter fell into the paper cup. Once the muffin tin was full, Cora loaded up the oven, and I set the timer.

"These are going to be so delicious." I kissed the top of Willow's head. She wriggled and pointed to the floor, which told me she wanted down. I lifted her off the island and set her down gently, and she toddled off to the great room, in search of her toys.

"That's progress right there," I told Cora as I watched Willow go for her dollies. "She feels comfortable enough to leave my side even when a stranger is here."

"Hopefully I won't stay a stranger for long." Cora tucked some hair behind her ear and leaned onto the countertop, her gaze across the room.

"You wouldn't be that much of a stranger, if Willow knew how to read the newspaper like me," I joked. Cora snickered, sending me a knowing look. "And at the risk of sounding like a stalker...I am curious how it's been going since you left the family business."

My heart pounded as soon as the question left my lips. I was far more interested in her response than was normal. This wasn't an innocent question, nor a way to fill the time until Trace came home.

Cora had left her family behind, and all their expectations.

I wondered if maybe her insight could help illuminate a path of my own.

Cora heaved a sigh, her gaze drifting off to some unknowable point that only she could see. "It's been...strange. I feel a hollow where my parents used to be. But the relief I feel alongside it is immense. Sometimes, it seems like it was too easy. Even though it wasn't easy at all. I don't know. I guess it has its ups and downs, but the sadness is balanced out by the joy I have from my life with Axel."

"So you'd say it was...worth it?" I asked.

Her gemstone gaze homed in on me, nearly causing me to stumble backwards. But I held her gaze, even though it felt like she was somehow seeing deep into my soul. I didn't know the particulars of her situation with her ex-husband. And surely she couldn't know the particulars of my situation with Caleb.

But somehow, they felt similar.

"It's always worth it if it brings you to your truest self," she finally said. "No matter how hard it is. Honoring that truth is the only path you can take."

Her words nearly made me crumble. I swallowed a knot in my throat and looked out toward the great room, hoping she wouldn't notice the sheen of tears in my eyes.

"And do you think you can survive?" I asked her, my throat suddenly tight. "Without the rest of your family, I mean. Without their...love."

She came around the island to face me, searching out my gaze. "Are you going through something, Mercedes?"

I nibbled on the inside of my lip, unsure how to respond. I didn't even know where to begin. And I'd just met this woman—all I knew of her was from the internet. This didn't seem right, much less *sane*.

"You don't have to answer that," she whispered, squeezing my wrist.

I needed a moment before I could respond, since the wall of tears in my throat was so thick. As I was composing myself, the front door opened. Trace was home. I gasped, rushing to Willow, just in case she reacted poorly to the sound of the door. I picked her up just as Trace came into the great room.

As soon as my gaze landed on his broad-shouldered figure wrapped up in a designer suit and topped off with derby shoes, my insides crumpled with relief.

This was the moment—and the man—I'd been waiting for. The man I'd *always* been waiting for.

My throat clamped tight again, this time for a different reason. His handsome features, which softened into a smile as his gaze landed on me and Willow, felt like coming home in a way I couldn't describe.

It had been this way since the beginning. And still was now. Even after so many reasons why it shouldn't feel like this. Why it *couldn't be* like this.

I hoisted Willow onto my hip and returned the smile. "Welcome home, Trace. We have a visitor."

His gaze swung toward the kitchen, where he found Cora. She offered a little smile, wiggling her fingers at him.

"Don't be mad," she said in lieu of a greeting.

His shoulders dropped slightly. "Cora. What a surprise."

She stepped closer to him, concern etching itself across her face. "I knew I had to come personally to ask this. Will you and Mercedes and Willow please come to our house in the Hamptons for dinner tonight?"

Trace's jaw clenched and I could see him mulling over her request.

"I'll send the helicopter. Or a car, if you don't want Willow wearing the earmuffs yet. I just know things have been tense with you and Axel," Cora added, "but this dinner is important to me. To us, as a family. Please come."

Trace studied her for a moment, then he said sadly, "I can't. I can't do it, Cora. Please don't take it personally. It has nothing to do with you."

Cora deflated visibly. "Are you sure?"

"I'm not sure when I'll be ready to see Axel again. But tonight is not the night. He got what he wanted from all his pushing. I broke. And I'll be out of the family business soon. Damian's coming with me."

Cora covered her face with her hands and shook her head. "No. This is not right. It can't be this way. I'm going to do whatever I can to make this right."

"I appreciate that, Cora, but I think this has been laid to rest."

"It's not over yet," Cora said, looking sternly at Trace. "I came here so I could get a head start at being an aunt, and Axel will be an uncle yet, I promise you."

Willow wriggled and reached for Trace, so he headed our way and took Willow into his arms. She nuzzled happily into his arms.

"I'd like to believe what you say," Trace said a moment later, "but Axel is the only one who can decide that. And I don't have much faith in him anymore."

Cora looked as dejected as if Trace had insulted her to her face. "I don't blame you for saying that. Just don't give up on your brother, please." She squeezed Trace's arm then she swung her gaze over to me. "Can we have a video date sometime? Maybe get lattes in our respective coffee shops?"

I laughed and nodded. It made me giddy that we'd connected so quickly and that she wanted to continue the conversation. "That would be great."

"Okay. I'll leave you three to your evening. This won't be the last you see of me." She rubbed Willow's back and then patted Trace's shoulder before she strutted toward the foyer, her heels clicking. "I didn't forsake my family just to see yours crumble, Trace," she called over her shoulder. "Don't forget that."

A moment later the front door swung shut, and Trace and I were left gaping at each other.

"So Axel sent an ambassador?" I finally said.

"Axel didn't send her," he mused. "Cora came on her own. If we'd accepted that invite to the Hamptons, we would have shown up to an irate Axel."

I grimaced, drifting closer to him. "So how did the day go?"

Trace sighed heavily, his eyes drifting closed. Now that Cora was gone, I could feel the sadness pouring off him, the thick waves of anguish. "Not great. Negotiations failed and Damian has decided to join me in leaving Fairchild Enterprises. So the entire company is set to dissolve and not a single soul knows yet but us. Except Axel didn't turn over the paperwork as promised."

"So what does that mean?"

Trace looked wearier than I'd ever seen him. "It means...nothing is settled yet. I need a few more days here to wrap things up. Is that okay?"

I nodded eagerly. It was more than okay. And it meant I could ditch the house viewing Caleb had scheduled, which was an unexpected perk. "It's totally fine. Don't even worry about it."

"Thank you. There's a lot Damian and I need to figure out, now that he's decided to join me." Trace sank into the couch, and Willow promptly wriggled off his lap and onto the floor, where she went back to address some of her forgotten stuffed animals. I sank onto the couch next to him, feeling every ounce of his sadness and conflict. I just wanted to take it all away, at least for a moment.

"I'm so sorry, Trace," I whispered, running my hand over his knee. "I wish I could help somehow."

"It's just the most epic failure that I could have imagined," he said softly, his gaze stuck on the carpet. "I thought there was one solid thing in life—my family. And even that is crumbling, no matter how hard I tried or how much I succeeded in life."

His words were heartbreaking in a way that I understood all too well. With tears in my eyes, I surged toward him and wrapped my arms around his broad shoulders. My hands barely touched around him, but I rested my head on his shoulder, hoping that I could relieve even an ounce of his pain.

"I'm so sorry, Trace," I whispered into the crook of his neck. As soon as the words left my mouth, a strange heaviness settled over me. Like a hot flash and drunkenness had descended at the same time. The scent of his cologne, spice and leather, flooded my senses, leaving me dizzy. Time and space seemed to contract, which pushed us even closer together. His breath hit the shell of my ear; goosebumps flared on every square inch of my body.

And then his strong arms went around *me*, scooping me into his lap. His thick biceps locked me in his embrace. I tilted my head up to see the drugging effect of his oak brown eyes from this close. My mouth parted; every cell of my body vaulted closer to this man, desperate to be near him, on him, consumed by him.

"Mercedes," he bit out, his voice coming out hot at my ear. I almost whimpered—or maybe I did without realizing, because the chuckle that escaped him next was amused.

I got lost in the swirl of his eyes, unable to speak or move, much less tear myself away from him. The only thing that managed to penetrate the fog of my brain was Willow.

Slapping at my arm, begging to be let into our group hug.

"Oh, my goodness." A maniacal laugh escaped me as my brain rocketed back to the present moment, the one in which I was a nanny and caretaker and not about to mount this god of a man. I pushed myself off Trace's lap and pulled Willow in between our bodies, where she settled happily, grinning up at us.

When I met Trace's gaze, I could read every desire in his eyes.

He wanted me.

And he didn't even know how much I wanted him.

CHAPTER EIGHTEEN
TRACE

Willow on my lap was akin to pumping the brakes. We had a two-year-old in our midst. We needed to act like rational, restrained adults.

But fuck, if Willow wasn't in the room? I would have fucked the legs off this woman by now. All these years apart, and now she draped her softness and sweet scent across me? I wasn't a caveman—unless Mercedes was around.

"I guess we should think about dinner…" Mercedes said, nibbling on her lip in the way that betrayed internal anguish. She'd started pacing the room, which meant she was still thinking about our illicit embrace. "What do you feel like eating?"

"Let's do takeout." I bounced Willow on my knee, giving her a big smile. She played with my tie, rubbing her fingertips back and forth over the silky fabric. "Thai."

"Perfect." She crossed her arms and tapped her fingers in a rhythm known only to her, staring out the wall of windows. "Sounds great."

"Take Willow for me and I'll order something delicious." I stood and met Mercedes by the windows. Before I handed Willow over, I leaned in close to whisper in Mercedes's ear. "We'll finish that hug later."

Mercedes's cheeks flushed, and she reached for Willow. *Score.* "If we know what's good for us, we won't."

"I never said anything about knowing what's good for either of us."

She dropped her chin, sending me a dark look. "I'm engaged."

"And there's nothing wrong with a little hug."

Her suspicious look told me exactly what was on her mind—*there's no way it'll stay a little hug*. We both knew it. And the sooner she was okay with that, the sooner I could silence this restlessness inside me, urging me to make Mercedes mine.

It didn't make sense. She hadn't chosen me. And she still seemed trapped in her world. I was still angry at her for the way things went down last time. But after the way everything had imploded in my personal life—particularly *today*—I no longer cared about standards or morals.

I wanted Mercedes when it didn't make sense. Even when I shouldn't.

And I was going to get what I wanted.

"Thai food." I scrolled through my favorite delivery app. "Pad thai for you? Dumplings and rice for Willow?"

Mercedes nodded. I remembered what she used to order back in the day and squared away her heat level at a medium, then I added my favorite green curry dish.

"It'll be here in thirty." I tossed my phone onto the couch and joined them at the window again. "So tell me, how was the visit with Cora?"

"Great." Mercedes's face opened up the way it always did when she was spilling a heartfelt response. "She's really astute. And so approachable, even though I kind of fangirled when she got here."

"You fangirled?"

"Only slightly." Mercedes hoisted Willow higher on her hip. "I've just read a lot of news. I know about her. She's felt...relatable because of what happened with her family."

This admission made my ears perk up. "Do you plan on leaving your controlling family behind for a Fairchild brother?"

Her mouth parted, jaw practically clattering to the floor. I could only laugh in the wake of her shock.

"*Trace.*"

"Sorry, that was a joke. I know you'd never go against your family. Especially not for a Fairchild brother."

Her chin dipped, the glower returning. At that, I felt the need for alcohol. I wandered to the dry bar nearby. "Can I interest you in a glass of wine? A shot of tequila?"

"I'm fine." She'd moved her steely gaze back to the skyline of Manhattan beyond the windows. "And just so you know, I *have* gone against my family, even if you think I haven't. And I was prepared to leave them behind for a Fairchild brother. Even if you think I wasn't."

I cleared my throat as I poured myself a finger of whiskey into a tumbler. A big, surly truth rumbled around inside me, and this time, I no longer had the capacity to restrain it. All my fucks had evaporated.

"Then why did you text me to stay out of your life after the fallout with your uncle?"

For a moment, the only sound that registered in the penthouse was the sound of the crackling fireplace and Willow's soft mumblings to herself as she played with Mercedes's hair.

"What are you even talking about?" Mercedes finally asked.

"After you saw me off from Louisville that last time. By the time I landed, you'd texted and basically told me to fuck right on out of your life."

Mercedes looked like I'd slapped her. "No I didn't."

I sipped my whiskey, knowing immediately I'd need another one in no time. "You sure did."

"That's ridiculous," she spat, then clamped her mouth shut and drew in a breath through her nose. She stroked Willow's hair for a moment before continuing. "Don't you think I'd remember if I told you those things?"

"One would think."

"I never said anything to that effect," Mercedes said, her brows drawing together. "Trace, I was ready to *marry you*. Why would I do the opposite of that?"

Her words landed like a surprise punch. I tipped more whiskey into my mouth. "Honestly, Mercedes, I've been asking myself the same question ever since. But clearly, my disappearance didn't bother you much. You texted me to break things off, I honored your wishes, and here we are."

Her nostrils flared and she took a defiant step closer. When she spoke, her voice was low and firm. "I texted you for *months* after you left. Don't talk to me about how it didn't bother me. I was *devastated*, and you were nowhere to be found."

I drained my glass, setting it on the bar. I shouldn't have brought this up—I knew better—yet here we were. Right in the thick of it.

"And conveniently none of those messages made their way to my phone? Sure. So why ask me to go away in the first place? Why break things off?"

"I never asked for that," she insisted, then looked down to check Willow's face. She had started to recoil slightly, and Mercedes sighed, shaking her head. "We can't talk about this right now. I don't want to upset her, and I know we will if we keep going."

"I shouldn't have brought it up. It was my fault." I poured a second glass.

Silence stretched between us. Willow babbled to herself as Mercedes and I stared hard at each other. Something wasn't adding up. One of us had to be lying, and it wasn't me.

But somewhere deep inside, I didn't think she was lying either.

Impossible. The likeliest answer is the simplest one. Mercedes told you to fuck off and is lying about how hard she bends to her family's will. End of story.

Sure didn't feel like the end of the story, though.

Willow wriggled out of Mercedes's arms and the two of them went to the coloring book at the little play station we'd set up. While they used colored pencils to scribble across outlined renditions of panda bears, I worked on my drink and waited for the food. After a while, the text notification came in: *Food is here, but can't reach the penthouse. Can you come down?*

"I've gotta head to the lobby," I announced. "They can't get clearance to come all the way up. I'll go down and grab the food." I could have told the doorman to let him up, but I needed the chance to clear my head. This penthouse had become a vortex now that Mercedes and I were face-to-face with the past. I needed to reset if I had any shot at making it out of this trip alive.

Mercedes nodded, moving into the kitchen where Willow had started removing pots and pans from one of the cupboards. "We'll be here." Just then the timer went off on the oven and Mercedes clapped her hands together. "The muffins are ready, sweetie! Yay!"

I smiled as Willow mimicked Mercedes' clapping. Once I was out of the penthouse and alone in the elevator, I took a few deep breaths, trying to shake off the intensity of the conversation we'd abandoned so I could return to the penthouse and continue not talking about the past in front of Willow. Because Mercedes was right. We'd been on a fast-track to getting heated. And there was no resolution in sight.

I met the driver, tipped him extra, and took my sweet time getting back up to the penthouse. I checked the mail, checked my phone, and then finally got back onto the elevator. I was as ready as I'd ever be.

Inside the penthouse, I headed for the kitchen to drop the bag, but the first thing I noticed was Willow. In the playpen in the great room. *Alone.*

"Mercedes?" I asked, glancing around. Nobody here. Willow babbled to herself as she played with two stuffed animals in the play pen. I figured Mercedes must have run off to the bathroom, but then I noticed the towels on the kitchen floor.

"Mercedes, where are you? Food's here." I headed for the hallway that led to the guest rooms, but both her bedroom and Willow's were dark. I crossed the penthouse, heading to the other side past the great room, just in case she was in *my* bedroom for some reason. I poked my head into my room. Nobody.

But I heard the rushing sound of water.

Curiosity consumed me. Clearly Mercedes had darted off to take a shower—but why? And why in my shower?

The temptation of finding out was too great to ignore.

"Mercedes?" I approached the bathroom door, which was ajar. It opened far enough that I could see the huge walk-in shower at the other end of the bathroom.

And there she was. On display. Glass doors revealing every curve Mercedes had, her creamy skin and soaked blonde hair beckoning to me, framed like a statue I could look at but not touch.

I gritted my teeth. The reset hadn't worked. I needed a reset for my reset.

Mercedes rinsed shampoo out of her hair, and once her eyes opened, she jumped. "Trace, my God!" She tried to cover herself with her hands, but there was too much body and not enough hands.

"I came back with the food and couldn't find you." I lingered in the doorway, unable to stop drinking in the view. My fingers curled and I swallowed hard. "Why are you in here?"

"Do you have to watch?"

"You're in my bathroom."

She huffed and dipped her head underneath the water again. My eyes migrated to the soft swell of her belly, the tightly trimmed patch of hair between her legs. My appetite for Thai had been replaced with a different appetite altogether.

"Willow jammed a spoon down her throat. She puked every-where, but most of it got on *me*." She ran her hands over the top of her head, squeezing out the last of the shampoo suds. "I knew she'd be safe in the playpen while I hopped in the shower. My clothes are gross—don't even touch them."

I couldn't rip my eyes off her long enough to even see where her clothes were. As far as I was concerned, there was nothing in this bathroom but her inside the shower.

"So why my bathroom? You just wanted another opportunity to remind me that you're engaged?"

Her shoulders slumped as she turned the water off. "It was closer. I was panicking."

I grabbed a new towel from the cupboard and walked toward the shower stall. She looked so wet and downtrodden, it was hard not to melt to butter in front of her. But I was nothing if not practiced at staying firm at all costs.

"I already brought a towel," she said, the door still closed. She pressed her forehead against the glass.

"Just trying to help." I moved the door slightly. When she stepped back, I slid it open all the way and held the towel open. I made no effort to hide the fact that I was gobbling up every square inch of her body. I was hard as fuck just from looking at her. I could already imagine what that wet skin would taste like against my tongue. The humid heat I'd find in the hollow of her neck. The dampness between her legs that had nothing to do with the shower.

"Trace," she whispered, holding my gaze like a warning.

"You're engaged. I fucking know. Have you noticed yet that I don't care?"

Her throat bobbed, and she stepped out of the shower. Her nipples were two tight, rosy points. I caught her once she stepped close enough, wrapping her up in the extra-soft, gray towel.

"Come here," I whispered, guiding her toward the wall-to-wall mirror above the double sinks. We faced ourselves in the reflection, her damp hair clinging to her face and neck, my big arms wrapped around her body over the towel.

"We need to get you dried off," I whispered, running my hands over the towel in slow, deliberate motions. Her eyes fluttered shut. "Keep your eyes open," I commanded. "So you don't forget how things would have been with Trace after you go home to Caleb."

Her throat bobbed with another swallow, her gaze stuck on her reflection. "What makes you think I'm going home to Caleb?"

I paused, one hand on her hip, the other cupping a breast through the towel. I stared at her through the mirror, noticing the way her chest rose and fell quickly as she held my gaze.

"I guess there's only one way to find out." I gripped her by the hip and turned her toward me, one of my hands moving to the base of her neck while my mouth descended and claimed her lips. *Mine.* I didn't even need to guess if she wanted it. She pushed herself toward me, welcoming the kiss, our tongues meeting instantly, teeth scraping as the hunger took over.

My fingertips dug into the back of her neck, and I pulled her closer, deepening the kiss. She whimpered, which acted as the gunshot to start the races. I hoisted her by the hips, the towel slipping away as I pushed her onto the marble countertop. Her bare skin squeaked against the surface as I filled the space between her legs. Her palms pressed against my chest before I could dive in for another kiss.

"No, Trace. No. This isn't right."

Her chest heaved and a wild look crossed her face. Her hands forced more distance between us, and I grunted, digging my fingertips into the fleshiness of her hips.

"Got it." My gaze washed over the scene—her naked body on the countertop, covered in goosebumps. Every inch of her wanted this...but Caleb was in the way. "There's my answer."

She squeezed her eyes shut. "You can't—"

"Get dressed. The food is here." I tore myself away from her before I made any other mistakes. I needed to stop putting myself on the line like this, but apparently, I was incapable of controlling myself around this woman. I stormed out of the bathroom, remembered she had no clothes, then headed for my closet and grabbed an old T-shirt and shorts, which I tossed on the bed. "Clothes are on the bed," I shouted over my shoulder and headed for the great room.

Willow was still happily playing. I tousled her hair before letting out a deep exhale and focusing on dinner. I needed to get her food ready. So that's what I worked on, and blocked all thoughts of Mercedes.

But the forced clear-headedness could only last so long. Once I'd gotten our dinners arranged and Willow set up in the highchair, Mercedes came slinking toward the kitchen in the oversized NYU T-shirt I'd laid out for her. She'd gone braless, the peaks of her tits visible through the thin fabric, and my workout shorts hung baggy on her. My gut wrenched. Seeing her in my clothes—another mistake. I was doomed to shoot myself in the foot with this woman.

"Smells good," she said as she joined Willow and me at the kitchen island where I'd set up the food.

"Willow is loving it," I said as I scooped another bite of dumpling into her mouth, followed by some chicken fried rice.

Mercedes settled into her bar stool, nibbling at her lip as she looked between Willow and me. The unspoken words between us weighed a metric ton. *Wine.* We needed wine. At least I did. Anything to distract me from how fucking badly I wanted Mercedes.

"Thanks for the clothes," Mercedes said softly, pushing at her food with the fork.

"Yep." I headed for the wine rack in the kitchen and grabbed a Pinot Noir. I wrested the cork out of the bottle and poured two generous glasses, which I brought back to our spot at the island.

"Thank you," Mercedes said, still nibbling at her lip.

"Drink. Or eat. Or don't. Whatever." I scooped some green curry into my mouth, frustrated by my own desire to pamper her. I wanted to give her the entire fucking world, and she wasn't even mine. Despite how sick I was of not having her, I couldn't stop myself from trying.

Which only sent my spiral of frustration cycling harder.

Willow tapped at her plate with her brightly colored toddler fork while I spooned more food into her mouth. Tension ballooned between Mercedes and me the longer I kept quiet.

"Trace—" she started.

"What?"

"Can I just say something about...what happened?"

"Will it change anything?"

She nibbled her lip and nodded.

"Go for it," I conceded, scooping up more food for Willow.

"I'm engaged right now. But I won't be shortly after I get back to Louisville."

I nearly choked on my curry. I cleared my throat and took a sip of wine. "Excuse me?"

"I'm going to end things with Caleb," she said shakily, staring at her food. "He sent me the engagement announcement to review today, along with some houses he wants to look at. But all of it just makes me...sad. No. It makes me profoundly unhappy. I've known for a long time that I didn't want to marry him, but it's only since you came into my life that I've been able to admit it to myself."

I tried to hide the immense wave of relief and pleasure her words provoked. I took another sip of wine and tried to fight back the grin. "I'll believe it when I see it, I guess."

"But I can't act like I'm not engaged *now*. I don't want to do that to someone who doesn't deserve that type of treatment." Mercedes swallowed hard, finally dragging her gaze over to mine. Her green eyes shone with emotion and the look on her face nearly tore me in half. "I want you more than I want air, but I'd hate myself forever if I did anything with you before I officially ended things with Caleb."

I ground my jaw back and forth, mulling over her words. I admired her moral compass, even though it didn't agree with my own sexual timeline.

"That makes sense," I agreed reluctantly. Willow slapped my forearm, which reminded me I'd delayed too long in serving up her next bite. "Sorry, sweetie," I said softly, spooning more rice into her mouth. "We're talking about grown-up things and not paying enough attention to you."

Willow offered me a cheesy smile in return, which prompted a laugh from both Mercedes and me.

Mercedes finally scooped a bite of pad thai into her mouth. She hummed a moment later. "Gosh this is good."

"My favorite place in Manhattan."

"Thanks for sharing it with me." She sent me a small smile, which just started my frustration-adoration cycle all over again.

Fuck it. She was going to be breaking up with Caleb, which meant I had to keep my dick in my pants for just a few more days. But I was done holding back in all the other arenas.

"There's plenty more I want to share with you," I admitted, bringing her free hand to my lips. She giggled as I set her hand down gently. "See? Chaste kiss. That's friendly. Not sexual."

"Right." She snorted and shoved some more pad thai into her mouth.

"Hugs are allowed. Gentlemanly kisses on the hand. Cuddling surely is allowed—you'd cuddle with your girlfriends, right?"

She smirked over at me. "I think that happens only in movies."

"Well, it sounds friendly and chaste to me." I needed to define the boundaries. I needed a fucking fix, and if left to my own devices, I'd have her naked in my bed thirty seconds after Willow was down for the night.

"No kissing," she said after she'd chewed and swallowed another bite of her food. "No S-E-X. No groping."

I tutted, smoothing my palm over her knee beneath the island. "That's all the fun stuff."

She sent me a secret smile. "What makes you think fun stuff isn't in store for the future? You just have to be patient." She looked too satisfied.

I grunted, scooping up another bite for Willow. "I've been patient for the past six years."

"Then what's another couple of days?"

I leveled her with a look. "Torture. And you know it."

CHAPTER NINETEEN
MERCEDES

WILLOW WENT DOWN EARLY that night, which I wanted to believe was unrelated to the sexual agendas of the adults caring for her.

But who was I kidding? I had an agenda. Once eight-thirty rolled around and Willow was softly snoring in her bedroom, all bets were off. Trace and I reconvened in the great room. There was no mistaking the fire in his eyes. The same fire that had almost incinerated me—and my morals—on the spot in the shower earlier.

Our wine glasses were refilled, both sitting on the same end table near the fireplace. Trace had changed into gray sweatpants and a simple black tee while I was putting Willow to bed. My stomach flopped, every inch of my skin coming alive under his gaze. His attention was both a whip and a caress. He challenged me as much as he made me feel safe. I barely understood it. I just knew that I needed more of it.

"Time for a chaste evening by the fire," Trace teased as I joined him. He handed me my wine glass, and we toasted. "Cheers to obeying the rules."

I smirked at him as he took a sip. "Why do I feel like that means you're *not* going to obey the rules?"

He ran his tongue over his bottom teeth. "Because you're right. I'm going to bend the rules until they snap."

His words sent a shiver down my spine. I took a drink quickly then set my glass down and eased onto the couch. Trace joined me.

"You can't possibly be warm sitting all the way over there." His mock look of concern was so exaggerated it was hard to bite back a laugh. He opened his arms, gesturing for me to come closer. I fell into his embrace and a sigh escaped me—deep, satisfied, blissed out. I'd missed the warm alcove of his arms too much to comprehend.

"This feels nice." I hummed in pleasure, sinking deeper.

"Just like how you used to sit with your friends at school, right?" His mouth glanced over the top of my head.

I laughed. "Right."

"Chaste and innocent."

"Mm-hmm." I shifted against him, cozying into his warmth even further, palming the solid planes of his chest through his shirt. My fingers itched from wanting to explore more, but I kept my hand in one spot. "But my hand isn't moving from this spot. Just so you know."

"Per the guidelines." He tightened his arms around me, which sent my eyes fluttering shut. After so long apart...this was heaven. I just wanted to enjoy it for tonight, consequences be damned. The second we returned to Louisville, there'd be the biggest shitstorm of my life to wade through.

"I'm not looking forward to the conversations that are waiting for me in Louisville."

"Why did you agree to marry him in the first place?" Trace asked.

I swallowed hard, picking at invisible fibers on Trace's shirt. "Because it seemed like the right thing to do. Because I knew my whole family wanted it so badly for me, and for themselves. Everything has been leading up to this for the past five years. It just seemed like an investment of time and…I don't know…planning that I couldn't say no to."

Trace tutted. "Did you ever want to marry him?"

Admitting these things out loud was hard. Harder than I ever imagined, even though the truths had been darting around inside the shadows of my heart like ghosts. Haunting my daily life with constant whispers.

"I thought I did," I forced out. "He and my brother have been best friends forever. I've known him my entire life. After college, he was there for me. If not him, then who?"

Traces lips brushed against the top of my head again. "I can think of someone."

"But you had walked away from me."

"I never walked away," he countered. "You told me to fuck off."

I sighed testily, wanting him to understand, beyond any ounce of doubt, that I was not lying about this. "Do you believe me when I tell you I never did that?"

Trace paused. "I don't know what to believe."

Emotion clamped my throat tight as I prepared to confess the last thing standing between us. The final truth that needed to be shared. "There's something I need to tell you. I called and texted you on and off for about four months after we last saw each other…I won't lie, my messages got increasingly more desperate."

"I never got a single one," he said, turning to me.

"Well, the reason I didn't back off, even when my better judgment told me I was acting crazy, was because…" I swallowed a knot in my throat. It had been so long since I'd talked about it with anyone. And finally, the person hearing it was Trace. I'd never believed this day would actually come.

"What?"

"I was pregnant." I frowned, looking over at him. My chin was already wobbling and I'd barely started the story.

Trace blinked a couple times, the confusion on his face softening into something else altogether.

"With our baby," I added, the words coming out on a whisper.

His brows made a slow trek to the middle of his face. "Wh...are you..."

"I wanted you to know so badly," I went on, my voice barely audible. "And then I miscarried, and I..." My voice faltered and tears filled my eyes. I looked down at my lap, rubbing my forehead. "I tried one more time to contact you and then I told myself I'd never try again."

"Mercedes." Trace's voice sounded so soft, so surprisingly tender, that it prompted the full cascade of tears I'd been beating back. A sob wracked my body, and his arms went around me, pulling me back into his warmth and security.

"I'm so sorry," he whispered, squeezing me tight. "I had no idea. I'm so sorry I wasn't there for you."

"I was four and a half months pregnant," I told him. "When he was born, he had fingers and—" My voice gave out. I cried into his chest, the solidity a reassuring foundation as my emotions spun into a freefall. I sobbed until my ribs hurt. And then I lay there, breathing deep, trying to collect myself.

I'd been twenty years old. Nineteen when I got pregnant. In a way, the humiliation and embarrassment of being the unwed pregnant girl in my family, of all families, was part of what gave me the push to allow Caleb into my heart.

He was what my family had wanted anyway. And after I'd disappointed them—even if it was in secret—I felt I owed it to them to do the right thing. Doing things my way had led to a fiasco.

Doing things their way seemed safe and came with the approval and support I desperately needed.

Trace dragged his fingers through my hair softly, repetitively. He stroked me until I was breathing normally again, and I relished the chance to just cry without some rebuke waiting for me on the other end. In the aftermath of the pregnancy, I had to keep all my anguish about Trace bottled up tight, because I didn't want my family to hate him any more than they did. But they weren't dumb. They knew I'd gotten pregnant, and that Trace was nowhere to be found.

Over time, the pregnancy—and miscarriage—became the thing we didn't mention. I'd never even talked about it with Caleb, though I sometimes wondered if Jericho had told him, as a friend or a future brother-in-law.

"I was so excited when I first found out." I dabbed at my eyes with a tissue Trace handed me. "Even though my family would be upset, you and I could have the life we wanted. But then when I didn't hear back from you...time and time again...I wondered if maybe it was because I was too young. Or maybe you had another girlfriend in New York that you didn't want me to know about, like I was the side girl in Louisville. Or maybe it was because my family wasn't right, or...or that maybe you just hadn't meant a single word you'd told me."

"It was never any of that." Trace's voice came out a hoarse croak. "Never any of that at all. I was a breath away from flying back to Louisville to hunt you down personally after I got the text. I called and called, but you never picked up. My brothers convinced me to let you go, because you'd made up your mind and I just had to accept it. I meant everything I said to you, Mercedes. Every last thing. I would have done anything for you, even if it meant listening to you when you told me to stay away."

Tears filled my eyes again as I looked up to find his heartbreaking gaze focused on me. There was so much emotion pulsing between us that I thought I might choke on it. Trace's big hands cupped mine, bringing my knuckles up to his lips.

"Mercedes, if I had known...I would have been there in a heartbeat." His voice cracked as he spoke. "I know I can never prove this to you. But please believe me. And please forgive me."

I nodded, warmth spreading through me, bliss mingling with the anguish. Trace knew the truth, and we were here sharing this moment, mending the past. Not everything made sense, but we were making progress.

"I do. I believe you, and I forgive you."

Trace pressed his lips to my knuckles in soft, tender kisses, watching me with so much emotion pooled in his big, brown eyes that I thought I might start crying again.

"I would have moved heaven and earth to be at your side. To raise our...baby boy." He shook his head, his throat bobbing. "Did your parents know it was ours?"

I nodded tersely. "They didn't want me to acknowledge you were the father publicly, though. They wanted me to either get an abortion or give the baby up for adoption. I refused. But their backup plan was figure out a way to help me raise the baby and concoct some acceptable backstory down the road. I hate saying it, but I think the miscarriage was a relief for them."

Trace's jaw flexed. "They would have been grandparents. That's what they're desperate for, right?"

"Not if the father isn't on the approved list," I said softly.

Trace let out a rueful laugh. He worked his jaw back and forth as he studied something unknowable across the room. "I think it's safe to say I'll never be on their approved list. Not after the way your uncle threw me under the bus."

"The bad blood from whatever happened between you two is permanent, I'm afraid."

"Your uncle pushed me to make some bad investments," he said, pulling his gaze back to me. "Atrociously bad. They were so risky, and I advised him not to do it. I mean, I put my foot down with him, Mercedes, in a way I never did back then with high profile clients. He had a lot of money on the line. But it was some gamble he heard about on a talk radio program, some investment scheme in central Asia. He forced me to move the funds; he was convinced it would pay off. I'm bound to follow my clients' directives, and I was too new to the work to feel I could fire him as a client. So I did it. When the investment tanked, he freaked. Like I knew he would. He lost millions. And then he turned on me, like he hadn't been the one begging me to make the investment. The rest is history."

"That's why you accused me of lying," I whispered, studying the fine lines of his face, the tiny dark hairs near his temple. I wanted to relearn every inch of his entire body again. "Because my uncle lied about the bad investment."

Trace smirked. "Thought it was a Hendricks trait."

I leaned back into the couch, drawing a deep breath. "Learning the truth is exhausting. I feel like I could go straight to bed."

"Then I think it's time for bed." Trace played with my hand, running his thumb along each of my fingers slowly, as if mapping the terrain. As if he was eager to relearn every inch of my body, too.

"Yeah. I think you're right."

"In my bed," he clarified, pushing his thumb into the palm of my hand in a slow, deep massage. When I sent him a look, he added, "After what we talked about tonight, there's no fucking way in hell that you'll spend a night under my roof without spending it in my arms. That's non-negotiable."

I couldn't fight the grin. "That doesn't sound so bad."

His lips brushed against my knuckles again. "Tonight we'll sleep. But after that, I can't make any promises."

The evil twinkle in his eye was both a warning and a promise.

Even though I could have stayed in New York indefinitely, I knew that Louisville couldn't come soon enough.

I was finally ready to end the previous chapter of my life and turn the page to the next one.

CHAPTER TWENTY
MERCEDES

THE NEXT MORNING I awoke slowly. Luxuriously. I was cozy and warm and absolutely buried in Trace's embrace. The clock at his bedside read five a.m., which was far too early for me to be waking up. Not when I had this delicious chance to sleep in, wrapped in the arms of my first—only—love.

I burrowed a little deeper, trying to return to sleepiness. But I couldn't. My mind had started with the jumping jacks and somersaults for the day—what needed to happen, what words I might use with Caleb, replaying the moment when Trace had me wrapped up in the towel pushing his hands all over my body.

The fire he'd lit in my low belly had not diminished even slightly. And according to my own wishes, we couldn't do a damn thing about it.

It only seemed just. But Trace was right. It was torture.

I tossed and turned a bit, barely able to keep my eyes shut amid the relentless thoughts. What rose above the rest was the horniness, though. So much unfinished business between me and Trace. So much tension and only one heated make out session to speak of.

I gritted my teeth, staring at the pristine ceiling of the bedroom. Trace breathed evenly beside me. Sleep was off the table for me, but I still had time to kill before anyone woke up for the day.

I knew how I wanted to spend it.

I gently removed myself from beneath Trace's arm and slunk off the bed, trying to be as quiet as possible. I did not want to be the reason he woke up at this ungodly hour, so I tiptoed out of the bedroom and scurried across the penthouse. I paused in the great room to gawk at the scene beyond the windows. Manhattan had turned into a sea of white snowfall. I took a few tentative steps toward the windows, unsure if this was a dream. It was a blizzard—but from this high up, it was positively magical.

I took a few moments to appreciate the snow globe moment, and then resumed my journey to my bedroom. I'd brought a vibrator for a reason, and I intended to use it.

Sexual energy filled me to bursting, and this was my only chance for relief.

I shut the door behind me, drawing a deep breath in the cool, still air of the guest room. The room was outfitted in the same sleek, modern style as the rest of the penthouse, with an outrageously comfortable king-size bed, an excessive number of fluffy pillows, and low, boxy furniture that made the room feel like it came from an episode of *Million Dollar Listing*.

I rummaged through my suitcase and grabbed the deep purple satin bag that held my secret best friend. Back home, I had a variety of vibrators stashed away in locations that nobody, not even the nosiest house cleaners, would be able to find. This was my travel-size one—easiest to hide, practically discreet. It was egg-shaped on the top with a curved silicone handle.

I'd slept in a thin tank top and cotton shorts, and I slipped off the shorts before crawling into my cold bed, leaving me in my tank top and panties. It already felt foreign and unattractive after one night spent in Trace's arms. There was nowhere else I wanted to spend the night. I hoped he'd make good on his promise to spend each night with me in his arms.

I eased between the covers, need pulsing between my legs. I'd been a raging ball of sexual tension since we set foot on the private jet, and finally, here was my release.

I pressed the button on the vibrator and settled back against the pillows, letting my head relax against the softness. My eyes drifted shut, immediately taking me to the moment in Trace's bathroom after he'd wrapped me in the towel. I'd been imagining nonstop how else that encounter could have ended. How it would have felt to have his hands slip under the soft fibers to meet my damp skin, to slide down to the V of my legs and find all the arousal he'd caused with his mere presence in the bathroom.

I rolled the egg in a slow circle around my clit, teasing myself. There was no need for a slow buildup. My whole body was tense, craving the release. A jolt of pleasure surged through me, making my back arch. A low hum ripped out of me.

I imagined Trace slipping his fingers into my pussy right there in the bathroom. Making me watch. Grinding his erection against me from behind while he slid his fingers in and out of me so slowly that I'd beg him to let me come.

My back arched again. I was so close. It had been mere *minutes*. I drew a deep breath and rolled my lips inward, trying to make sure not a peep of noise escaped. Everyone was asleep, so it was an unnecessary precaution. I clamped my thighs around the vibrator, arching again as I imagined Trace bending me over. Pulling his pants down to reveal his thick, cut penis. I'd always loved his dick—he was the only man who I could say had an *attractive penis*. Most were unsightly, strange at best. But not Trace. His was handsome. It was *sexy*. And just the thought of it had me nearly tipping over the edge again.

I felt the pleasure balloon inside my chest. And then when I pushed the vibrator in just the right spot, the pleasure popped—all my limbs went hot and sparkly. A shudder wracked my body, and I was distantly aware of making a noise, but the orgasm was too loud between my ears for me to notice.

I tipped my head back, breathing heavily as I recuperated from the high. *Holy shit. Holy shit.* That's how good it was when I was just imagining Trace. I was sure the real thing, six years after our last lovemaking session, would be ten times better.

A noise caught my attention, a *swoosh*, and I opened my eyes.

My door hung open.

And Trace was there.

A gasp rocketed out of me, and I jolted to sitting. My first thought was that this was a hallucination—something inspired by the mania of that orgasm. There was no way Trace could be here, because he was sleeping, and I'd been quiet.

But his gaze sizzled over me, amused but tired. Recognition colored his expression. I was caught.

"Trace," I forced out past dry lips. "What are you doing here?"

"You called my name," he said slowly, stepping inside the bedroom. "So I came in."

I let my head fall back on the pillow. Each passing second compounded my embarrassment. There was something about being *caught* masturbating. Especially when I'd brought a vibrator on a work trip.

"What were you doing in here?" He stepped closer, coming over to the bedside. He towered over the side of the bed, the intensity of his attention growing by the second.

"Nothing," I said, knowing this was already a hopeless battle. "Why are you even awake? I thought—"

"I woke up when I got cold," he said. "And then I noticed you weren't in my bed, so I went to the bathroom. And that's when I heard you making noises."

I squeezed my eyes shut. I was so caught.

"Mercedes...what is going on under here?" Trace tore back the covers, revealing the vibrator in my right hand. "What were you doing?"

I sighed loudly, unable to meet his gaze. "Do you have to be so pushy?"

"I just want to hear you say it." His brown eyes were alive and aware, sparkling with mischief. I couldn't stand him as much as I wanted to devour him.

I huffed, sitting up with the intention of tossing the vibrator back toward my luggage. But Trace caught my wrist when I moved to toss it.

"What are you doing?"

"Trace, I'm embarrassed. This isn't how I imagined things going."

The corners of his mouth turned up. He moved his hand down my hand to the vibrator, enclosing it in his grip. "There's nothing to be embarrassed about. Let me help you."

I swallowed hard. "Help?"

"You're sexually frustrated. The one cock you need, you can't have. I'll make sure you can still function until you take care of things in Louisville and then I can bury my cock so deep inside you it'll touch your skull."

Heat zipped through me, igniting every inch of my body. I'd forgotten about Trace's mouth. I drew a shaky breath as goosepimples sprang to life on every square inch of my flesh.

"I already...got off," I said softly, still unable to meet his gaze.

Trace reached for my chin, guiding my face upward until he forced our eyes to meet. "Then you'll get off again. I'll make you come so hard that you scream my name like it deserves to be screamed."

It was hard to argue with him when he laid it out like that. It was all I wanted to do. But there were rules, even though it felt like they were rapidly evaporating.

"We can't," I whispered, getting lost in his brown gaze. "I'm trying to do this right."

"I won't touch you," Trace said. "The vibrator will. And what's the difference if I'm the one using it instead of you? We won't even kiss. No groping. We won't break a single rule."

I knew it was wrong. But his subversion of the rules was elegant and irresistible. Trace knew what he wanted, and I wanted to give it to him.

"Promise me," I said.

His wicked grin was the stuff of fantasies. "Promise."

He eased to sitting on the side of the bed, my vibrator almost comically small in his big, manly hand. He toyed with the settings for a moment, turning it on, playing with the speeds, until he knew all he needed. He jerked his chin toward me.

"Lay back."

I did as I was told, my head sinking into the softness of the pillows again. It would almost be relaxing, if my entire body hadn't been electrified with awareness and need.

"Spread your legs." His voice was a sexy rumble as he clicked the vibrator on to the lowest speed. He tilted his head, his gaze coasting up and down my body. He dragged the vibrator over my inner thigh, dancing it around the swollen lips of my pussy. I inhaled sharply as he danced the tip of the vibrator so perilously close to my clit, barely glancing it.

"You're soaked." He brushed the vibrator gently against my clit through my panties; infuriatingly gently. His dark gaze raked up my body, lingering on the tight points of my nipples visible beneath my tank top. "What were you thinking about?"

"You," I blurted.

"What were we doing?" He drew lazy circles around my clit, which caused me to buck, seeking the friction.

"I thought about when we were in the bathroom yesterday," I whispered. "When you kissed me."

"I wanted to fuck your mouth with my tongue." He held the vibrator against the underside of my clit suddenly, the sudden jolt of pleasure causing me to buck forward and cry out. He pulled it away after a moment. "I could kiss you for an entire month, Mercedes, and it still wouldn't be enough."

I hardly had words after what he'd just done to me. I clamped my knees against his arm, trying to keep the vibrations in the right area. He smiled slyly.

"You're so wet I can feel it on my fingers. That's a no-no, Mercedes. Remember?"

"I can't help it," I said with a little laugh. "And it's your fault anyway."

"I think these panties are ruined." He tilted his head, looking between my legs. "Won't be the last."

His words sent a shiver through me, and I bucked toward him again. "You know you could turn the speed up on that thing."

"Oh I know. I'm not going to."

I huffed, the urgency pulsing through me. Even though I'd just come, I needed the next orgasm almost as much as I needed air. Trace was too good at pushing my buttons. "This isn't fair."

"I hardly think it's fair that you call me in here only for me to find out you're masturbating by yourself under the covers." He glanced the vibrator over the top of my clit, the corners of his lips turning up.

"I didn't want to wake you up," I told him.

"Let's be clear on this. You can wake me up anytime you need to get off." His eyes went hooded as he rolled the vibrator over the crotch of my underwear. "But since you didn't wake me up, I'm not even sure I'll let you come."

I groaned, bucking my hips to find more of the friction I so desired. "*Trace.*"

"There's some of the enthusiasm I like to hear."

I huffed, rolling my hips closer to him. "You're such a tease."

"Just like you've been." He rolled the egg over the peak of my clit so slowly that it sent a gale force jolt of pleasure through me. Just shy of an orgasm. I didn't know how he knew me so well, but he did, and I hated him for it. "Teasing me with that stupid ring you used to wear. Teasing me by acting like you didn't want it when clearly"—he slipped the vibrator beneath my panties and into the slick channel—"you absolutely do want it."

I threw my head back and moaned. "Pleaaase, Trace." It was already a horribly painful tease that he wasn't using his fingers, his mouth, his tongue. I wanted so much more from him—in every way. I always had.

He pulled the vibrator out and looked at it before turning it off. I gasped. "What are you doing?"

"Convincing myself to stick to your rules." He sent me a deeply desirous look and surged to his feet. His pajama pants tented over his cock until he reached into his underwear to adjust himself. The swollen head of his cock peeked past the waistband and my lips parted.

"Don't go," I pleaded. "I'm so close."

"Good. I'll be right back," he promised. "But don't touch that vibrator."

With a stern look, he headed out of the bedroom, disappearing into the gauzy light of the hallway. Dawn had crested sometime between solo masturbation and Trace-aided masturbation. I struggled to catch my breath as I waited for him, trying to orient myself. Who was I? What was going on? Did I want this?

Mercedes. You're bending the rules with the first and only man you've ever passionately loved. And yes, you want this more than life itself.

My chest heaved as I waited for Trace to return. The clock on my nightstand said six a.m. I'd been lost in the pursuit of orgasm for an hour now. This was insane. Yet somehow perfect.

Trace returned a moment later, pulling the plastic wrapper away from something in his hand. As he neared, I saw that it was a chocolate bar.

"Are you hungry?" I asked.

"No." He revealed the long chocolate bar, his greedy gaze settling on me again. "But I want to taste you. If I can't eat you out properly, this is the next best thing."

His words thrilled through me, igniting question marks beneath my skin. "What...what do you mean?"

His evil smile stretched ear to ear as he kneeled at the bedside once more. "You can't come on my fingers, or my tongue, or my cock, as God intended. So this is our stand-in."

My brain still struggled to synthesize this information. All I could think about was how glorious it would feel for him to plunge his tongue inside me right now, followed by his cock. My gaze drifted to the swollen cockhead still visible above the waistband of his underwear. Anything to relieve the pressure he'd painstakingly built up.

"No touching." He moved my hand away from his crotch, which I hadn't even realized I'd lunged for. He was making me delirious. "Remember?"

I groaned. "You'll need to tie me up."

"Say no more." He headed to the closet on the far wall of the bedroom. He slid open the door with a low *swoosh* and contemplated the interior. "Tying you up for our first real sexual encounter after six years has a nice ring to it, doesn't it?" He grabbed a silk tie from a collection hanging inside. "We didn't fuck in the traditional sense, but I was still able to tie you up and fuck you with a chocolate bar. Because that's following the rules."

I inhaled sharply, his words as hot as though he'd brought the vibrator out again. I was so close. I pushed a hand into my panties, seeking the hard peak of my clit since Trace was so insistent on denying me what I needed. He tutted, stilling my wrist with one firm swipe of his hand when he arrived at the bedside.

"You *do* need to be tied up. Take your panties off first."

I did as he instructed, shimmying out of them quickly and tossing them over the edge of the bed. I whimpered as he deftly lifted my arms above my head and secured them with the silk tie. He secured the tie to the headboard somehow—I couldn't even spare enough attention to know what he was doing, since every pulse of blood through my veins was directed to my pussy. I jerked my hands against the restraint—firm. A satisfied smile curled at Trace's lips.

"You can't touch yourself *or* me." He palmed the length of his hard-on through the front of his pajama pants as his gaze washed over my half-naked body, settling on my bare pussy. His attention electrified the area, sending heat streaking through my veins.

"Let me see it," I breathed, my gaze stuck on the thick ridge visible through his pants. "Please."

He tutted, shaking his head. "Not yet. Not while I'm looking at how gorgeous you are, half-naked, tied to *my* bed. I should take a picture. Just to send to Caleb."

My skin prickled as his gaze sizzled over me. Every baritone word from his lips pushed me closer to the edge. I could have gotten off just from squeezing my thighs together while I looked at the bulbous head of his cock peeking out from his waistband. *Almost.*

"Ohh, Mercedes. I'm going to fucking devour you when we get back to Louisville." He sat on the edge of the bed again, reaching for the vibrator. "You won't even be able to walk after I'm done with you." He pressed the button and the vibrator hummed quietly. He eased my legs open, rolling the vibrator back and forth across my clit, guiding it with his palm. With his other hand, he grabbed the chocolate bar.

It happened so quickly. He held my gaze as he played me like a fiddle—plunging the chocolate bar deep inside me. Pushing me over the edge with the vibrator. Fireworks burst behind my eyelids and my entire body clenched. I screamed, I was sure of it, though I wasn't fully aware of it. I pulled at the restraints as the orgasm tore through me, leaving me a quivering, quaking mess.

My chest heaved as I struggled to get my breath. When I opened my eyes, Trace looked like he'd reached the end of his personal restraint. He slipped the chocolate bar out of my pussy.

And then he took a bite.

"Mmmm." He looked drugged as he chewed. "You taste so fucking good, Birdie."

The reappearance of his pet name for me was an extra squeeze around my heart. I hadn't heard that name in so many years, and that word from his lips was a relief I hadn't counted on. For whatever reason, the fact that he was still on board with this—with *me*—meant that I wasn't crazy. This was real. This was worth fighting for.

He feels it too.

I sighed deeply, my heart still pounding.

"Do you want a taste?"

I laughed. "Not really."

"Come on. This is a once in a lifetime opportunity." He offered me a bite, which I took reluctantly when he brought it up to my lips. It just tasted like chocolate to me—albeit one with a floral...*essence*. Just knowing that my juices were on there gave it an extra dimension.

"Thanks." I chewed with a grimace. "This is so weird."

Trace took another bite, nodding. "It is. In the best way."

We smiled at each other for a moment, until I realized I was still tied to his headboard. "Are you going to untie me someday?"

He shook his head.

"Trace."

"I'll untie you on one condition." He downed the rest of the chocolate bar before he sent me a serious look. "The first thing you do when we get back to Louisville is end it with Caleb."

"That's the plan," I said quietly.

"I'm talking straight to his house or your parents' house, or wherever you need to have the conversation. Because, Birdie..." Trace's nostrils flared as he dragged his fingertips along my arm, heading for the tie. "I can't keep pretending to the world that you're not mine. I've spent the last several weeks pretending otherwise, but time's up. The truth is you're mine. And you have been since I fucking met you."

I squeezed my eyes shut as he spoke, emotion overwhelming me. He was right. He was so fucking right. I'd been his and he'd been mine before it even made sense. And now here I was—tied to a bed after being fucked with a chocolate bar—because we couldn't keep pretending. A tear escaped my eye, and Trace's thumb brushed against my cheek before I could open my eyes.

"I didn't want to upset you," he said softly.

"You're right, Bear." His pet name had finally escaped me, and it prompted a chest-hitching sob. Trace undid the tie quickly, releasing my wrists. He scooped me into his arms, pulling me into his solid, masculine heat. I collapsed against him, feeling protected at my most vulnerable moment. Not only had he taken me to the heights of pleasure, he'd accompanied me to the depths of our pain.

Trace was the man I trusted to be at my side.

"There's never been anyone for me but you." My voice came out shaky. He swiped a tear from my face as our eyes met, the emotion and sincerity in his eyes as much of a relief as a gut punch. "It's always been you."

CHAPTER TWENTY-ONE
TRACE

A FULL-BLOWN SNOWSTORM HIT New York that morning. The entire city was coated, white, dangerous. I couldn't have cared less, because I had all I needed in this penthouse: Mercedes, Willow, and plenty of reading material.

After I finished punishing Mercedes for pleasuring herself without me, I headed straight for the shower—served extra cold, just this shy of ice cubes—to settle my nerves and coax my cock to settle down. It wouldn't be seeing any action in Manhattan, and it needed to get the message.

When I stepped out of the shower, Mercedes was there. She met my gaze like a challenge, her arms crossed over her tank top.

"Just came to watch me towel off, huh?" I grabbed for the gray towel hanging next to the shower and ran it over my head then along my arms. Just seeing her tits in that thin tank had me half-hard already, ruining the desire-dousing effects of the cold shower.

"You didn't get off." She lowered her chin, her tone accusatory.

"Correct."

"Let's change that."

I chuckled, shaking my head as I wrapped the towel around my waist. "I know better than to wade into those waters."

"You got me off. Fair is fair. And I should be able to watch, since obviously I can't help you."

Her innocent negotiations amused me. I paused at her side, towering over her as I forced her to tip her head back to meet my gaze. "You better get out of this bathroom or I'm liable to break some rules."

She pouted. "Okay fine."

"Don't be impatient, Birdie." I squeezed her chin before moving to face the mirrors. Funny advice to give, considering how absolutely ravenous I was for her. "What did you tell me yesterday? We've waited six years. What's a few more days?"

"But what if this snowstorm keeps us here even longer?" She nibbled on her lip, her gaze drifting to the long, narrow window overlooking the city at the far wall of the bathroom. "It looks bad out there."

"Isn't that what you wanted? To be snowed in and trapped with books?"

She pursed her lips. "My fantasy involved slightly different circumstances where *this*"—she gestured between our bodies—"was concerned."

"Then we'll just have to fester in our sexual frustration and do nothing about it." I smiled evilly at her through the reflection. "You wanted these rules, after all. And I'm going to make sure we stick to them."

"You weren't such a stickler before," she teased with a coy smile, sidling up beside me. She let her gaze fall to my naked torso, sending another near-fatal surge of desire down my spine. There was nothing more that I wanted in life than to be appreciated. By *her*. "What changed?"

"It turns me on to see you squirm. And I realized I have some rules of my own." I applied my deodorant as we spoke. Then I set the container down and turned to her, grabbing her by the chin.

"I won't fuck you until that little ring he gave you is in the trash. Because once we fuck, there's no turning back, Birdie."

Her cheeks flushed but she held my gaze. "I was always yours."

"But he needs to be made aware before I bury my cock inside you."

Her eyes fluttered shut, and she drew a deep breath through her nostrils. "Should I tell him that you're the man I'm leaving him for?"

I knew the answer—*of course you fucking should*—but I paused. There was more at stake here than just leaving a fiancé. The history between her family and me necessitated some finesse.

"Not right away," I said, pushing my fingertips along her jawline, up into her silky hair. "I know that's going to be a bumpy transition."

"But you'll help me?" she whispered.

"Help you?" I chucked softly, brushing my thumb gently back and forth across her lips. They were my weakness. "Birdie, I'll do whatever it takes for us to pick up the pieces of what we left behind six years ago. I'll move Heaven; I'll move Hell. I'll move Caleb to his rightful position, which is out of your life."

She smiled, but it was the sad kind. "It's going to be hard. My family will be furious."

"*You* should be furious with *them*."

Her brows furrowed. "I am. I think even I don't realize just how much, too."

I leaned down and pressed a kiss to her forehead. "Chaste kiss," I murmured against her skin. "This is allowed."

Mercedes slid her arms around my bare torso, cinching me into a tight hug. She laid her cheek against the flat plane of my chest and sighed deeply. I wrapped my arms around her and held her, a thought rumbling to life.

On the plane ride here, she'd asked me if I'd been truly happy when we'd been together. I couldn't answer her then because it would have broken me. I hadn't believed the glimmer of hope on the horizon when it came to her and me, even though it was just a couple days ago. And sometimes, allowing hope in was just as painful as having hopes dashed.

But now?

I wanted to tell her the answer.

"Birdie. Do you remember when you asked me if I'd been truly happy when we were together?"

She nodded, propping her chin on my chest to look up at me.

"That was one of the happiest times of my life. It's why I never stopped thinking about you all these years. Even when I desperately wanted to."

Her eyes went shimmery. "It was the happiest time of my life too, Bear."

Seconds bled into minutes. We could have passed an eternity there, warm in each other's embrace. I stroked the top of her head until a distant wailing broke through our reverie.

"Willow's awake." Mercedes drew a deep breath. "I'll go get her and we can make breakfast."

My heart swelled. There was nothing that sounded better. Well—fucking Mercedes until sunrise the following day sounded slightly better. Having her come around my cock instead of a chocolate bar sounded *way* better. But given the circumstances, this would have to do.

"Go before I kiss you for real."

She grinned and tore herself away from me, hurrying out of the bathroom. I finished my morning routine, and went to get dressed. Once I'd pulled on briefs, sweats and a T-shirt, I headed out into the great room to find Mercedes at the window with Willow on her hip, pointing out at the snowstorm.

"Hey, girls." I wrapped my arm around Mercedes's waist and kissed the top of Willow's head. She wriggled in Mercedes's arms, reaching for me, and I picked her up easily. "Did you sleep well, sweet girl?"

Willow slapped at my collarbone, speaking gibberish in return.

"We didn't sleep well," I told her, smoothing her blonde curls. "In case you wondered."

"Yeah, the storm really...kept us up," Mercedes offered with a laugh.

"Mmm. Yes. The storm."

"Do you want some coffee?" Mercedes asked.

"I'd love some."

"Frighteningly strong espresso or oat milk latte?"

"I want what you're having," I told her.

Mercedes winked and headed for the kitchen while Willow and I considered the city through the windows. She jabbed her index finger against the glass every so often, her gaze tracking an unknowable number of snowflakes. It was mesmerizing, in a way that felt so completely warm and fulfilling I hardly knew what to do with the feeling. It was almost too big. Too good. Too real.

This is what you've been waiting for. What you almost had six years ago.

I swallowed a sudden knot in my throat, studying the contours of Willow's face. She didn't seem to notice me getting lost in my feels. It hurt to imagine what my life would have looked like now if things hadn't been derailed six years ago. Would Mercedes and I have a five-year-old now? Would we still be together? Would the miscarriage have pushed us apart? Brought us even closer together?

The possibilities were dizzying. We'd almost started a life together once.

And now here was our second chance.

"Whatcha thinking about?" Mercedes appeared at my side, handing over a mug of steaming black coffee. "You look deep in thought."

"What do you want, Mercedes? Like truly want." I took a sip and set the mug of coffee down on a nearby end table. "If family were no issue and we were living in a perfect world without barriers. What would you have?"

She drew a deep breath, contemplating the snowy world beyond the window over the top of her steaming coffee. "Well that's a big question."

"Take your time."

"There'd be no wedding," she blurted.

I grinned. "You didn't need any time at all for that one."

"There'd be no wedding, and I'd be working full-time. I'd...have my own place. Wherever I lived. Because I'd be going to school during the day, working at night. Something like that. And uh..." She took a drink of her coffee, eyes fastened on the snowstorm. "I'd be with you. My family would accept it. And we'd spend every night in each other's arms, then reading books together in the ungodly early morning hours."

I couldn't fight the grin. "Oh. Is that all?"

"Yeah. That's all." She smiled and sipped at her coffee.

I dipped down to kiss her hairline. "Chaste kiss of acceptance. Allowed via technicality." Willow patted the top of Mercedes's head, joining in on the lovefest. "I want to give that to you, Birdie. As much as I can. What destination should we visit to celebrate this reality?"

Mercedes grinned up at me, stars in her eyes. "Aren't we doing a Chilean wine thing?"

"No, that was for Petit Verdot appreciation only. This is specifically celebrating our perfect future."

She leaned into me, giggling. "Oh, right. How could I mix those up? Let's see....I think I'd go to...Puerto Rico!"

"Puerto Rico?"

She nodded. "I've always wanted to go since I was a little girl."

My brows drew together. "And you still haven't been? With how easy it is to get there?"

"My parents aren't big on long flights."

I nodded, snaking my hand around the curve of her neck. I dug my fingertips in until her eyes went a little hooded. *Mine.* "Consider it done."

"Dah," Willow echoed.

Mercedes's eyes lit up and she tickled Willow's belly. "What was that, sweet girl? Are you saying *done*?" We prompted her for a few moments, trying to get her to repeat the word. But she'd had enough soon, and she focused on the snow again.

"Okay. We'll stop bothering you." Mercedes rubbed Willow's back, her gaze drifting up to meet mine. "So what's your perfect future, if everything were possible and no barriers existed?"

I grinned, knowing she'd return the question. "I don't know if I can say it out loud."

"You'll have to. I said mine; now it's your turn."

I hoisted Willow a bit higher in my arms, absorbing the fascinating depths in Mercedes's green eyes. "We're planning *our* wedding. At the winery. But it's small and intimate and it's so fucking easy to figure out, it's stress-free. My brothers and I would be opening Fairchild Solutions together, in Louisville, because we..." I cleared my throat, my gaze dropping to the floor. "Because we've reconciled. And Willow is still with me. She's the flower girl in our wedding, obviously. She starts school in Manhattan because I get permanent custody somehow. And..." *I don't go to prison.* Those were the words I couldn't say. I was too afraid of their outcome to even go there. I wasn't even sure Mercedes knew what I was up against, and now didn't seem like the time to bring her up to speed. "Life is good," I finished up.

Mercedes nodded, her eyes brimming with emotion. "That sounds lovely. I'd like to make that happen too."

I pulled Mercedes into me with my free arm. My heart throbbed, my chest tight from a combination of baring my soul and feeling too full. Strange how sometimes happiness could come on the heels of feeling more broken and empty than ever. How choking happiness could be. I'd lost a brother but gained a niece and found the one who got away. As a man of numbers and logic, it didn't make sense.

But maybe it didn't have to.

Maybe just having them in my life, in this weird and unexpected way, was enough.

CHAPTER TWENTY-TWO
MERCEDES

THE SNOWSTORM KEPT US trapped in New York for two more days. They were as wonderful as they were challenging. Going to sleep and waking up in Trace's bed was a beautiful thing...until the brakes invariably had to be applied because going further required a conversation that could only happen in Louisville.

The snow cleared enough for us to travel on Saturday. We packed our things, and I said a sad goodbye to the Tribeca penthouse, which had been, and might always be, my fantasy getaway nest. Though I knew Trace and I could visit here again when we wanted, I feared the situation with his brothers would keep him out of New York for the foreseeable future.

We spent the plane ride home cuddling as a family of three, with Willow on my lap and me nestled into Trace's arms, gazing out the window. I wasn't sure I could exist away from his heat or his security anymore, but I'd have to, once we touched ground in Kentucky. Because my only destination from here was my parents' house.

Nerves had been tightening inside me for days. By now, my belly was a tangled mess, and I knew it would only get worse from here. This was what needed to happen—what I *wanted* to happen—but it didn't mean it would be easy. In fact, I fully expected a nuclear meltdown from Caleb and my parents.

But it was preferable to the nuclear meltdown that would be my innards if I didn't cancel this wedding.

We landed in Louisville mid-afternoon. Trace held my hand the entire drive to my parents' house. He parked on the street the same way I'd instructed him before we left for New York—one house down, mostly out of view of their gated driveway.

"Let me help you," Trace said, reaching for the door handle, but I shook my head.

"No. I can get my things. Just pop the trunk."

His jaw ticked and he held my gaze. "Are you sure you don't want me to come with you?"

"Absolutely sure." I squeezed his wrist. "They wouldn't even let you through the front door. I appreciate you wanting to help, but I need to handle this on my own."

He looked like he was about to say more, but his phone vibrated and distracted him. He let out a terse sigh and declined the call. I slipped out of the car as the trunk popped open. A moment later I heard Trace answer his phone with a short: "Who is this?"

I collected my things and peered around to look at him before I walked away. He was frowning down at his phone, so I tapped the driver's side window and waved before I hurried toward the wrought iron gate entrance. I punched the code into the security pad, and the gate clanked as it slid open. I hurried down the long, winding driveway, my rolling luggage clicking behind me, breath coming out in quick puffs.

Every step against the pavement reminded me of what lay ahead. *It's. Time. It's. Time. It's. Time.*

I couldn't lie. I was scared shitless. I'd avoided this moment for so long, even while knowing I didn't want to go through with the wedding, because at the time, suffering through a relationship I didn't want was still easier than going after the life I wanted.

Now I had no other option.

Trace had lit that fire inside of me again. Regardless of what happened with him…regardless of how our love story panned out…I was doing this.

I paused near the house, feeling a burst of resolve. I texted Caleb before I could think twice.

MERCEDES: I'm back in L-ville. Are you coming for dinner tonight? I really want to talk. Maybe you can come early. I need to see you urgently.

I had no handbook for how to handle this stuff. I hoped I was doing it right.

I entered the sprawling colonial mansion via the overhang connecting the house and the garage. I stepped into the warm hallway and spotted a few people in the kitchen. Something felt odd, though I couldn't put my finger on what. At this time of day, on a Saturday, there weren't usually visitors, much less people congregating in the kitchen.

I left my bag by the door, since I'd be leaving through there to get to my detached pool house later, and unbuttoned my coat as I went to the kitchen. "Hello?"

Someone inhaled sharply. I found my mother and aunt Rosie with their heads together in the kitchen. Maddie was there too, bouncing Grace on her hip.

"Hey there," I said slowly. My mother avoided my gaze, and she sniffed, a tissue clutched in her hand. "Is everything okay?"

Aunt Rosie drew a deep breath, gliding my way. "Hi, Mercedes. Everything's fine for now. There's just…been a scare."

Fine for now? I blinked, looking at my mother, who leaned against the countertop like she might faint. "A scare? What kind?"

"Your Gramma Kay," Aunt Rosie said softly, squeezing my arm. "She was in the hospital for a couple nights this week—she just got home this morning, and we've been getting things settled."

I blinked even more rapidly now, looking between the three women in the kitchen. I wasn't sure whether to laugh or cry. "I'm sorry...what did you say?"

"It was her blood pressure," Aunt Rosie went on. "They're thinking it might have been, I don't know, a mini-stroke..."

"She was in the hospital for a couple nights and nobody told me?" I asked, unable to keep the hard edge out of my voice.

Maddie's mouth turned downward, and her gaze fell to the ground. My mother shielded her eyes with her hand.

"I can't have this conversation right now," my mother said, sounding wearier than I'd ever heard her.

"Somebody couldn't have sent a text?" I spat, throwing up my palms. "Even Jericho? What about Dad?" I started sputtering. "For God's sake, I left town for less than a week and I don't even get the courtesy of hearing about the fact that my gramma had a *stroke*?"

My mother's mouth turned into a frightening thin line and she took a menacing step forward. "Don't make this about you," she hissed. "Now is *really not the time* to make this about you."

"I'm not making this about me," I barreled on. Somewhere deep inside, I was shocked I had the balls to speak to my mother this way. But I was angry. No, I was furious. This felt like a betrayal, and I hated that she couldn't see that. "Why would you exclude family for something like this? How am I not on the call list?"

"Because you were gone," my mother nearly shouted. Her nostrils flared, and suddenly she was seething. "You've been so absent recently, I didn't think I needed to hunt you down from wherever you were."

"I was in New York," I said, my voice wobbling slightly. The emotional tears were on their way, and I had limited time before I fully lost it. "There was a snowstorm. We couldn't travel back on schedule. I can't believe that would exclude me from news like this, in your eyes."

"You've been so different lately," my mother said, waving her hand dismissively in my direction. "And here we are again. You get home and find out that your grandmother had a medical scare and all we're talking about is why *you're* upset."

I clamped my mouth shut, trying to tamp down the anger skating through my veins.

"I don't know where your manners have gone," my mother continued, crossing her arms.

I closed my eyes, trying to reel myself in. Not only would this conversation go nowhere, it was unfolding in front of Aunt Rosie and Maddie and Grace. I felt justified in my anger—but maybe my mother had a point.

Maybe I was the wretched one out of line again. *Like always.*

"I'm sorry," I said, once I found my voice. "This is just so shocking. I wanted to know. I wouldn't have been able to come but—"

"It would have just made things harder if you'd known and couldn't come," Aunt Rosie said, touching my arm softly. "I know it would have eaten you up."

I deflated. She was right. But that wasn't why my mother had kept it from me, which meant Aunt Rosie's words were just a band-aid that was already falling off.

"I'm just thankful the wedding isn't far off," my mother whispered after a painful silence had stretched across the kitchen. She dabbed at her eyes with the tissue. "I don't know how much longer Mom has. It would kill her if she couldn't make it to your wedding."

I squeezed my eyes shut, my mother's words a spear forged from iron and guilt. It nearly split me in two. I drew a deep breath and realized I needed to get out of here. Immediately.

"Can I go see Gramma Kay?" I asked.

"She's resting," my mom said. "Now's not a good time."

I nodded, swallowing a knot in my throat. "I'll go get unpacked and try before dinner." I saw myself out of the kitchen, grabbing my suitcase before leaving the house and heading for the pool house where I lived. Once I was back in my familiar bedroom, all my things just as I'd left them, the waves of emotion I'd been holding back finally pummeled me.

I sank to my knees at the foot of my bed, all the worries and hopelessness barreling down on me. My family was already showing me just how well they could shut me out, and I hadn't even told them the news. Not to mention I now had to come to terms with the fact that I was single-handedly detonating the one thing my grandmother wanted before she died—to see me marry Caleb.

Mercedes, what are you doing?

It felt so horrible, in so many ways, but even after what had happened in the kitchen, breaking it off with Caleb didn't feel wrong. Maybe even because of what had happened in the kitchen.

That, for now, was what I'd run with. Trace, Damian and Jessa, and Cora had included more in their family than my own had. Had shown more compassion than my own mother.

I cried into my bedspread until the tears stopped coming. Then I blew my nose, wiped away the mascara trickling down my cheeks, and hauled my suitcase onto my bed. A text message came in as I unzipped the bag.

CORA: Hope you don't mind that I'm reaching out. I was just thinking of you and wanted to touch base. Are you back in Kentucky?

My heart skipped a beat as I reread the message. Cora had texted me during the snowstorm, and we'd chatted about Willow and how those muffins had turned out. Word must have traveled fast in the Fairchild family, because she'd also asked me about my counseling ambitions.

MERCEDES: Just got back to my house in Louisville. Thinking I made a mistake.

CORA: Oh yeah? How so?

MERCEDES: New York is really calling to me. But if I want to be there someday, I need to get myself out of a very messy situation here first. A messy situation I put myself in.

There was something about the rawness of my previous anger, combined with that good, solid cry, that made me more honest and open with Cora than I might have been otherwise. What was there to gain by hiding? Besides, this woman had bared it all—to the world, no less. Maybe I was taking a page out of her book.

CORA: Should we talk on the phone? You can call me if you want.

I didn't even have to think twice. A moment later, the phone was ringing, and I had it pressed to my ear. This felt both surreal and impossible. I was calling Cora Margulis, real estate heiress, on the phone. What alternate dimension had I woken up in?

"Okay, girlie," Cora said, sounding like she was getting down to business. "Let's hear it."

I sat with my back against my bed, bringing my knees up to my chest. I opened my mouth, but nothing came out. The words began piling up in my head, higher and higher until they finally spilled out. "I'm going to tell my fiancé that I can't marry him."

She let out a breath. "Wow. You know how to start a conversation off. Why are you calling it off?"

"I never wanted to marry him," I whispered, clutching the phone so hard I felt my knuckles straining. I looked toward the door in case anyone from my family had suddenly appeared and witnessed me speaking this truth for the first time out loud. "I mean, I *thought* I wanted to marry him, but once I got real with myself, I realized I was going along with it because I thought I should. Because my family wanted me to."

"I know a thing or two about that," Cora murmured.

"That's what makes it so hard. Everyone loves him and wants him to be a part of this family. I just wish he could marry someone else. A different sister that I don't have. I'm just not the woman for him."

"Do you need help with breaking the news? What's the plan?"

"I...don't know." Anxiety churned slowly inside me; the whole concept felt surreal still. Viscous, like sludge that lurked beneath the surface of my mind. "He's coming over soon. I'm going to tell him then. I don't think I've ever actually been in love with him."

"Is there someone else?"

Tears pricked at my eyes. "Of course there is. The man I've been in love with since I was nineteen."

Cora paused. "Is it..."

"Trace," I breathed, a sob following his name.

"Oh, honey. I'd hug you if I could. Those Fairchild men are hard to get over."

I laughed a little, dabbing the corner of my eye. "Yeah. They stain."

"For life," she added.

Cora listened as I whined and wailed about my predicament. We talked for a half hour. I hadn't realized that I could be on the phone that long with anyone, much less Cora Margulis. But by the time we hung up, I felt sturdier. More capable. Ready for whatever came my way.

Caleb showed up at my door about a half hour before dinnertime. As high as Cora had boosted me, my stomach still felt like a zipper of nerves. Half an hour wasn't enough time to break the news to him.

But it would have to do.

"You in here?" Caleb pushed into the room, his gaze bouncing around the walls quickly before settling on me. His smile was brief. Half-hearted. "Hey there. Welcome back."

I swallowed hard, not moving from my spot on the bed. I hadn't finished unpacking because part of me thought I might need to pack even more and just leave altogether. "Did you hear about Gramma Kay?"

He nodded, his gaze falling to the floor. "I wanted to tell you..."

"When did this entire family turn against me?"

Caleb cocked his head. "Don't be so dramatic."

It didn't feel dramatic. Not after a lifetime of being squashed and silenced. But despite my resolve, a voice at the back of my head still sounded the alarm.

How could you do this today when Mom is still grappling with Gramma's medical issue? How selfish. Your mother is right. You always have to make things about you.

"Nobody wanted to tell you because you were three states away. What could you have done but worry yourself sick?"

Caleb's smooth, reassuring tone did nothing for the jangle of nerves inside me.

"Honestly, this is part of what comes with working the job you have," Caleb said, easing onto the bed. He reached out and squeezed my ankle. "One of the many reasons why we should look at you just...not working."

His words kicked my frustration back up to a boil. "But what if I want to work?"

Caleb looked confused, as if he'd never heard those words before. "Mercedes—"

"Caleb, I have to tell you something," I said, forcing the words out before they withered inside me. They tumbled from my mouth, bulky and uncomfortable. I wasn't even standing up, and my legs felt heavy. "I'm having second thoughts."

He blinked slowly. "About what?"

"About...this. About all of it. I feel like what you want from me and what I want for me are two separate things."

His brows began a slow trek to the center of his forehead. "Is this because I think you should be more present when our kids are young?"

"No," I hissed, "It's not *that*. Of course I would want to be present when our children are young. It's just that—" I paused, pressing a hand to my forehead. The emotion thumped so loudly inside of me I almost couldn't hear past it. "I feel like we want different things. You want me to be a stay-at-home mom. You want us to live some replica life of my parents'. Caleb, when's the last time we actually had a conversation?"

He laughed like maybe this was the start of a joke he didn't quite understand yet. "What does that have to do with anything?"

"You guys haven't listened to a single thing I've had to say about this wedding, either." I knew that everything was just tumbling out now, a graceless fall from inside the cage where I'd held these feelings hostage for too long. "And during the wedding planning, I realized you guys don't listen to a single thing I have to say about...anything."

"That's ridiculous," Caleb said, his mouth turning into a sneer. "How could you even say that? Literally everything I do, I do for you."

I swallowed hard. "I just think we might not be right for each other. It doesn't mean I hate you, or that I even dislike you. I just…" My whole chest vibrated as the words came to me, begging me to speak them. "I'm just not in love with you."

Caleb stared at the floor blankly, a deep silence settling between us. After a moment, he shook his head. When he swung his gaze to me, he looked vacant. Resigned. "Wow. So this is what I get for spending every last dime on you, doing everything I think you want, and trying to give you the best of everything?"

Guilt crashed through me, and I buried my face in my hands. "This isn't a punishment, Caleb. I'm trying to be honest."

"You're trying to be *honest*? Well your honesty feels a lot like cruelty. This is so ridiculous." He surged to his feet and started pacing, dragging a hand through his hair. "Or maybe this is a joke? This has to be a joke."

"Caleb—"

"We're months away from the wedding and you spring this on me *now*?"

"We wouldn't be months away from the wedding if anyone had asked me what I thought about it!" I shouted, the rawness in my voice surprising even me. Caleb stopped walking and stared at me.

"What did you think we were doing together all this time then?" He threw his hands out to his side. "Like we've just been dating for years for fun? Didn't you think I'd ask you to marry me? Why wouldn't we jump straight to the wedding if we can?"

His questions deflated me. I drew a deep breath. "It's my fault for not being honest with you earlier. I'm sorry."

He laughed without humor, shaking his head. "There's someone else, isn't there?"

"Excuse me?" Fear prickled through me.

"Who is it? Are you seeing someone else?"

"Do you really think I'd cheat on you?" I asked slowly.

"I don't know anything anymore, Mercedes," he scoffed. "Who is it?"

"I'm not saying this because of someone else." My entire body was warm, and I forced myself to speak louder, to erase the waver from my voice. "I'm saying this because we aren't right together, and I'm done being silent."

Caleb kicked at my wastebasket as he resumed pacing. "So what are we supposed to do now?"

"I don't know," I admitted. "Go our separate ways? I just...I don't want to do this anymore. I'm sorry, Caleb. I'm so, so sorry."

"Yeah right, you are," he muttered, swinging his head to look over at me. Hurt had creased itself across his face, his hazel eyes shining with a hardness I didn't recognize.

"I wanted to be the woman of your dreams," I told him softly. "But I can't be myself and be the perfect woman for you at the same time. Because the truth is, we want different things. We just do. I don't know how else to put it."

"So you've just been lying to me for years then."

He wasn't entirely wrong. "I was lying to myself for years, too."

Caleb sniffed, turning to me with his hands on his hips. "I think you're just going through a phase. You're going to change your mind. And the stupidest part about all this is that I'll take you back once you remember what we have and where we're going together in life."

"I'm not going to change my mind," I said.

"We'll see about that." He pinned me with a hard look and then tore open the door, storming away. He left the door hanging open, cold air billowing inside. I leapt to my feet to shut it behind him, pressing my back to the door. My heart pounded like I'd just sprinted a lap around the property.

You did it.

But I wasn't quite done. I still had to inform my parents. And that would be harder than telling Caleb.

I took a few moments drawing deep, cleansing breaths. Letting the reality sink in. Coming to terms with the new truth. *You broke up with Caleb.*

I didn't feel sad about it. Not in the way you'd expect after losing a fiancé—in that gut-ripping sense of loss way. I felt sad for letting Caleb down; for knowing that I wasn't giving my family what they wanted. And that, perhaps most of all, was the indicator that it had been wrong for me. Caleb had looked good on paper...but he'd never been right for *me*.

I lingered in the bedroom, gathering my strength. Dinnertime came and went, and nobody came for me, which told me that Caleb had probably spread the news. I was too anxious to eat anyway. So I hid.

Waiting for the biggest blow of all.

Facing down my parents.

By 7:30, I knew I couldn't put it off any longer. I prayed they'd all have finished eating by now. I slid on my coat before pulling open the door, my heart in my throat. Caleb's car wasn't in the driveway, but Jericho's was. I shivered against the sudden whoosh of cold air and jogged to the house. In the hallway, the low murmur of voices drifted toward me from the dining room. I hooked my coat on the rack near the door and hurried to the dining room, my belly twisting into eternal knots.

When I rounded the corner, I found my mother, father, and Jericho at the big table. The plates were cleared and judging from the tension in the air, they'd been discussing something serious. My mother glanced at me and then immediately looked away. *Shit.* They definitely knew.

Anxiety swarmed me. I had no idea how to launch this—so I tried to act normal. Like this was just any old day.

"Hey, guys," I said. "Did everyone eat already? Where's Maddie and Grace?"

"Grace is sick, and Maddie took her home." Jericho didn't look at me as he spoke. My father cleared his throat and crossed his arms.

Nobody said anything for an eternal moment.

They were waiting for me.

I drew a shaky breath. "Well, I just wanted to come share some news with you."

My mother drummed her nails against the table, her gaze fixed on her hand.

I'd never felt more disconnected from my entire family.

"I, uh....I've ended things with Caleb," I said, my voice swallowed up by the black hole of their displeasure. "I thought you should know."

"Caleb told us," my mother said, her voice raw. Then she dragged her gaze up to me. Staring daggers from behind black lashes and perfect winged eyeliner. "Let's mark the calendars. Because I can honestly say I've never been more disappointed in you than today."

I swallowed a knot in my throat, reminding myself to stand tall. There had never been anything more symbolic than this. Me at the head of the table against *them*. Struggling for recognition, for acceptance, for support, and instead being met with iciness and disappointment.

Other parents might have asked why—if something had been going on beneath the surface that nobody was aware of. Or if I was all right.

Not my family.

"Things hadn't felt right for a long time," I said slowly, though I could tell they were already losing interest.

"I just don't understand what's gotten into you," my mother blurted, clipping my last word.

"You understand that we paid for the venue *in full* already?" my father asked, his voice coming out a gruff roar. I swallowed and nodded, but he wasn't done. "Along with the designer gown. The catering and the florist. All the announcements sent to the papers, the band paid for. This was going to be a seven-figure wedding, Mercedes."

All things I'd never agreed to or helped select. I never asked for that.

"I'm sorry," I said, but my voice disappeared in the wake of their disgust with me.

"She is so incredibly selfish I can't even stand it," Jericho muttered. His words cut more than I wanted to admit.

"I don't want to spend the rest of my life miserable," I bit out. "If that makes me selfish, so be it. I need something else."

"And what is *something else*?" My brother used air quotes, the sarcasm thick in his voice. "You want to run off and take a woman lover? Go travel Europe and *find yourself*? What else could you possibly need that you haven't been fucking offered on a silver platter?" He scoffed, turning to our father. "This is what you get, you know. When you constantly tell them what a good job they do, how pretty they are, all of that."

His words landed like a hammer. That was the heart of it all. I didn't deserve to be dissatisfied because I'd been given everything. But only what I never wanted.

"Room to breathe?" My voice came out louder than I intended. "I don't know what it is yet, but I'm going to find it."

"Maybe she already found it," Jericho said with a sneer. There was something behind his tone that lit a spark of fear inside me, though I couldn't say why.

My mother laughed low, but it was an empty sort of laugh. "I don't even want to look at you right now. After what we've been going through, I can't believe you decided to bring this news to our house *now*. As if we needed more to deal with after Gramma Kay."

Guilt piled up around me. Deadening my limbs, making it hard to breathe. The tears were joining now too. I swallowed hard and looked at the ground.

"I'm sorry." It was all I could offer. But it didn't make a difference.

I tore myself out of the dining room, racing back to my bedroom, the weight of their glares the only thing I could feel.

CHAPTER TWENTY-THREE
TRACE

I BARELY SLEPT THAT night, wondering what had happened over at the Hendricks' household. Mercedes's text at nine p.m.—*I did it. It's done.*—had been equal parts reassuring and nerve-wracking. My ensuing texts—*Do you need me? I'll come now. I'll sneak in if you need me or send a car if you want to come here.*—were met with a promise to share everything the following day when she showed up to care for Willow.

It wasn't like I didn't trust her to break things off. I was afraid she wouldn't tell me when she really needed me.

And if it hadn't been for Willow asleep in her crib, I would have raced to her parents' house and snuck into her bedroom anyway.

Not only did I not sleep much that night, I also awoke extra early the following morning. I tried to while away the extra time by reading, but I could hardly focus on the words. So instead I made espresso and started my research into Puerto Rican resort destinations until Willow woke up. Then I gently got Willow ready for the day—cuddles followed by getting her dressed, preparing milk, cutting fruit for her breakfast.

I had a whole trip arranged by eight thirty. If Mercedes wanted to go to Puerto Rico, I was taking her there immediately. There was no question about it.

Mercedes was mine now, and I had a lot of lost time to make up for.

When the knock sounded on the front door, I sent a wide-eyed look to Willow. "Do you know who that is?" I asked her. "It's Mercedes. *Mercedes.* The woman who's practically become your mama."

I scooped Willow into my arms, my heart pounding as I headed for the door. I felt like a teenager going on a first date. After how restrained we'd been during our time in New York, this was practically our first day together—at least with her as a single woman who could behave as she wanted.

I pulled open the door, my breath disappearing as I beheld her. Her green eyes found mine immediately, a shy smile morphing into a cheek-busting grin.

Everything inside me rioted. *Finally.* It seemed years had passed since I'd last seen her. Not just because I'd felt every excruciating minute without her at my side, but because she looked different now, less than a day later. The glow of a woman who'd dumped her fiancé and dashed all her family's expectations. She moved toward me, but I bridged the distance in one strong step. I hooked her at the waist with my free hand, bringing her against me, where she belonged, as the door fell shut behind her.

I dipped down and covered her lips with my own. This time, instead of shrinking back and wanting time, Mercedes opened up.

She tilted her head back and kissed me. Like it was the first, or maybe last, time. Her tongue pressed past my lips as my free hand migrated up the side of her body, her neck, until my fingers tangled in the soft strands of her blonde hair. I knotted my fingers there, which tilted her head back even further. Our lips disconnected and she gasped, a grin playing at the edges of her lips.

"Welcome," I said, our lips brushing.

She laughed and straightened, her gaze moving to Willow. She cleared her throat. "Hi, sweet girl."

Willow looked a little enthralled. She clapped her hands then and reached for Mercedes, signaling the close of our intimacy window. "Mama," Willow said.

Mercedes's eyes went round as she held out her hands and Willow slipped into her arms. I felt every bit as stunned as Mercedes looked when she gasped, "What did you say?"

"Ma," Willow repeated, clapping again.

Mercedes's stunned gaze moved to me. "Did you hear that?"

My heart swelled, nearly to bursting again. I nodded. "I had just told her that you'd practically become her mama."

"Mama," Willow said again.

Mercedes clamped a hand over mouth, tears welling in her eyes. "Oh, she's gonna make me cry. Sweet girl, you're definitely going to make me cry." She snuggled Willow to her chest as we drifted deeper into the apartment.

"Tell me everything," I told her, guiding her to the kitchen island with a hand on her hip. Now that I could, I'd be touching her every moment of the day.

"Oh, it was just one of the worst nights in recent memory," she said with a little laugh. "It started with finding out that Gramma Kay had a mini-stroke of some sort while we were in New York. Nobody told me. According to them, they didn't want me to worry. But it was their way of punishing me for not being there. I broke up with Caleb, and he insisted I was having an affair. My family thinks I'm selfish. My mother said she's never been more disappointed in me. All in all, a pretty defeating evening."

I wrapped my arm around her waist again and pressed my lips to the top of her head. "It sounds rough. Is your grandma going to be okay?"

"I don't know. They wouldn't let me see her." Mercedes's chin wobbled, which I took as my sign to kiss her. So I did. Without hesitation. Her eyes fluttered shut as I brushed my lips against hers.

"I bet she'll recover in no time," I reassured her. "And your family will calm down eventually. They have to.'"

"I appreciate your positivity," she said softly, "but I just don't know."

I let my hand drift from her waist down over her hip, over the swell of her ass cheek. She tilted her head, smiling up at me. "Are you trying to distract me?"

"Maybe."

"Well, it's working." She hoisted Willow higher on her hip. "But we have to pump the brakes for another reason today. I don't want to be responsible for traumatizing the youth."

I smirked. "We'll have none of that. Especially since I have an appointment in roughly two hours that I absolutely should not miss, since it may be my new office if all goes well."

Her eyes lit up. "You found an office space?"

"I did. It looks excellent in the pictures, and I snagged a quick viewing before our trip."

This time, her eyebrows shot up. "*Our trip?*"

I smirked. "Come on, Mercedes. You had to have known that I wouldn't waste a single second in giving you everything you ever wanted."

The look she gave me so pure, raw, and happy, that I couldn't help but claim her lips again.

"You're going to have to repack," I whispered against her lips. "Because we're catching another plane this evening."

I brought Mercedes and Willow downtown with me, since Mercedes wanted to take Willow to the library's play area before lunch. I dropped them off with another kiss and a promise to pick them up in an hour and a half. As I drove away, gripping the leather steering wheel with a satisfied smile, I contended with that too-full feeling again. The pressure was almost uncomfortable. Like the happiness could burst inside me at any moment and turn fetid.

But I'd have to get used to it. Things in my life were far from resolved, but I wanted to hang on to this feeling. Things were at least coming together. Mercedes had made big moves, and Willow had made a big improvement too. Two major wins for the women in my life.

I pulled up to the building with space for rent, not far from where Aurora's Nannies sat. I was able to park my Benz just a few spots down from the main doors, which was a plus. I pulled my winter coat tighter around me as I strode toward the front door.

Inside, the gray vinyl plank flooring paired well with crisp, white walls and the vestiges of matte black decorations. The realtor turned when the door opened, a bright smile fading quickly. He was a tall, lanky man, with thin brown hair and very expensive shoes. I strode up to him as he seemed to shrink away.

"Hi there," I told him, heading with my hand outstretched. "Trace Fairchild for the ten o'clock."

"Hello. Yes. That's right." He shook my hand but seemed reluctant. His smile looked strained. "I'm Rowan."

"Oh. Rowan?" I pulled out my phone, beginning to swipe to my emails. "I'd been speaking with David..."

"He had a last-minute issue come up with a showing," Rowan said, his smile tightening by the second. He was completely average in every way except for chipmunk-like cheeks and front teeth that seemed abnormally small. "He asked me to come instead. So *you* were the one interested in renting here or is it for...someone else?"

Something in Rowan's tone grated at me. I flexed my jaw and shoved my hands into my coat pockets. "It's for me."

Rowan sniffed, his gaze skating across the room. "For what company?"

"Does it matter?"

"The owner is interested in the use of the building. So yes."

"Wealth management firm," I told him.

Rowan scratched his nose, grimacing. I caught another glimpse of his excessive gumline. "Listen, I don't normally do stuff like this but...between you and me? This place is basically a no-go."

I blinked. Was this guy serious? How was he in the business of selling or renting buildings with an attitude like this? "Excuse me? Are there structural issues I'm unaware of, or—"

"The owner has pretty much made up his mind about the next lessee. They haven't formalized the arrangement, but it's a matter of time. So it would be a shame to show you the building when there's just...no chance."

I squinted at him. Something was off. Rowan stuffed his hands into his pants pockets and held my gaze like a challenge.

"And you're not soliciting competitive offers for this space...why?"

"Listen, I'm doing Dave a favor. That's all. I don't want to waste our time."

I looked out toward the sidewalk through the windows. Rowan didn't want to show me the building, despite being told to specifically come downtown and look at this available listing. Something wasn't making sense, and I needed to find out why. "So what is the nearest listing that you *could* show me?"

Rowan assessed the street visible outside the window, tipping his head side to side as he thought. "I know of a nice lead on an office space in Lexington."

"Lexington?" I laughed. "That's two hours away."

"It's very similar to this space; would be a great fit for whatever operation you're trying to run out of it."

I looked over at him. *Whatever operation.* Like my business was a scam or something. "Are you unfamiliar with wealth management firms?"

He shrugged, fixing his gaze on me once more. "Not with actual businesses that manage people's wealth, no. However, what you do is...something different."

The pieces finally clicked together. This was why I needed Axel at my side—and Damian for good measure. Axel the bloodhound would have sniffed this out as soon as he set foot in the building. Me, on the other hand? I played the mediator too well.

But I was tired of the weight of this infamy.

And if they hated me already, it didn't matter if I played the nice guy.

You couldn't mediate a bad reputation.

"Your ignorance is embarrassing," I sniffed. "And I'll speak with David directly about the piss-poor excuse of a replacement he sent my way today. So do you have anything of value to add here or can you send me to a realtor who actually knows how to do his job?"

Rowan's gaze darkened. "It doesn't matter who you get. Everyone knows who you are and how you operate. People don't want a business like yours anywhere near theirs."

I cleared my throat, once again hearing Axel in my head. *Punch him, Trace. Just do it. His teeth are ugly anyway; you'll just be doing him a favor.*

"You don't scare me," I told him. "I know more people than you think. And I'll be moving into my new office space before long. Guess you and your embarrassing network will just have to cower in fear from sharing the block with me."

Rowan's lips twitched. I heard Axel again: *Ooh, we missed the gumline.*

I almost laughed. Imaginary Axel was making it hard to concentrate.

But I was done here. I spun on my heel and strode toward the front door. As my hand hit the handle, Rowan called out, "We don't want the Fairchilds here."

I looked over my shoulder. "Too bad. The Fairchilds are already here."

The door clanged shut behind me. I mulled over my words as I stormed back to my car. What I'd said wasn't technically wrong—I was a Fairchild, and I was here. But what echoed painfully inside me was that it wouldn't be all of the Fairchilds. Reflecting on this only added to the maelstrom of emotion as I got into my car and drove away.

Louisville, despite how close it was to my parents and the fact that it had brought me back to Mercedes, didn't feel quite like it fit.

And the longer I tried to ignore this, the more forcefully the truth presented itself.

I needed my brothers.

No matter how much I wanted to strike out on my own and launch this on my own terms…I fucking needed my brothers. Now more than ever.

CHAPTER TWENTY-FOUR
MERCEDES

I'D JUST BEEN IN New York City.

Woken up in Louisville the next day.

And I'd fall asleep in Puerto Rico.

This is the life of dating a billionaire. The thought ran through my head like a marquee as I took in our surroundings. Trace smiled down at me, his thick forearm wrapped around my waist as he pushed Willow's stroller over the slatted, raised wooden walkway. We followed a resort employee, leading us to our lodgings. Behind us, a bellman brought our luggage.

And before us? The sprawling, unchecked Atlantic ocean. The most pleasant humidity wended its way through me, filling my lungs and my heart. Lush greenery leaned in toward the pathway. I wasn't sure if we were walking above a swamp or a bog or remnants of the rain forest itself. Whatever it was, it was a million times better than the festering swamp I'd left behind in Louisville. I was pretty sure my parents were ready to disown me.

"I booked us a private residence," he murmured into my ear. The sun had started to set, the bloated tropical sun sinking toward the horizon. I still couldn't believe I'd been in Louisville mere hours before. This was what surprised me the most about Trace's life: the speed at which things occurred when not burdened by layovers or waiting on literally anybody else. He made things happen in an instant.

Which explained his supreme impatience—and frustration—waiting for me to break things off with Caleb.

"This place is already the most magical destination of my life," I breathed. Palm trees shot up at intervals around us as we followed the pathway to an angular, modern house. It was built of pure glass and oceanfront, it seemed. An infinity pool tickled at the edge of my view. Giddiness coursed through me, swift and thrilling. Trace had wanted to keep the details a surprise. I didn't even know we were in Puerto Rico until I'd seen the shape of the island through the window of the private jet.

"I thought you'd like it." Trace kissed the top of my head as we came to the front patio of the residence. The resort employee showed us inside, handing over the keys while the bellman offered to put our luggage in specific rooms.

"Whichever room has the best view, that one will be ours," Trace told him. He seemed a little undecided at first but eventually wandered off into the depths of the house, carting our luggage behind him.

"How many bedrooms does this place have?" I asked, eternally twisting my neck to see more.

"Five," the resort guide told us, "though one could use the movie theater room as a bedroom as well. So, up to six."

I laughed just as Willow began demanding angrily to be let out of her stroller, shaking the front restraint bar. "Ma!"

"Coming, sweet girl." I unbuckled her restraints and pulled her into my arms. She immediately smiled over at Trace as though saying *Look where I made it.*

Once our luggage was deposited, Trace handed over hefty tips to both employees and sent them on their way.

And then it was just us.

"This is the most spectacular place I've ever seen." I looked up at him, getting lost in his deep, brown eyes. "And to think we woke up in the cold in Louisville."

He pushed his fingers through my hair, smiling softly at me. "I think waking up here will be much nicer. Though really it doesn't matter, as long as I'm waking up with you."

I bit my bottom lip. It was no secret that the first item on our collective agenda was *fuck until sunrise*. But we weren't heathens. We needed to do things like take care of Willow and have dinner. I knew our moment would come—I'd been secretly imagining this for the past six years.

"You'll be waking up with me as long as I can help it," I promised him, nuzzling my face into his warm palm. He dug his fingertips into the back of my neck, sending a jolt of heat through me. I loved it when he touched me like that. With possession. Like he was claiming me.

"Mama!" Willow broke through our heated moment, pointing urgently through the floor-to-ceilings windows looking out toward the ocean. "Mama!"

"What is it, sweet girl?" Trace took her from my arms, and we followed her urgent pointing. It led us to the beachfront. Willow wanted *sand*.

Trace laughed and plopped down onto the sand with Willow between his legs. I joined them, pushing the fine, white sand back and forth between our fingers, making mounds, sprinkling it over toes. The sun sank to the horizon in a blazing display as we laughed and played together.

Strange how full life could feel mere hours after yanking something so large from one's life.

"Are you girls getting hungry?" Trace asked us, just as the sun touched the edge of the ocean.

"Definitely. Should we check out some of the resorts' restaurants? Or—" I paused, mischievous glee lighting me up "—should we order room service?"

"Room service," Trace decided. "Whatever makes you look *that* excited, we need to do."

I giggled into my palm. "Is there any other option but room service when we're in a private residence like this?"

"No," Trace said, the look on his face so tender it nearly split me in two. He reached for my hand, bringing my knuckles to his lips. "Because whatever Birdie wants, Birdie gets."

The entire night unfolded around us, nothing short of magical. There was no other word for it, which frustrated me; given how many books I'd consumed in my life, I should know enough words to convey how special this was.

But I fell short. I was simply at peace. My cheeks hurt from how hard I smiled, how much there was to explore and discover and enjoy with Trace and Willow at my side. I changed into a beautiful sundress that Trace surprised me with—mint green and jade, with tie straps and the softest, most luscious material I'd ever felt. The look of adoration on his face when I came out of the bedroom in it was one I'd never forget.

We ate scallops by the ocean while torches burned gently along the elevated boardwalk, casting an ethereal glow to the night. Our infinity pool glowed the most surreal shade of lavender, which only complemented the mood lighting in our house after dusk, shades of cerulean and baby blue and royal purple.

We put Willow down late—because *Puerto Rico,* of course—and the moment she was asleep, Trace descended upon me like a lion on fresh meat.

He had me pressed up against the wall just outside Willow's room, our lips engaged in a hungry, unending dance. His teeth knocked mine; our tongues met sloppily in the middle. His fingertips skated up my jaw while I wrapped my arms around his waist and yanked him closer.

I needed every inch of this man. Immediately.

Trace cupped my face in his big, warm palms. Our kiss deepened somehow, igniting a fire deep inside me. I realized that no matter how much he kissed me, I'd need more. I'd always need more from him. And that scared me.

He was the only man who had ever inspired such a sensation.

Trace broke the kiss, our chests heaving as we stared at each other from millimeters away. "Come with me, Birdie. We need to go somewhere else. You're going to be far too loud."

"Wh…" My brain function had been reduced to a murky slog. "What do you mean?"

"When I have my way with you." The evil smile licking at his lips clarified everything. "Let's go."

He led me through the two-story living room, out toward the patio that faced the infinity pool and the beach beyond. He paused to assess the enormous patio, and then veered toward a lounge area at the far edge. A king-sized daybed was flanked by palms, and throw pillows littered its soft, sumptuous surface. Trace sat at the edge and pulled me between his legs. He tipped his head back and watched me as he trailed his hands up my legs beneath my dress.

"Before we get started," he said, his voice a husky rasp, "these need to go."

He hooked his fingers around the waistband of my panties and tugged them down to my ankles. I rested my hands on his shoulders as I stepped out of them, never breaking his gaze. He tossed them aside then pulled me down on top of him, my legs spreading to straddle him, knees sinking into the foam.

A low hum erupted from him as his big hands pushed up the backs of my thighs, over my ass, and along the ridge of my spine. "This is where I want to be, Birdie."

I nestled into place on top of him, the hard ridge of his cock finding my most sensitive area even through his linen shorts. "Me too."

"Can you see the ocean?"

His question reminded me there was a world beyond him, beyond these exquisite sensations. I looked over his shoulder, into the abyss of the tropical night. I could see the path lights leading to the water. And beyond that, the dark, roiling churn of the ocean. Featureless and enormous. So present it nearly drowned me just from contemplating it from a safe distance.

"I can," I whispered.

"Good." His lips skated up the side of my neck, until his teeth landed on my earlobe. "I want you to have a view once I bury my cock inside you."

I grinned, my nipples going taut beneath my bra as he worked to undo the hooks. "Like you aren't enough of a view?"

"This is our first time in six years, Birdie. It needs to be special."

I looked down at him, cinching my arms around his neck. "How could it be anything but life-altering?"

"I'm not taking any chances." He gripped my hips, grinding me in a slow, torturous circle on top of the hard length in his pants. That thick steel against my clit made my breath hitch. He tugged at the ties of the sundress straps, loosening them until they crumpled at my sides. He unhooked my bra and tossed that aside as well. His lips found each nipple in turn, and he grazed his teeth against them.

I tossed my head back, now rocking against him as hard as he ground against me. I felt so greedy—so hungry—as I rubbed my pussy shamelessly against him. He watched me, rapt, as I took what I wanted, my tits swallowed by his big hands as he occasionally dipped down and covered a nipple with his tongue.

"You're making a mess on my pants, Birdie." He said it with a wry grin.

"I'm sorry..." I breathed.

"Don't be." He gripped my ass cheeks in his hands, fingertips curling into flesh dangerously close to my swollen folds. "This is what I've been waiting for."

He ground up into me at the same time his teeth scraped against my nipple once more. Of course it didn't take long. I came like a firework. Bright, fast, dazzling for only a moment. Once the pleasure had shuddered through me, he smirked.

"First one down," he murmured, "a lifetime's worth to go."

I draped my arms around his neck as I laughed into his collarbone. "That was so quick. I'm so sorry."

"You haven't been with someone who can take care of you for six whole years." He shifted beneath me. "But that's changed now."

The magnitude of his words hit me with a wall of emotion. I tugged at the hem of his shirt, suddenly desperate to feel him against me. All of him. I felt like I might die without his touch. He was the only person who could soothe me, make me feel complete. "I need you, Trace. I need you right now."

He tore off the shirt—it landed somewhere among the bushes with the rest of my undergarments—and scooped me up into his arms, his heat soaking into me. My bare breasts smashed into his chest. But topless was only halfway there. I fumbled with the button of his shorts, trying and failing to undo them.

"Let me," he said, grabbing my wrists. "You're too excited."

I laughed in defeat. "Can you blame me? You haven't even let me look at it. The only time I've seen it was on accident when I walked in on you jacking off."

His eyes widened. "So you did see me that day."

I bit my bottom lip, nodding. He sucked at his teeth and scooped me up, flipping me onto my back on the daybed.

"I fucking knew it. I had a suspicion you'd spied on me."

I giggled, nestling into the soft surface as he sat back on his heels and worked at his button. His gaze fell to the smear across the fly of his shorts—all my juices. My cheeks heated up.

"I use the memory of you in the shower in my fantasies," I admitted.

The corner of his mouth turned up, and he stood to pull his shorts off. His cock tented his boxer briefs, and he palmed it through his underwear.

"I knew you would. I could tell you were dying for it." He pushed his briefs down then, exposing his thick cock, swollen head and all. "Why didn't you say anything?"

I swallowed hard, my gaze dropping to his cock bobbing gently in the air. His cockhead was swollen, almost purplish. The hair around the base was neat, dark stubble. And just like I remembered, he looked way too big to go anywhere but in a fist.

But it had fit many times before. It had to fit again.

"I was still trying to convince myself I could go with the grain," I whispered, reaching for his dick. This time, he let me grab it. His eyes went hooded as I smoothed my hand over the ridges of his shaft, up to the swollen head. His nostrils flared as his gaze fell to my hand.

"I would have fucked you senseless in the shower if you'd come in," he growled.

"I knew that. It's why I turned around. Even though I wanted you to fuck me senseless."

He sucked at his teeth, tugging the sundress down over my hips until it, too, joined the rest of our clothes draped across the bushes. I was laid bare for him, goosepimples rising under his attention. He climbed onto the bed, his knees indenting the plush surface. His lips dropped to my shoulder, leaving a damp trail along my collarbone.

"You look so fucking good spread out for me like this," he said, his voice gritty. "But I need you on top, Birdie. I need you to ride me."

A shiver raced down my spine. I couldn't help the silly grin that erupted. Trace was pure sex appeal, and to hear him *need* me like that was nothing short of dizzying. He was the only man who'd ever made me feel that way. Ever.

"I have no objections," I said before he swooped down and captured my lips in a kiss. Our tongues met, urgent and seeking. Trace's arms went around my body and scooped me up effortlessly as he turned and sat on the bed, pulling me on top of him again.

This time, when I settled there, all I felt was the velvet steel of his cock, pressed right against my swollen clit. His heat flooded me, made me dizzy and dumb. I could hardly speak or think for how much I wanted him. I closed my arms around his neck, flattening my chest against him.

Trace buried his head in the hollow of my neck, groaning. "You make it so hard to think straight."

"What do you need to think straight about?"

"I brought condoms." He pointed to the bush. "But I threw them over there."

I rolled my hips in a slow circle above him, enjoying the way the hard length teased at all the sensitive areas of my pussy. "Do we need them?"

He opened one eye to peer up at me. "Come again?"

I smirked, dragging my folds along the length of him. His eyes fluttered shut again, and I knew I couldn't hold out much longer either. "That's exactly what you're going to make me do. I don't want to use a condom, Trace. Do we have to?"

His eyes snapped open, something dark and dangerous swimming there. "Of course not, Birdie. Not when you're mine."

Trace's hand fit over my hips like they were made for me. He guided me up, and then a moment later the fat tip of his cock pressed at my dripping entrance. I gasped at the sensation of being stretched. Ever so slowly, he pushed himself inside me, murmuring sweet nothings as he did. He never released his grip on my hips as I eased down, down around him.

"Christ, Mercedes. You are so perfect." He tilted his head, watching the show as I sank farther down, his cock igniting every millimeter of space within me. The deeper I sank, the more the fireworks went off. His head tipped back, the expression on his face drugged and desirous.

I whimpered as he found the last couple inches of space. The feel of him inside me—filling me—had me on the edge already. My entire body quivered from the fullness, the intensity. I dug my fingernails into his biceps as he flexed his hips against me.

"You good, Birdie?"

I nodded, feeling wisps of my hair stuck to my lips. I couldn't gather enough focus to brush them away.

"You're in outer space," he told me.

"You take me there."

His lips quirked up. "I'm your rocket, huh?"

I squeezed my eyes shut, hit by how true it was. How poignant. He'd always been the person to blast me out of my world. Into the scary new frontier. He was my rocket and then some.

"You're everything, Trace," I told him, my entire body caught between a scream and a sob. I felt like the smallest movement could catapult me into an orgasm. He rocked against me slowly, his eyes never leaving me.

"I'm your everything, and you're mine." He gathered my hair at the nape of my neck and tugged gently, forcing my chin to the sky. "Let the rocket take you to outer space again, Birdie."

My gaze got lost in the inky black sky above me and the immense expanse of stars that I hadn't even noticed until Trace guided my attention there. I'd been too focused on him, on us. A whoosh of air left me, all the bodily sensations amplifying as my head got lost in the cosmic swirl above.

Trace filled me—and fucked me. Our bodies bumped and rocked together, the pleasure building so quickly I had no way to beat it back. This type of orgasm was something different—it wasn't a firework, it was a forest fire. Long, sustained, destructive at the same time it was regenerative. He was scorching me from the inside out.

My mouth gaped as the first tendrils of pleasure began to unfurl. A low moan escaped next, every inch of my body going alert and taut. And then I was gasping. Crying out. Moaning and clawing, equal parts desperate for the orgasm and terrified of how big it felt racing up on me. Trace tightened his grip around me, our bodies soldering together. My head dropped to his shoulder as he drilled up into me, driving the pleasure even deeper.

His breath came out in soft grunts at my ear. Heat wound its way through me from head to toe, until that heat turned into flame, and the orgasm zipped through my veins, white hot and loud.

I cried out. Head to the heavens. I saw stars, in every way imaginable. Trace ground into me, over and over again, pushing my orgasm to its limit. I was a rag doll in his arms, helpless and loving it as he wrung every last drop of pleasure from me.

I knew when he orgasmed too, from the gruff moan and the way his arms circled around me like roots. Grounding me. Keeping me. His hot release coated my insides, spilled out from between my legs.

I laid my head on his shoulder, chest heaving as I struggled to come back to Earth. His breath came out in quick puffs at my ear. And then the kisses started. Light, feathery, reassuring kisses, along my cheek, to my chin, across my lips, and around the other side.

"Oh, Trace." A sob escaped me, the overflowing emotion that knew no other way out. His kisses moved to my forehead.

"Did you see stars, Birdie?"

I laughed into his chest, too wrung out to even lift my head. "I did. Did you?"

"Every time I look at your perfect face." He ran a thumb across my cheek, wiping away tears I didn't realize had fallen.

We stayed like this, his softened dick still inside me as I relished the aftermath of the orgasm in his arms. Once our breathing had evened, he whispered, "Stay here," and lifted me off him, winking at me. He padded barefoot back into the house, his muscular ass cheeks flexing with every step. I collapsed back on the bed, staring up at the inky black sky, getting lost in infinity.

This was bliss.

I never wanted to forget what this felt like. To be showered with all the things I'd been made to believe I didn't deserve. Life couldn't possibly be more perfect than this.

But as Trace came back out, I realized it could get better. He was an expert at making things better. His soft, sexy smile seared itself into my memory as he sauntered back carrying a bottle of wine, two glasses, and a book tucked beneath his arm. A rag was draped over his shoulder. He set the bottle and glasses down on the end table, set the book next to me, and then said, "Lie back."

I did as I was told. He washed me gently, cleaning up the mess he'd left between my legs. I almost cried from the care he took. When that was done, he tossed the rag to the ground and lay next to me, arranging pillows beneath his head.

"I brought us wine if you want some. Your book if you want to read. And me if you need a pillow."

Tears came to my eyes. I propped myself up on an elbow and leaned in for a kiss. He grabbed my chin between thumb and fore-finger, giving me a kiss so deep it almost had me ready for another round.

"You're the best," I whispered, reaching for the book. He leaned back on the bed with a satisfied smile on his face. I cuddled up at his side, resting my head on his chest as I opened my book to where I'd left off.

I wasn't sure I had the concentration to read right now. But it didn't matter.

Even if I just read a few words, it was proof that such perfection could exist.

Proof that this man had always been the only one who knew the interior of my heart.

CHAPTER TWENTY-FIVE
TRACE

Four days in Puerto Rico bled into two more days lounging in Louisville. We lived in a blissed-out bubble, and we were hesitant to burst it. Plenty ofthings waited for us in the real world beyond this cocoon. I was amassing a collection of missed calls from Axel and warning texts from Damian about how disgruntled Axel was becoming, but that the tides could turn soon. Mercedes was confronting the opposite but equally unsettling: despite frequent check-in texts about her grandma, she received a total lack of communication from her family.

And I'd received a weird email from an unknown sender our first day back from Puerto Rico that simply said "GET OUT." I'd deleted it before it could penetrate my happiness.

And after almost a full week in honeymoon mode, actively rejecting the real world and being lost in domestic—and orgasmic—bliss, it only seemed right that Mercedes move in with me.

On Sunday morning, our last day before returning to the world, I mixed up batter for chocolate chip pancakes and Mercedes whipped cream.

"Is it too early for you to move in?" I asked.

She stopped whipping and looked up at me, her eyes green saucers. "What?"

"It would be better that way, right?" I shrugged, trying to act nonchalant even though my heart was pounding. At my side, Willow tugged on my shirt, pointing insistently at the countertop where I'd been doling out individual chocolate chips to her on the sly. Mercedes didn't like her to eat pure chocolate, but I had a hard time saying no to Willow. "You wouldn't have to worry about how angry your parents are."

She smirked at me. "One week is a little fast, don't you think?"

"It hasn't been one week. It's been six years and then some."

Mercedes smiled at me warmly. "True. But..." She sighed, shoulders slumping. "I don't want them to stay angry at me. I'm going to fix it. I just need to be around a bit more consistently. That's why I'm planning on going to Sunday dinner tonight."

I winced. "Are you sure that's a good idea?"

"I have to, Trace. I should spend a night or two there."

"Okay. Just promise you'll call me so we can fall asleep together on speakerphone."

She snorted. "Are we *that* couple already?"

"Not quite yet, but with a little effort, we will be," I teased. Willow started making noise again, wanting more chocolate chips. I looked down at her—I'd already slipped her seven or so—and sent her a look, trying to subtly inform her to not draw attention to us. But there was no hope. After a few angry grunts and one stomped foot, Mercedes was onto us.

"What does she want?" Mercedes asked.

"Oh...nothing." I held Mercedes's gaze as I reached for the chocolate chips in the bowl. Mercedes gasped.

"Are you giving her straight chocolate chips?" she asked, sounding equal parts horrified and amused.

"Maybe." I slipped Willow two more.

"*Trace.*"

"She likes them. And we're making chocolate chip pancakes. How can I not?"

"That's why you're making her the plain ones, because of the sugar content," Mercedes insisted. But it was followed up with a laugh. "I have to admit, even though you shouldn't, it's too cute when you do."

Willow grinned up at me as she chewed her contraband, melting my heart further. I ruffled her hair. "How can I say no to this chocolate-smeared face?"

Mercedes let out a terse sigh, but I could tell she wasn't as annoyed as she tried to sound. "It's hard to, that's for sure."

Mercedes finished preparing the cream, then cut up strawberries, making a big display of slipping "an acceptable secret snack" to Willow. I loved her ribbing; it filled my heart and made me grin so hard my cheeks hurt.

We had a lot of lost time to make up for. And I already knew I wouldn't be able to get enough time with Mercedes—hence the offer to move in. I knew there were a lot of details to arrange—like how this would affect Mercedes's employment at Aurora's—but we'd figure them out. Together. I had no doubt.

Things were clicking into their rightful place.

Once the batter was ready and I'd cooked one set of pancakes, Mercedes shooed me away from the stove, insisting on cooking the rest herself. Apparently she disagreed with the amount of butter I used—"a ridiculously excessive amount"—so I followed Willow into the living room. I lounged on the couch, both my favorite girls in sight, and pulled out my phone. I'd gotten a new email notification during my batter session.

It had no subject line and came from an unknown sender with an email address that contained so many consonants and numbers it looked like it came from the dark web. My stomach pitched to my feet as I opened it up.

You're not getting the fucking hint. GET THE FUCK OUT OF OUR CITY OR WE'LL MAKE SURE YOU LEAVE OUR-SELVES. NOBODY WANTS THE FAIRCHILDS HERE.

I stared at the message for too long, my mind racing a mile a minute as I pored over the implications, potential consequences, and ideas for how to respond. The messages were ramping up. This was the second email, and these had come on the heels of various creepy, anonymous calls. Judging by my reception in this city in general, any number of people could be behind this. Even though part of me wanted to blame Jericho and Mercedes's family as the most likely culprit, logically speaking, I knew that they still weren't aware she and I were together. When a run-of-the-mill realtor didn't want to lease me a building, it seemed like my reputation had turned into a noxious gas cloud.

And really, the *who* didn't matter as much as the *now what?*

I need to figure out the next steps. Today.

Because something about this email told me they weren't going to stop at just calls and digital correspondence.

I cleared my throat and pocketed my phone, making my way back into the kitchen.

"What would you say if I hired a bodyguard for us?" I asked Mercedes, coming up behind her and placing a kiss on the top of her head.

"A bodyguard?" She laughed a little, moving the last batch of pancakes from the griddle to the serving plate. "What for?"

"For protection."

"From what?" she asked, sounding a little shocked.

"From...anything. Who knows? I've been getting some pushback from certain people in the community since I arrived. A few strange calls and emails. I just want to be prepared."

She snapped off the stove and turned to me, brows knit together in confusion. "Strange calls and emails?"

"Yeah. They're probably nothing, but I don't want to take a chance. I've got the resources. So I want to do it."

She nodded. "Well it sounds like you've made up your mind."

"I think I have too." I took the serving plate and carried it to the dining room table. Willow ran screeching up to me, arms outstretched. That was how I felt about pancakes, too. Especially the chocolate chip kind.

"It's not a bad idea. If you think you need it. I guess it will just..." Mercedes set the spatula in the sink and dried her hands off before shrugging. "Take some getting used to?"

"I'll make sure I hire someone great," I promised her, lifting Willow into the highchair. She started pounding at the plastic tray, impatient as hell. There was no greater revelation from fostering my niece than the impatience of a toddler when it came to food. "Hang on, Willow. It's coming. I promise."

Mercedes brought over the syrup, butter, strawberries and cream. I grabbed plates and silverware. Soon, we were all seated at the table, each one of us flanking Willow, tucking into steaming pancakes with the perfect syrupy drizzle on top. Although Mercedes made sure to only put a few drops on Willow's.

"Sugar just makes them so crazy," she murmured as Willow pointed insistently at the jar of syrup.

I shoveled a bite into my mouth, chewed, and then said, "Maybe I'll eat a few extra chocolate chips for brunch. Then you'll get the benefit of the sugar rush once Willow's down for a nap."

Mercedes's lips curled into a sexy smile. "I don't mind *those* sugar rushes."

The pancakes didn't last long. Once the plates were cleared and the kitchen cleaned up, we switched back into lounge mode. Willow started yawning around one, and Mercedes was quick to scoop her up and carry her off to naptime.

Left on my own in the living room, my analytical brain kicked into gear again. I re-read the email, compared it to previous emails, then sent them both to Damian with a note that simply said: *Any info you can glean on these?*

If anyone could do some digging, it was him. And then I began looking for a bodyguard. Someone who could kick some ass and protect Willow, Mercedes, and me if need be. Someone Mercedes would be comfortable around, someone with experience. Price was no issue. Quality was my priority.

I was knee-deep in the bodyguard hunt when Mercedes startled me. She appeared in front of me, pushing my knees apart as she knelt on the floor. Whatever surprise I felt was immediately replaced with *fuck yes.* The look in her eye told me everything I needed to know.

"Put that phone away," she whispered, dragging her fingernails up my legs. "And take these sweatpants off."

"Yes, Miss Hendricks," I teased, popping to my feet and tearing off my sweatpants. I took off my underwear and T-shirt for good measure too. Because why not? She looked hungry for the opposite of something soft and doughy now.

She pushed at my hips so that I fell back on the couch again. My cock was already at half-mast just from her merely breathing in my vicinity. She pushed my knees apart and filled the space between my legs, looking at my cock like it was the next round of brunch.

"You look like you didn't eat enough pancakes, Birdie." I pushed my fingers through her hair, gathering her silky blonde tresses to one side. Her small, cool hand wrapped around my dick, causing my abs to tense. She looked up at me with doe eyes as she dragged her tongue along the seam of my cock.

"I'm definitely still hungry," she purred. The whole sex kitten vibe she had going on made my balls tighten and my dick stand taller. "I need my dessert."

She covered my swollen cockhead with her mouth, never breaking eye contact. I grunted as the first wash of pleasure ran through me, grabbing a fistful of her hair.

"Fuck." I rocked my hips beneath her as she dipped her head down and took almost my entire length into her mouth. Then she pulled back, her lips releasing my cock with a pop. She laved the underside of my cockhead with her tongue, back and forth, before going in for another deep pull. I rocked my hips beneath her, looking for more depth in that velvet mouth.

"Yes, Birdie," I told her as she dipped down for another round. "You suck me off so good." I rocked my hips toward her face while she slurped at my cock and used her other hand to jack me off. My balls tightened even more as the orgasm swirled just beneath the surface. I was a sucker for a surprise cock-sucking session—and just the sight of her between my legs was the image I'd get off to for years.

She mumbled her response, since my dick was filling up of her mouth. She pulled her head up and disconnected, drawing a deep breath.

"I want on."

I grinned at her, waving my cock in the air with both hands wrapped around the base. "Oh, on this?"

She was already shimmying out of her leggings and pushing her panties down. I loved that fire in her eyes. It had been there since the day we met. The connection between us hadn't just sparked, it had sizzled and burned. I'd known it in the first hour, even though it sounds ridiculous to say. How could I have known when she was nineteen and I was twenty-five? But I did.

I fucking did.

Mercedes eased on top of me, her smooth, warm thighs gliding against mine as she sank down, her pussy settling against my hard, seeking cock. Her arms went around my neck, her breasts smashed against my chest. She sighed as I encircled my arms around her waist and squeezed.

"This is my favorite spot," she whispered into my ear.

"Mine too." And then I flexed my hips, my cockhead slipping inside her as I coaxed a deep, hungry kiss from her. Mercedes was pure juice and heat, and her legs spread wider as she welcomed me deeper. I slid into her tight, slick core, our tongues dancing as I filled her until there was no space left to claim.

Once I was buried to the hilt, I grunted, squeezing my arms tighter around her. "You're perfect, Birdie."

"You are," she said breathily. "And not only that. You're perfect for *me*."

I rocked my hips in a slow circle beneath her, watching the fascinating play of expressions on her face. Being buried so deep inside her allowed me to feel every flex and movement she made. I brushed my lips along her collarbone, palming the feminine dips of her waist, her lower back, her delectable ass. I grabbed both cheeks in my hands and guided the slow roll on top of me. She whimpered, her eyes fluttering closed.

"Oh, Traaaaace."

"You like it when I grind you against me like that?" I tilted my head to watch the way our bodies bumped and collided. This still felt too good to be true—that she was here, my cock swallowed inside her, our skin glistening and gliding against each other.

"I love it," she moaned, her head tipped back.

"I love *you*." The words had tumbled out without a second thought. Because it was true. It had always been true. Since she was nineteen and it didn't even make sense.

She inhaled sharply, her heavy-lidded eyes finally opening. "I love you too Trace."

"I know." I pressed kisses up along her throat, grinding up into her so hard that her eyes shut again. "I can feel it."

She whimpered, and I lifted her off me, eager to change positions. My cock slid out of her with a slick noise and I jerked my chin toward the floor. She wobbled onto the floor like a newborn colt, and I joined her there, snagging a pillow to place beneath her head. She was limp and pleasure-drunk, grinning like she knew a secret, as I arranged our bodies. Once I slid between her legs and pushed myself back inside her, another low, sexy moan erupted.

"Legs up, Birdie." I knew this angle would be my undoing, but I needed it. We both did. Urgency prickled through my abdomen as I gathered her legs against my chest and then sank into her. Her face contorted with pleasure, with adoration, with relief. I only lasted a few pumps before the prickles turned to fireworks.

She came first—as always. Her pussy clenched, and I released. I dragged my lips along the inside of her leg as I emptied my rounds into her. Her green gaze was swirling, hazy. I let her legs fall back to earth and I lowered myself for a long, sweet kiss.

"That...was...."

The fact that she sounded a thousand miles away made me smile. "That's what you get when you come in here looking gorgeous and wanting to suck my cock."

She giggled and I kissed her again. And again. When I finally slipped myself out of her, I told her to stay there so I could clean her up. I grabbed a warm cloth from the kitchen, cleaned her up while she grinned at me with ruddy cheeks, and then walked back to the sink to clean up. On my way back to the living room, where Mercedes was slowly dressing, a new email notification broke through our pleasant reverie.

I'd forgotten all about the stress, the worries, even the bodyguard hunt. I swiped my phone on without thinking, pulling up the new email.

Another no-subject email with a complicated email address awaited me.

WE SAID GET OUT. AND THAT MEANS NOW.

CHAPTER TWENTY-SIX
MERCEDES

I ARRIVED AT MY parent's house that night with my belly in knots. I'd sent some texts to my mother over the past few days, trying to test the waters. I knew she'd been mad, but she would ultimately respect my decision...*right?*

Appearing at the weekly Sunday dinner was the only way to ensure I'd run into them all and start to put the fractured pieces back together. I'd dealt them a devastating—and surprising—blow. And I hated that I'd hurt them. Especially while Gramma Kay was recovering.

I carried this guilt and tension with me across town and into the driveway of my parent's house. I entered the house cautiously, my anxiety immediately spiking. Something felt off again, like when I'd gotten back from New York. I hurried down the hallway, pausing to hang my coat on the rack. The scent of roast beef and cooked vegetables hung in the air, lending a strange sense of normalcy to what was sure to be the most abnormal dinner of all time. I followed the sound of voices into the dining room.

As soon as I stepped inside, the conversation stopped.

The gazes of my mother, father, brother, and Maddie all landed on me. Grace, sitting in Maddie's arms, was the only one who didn't react.

"Hi, y'all," I said softly.

Jericho's eyes went wide before he rolled them. My father's gaze dropped to the table, and he cleared his throat, shifting in his seat. My mother watched me for another moment before looking back at my father.

Maddie just looked at the ground and continued patting Grace's back.

"What are you doing here?" my father demanded gruffly.

"Just came for Sunday dinner?" It seemed so stupid now. I should have known they would all turn on me like this. That my personal decision about my future would be taken as a collective insult.

"I can't believe you even dared to show your face here," Jericho muttered. He crossed his arms, seated to the right of our father. "After everything you've done."

"I stand by what I did," I said, straightening my back. "I didn't want to marry Caleb. I'm not going to."

"So what do you intend to do instead?" my mother asked, incredulity dripping from her words. "Just dip in and out of our house, our lives, when it suits you?"

"You owe them so much more than that," Jericho spat.

"I don't *know* what I intend to do." The heat rose fast inside me, flaming my cheeks, nearly exploding out of the top of my head. This was a four-alarm emergency already, and we'd barely started talking. "I'm figuring it out."

"Just *finding herself*," Jericho sneered, looking at my father.

"Finding yourself here for a dinner, then gone for a full week, then back for a dinner..." My mother scoffed, crossing her arms. "No accountability. No warning."

"Completely selfish," my father said as he closed his fist on top of the table. "You've lost your way, girl. How did this happen?"

"I-I-I *haven't* lost my way…" My words evaporated under their intense displeasure. The irony vibrated through every cell of my being. *I didn't lose my way—I found it.* How could they not see it? Or at the very least back down when I said I wanted something different? "I reached out. I tried to contact you. I've been checking in on Gramma Kay—"

"I find it ridiculous that you think you can pull stunts like these under my roof." My father's gaze zeroed in on me, slicing like a knife. "It's insanity. A lifetime of money, clothes, schooling, opportunities, networking…all of this tossed aside, flushed down the toilet, and for what? For a chance to struggle and fail on your own?"

I began to understand why nobody had been responding to me over the past week. They'd been festering. Letting their distaste and anger ferment into something different. A bubbling, dangerous brew.

"It just makes me wonder if you've ever valued family at all," my mother said, her voice low and mournful. She still wouldn't look at me. "After how you've treated yours."

Their over-the-top response to me diverging from their preferred path made my head spin. But this is how they were. They wielded disappointment and judgement like a battleax as a way to grind me into submission. "I'm sorry for bringing this to you while Gramma Kay is sick," I said, already hearing the wobble in my voice. "But I couldn't stand it a minute longer. I can't marry Caleb, but that doesn't mean I'm not still your daughter. I'm not trying to leave the family."

A weird tension pulled taut over the table. Jericho laughed sarcastically, so sharp and pointed that it practically left papercuts.

"You are so fucking *stupid,*" he spat.

I inhaled sharply, looking over at Grace. "How could you speak that way in front of your daughter?"

"Is it any better than what you do in front of your entire family?" Jericho asked, something dangerous edging his words. "You think we're dumb, Sadie. But we're not. We know what you've been up to."

Tension prickled through me, slow and winding. "What are you talking about?"

"You want to live life on your own terms. As a fucking liar and cheat, apparently." Jericho's words were so fierce that Grace started whimpering. The tension of the moment had affected her, even though she was too young to understand.

"Can you please tone it down? You're frightening your daughter," I hissed.

"It's your fucking fault," Jericho said, louder and more aggressive than before. "You're the one who brought this here."

I rolled my lips in, staring at him fiercely in an attempt to stave off tears. "Why would you say that to me?"

"You did Caleb fucking dirty." Jericho jabbed his finger as he spoke, a fire in his eyes that I hadn't seen before. I didn't think I'd ever seen him this angry. "My best friend. Your *fiancé*."

"I didn't do him dirty," I said, my voice wavering. "I did him a favor. Why would he want to marry someone who doesn't want to be married to him?"

"You are so fucking stupid." The phrase hurt worse the second time. I wiped at a tear that had spilt as Jericho pulled his phone out, swiping idly. "I already showed Mom and Dad. We all know what you've been doing. I haven't told Gramma Kay yet because I don't want her to die of a broken heart, which absolutely would be your fault. You could at least have had the decency to *tell us* you've been seeing Trace Fairchild, instead of acting like a goddamn fool about it."

I clenched my teeth as his words wound their way through my body, leaving everything stony in their wake. My entire body felt frozen and heavy. My gaze darted between Jericho and my parents.

I had no idea what to say. Because it was true. And I really was fucking stupid.

"Sad that I have to hire a tail on my own sister," Jericho said, flipping his phone so I could see the screen. It was a grainy shot of the airport. Trace and I stepping off the private jet, him on the ground, me on the third step, leaning forward to plant a kiss on his lips.

It would have been beautiful—something fit to frame—if it weren't so utterly horrible and damning.

My stomach twisted harder. "Nobody asked you to do that."

"Well turns out I have to, if I want to get any goddamn answers." He slid his phone back in his pocket and scowled at me. "Can't trust you to be truthful about anything."

My mother sat with her hand pressed to her forehead. She shook her head. "That's the worst part. Zero trust. After everything we've done for you."

"It's goddamn humiliating is what it is," my father grumbled.

I gnawed at the inside of my lip, fighting the tears with all my might. I was surprised my chin didn't wobble right off my face. "I broke things off with Caleb the first chance I had. I don't know what else to say other than I'm sorry."

"You were supposed to marry Caleb," Jericho said, that sneer still fixed firmly on his face. "That's what's best for everyone in this family. Trace disappeared from your life once already—what makes you think he won't do it a second time?"

His words prompted a strange sensation inside me, something metallic, tinged with fear. "He won't."

Jericho scoffed and paced behind my father's dining room chair.

"How many people know you've been seeing that man?" my father demanded.

"N-nobody. It's very new. It's...not public, per se. I've been working for him—"

Jericho barked out an incredulous laugh. "*Working* for him? *He* is the 'family' you've been working with?" He used exaggerated air quotes around the word "family." His eyes nearly popped out of his head. "This is fucking absurd. That guy is a predator. And you're taking care of his...what? His mutant offspring?"

I was so appalled I didn't even have a response for him. All I could do was gape at him.

"Mercedes, it isn't too late to change your mind," my mother said slowly, looking up at me with a pained expression. "We can put this behind us. We can pick things up right where they left off. Time is running out—don't you get that?"

"That's incredibly gracious of her to offer that—I hope you realize," my father rumbled.

"You think you could really trust her though?" Jericho asked, sarcasm dripping from his words.

"Mom, I—" My voice gave out and I could hardly say the words. *Do it. Tell them. You need to tell them.* "I don't want to pick up where I left off. I want something else."

My father laughed bitterly. "Something else. Being handed every single thing you could ever want wasn't enough, was it?"

Jericho scoffed in solidarity. I hung my head, more than ready to end this verbal assault.

"I think it's best that you leave," my father went on. "To be honest, I don't even want to look at you. Not until you start making better choices and you have something positive to bring to this family."

"Once you start pulling your weight," Jericho added.

A few tears escaped, and I brushed them away quickly. I looked up just in time to see Maddie turn away, concern etched across her face.

"Fine," I said, my voice thick with tears. "I'll go."

I tore myself out of the dining room, away from the comforting scent of dinner and all the familiar surroundings that reeked of family. No house was a home when it was filled with vitriol like that.

Jericho was right. I *was* stupid.

Stupid to think I'd be able to find a happy medium right now.

I tore my coat off the rack, tears streaming down my face as I shrugged it on. Each beat of my heart felt like an anguished scream. I'd never felt worse. More rejected. The biggest failure and disappointment.

I couldn't have done worse if I'd tried.

"Mercedes, wait." Maddie's soft voice made me stop just as my hand hit the doorknob. Her soft face was wrought with concern as she clutched Grace close to her chest. "Are you leaving for good?"

"I have to. You heard all that." My voice was raw. I wiped tears off my cheeks. "I guess the only consolation is I don't have much to pack. So I'll be out tonight."

Maddie's mouth turned downward. She looked over her shoulder briefly then stepped closer. "Please be careful. I don't want to see you hurt or worse."

From inside the dining room, Jericho bellowed, "Maddie! Where are you?"

Maddie winced, her entire being constricting at the sound of his voice. She looked like she'd been slapped.

"Are things okay with you and Jericho?" I asked softly, touching her wrist.

She swallowed hard and straightened her back. "I don't know. I should go back in there."

"Do you need to leave him?" It came out automatically, because I couldn't imagine anyone wanting to be with the beast he'd just been in there, but the pain in her eyes told me he might not only be that way with me. "Because you can walk out this door with me right now if you want to."

She shook her head, her mouth turned downward. She looked sadder than I'd ever seen her. "I can't, Mercedes. Not like you." She backed up toward the dining room. "Be safe. Promise me."

I nodded, watching as she slipped back into the dining room.

I didn't know when I'd ever be welcomed back here...or if. I wanted to say something to Gramma Kay, but I didn't know what. As the family's black sheep and biggest failure, I felt the best thing to do would be to just disappear.

So I pushed the door open and stepped back into the cold.

I couldn't give them what they wanted, so I'd give them the next best thing: the gift of my absence.

CHAPTER TWENTY-SEVEN
TRACE

M ERCEDES'S FIRST NIGHT AT my penthouse, with all her bags tossed into the spare room, was spent with a lot of crying in my lap. I stroked her hair while she cried, reminding her that her parents were shit and her brother was even shittier.

Willow joined in the consolation the next morning, wrapping her arms around Mercedes's shoulders and patting her back, murmuring something that sounded a lot like "no no."

I knew this had to be for the best, even though it hurt. But I couldn't see a downside to her breaking away from a family that wanted her to marry someone she had no feelings for. A family that pushed her to conform, even to her own detriment. A family who could speak such cruel words to her.

I cancelled everything the next day so that I could tend to her. Mercedes mostly stuck to the couch under a blanket, so I did what I could in the way of preparing her favorite tuna salad sandwich and waiting on her hand and foot. I would have used the bathroom for her if I could. I hated seeing her so down. So broken.

I only hoped that she viewed what grew between us as worth the strife.

But as always, my delightful inner critic had plenty to say.

Second chances are just a second chance to fail.

I pushed the cruel words out of my head. I was a perfectionist to my core, even when I didn't want to be. I didn't want to believe Mercedes and I would fail this time around. Not now that we were older, wiser. Not now that the truth was laid out on the table.

This is our second chance to flourish. I had to repeat it to myself. Make it stick. I wanted to hang onto *that* thought. Even though our opportunity to flourish came on the heels of her personal devastation.

After Mercedes had eaten her lunch and started a new round of sad movies, I put Willow down for her afternoon nap. Then I stopped in to check on Ferdinand and the leopard slug gang before joining Mercedes and continuing playing the emotional-support role. I enjoyed it a little too much. Not that she was hurting, of course. Just that I could be of service in her time of need.

"Willow went down." I bent to kiss the top of her head from the back of the couch. "You need anything, Birdie?"

She sniffed and shook her head. "Thank you for being the best human being on the face of the planet."

I cracked a grin. "I don't think I'd say *the best.*"

"At least the top five."

"I'll accept that." I sat on the far end of the couch, encouraging her to put her feet in my lap. She did so with a little smile, but it faded quickly.

A moment of silence passed before she blurted, "I think what hurts the worst is that they can't even fathom that I want something different than what they've offered."

I nodded. "They must think they're...doing their best. Or something." I wasn't entirely sure how to empathize with her family, but I wanted to help connect the dots if I could. If it meant it would make her feel better.

"I've felt so guilty for not wanting what they've given me. But I'm not wrong for wanting what I want." Her throat bobbed and her gaze fixed on me. "Right?"

I squeezed her ankle. "Not wrong at all."

She stared across the room for a moment before more words tumbled out. "I keep asking myself why I didn't say anything sooner. Why I couldn't pinpoint that my needs and their plan were incompatible earlier. And I think I just thought that I was supposed to want all the same things they did. And that there was something wrong with me, something I could fix if I just tried harder."

I nodded, gently stroking her calf as she spoke.

"And now, after being with you..." Her voice broke, and she wiped away a tear. "I realize that I've spent these last few years asleep. By choice. Just waiting for it all to click into place."

"It was never going to click into place that way," I whispered.

She shook her head, wiping away another tear as she sniffed. "I think the biggest difference between my family and me is that they live for the external. They want it all to look picture perfect. They want to be able to flaunt their facade at galas and have it published in the magazines, in a way that fits into everyone else's lives around them. I think that's how Caleb is too. From the beginning, he was setting up our relationship to be the same. And that's when I went to sleep."

I drew a deep breath, reaching for her small hand. I gave it a squeeze. "You didn't do anything wrong, Birdie. You were doing what you thought was right. It's hard to go against the grain. It can feel like dying. But then a reincarnation is waiting for you on the other side."

She laughed softly, wiping at the corner of her eye. "Yeah, my family isn't a big supporter of the reincarnation theory. In more ways than one." She drew a deep breath, burrowing into her spot. "I'm sorry I'm a potato bug."

"You're the sexiest potato bug I've ever seen." I squeezed her ankle. "So I'm not complaining."

She laughed at the same time a pounding sounded on the door. I twisted to look back at the door, confusion making slow steps through me. I wasn't expecting anyone. And I hadn't gotten an alert from the doorman, who always called when anyone not on the approved list came to the building.

"You expecting anyone, Birdie?"

She shook her head. "Maybe it's the mail and there's a package?"

I checked my watch. "That could be it." I sighed, setting her feet aside. I'd been planning on digging into the bodyguard hiring process—I needed that item off my to-do list. "Don't you move. I'll be back to continue the potato bug agenda."

She giggled and burrowed into her soft blanket, puckering her lips at me in an air kiss. I headed for the door as another urgent knock sounded. My hand hit the door handle, but something niggled at me to check the video monitor before opening. *Just in case.*

I pushed the button to check the front door camera. I grunted when I saw who waited for me on the other side.

"Son of a bitch," I muttered.

"Who is it?" Mercedes asked, sitting up a little so she could see over the back of the couch.

I pressed my palm against the door and drew a deep breath. The knocking sounded again.

"Trace?" Mercedes asked.

I swung my head to look at her, running my tongue over my bottom teeth.

"It's my brother." I cleared my throat. "Axel."

I drew a deep breath, silencing the doubts and worries and shock. I didn't plan on leaving him hanging. Not when he'd clearly made an urgent trip all the way from Manhattan. But I won't say I didn't have to muster some courage.

The door creaked slightly as it swung open.

And then, there we were. Two brothers. Staring each other down, the weight of the world sagging between us.

"Axel," I said. But I had nothing to follow up. I was too surprised.

He held out his palms, his icy blue eyes lasering in on me. "Trace."

I leaned against the door, gesturing at him. "What are you doing here?"

"Can't a guy come visit his brother?"

I hefted with a laugh. "Not when we left things like we did. How did you make it past the doorman without him telling me?"

Axel's shit-eating grin came out to play. "I have my ways. CEO of Shmoozing at your service."

I sighed, shaking my head. I should have warned my doorman not to believe a thing Axel told him, but I'd never expected him to actually come out here to see me.

Axel sized me up, his jaw flexing. "You gonna invite me in or what?"

"Sorry." I stepped aside, gesturing for him to come inside. "Color me shocked. Axel Fairchild dared to show up at my Louisville penthouse."

He strutted past me, pinning me with a satisfied smirk. "I know this is very thrilling for you."

I laughed. Genuinely. Some of the old, familiar energy revved back to life between us. But I knew better than to trust it. After how bad the last few months had been between us, I couldn't act like everything was okay.

"Oh." Axel stopped in the middle of the foyer, looking over at Mercedes, who peeked at us from above the edge of the couch. "That's the one who got away, huh?"

"Found her again." I shut the door behind him and headed for the great room. "Mercedes, you remember Axel, right?"

She cleared her throat, arranging her hair, sitting up like she hadn't been in the depths of a pity party all morning. "Of course! Axel, how are you?"

"Been a long time, Mercedes. How you doing?" Axel smiled over at her.

"Oh, you know…" She looked at me, laughing in spite of herself. "Pretty good, all things considered."

"I like that attitude." Axel nodded vehemently. "Cora talks about what a good attitude you have."

"Cora?" I asked, looking between Axel and Mercedes. "How does she know about Mercedes's attitude?"

"She and Mercedes are constantly texting," Axel scoffed.

"We have a group chat," Mercedes admitted with a guilty smile. "Me, Cora and Jessa."

My brows lifted—this was certainly news to me.

"I meant to tell you," Mercedes hurried to add, "but so much has been going on."

"Let the girls talk," Axel chided me jokingly. "They need an outlet, being around us all the time."

I arched a brow. "Okay, Mr. People Pleaser. What's up?"

Axel smirked. "Can you please control that eyebrow?"

I laughed again. Axel was good at things like this. Defusing tension, wooing people. When he *wanted* to. "I just want to know why you're here. You have no business in Louisville, and we both know it. Now spill."

"I just came to spite my brother." Axel shrugged, looking as nonchalant as they came. "Is that a crime?"

Mercedes giggled behind the couch cushion.

"And, you know, maybe make amends." Axel sniffed as he inspected his nails. "If there's time."

I hadn't seen *that* coming. Damian hadn't even warned me. I was speechless—I had no idea what to say. How to start. Where to begin.

"Where's my niece?" Axel demanded suddenly, looking around. "And my nephew, Ferdinand?"

I couldn't fight the warm smile that crossed my face. Mercedes caught my eye and sent me the sweetest smile I'd ever seen.

"I can take you to see one of them," I told Axel. "But only one. The other one is asleep, and I'll let you hazard a guess as to which one."

"Ferdinand," Axel said without missing a beat. "He's always been a lazy bastard."

I led Axel to the hallway, heading for my office, head swirling. I pushed open my office door, the big tank front and center.

"There he is," I told Axel. "Humid and ready."

"Just like I like 'em."

Axel strutted up to the tank, peering through the thick glass at Ferdinand's moist, black body. I shut the door behind us.

"Why did you really come, Axel?"

Axel expelled a breath, straightening his back. He took a moment before he swung my way. "I already told you. I came to make amends."

"You think one visit to Louisville is going to make up for the months of bullshit you've been doling out?"

Axel didn't blink, holding my gaze. I could see the conflict swirling in his gaze. All the unspoken thoughts swimming underneath the surface. "Yes," he finally said.

"Well at least you're honest." I ran a hand through my hair. "And if you're being honest, I can be honest." I went to my desk chair and sank into it, suddenly feeling too tired to stand. "Shit's not right without you and Damian."

"Severely not right," Axel agreed. His gaze drifted to the floor, a thick but not unpleasant silence settling between us. "Trace, I...I'm sorry."

I let the apology linger in the air. Savoring it. I honestly hadn't thought this day would come. I'd given up entirely on the idea of Axel recognizing that he'd been the engineer of this rift. "Thank you for that. It's...appreciated."

"I get caught up in my grudges sometimes," Axel went on. "But I was only hurting us all with this one. I'm not gonna lie—I was fucking pissed about the whole fallout with Ian and Dad. But Cora has helped me see that you were just a teenager doing the best you could with what you had at the time."

I nodded slowly. "Yeah. That."

"And besides, I'm ready to be an uncle." Axel sent me a shit-eating grin. "Cora said Willow is a cutie, and it would be wrong not to spoil my first and only niece. You know? She's both the world's luckiest and unluckiest girl, being born into the Fairchild family. We need to celebrate appropriately."

I rubbed my face, my body shaking with laughter. "Right. Equal parts celebration and consolation."

"Hey. All her uncles might go to prison. No big deal. She deserves a shopping spree. Three hundred princess dresses or something."

Axel and I held each other's gazes, silly grins on our faces. What else could we do but make light of it?

"I don't think Willow will complain one bit," I told him. "How long are you here for?"

Axel shrugged. "I've got an overnight bag in the car. I'd like to stay for a few days, if you don't plan on kicking me out."

Warmth spread through me. "And what about Fairchild Enterprises? I never got that dissolution paperwork."

"Yeah, I never even hired the lawyer to draw that shit up," Axel admitted, rubbing at the back of his neck.

"So full of shit."

"Bursting with it, I'm afraid."

I drew a breath. I needed to stick to business, or else I'd break down into tears of relief on the spot. Part of me didn't want to even admit how much this whole saga had affected me. But with my brothers, there were no secrets.

"Are you gonna cry, Trace?"

I laughed, rubbing at my forehead. "How could you tell?"

"Your judgmental eyebrow turned into the emotional eyebrows."

I pinched the bridge of my nose. "You're such a twatnugget."

"Takes one to know one."

I swallowed a knot of emotion in my throat. "You want to help me scout a new location for Fairchild Enterprises? It'll be our Louisville location, since I'll need to stay here most of the time until I get full custody of Willow."

"Consider it done."

"I need to hire a bodyguard too. You think you can help me out there?"

Axel cracked his knuckles. "Love this Axel-Do list. I'm on this shit, brother. What else is on the list?"

I couldn't even think of anything else. Not when I had this warm, buzzy feeling in the center of my chest, growing stronger by the second. It was surreal to be facing Axel again, after so much time apart. Much less to be *smiling* at him.

But this was what brotherhood was about. It was a choice. I'd chosen Axel once, and I'd choose him again. And I chose to let the past lie so that we could create a better future together.

"I think the only other thing on your agenda is to sit back and learn how to be an uncle," I told him, my cheeks hurting from how hard I smiled. "And honestly, I think you're gonna love it."

Axel wasn't just my brother. He was a necessary support beam in my life. One that I relied on as he accompanied me to visit another building that had come on the market as a Fairchild Solutions Louisville headquarters candidate.

"The last time I did this, it didn't end well," I warned him as we headed to a ground floor office space in the downtown area. "The agent all but told me we were operating a racket that should relocate to Timbuctoo."

Axel scoffed, pulling his long winter coat tighter around him as we braved a gust of spring wind. "He's lucky I wasn't there to *make* a racket."

"You were, in spirit." We passed slightly tinted windows, heading for the matte black door of our destination. As I pulled open the door, a car on the street began honking loudly.

Over and over again.

"Jesus Christ," Axel muttered, scowling at the black SUV, which had now come to a complete stop just outside of the office building. *Honnnnk. Honnnnk.* "Shut the fuck up!" Axel yelled over the din, but it was pointless.

One of the tinted windows rolled down. A man wearing a black ski mask chucked something out of the window, which exploded on the pavement right in front of Axel's feet.

"No Fairchilds!" His shout was gruff, and then the car sped away.

"What the fuck?" Axel peered down at his feet. Something suspiciously brown streaked the pavement, along with what looked like egg yolk. "Were we just egged?"

I glanced up down the street. Regular traffic had resumed, but a pit had formed in my stomach. "Let's go in."

"Fuck, it splattered my coat." Axel groaned as I pulled open the door. He went inside, where the wide-eyed realtor awaited us, a thin but well-groomed man with very round eyeglasses.

"Hello," I started, unsure how to segue into *Could we wipe egg yolk and what looks like dog shit off somewhere on your premises?* "You must be Jack."

"Did you know those people?" Jack looked horrified, peering down to inspect Axel's coat and shoes.

"No idea who they were," Axel said. "But they knew who we were."

"They did?" Jack nearly screeched as he swiveled his head between me and Axel.

"Not a very nice welcoming committee, huh?" Axel mused. "Where's your nearest restroom?"

Jack pursed his lips and pointed to a set of doors along the far wall. "But stick to the floor. I don't want any of that getting on the carpet." Axel headed to the bathroom, and I drew a deep breath, offering a smile to Jack.

"Let's start over. Hello. I'm Trace Fairchild. Your two o'clock." I stuck out my hand.

He took my hand, realization cresting over his face as he shook it firmly once. "Fairchild. That's right. That's how they knew you."

"Excuse me?"

Jack cleared his throat, looking around like he'd lost something. He scurried over to his paperwork and flipped through a folder. "Oh my goodness. Hang on a second. You know what, I totally forgot I have a different appointment right now. I came to the wrong address!"

I blinked. "But you and I spoke on the phone…"

"That was a different Jack at the firm. This is an embarrassing mix-up, and if I don't hurry I'll miss the client across town." Jack winced, packing up his things into a messenger bag. "So sorry. My bad. Someone will be reaching out soon to fix this."

Before I could protest, Jack was out the door.

And I was back to square one.

The toilet flushed a moment later, and Axel emerged from the bathroom with a sigh. "That was definitely shit."

I worked my jaw back and forth, contemplating the street through the windows. "Dog or human?"

"Undecided. Hey, where's our realtor friend?"

I frowned over at Axel. "He left."

"The showing is over already?" Axel exclaimed. "I was in there for two minutes."

"No. He bolted. Claimed there was a mix-up with the showings and went meet his 'real client.' That was after I told him our last name. I think he connected the dots on the dog shit attack and got scared."

Axel strutted my way, brows furrowed in thought. "You weren't kidding about people not wanting us to move here."

"I feel like we're up against the entire city." I sighed, rapping my knuckles against the bar-height reception desk. "This shit is just getting worse. *Literally.* Do you think we should nix the idea? I mean, maybe now's not the right time." I looked out to the city street beyond the windows. "I thought this would be my off-shoot business since you wanted me out of the New York office. But maybe it's not worth the effort."

"A little dog shit doesn't scare me," Axel said. "We've overcome worse, haven't we?"

"We have," I admitted.

"I think this is a good expansion," Axel said. "As the CEO, I approve of showing our clients and the world at large that we're not shrinking, we're growing. Besides, this just means it's time for that bodyguard. What was his name?"

"Seven. I can't tell if it's his military code name or not."

Axel snorted. "Or maybe it's how many people he's killed."

"It could be how many felonies he has," I countered.

"That's a good quality to have in a bodyguard. Means he's got connections and not afraid to take drastic measures when required. Anyway, sounds like Seven is gonna be the antidote we're looking for. When are we meeting him?"

I checked my watch. "At four. He texted me the address just a little bit ago."

"Ah. The neutral location." Axel grinned. "He's totally military."

"Unless we make Seven run screaming too."

"If we can scare off a man named Seven, then I think we should add that shit to our resumes." Axel wandered over to the carpeted area and stomped across it, making a big display. "And that's just for our realtor friend. He wasn't here to stop me, so that's what he gets."

I pushed Axel toward the door, laughing along with him. Even though our reputation was a heavy burden to carry, with Axel here at my side and Damian promising to visit soon, I knew I could handle whatever new surprising parcel of dog shit life decided to chuck out the window at me.

And if Seven proved to be a good fit, even better.

Axel was right. We'd overcome worse. It wasn't the first time we had life telling us we didn't fit or weren't good enough. We'd spent our entire lives clawing our way up from the bottom. And though I hadn't expected to have to do it again in Louisville, I wasn't opposed to it.

I was, after all, an expert at it.

CHAPTER TWENTY-EIGHT
MERCEDES

Days bled into weeks, and a wintery March bled into an almost springlike-April. Amid the sad trudge of family estrangement, I found a blissful new normal living with Trace.

We'd gone from zero to full-fledged family...with a twist. Just like it happened the first time around, though Willow hadn't been involved then. And neither had Seven, the bodyguard Trace had folded into our lives. I supposed there was no happy medium with us. It was either everything or nothing. Which was why we'd both known the arrangement for me to be Willow's nanny—and stay engaged to Caleb—had been a farce destined to unravel.

Now we were simply an unlikely family of three—plus Seven.

When I wasn't taking care of Willow, I was researching grad schools for child psychology and spending every possible second wrapped in Trace's arms, enjoying the slow transition from our snuggly fireplace-and-couch sessions to seeing the tiny signs of spring unfolding in the city. The planters already burst with green foliage. The pop of white squill flowers in the landscaping outside of Trace's apartment building. The tight buds of the lilac bush further down the street, already close to opening.

Anytime we left the house, Seven came with us. He drove us to the grocery store. He trailed behind us as we walked the park. And most importantly, he was always alert. Scanning for threats. The broad-shouldered, dark-haired bodyguard that barely cracked—except for when Willow toddled up to him and offered him a dolly. That was the only time I'd seen a boyish grin cross Seven's face.

Life was perfect. *Almost.*

The deeper Trace and I sank into domestic normalcy, the further away from my family I grew. I hadn't seen or spoken to my grandmother in weeks. Whenever I called the house phone, it rang and rang. My mother didn't even pretend to want to talk to me, leaving all my text messages on read and refusing to answer any call to her cell phone.

I didn't bother with my father or Jericho. Part of me wondered if my relationship with Jericho could ever heal. Maddie was the only one who dared speak to me, and only through an app that erased conversational history daily.

I was desperate to smooth things over with them in some way. I couldn't let another week go by with no word from anyone, or without seeing Gramma Kay. I had to figure out some way back into their hearts.

Because I believed I could find a way to have it all. I could be with Trace, and I could be on speaking terms with my family. *It can happen.*

On a late April morning, when the tang of humidity had it feeling more like summer than early spring, Willow and I were taking a lap around the block. She no longer wanted to be in her stroller, and instead preferred sitting on a combo stroller/tricycle Trace and I had purchased recently, grunting angrily when it didn't move, while refusing to let me push it for her. It made for a very fun time for all parties involved. While I was coaxing her to pedal, a familiar figure strode toward me on the sidewalk.

My broad-shouldered love, dressed in a long-sleeve button down and dark slacks. I smiled at him as he approached, caught in the captivating grip of his gaze. His brown eyes were so warm, so deep, that the rest of the world fell away.

"There's nothing better than running into you two out here," he said as he approached, leaning in for a kiss. I accepted his warm lips eagerly. Willow whined and opened her hands toward Trace, demanded to be included.

"Ta-Ta!" she shouted.

Trace's brows went up as he hefted her into his arms. "Did you just say Dada?"

Behind him, I saw Seven standing at attention, his hands clasped behind his back.

"Hi, Seven," I called out, wiggling my fingertips in his direction.

He jerked his chin into a nod. "Morning, Mercedes. How's the day?"

"Pretty great so far." I grinned up at Trace. "Hopefully you two have had an uneventful morning?"

Trace scoffed, shaking his head. "I'll tell you about it inside."

"Uneventful and secure," Seven confirmed.

"Well at least we have that," I told Trace. "No more threats or dog shit bombs this morning counts as a win."

The threats had increased in the past couple of weeks. Whatever Trace had been receiving in the beginning, he'd downplayed it so effectively I hadn't even realized. So once Seven came into our lives, it was because it had gotten *bad*.

And though Seven was a huge help in our daily routines, things were getting overall worse.

"You know you shouldn't be walking out here by yourself," Trace murmured to me, sending me a stern look.

"Willow was so restless," I told him. "Besides, you're the target. They don't care about us."

Trace nodded, looking down at Willow in his arms. "I just don't want to take any unnecessary chances."

"It will be harder to stay indoors as the weather gets nicer," I told him. "Maybe you should consider…"

"Bringing you both with me every time I leave the house?"

I laughed. "Sure. Just add us to your schedule, constantly."

Trace tipped his head toward the building. "Let's go inside."

"Can't we take a walk together? It's so warm out, finally. And besides, Seven will be with us. You haven't been able to enjoy watching Willow refuse to let us help her on the tricycle." I gestured toward the pink trike. "It's your turn."

Trace grinned, leaning in for a kiss. "I can't say no to a proposition like that." He looked over his shoulder. "Seven, we're gonna take a lap."

Seven dipped his chin, his dark, trendy sunglasses glinting briefly in the sunlight. His biceps bulged even through his conservative black long-sleeve shirt. The man had been a part of our lives for a couple of weeks, but I barely knew anything about him.

Trace attempted to arrange Willow on the tricycle again, which invited some light whining. Once she was safely tucked into the seat and he'd managed to push her a few feet, I said, "So how was your morning? Any luck with the newest potential office?"

Trace sighed, shaking his head. The brothers had been trying new tactics to acquire an office space, after three more realtors blocked Trace and Axel from leasing. Or in Axel's words, *cockblocked.* "Still nothing. Luckily some of the new clients I brought on are okay with virtual meetings for now. But it just looks so damn amateur."

"The important thing is that you're making progress. New clients is all we need to hear." I rubbed his back as we made our way over the sidewalk. A lilac bush to my left was nearly ready to pop.

"What about you?" Trace looked down at me, a soft smile tugging at his lips. "How was your morning?"

"We've had a good morning. Cora and Jessa and I were chatting. We want to plan a ladies' night when they're here for the Derby."

Trace nodded. "That's right. A month away now"

"Less!" I couldn't keep the excitement out of my voice.

"You love the Derby so much, don't you?" Trace asked.

Love was an understatement. The Derby was my favorite annual event in Louisville. It had been *the* event of the year for me as a child and throughout my adolescence. I loved getting ready for it, picking out the hat, arriving to see everyone in their Derby best. It was wrapped up in so many warm memories that had nothing to do at all with the races happening center stage. The fact that Cora and Jessa were planning on coming seemed almost too good to be true. Because this year, the Derby would be my debut as Mercedes, instead of the Hendrickses' daughter. The pieces of the life I chose were assembling.

I hoped that it would also mark the official beginning of my family accepting the Fairchilds in my life.

As Trace and I neared the apartment, an incoming call vibrated in my purse. I slipped my phone out and saw Maddie's name on the screen.

"Oh, I need to take this." Anxiety stalked through me, whispering menacing things. Maddie never called—not anymore.

"Of course." Trace pressed his hand to the small of my back as I slowed and answered.

"Maddie?" I answered the phone tentatively.

"Mercedes. How are you?"

"I'm good," I told her. "Is everything okay?"

"Not really," she nearly whispered. My stomach sank to my feet like a rock. "I think you need to come home. Gramma Kay isn't doing well."

"Not doing well how?" My voice barely made it past my lips. I'd stopped walking altogether, and Seven paused behind me, standing far enough away to respect my call.

"She's having a lot of fainting spells. She had a seizure recently too. They say it's all related to the stroke, but there isn't much they can do. They're just taking care of the symptoms until…"

A wave of emotion clamped my throat shut. I pressed a hand to my forehead. "Until…"

"Yeah." A breath slid out of her. "I didn't think anyone was going to tell you. And I thought you should know."

I pressed my fingertips to my forehead, fighting a swell of despair. I needed to fix this rift in my family. I needed to be there for Gramma. The truth pounded through me, urgent and loud.

"I really appreciate that. Deeply. Thank you."

"I felt like you would do the same for me, if it ever came to that," she said.

"I'm thankful you even think of me." Tears rushed to my eyes. "Everyone else has been very content pretending I don't exist."

"It's hard on all of them," Maddie said. "We're still coming every Sunday for church and dinner, and whatever else happens to be going on. I see how hard it is on your mother. I feel like she's…softening about the whole thing. If you know what I mean."

"You think so?"

"I think now would be a good time to try to come back. We all miss you, even if nobody has said it."

I squeezed my eyes shut. "I never wanted to bring this drama to the family. But I couldn't go through with it. I was with Caleb because I felt like I had to be. I—"

"I don't blame you," Maddie said softly. "In fact, I'm trying to hang onto this. As inspiration. Because I think I need it."

Her words took a moment to fully register. I blinked a few times before I was able to say, "Are you thinking of leaving Jericho?"

Silence thudded through the connection.

"You don't have to talk about it, if you don't want to..." I began, suddenly wondering if I'd misread things.

"No, it's fine," she started.

"Just know that I am always here, Maddie. If you ever need to talk, or cry, or vent, you can call me. Okay?"

"Okay." She sniffed. I wondered if she'd been crying this whole time.

"I wish I could give you a hug."

"Me, too." A laugh came out, but it sounded part-sob, too. "Hopefully I'll be seeing you soon."

After the call ended, I stared at the cement of the sidewalk for so long that Seven cleared his throat.

"Miss Mercedes, we should head inside." The low rumble of his voice snapped me to attention, and I looked up, nodding.

"Right, right. I'm sorry."

My head swirled with worries—and ideas—as I hurried ahead to meet Trace, who had paused at the main entrance of the building. Willow waved as I approached, shouting a greeting that sounded a lot like "Ha!"

Trace's brows drew together in concern as I approached. He closed the last steps of distance between us. "What happened?"

I looked up into his eyes for a moment before the emotion escaped. Tears spilled out as I forced the words out. "Gramma Kay isn't doing well. She might not have much longer to live."

"Oh, Mercedes. I'm so sorry." Trace's arms went around me, wrapping me in his thick, masculine warmth. I melted into him, clinging to the security he offered me.

"I think I have to go back, Trace," I said, once I'd dragged my head up and found his gaze waiting for me. "I have to try. I won't be able to live with myself if Gramma Kay passes and I didn't see her or make an effort. I'd die myself."

"Of course. I get it." He cupped my face in his big, rough hand. "What do you need?"

My eyes fluttered shut. His offer was both a relief and a joy so large I could hardly bear it. Instead of fighting me, instead of disagreeing, he just looked for ways to help. I loved him so much in that moment I could scarcely form words.

"I just need a few days. Or more. I want to go back and see if I can be with her. I'll try to...I don't know...mend the fences that I can."

He nodded, his gaze searing so deep I thought I'd be split in two. "Just let me know when you need me. We'll be waiting for you when you get back."

"You are the absolute best," I forced out around the lump in my throat. "Thank you."

Trace pulled me into another hug. Deeper, harder, more intense.

Because this time, it wasn't just to make me feel better. It was goodbye.

CHAPTER TWENTY-NINE
TRACE

I thought Mercedes would be gone for a few days.

It actually became almost two weeks.

Her grandmother was seriously unwell, and once Mercedes elbowed her way back into her parents' house—literally, no doubt—Gramma Kay only wanted *her* to help with things. Which meant Mercedes became her grandmother's full-time caretaker in her final days, a role Mercedes was more than willing to take on.

She apologized no less than daily for leaving Willow and me in the lurch, but I got it. I really did. Even though Willow didn't understand, and asked for *mama* at least thirty times a day. Gramma Kay had been the one drama-free person in the family. Even though the woman herself was extremely traditional, she had at least been a safe haven for Mercedes when it came to understanding that it was okay for her to want to do something different.

Luckily, my mom volunteered to come back to Louisville and help out with Willow until Mercedes could rejoin the fold. And her reception from Willow this time was much better.

"Peek-a-boo!" Mom revealed her face with a flourish, which caused a peal of giggles from Willow. "There I am! This game doesn't get old, does it?"

I grinned over the top of the book I read, sitting on the couch as they played on the rug. "I think we've played that game eight thousand times since she came to stay with me. And each time it's as fun as the first."

"That's the joy of children." Mom executed another round of peek-a-boo, which elicited even more belly laughs from Willow. "Because the sound of this laughter never gets old, does it?" She tickled Willow's belly, and Willow clutched at the front of her frilly yellow dress, shrieking with delight.

"Maybe she'll start calling you Grandma soon," I said.

"Well if she called Mercedes 'Mama' and you 'Dada,' then I'm sure it's not far off. Does she have a name for Axel or Damian yet?"

"She's only seen them each briefly. It'll take months before she has a name for them, I bet."

"I guess we'll find out soon, won't we?" Mom dove in for another round of tickles, and Willow fell backward onto the rug with laughter. As soon as my mom stopped, Willow demanded more. Looking up at me with a grin, Mom went on, "When does the crew get in, anyway?"

I checked my watch. My brothers and their better halves were arriving in Louisville today for an extended pseudo-cation. Since the Kentucky Derby was around the corner, we'd decided to use that as the focal point of a big family get-together. Axel and Cora would stay at my condo, while Damian and Jessa had rented a restored luxury loft that was in the middle of a stretch of exciting bars and trendy restaurants. Mom planned to stay with us too, because why not? This was a bona fide family affair now, and after so much time away from everyone, I was more excited than I was able to admit out loud.

"I think they'll be here around four. Axel has been pestering me about dinner plans."

"I'll make something," Mom said with a shrug. "Why not? I'll have all my boys in one place, I think that calls for pork chops and spoonbread."

I covered my heart with my hand. "Mom. You're too good to us. I'm already starving."

She winked at me then went back to tickling Willow. With giggles floating in the air, I pulled out my phone and fired off a message to Mercedes. Two and a half weeks without her here had been excruciating. I missed her soft presence and sweet kisses more than I'd expected, and I was dying to have her return to where she belonged—with me, in my arms.

TRACE: Can I call? I need to hear your voice.

Mercedes didn't answer right away. In fact, a full hour passed before she responded. This was common since she'd gone home. She said she spent most of her time tending to Gramma Kay, and the time she wasn't helping her to the restroom or feeding her, she was sitting quietly in her room, reading. Things remained frosty between her and her father and Jericho, but her mother had opened up slightly to reconciliation.

She never mentioned Caleb, and I didn't ask. I didn't believe I had anything to worry about as far as that sorry piece of her history was concerned.

MERCEDES: I'm sitting here with Gramma while she takes a nap—she asked me to stay near her. Let's just text for now. I'm finishing up my applications for U of L and Eastern Kentucky right now. Then I'll work on the one for Cinci. Deadline is in two days!

TRACE: That's my good Birdie. What about NYU?

MERCEDES: But you'll be in Louisville.

TRACE: But you dream of living in New York City. And I have a house for you above Barnes & Noble. With a crackling fireplace and a bookcase waiting for your entire collection.

MERCEDES: Did you literally fall from heaven? Because you are too perfect for words.

TRACE: Apply to NYU.

MERCEDES: I will. I hope at least one of them accepts me!

TRACE: They all will. And we'll celebrate when you're forced to make a decision. Any chance you could escape tonight? The NY crew will be here soon—Mom is planning pork chops and spoonbread. Won't be complete if you're not here.

MERCEDES: I'll try! I miss you so much Bear. I feel like I haven't seen you in a year.

TRACE: Me too Birdie. Things aren't right without you here.

MERCEDES: Jessa and Cora and I have been texting. Outfit planning! You're gonna freak when you see my hat.

TRACE: I'm gonna freak when I see your ass, too.

MERCEDES: <blushing emoji>

TRACE: I'm going to hold you hostage in the bedroom for a full day when I see you next, you know that?

MERCEDES: That will be a little awkward for the visitors. But I'm okay with it.

TRACE: I'll set you a place at the table tonight. Hope your sweet ass fills it.

I set my phone aside, only marginally sated from our text interaction. I wanted Mercedes back in my daily life more than I wanted air. But sometimes, my perfectionist nature worked against me. Asking what I thought I was offering her with this restricted existence? Sure, we had plenty of money at our disposal—but for how long? If we couldn't even leave the apartment safely, or without an ex-military escort named Seven, did that count as truly living?

The threats had been steadily increasing. I received multiple emails daily, all sent through untraceable hacker accounts, according to Damian. Somebody with resources or know-how. So many threatening phone calls poured in that I had changed my number a few days ago. Seven had blocked at least a small handful of suspicious characters from approaching my apartment door.

It felt like things were spiraling, and I didn't know how to stop it. And the worst part was, I wasn't sure where the threats were even coming from.

It felt like everybody in the entire world was against me. And my only recourse was to forge ahead. Ignore it. Try not to let the anxiety erode me entirely.

Mom and I spent the afternoon preparing for Axel and Damian's arrival. I ordered the groceries she needed via delivery, and once Willow was down, we made sure the apartment was ready for guests. While she prepared the spare bedroom for Axel and Cora—the room that Mercedes had used a time or two before I swallowed her entirely into my own bed—I vacuumed and tended to Ferdinand and crew.

Hours passed. Willow woke up with some tears, but calmed quickly once she was in my arms. As I put the finishing touches on the house with Willow accompanying me, Seven called.

"Hey. I've got visual confirmation of your brothers. I'll be escorting them straight to your place, no stops."

"Awesome. Thanks, buddy." I paused, realizing immediately that wasn't the right word to use. Seven was the hired muscle. He wasn't my *buddy*, he was a 280-pound slab of lean meat that could karate chop my head off at any time, for any reason. If anything, he'd be calling *me* buddy. "Muscle buddy, is what I meant," I clarified, but sighed when I realized how wrong *that* sounded too. "Whatever. We'll see you here."

I pocketed the phone, heading to the kitchen to find Mom, where she was unwrapping a stick of butter. Flour dusted the countertop, and the wide array of mixing bowls and measuring spoons told me she was elbow deep in the spoonbread recipe.

"Everyone just landed at the airport," I told her, hoisting Willow higher in my arms. "They should be here in about twenty, depending on traffic. Seven promised no stops."

Mom smirked. "And we should believe him. That man sticks to his word."

"That's what I hired him to do."

Mom's tongue stuck out past her lips as she carefully measured a teaspoon of salt. "What does that man do in his free time? Anything? Does he even *have* free time?"

"Not really. But I let him manage his own schedule. What he does when he's not here isn't really my concern."

She shrugged. "It'd be nice to know more about him, considering he's single-handedly protecting you from these Louisville weirdos."

"We can invite him to join us for dinner," I offered. "Then you can ask him yourself." Truthfully, I *was* curious. But Seven made it a point not to engage too much. He didn't want us distracting him with conversation while he was in protection mode. Which I respected. Hell, that's what I *wanted*. But Mom had a point.

"That man needs some spoonbread," she said, reaching for a spoon to mix the dry ingredients. "And I intend to feed it to him."

Mom moved on to preparing the rest of the meal—chopping vegetables and readying sauces in advance of everyone's arrival. I did what I could to assist, but she was the expert in the kitchen, and I was the mere underling. Besides, I needed her all-business command of the kitchen to keep me from drowning in my sorrows, mourning the fact that Mercedes wasn't able to share this prep time with us. I was desperate for Mercedes and Mom to connect, and it still hadn't happened.

My phone vibrated.

SEVEN: Approaching in five.

"You ready for all your boys under the same roof again?" I asked her. "Because they are minutes away."

Mom sent me a warm smile, a wisp of her gray hair sticking to her cheek as she whisked the secret marinade she loved to use for her pork chops. "Been waiting too long for this moment, son. Just promise me you three will never pull this shit again, huh?"

I bit my tongue before making a sarcastic comment about Axel—after all, he was probably steps away from my front door, and we'd made amends. He'd probably hear me if I talked shit about him now. "Promise."

I had Willow in my arms before the knock on the door sounded. Then we hurried to the door to answer it, four familiar, beaming faces shining back at me—plus Seven, facing the length of the hallway as he continued his vigilance.

"About time you guys got here," I said, wrapping my free arm around Axel, and then Cora. Damian and Jessa came next, everyone cooing their greetings and making bright, smiling faces at shy Willow.

"Trace already ate all the spoonbread," Mom announced as the crew filed her way for hugs and kisses.

"Feud's back on if that's true," Axel deadpanned, sending me a pointed look.

"She hasn't even baked it yet," I informed him. "But I'd eat it if I could." I stepped through the door, angling my head toward Seven. "Hey, you wanna come in for dinner?"

He sent me a wry grin. "You know the answer to that. I'd love to, but I can't."

"Promise me you'll eat some spoonbread, at least. My mom is dying to feed you."

Seven nodded, which prompted the muscles of his neck to ripple. "I can do that much."

I shut the front door and rejoined the family. The six of us moved to the great room, where Willow sat shyly in my lap, her face tucked into my chest, while we all caught up. Cora's theater program had officially started accepting applications from potential students, now that the renovations on that floor of the building were nearly done. Jessa had started designing a personal line of evening wear for a big-name client, with the possibility of her designs making it to a well-attended show at New York Fashion Week the following year. And Axel and Damian and I...well, we were finally back to being brothers again.

"Where's Mercedes?" Cora asked, once Mom had returned to the kitchen to cook the pork chops. "I thought she'd be here by now."

"I'm not sure she'll make it tonight. Her grandma has been getting worse." I stroked Willow's hair. "But maybe she'll surprise us. Willow and I have missed her, haven't we?"

Willow didn't respond, and instead snuggled deeper into my arms.

Jessa frowned. "Too bad we can't be there for her."

"I know she'd like that, but I don't think any of us would be very welcome at the Hendricks household," I said with a bitter laugh.

"That's the price we pay for so much awesomeness," Axel quipped.

"And sexiness," Damian added.

"And massive, throbbing, earth-shattering intellect," I rounded out.

Jessa's brows lifted. "I really did not think that was the word you were going to use."

Mom cackled from the kitchen as she closed the oven door. "These Fairchild boys sure are confident, aren't they?"

Cora smiled over at Mom. "You raised them right!"

I slipped my phone out of my pocket to see if Mercedes had texted an update. Still nothing. My heart sank—I wanted her here more than anything else. To feel the loving embrace of my family, to be accepted without question. I knew the time would come—but damn, I was impatient.

As I was pining for Mercedes, a call came in from FIELDS LE-GAL. My stomach sank to join my heart at the soles of my feet. *Fuck fuck fuck.*

"What's wrong?" Damian asked.

"It's the lawyer," I forced out, my mouth suddenly dry. Every-thing inside me twisted as I swiped the phone to answer. "Hello?"

"Trace. It's Robert. I have news," he said, his tone brusque as usual. But today, I sensed something else beneath his words. Or maybe it was just my own eternal foreboding when it came to the SEC investigation.

"Okay. Hang on. I'm here with everyone and I'd like to put you on speaker phone." I stood and headed for Mom in the kitchen, handing Willow off without a word. She accepted her with a nod, like she had read the seriousness in my face. I hurried back to the great room, turning the volume up as loud as it would go so everyone could hear. "We're ready."

"I'm not going to sugar coat this," Robert started. After a brief pause that sent my gut shooting to the ground floor of the apartment building on a rollercoaster, he said, "This isn't the news I wanted to deliver."

I found Axel's and Damian's worried gazes. Axel covered his mouth with a fist, while Damian looked ready to crumble.

"The SEC has decided to proceed with filing charges for financial fraud," Robert said.

The news entered like a sonic boom. Enormous in its arrival, blinding and deafening for a few moments afterward. I blinked rapidly, trying to understand the sick, sludgy feeling pumping through my veins. Cora covered her face with her hands while Jessa's chin began to tremble.

"They've determined that there is reasonable suspicion the algorithm fueling the investment decisions is an indicator of fraud," Robert went on. "News hasn't leaked yet, but it will over the next couple of days for sure. But if you choose, we can take it to trial, which means you won't be heading to jail anytime soon. At least we have that."

Nausea crept up my throat, threatening to eject itself from my body. The sheer dismay on my brothers' faces as we processed the news was almost worse than the news itself. I'd never seen these looks on their faces. So raw. So helpless. So *fucked*.

I cleared my throat a few times before I found my voice. "We, uh...I don't know what to say."

"We were definitely hoping their investigation would uncover no evidence of fraud," Axel added a moment later.

"We all were," Robert said. "But now from here, it could go one of two ways. There's a lot to think about. Your options are plea bargain, which will involve some jail time no matter what, or take it to trial, which could also result in jail time. It's a matter of strategy now," Robert said.

"Why do I keep hearing jail time?" I asked, my voice raw.

"How much time do you uh," Damian pinched at the bridge of his nose, "how much extra time? I mean, with our...freedom?"

"If you guys opt for the trial, it'll buy you several more months for sure. Possibly limitless freedom, of they decide not to convict after the trial. That would be the best-case scenario," Robert said.

"But if they do decide to convict..." Axel started.

"Listen, we're going to fight this," Robert said. "Let's strategize when you're back in New York. But I wanted you to hear it from me first, before it hits the news outlets."

"Thank you," Axel said, his voice raw.

Damian nodded, his lips rolled inward, but didn't say anything. I ended the call. Nobody said anything, our gazes flitting between each other.

Jessa rubbed Damian's back as she sniffled. "We can fight this," Jessa finally said.

I believed her intellectually. But down to my bones, I knew the fight was over. All I'd absorbed from that call was 'jail time'. And from the looks on my brother's faces, they had too. Cora's body wracked with a sob as she leaned into Axel, wrapping an arm around him. At that moment, I would have given anything to have Mercedes here.

Mom squeezed my shoulder then, and I twisted up to find her red-eyed and frowning. "I'm so sorry, baby," she whispered. "But if you let it go to trial, there's a chance..."

Tears swam in my eyes. I couldn't form words, much less full sentences. There was too much swirling in my head. All the worst-case scenarios I'd been entertaining, all the hatred that I'd been beating back flooded forth and consumed me, a white-water rush of negativity.

All I could think of was Mercedes. If her family had hated me before, now I'd be absolutely despicable to them. And what about these threats? Would they get worse now that the SEC wanted to prosecute?

I didn't know how to tell her. I wasn't even sure I'd be able to speak for the rest of the evening. And I certainly couldn't fucking text her news like this.

If I'd been uncertain before about what I could offer Mercedes, now I was certain that the answer was bleaker than I'd imagined.

I could offer her a restricted existence, one scarred by threats and fear, at the side of a financial fraudster who'd be locked behind bars.

You can give her nothing.

CHAPTER THIRTY
MERCEDES

Something was wrong with Trace.

I felt it in the air, like the distant rumble of a thunderstorm. I'd missed the Fairchild family dinner because Gramma Kay had fallen during her transfer from the bed to the shower that night. I'd called an ambulance and accompanied her to the hospital.

Things were only getting worse with her. She didn't have much time left.

But Trace needed me too. And he wouldn't tell me why.

I finished up with Gramma Kay at the hospital around one a.m. She needed to stay overnight, and I couldn't stay with her, so instead of going back to my parents' house, I went to Trace's apartment. I let myself inside the building and hurried upstairs, knowing that I'd likely find drunken brotherly bonding at this hour.

Seven wasn't at the door when I showed up; an unknown man, just as beefy and foreboding, stood at attention. I smiled brightly as I approached, as though this would convince him of my harmlessness.

"I'm part of the Fairchild crew," I explained at the door.

"Name?"

"Mercedes Hendricks."

"ID?"

I rummaged around inside my purse, producing my driver's license. He scanned it quickly and then asked, "Nature of your visit?"

I laughed to myself—part of me was dying to say *booty call.* "Trace is my boyfriend. And this is a surprise, so if you could avoid calling him, I'd appreciate that."

He jerked his head toward the door. "Go on."

I let myself inside the apartment quietly, hoping that interaction wouldn't ruin the surprise factor. But as the door swung open, a dark, still apartment greeted me. The only sound I heard was the low hum of the refrigerator. An empty bottle of wine sat on the countertop—the only sign of the dinner I'd missed.

I scurried through the apartment silently, knowing that Trace was likely asleep, which meant I'd have to wake him up with kisses and hugs. I slipped into the room, my heart pounding against my ribs as I saw him tucked under the covers. He was a dark lump, lit by the faint moonbeams streaming in through the window, facing away from me on his side. I gently set my purse down, toed off my flats, and then got to work undressing as quickly as I could. I stripped down to panties only and slipped under the covers with him.

Trace stirred as I sidled up against him. The first whiff of his scent almost undid me—leather, bergamot, and that indescribable edge of pure man. The warmth of his body sank into me as I wrapped my arm around his waist.

"It's me, Trace," I whispered into his ear as I spooned him. He startled, inhaling sharply at the sound of my voice, and twisted to look back at me.

I grinned at him so hard I thought my cheeks might split.

"Mercedes?" His voice was thick with sleep and confusion. He rubbed at an eye.

"You're not dreaming. I'm here." I ran my hand along his jaw, down the sturdy line of his neck and over the ridge of his shoulder. "I'm so sorry I missed dinner."

He stared at me another moment through the hazy light of the full moon. "You're really here."

"Yes, Bear." I laughed, dragging my fingertips down his chest. "Now are you going to kiss me?"

That seemed to help him put the pieces together. He pulled me into his arms like there was real danger on the other side of me, bringing me roughly against him. Our lips met hungrily, tongues dancing as we kissed each other as if the time apart had been years instead of weeks.

He rolled on top of me, caging me with his powerful arms. The thick ridge of his arousal pressed against my hip. I circled my arms around his neck as he kissed me so deeply I thought I saw stars.

"I've missed you so fucking much, Birdie." He moved his kisses to my cheek, my jawline, down my neck. Shivers erupted along my body as I relished this outpouring of love and attention. "I thought I might not survive without you."

His thick arms went around me then, pressing every inch of our bodies together. He buried his face in the hollow of my neck, still for a moment. I dragged my fingertips through his hair.

He didn't move.

"Is everything okay, Bear?" I asked.

He didn't answer me. When he finally pulled his head up, I thought I saw tears shimmering in his eyes. I ran my knuckles along his cheek.

"Talk to me."

He drew a deep breath. "I didn't want to tell you yet. I don't want to ruin seeing you again. But this is...this is going to ruin everything, no matter when I tell you."

Panic zipped beneath my skin. "What are you talking about?"

His throat bobbed. "Our lawyer called before dinner today. They found enough evidence to file charges for financial fraud. It's...I..." His voice gave out and his head dropped. I wrapped my arms around his neck and pulled him down on top of me again, encircling him in a tight hug.

"I'm so sorry Trace." Tears stung my eyes as I held him, wishing for all the world I could absorb his pain and fear. It radiated off him in thick, choking waves. I didn't know if it was the hour of the night that made me more sensitive to it, heightening our vulnerabilities, but my man needed to be held. And I planned to do that for as long as I physically could.

He pressed his forehead to mine, drawing deep, even breaths. I couldn't imagine the war going on inside his head.

"We plan to take it to trial." His voice sounded strained. "It'll buy us some time. But...it won't...it might not..." His voice cracked. "I don't know how long I'll go away for, Birdie."

His chest hitched, and I tightened my arms around him. He drew a deep breath.

"I'm sorry I wasn't here when you got the news." I nuzzled into the hollow of his neck. "I should have been here for you."

"You're here now." He rolled onto his back and dragged his hands down his face. "And you probably wish you hadn't come back."

I frowned, propping myself up on one arm to look down at him. Concentration etched his handsome features as he studied something invisible across the room. "That's not true at all. I've been dying to come back here. But Gramma is...well...dying."

Trace cleared his throat, pinching the bridge of his nose. "I'm so sorry. No improvement?"

"Things are only worse, I'm afraid," I whispered, running my palm across the smattering of dark hairs on his chest. "She fell last night and might have broken something. She's at the hospital now, on some serious pain meds and sedated. I'll have to go back in the morning to meet with the doctors."

Trace nodded, running his hand up and down my arm. He seemed vacant. Checked out. And for good reason.

"You should have just stayed with her," he whispered.

I frowned. "Bear, let's sleep. You need it."

He took my hand in his, bringing my wrist to his lips. "I planned for my first night with you to be much different."

"That was before you got the news you did," I whispered, lying down next to him. "Just sleep, Bear. You'll ravage me another time."

He turned toward me, pulling me into his arms for one last passionate kiss. I snuggled up into his embrace—the only place I'd found that could melt away the anxieties and doubts of the outside world.

I didn't know what tomorrow would bring. I sure as Sunday didn't know how to handle the big news he'd received, either.

There had to be a way forward for us. I believed it.

But does he?

Visiting hours at the hospital began at eight a.m., which meant I was able to catch a very quick morning coffee with Cora and Trace's mother before I darted off again. It was something—better than nothing. Especially since the three of us were able to bond a bit more while processing the SEC news. Trace stayed in bed, as did Axel. Understandably, the Fairchild brothers were still in shock. But under close watch. I didn't even get to hold my sweet Willow girl before I darted off to meet Gramma Kay's doctor, instead just pressing soft kisses to the top of her head as she slept.

It's okay. The Derby is in two days. This will work out somehow.

I was bound and determined not to miss the Derby. We all needed it now. After almost three weeks of full-time caretaking for my grandmother, and after the atrocious news the brothers had received, Derby would be a welcome respite. I just hoped Gramma Kay was in a good enough condition that I could slip away for the day.

It wasn't that nobody else was qualified or interested in taking care of her. She was just a fiercely vocal lady, and even in this advanced stage of deterioration, she made it very plain that she only wanted me handling her "intimates," as she called it.

So if Gramma Kay insisted I miss the Derby, I would. Even if it broke my heart.

Gramma Kay was sent home for bedrest due to a hip fracture, with a strong recommendation for a professional in-home care team. Naturally my family implied that her fall had happened because I had been the one overseeing her care, at least according to the comments Jericho had let slip while he was down the hallway.

Gramma Kay needed round-the-clock help now. It had gone beyond the realm of keeping it in the family. Which was both a blessing and a burden. Because even though I didn't logically agree with Jericho—I knew that falls were common with elderly people—part of me wanted to believe that if I'd just done things right, done things *better*, we could have avoided it. And now I had something I needed to make up for.

The reason things aren't good right now is because of you.

The sentiment weighed heavily on my heart. The way it had my entire life. So when the morning of the Kentucky Derby arrived, and Trace was texting me to confirm plans, the first person I went to see was my grandma.

"Gramma Kay." I let myself into her room quietly. She was still asleep, so I sat at her bedside and held her hand. "It's time to wake up for your morning medication."

She stirred at my side, her brows furrowing as she roused. "Mercedes?"

"It's me, Gramma Kay." I pressed a kiss to the back of her hand. "Good morning."

Her gaze landed on me, and she sighed. "Oh, thank goodness. I couldn't stand to spend another morning with that awful lady."

My heart sank. "You mean Miss Priscilla? Your new nurse?"

"Yes, her." Gramma Kay sighed and tried to sit up. I helped put enough pillows behind her back until she was comfortable. "She's so dry. Couldn't smile to save her life. Pass me that water, dear."

I handed her the glass at her nightstand, nibbling on my bottom lip as she drank. I got out the pillbox next and handed her the morning dose of medication, which she dutifully swallowed. Once she'd settled back into the pillows, I said, "It's Derby Day, Gramma."

"Is it?"

"It is." I swallowed hard, wondering how I should phrase it. "I was hoping to go."

"Well then." She said it matter-of-factly. "You should go."

"But then Miss Priscilla will be back."

Gramma Kay sighed exaggeratedly. "I can stand a day."

I scooped up her hand in mine and kissed it again. "Are you sure?"

"Only if you promise to take pictures of your hat. Will you see Caleb there?"

The question floored me. She and I hadn't talked much about him over the past few weeks, though she was aware of our broken engagement.

"I-I'm not sure," I forced out.

She patted the top of my hand. "Go make up with that boy. He loves you so much."

I dropped my head. "I'm not so sure about that, Gramma. But if I see him there...I'll be nice to him. And I can see about Mom staying back with you today instead of me or Miss Priscilla."

Gramma Kay nodded and smiled softly. I helped her get another drink of water before I promised to get breakfast sent up for her and that I'd see her the following day.

And with that, I was released.

I raced back to my old bedroom in the pool house, where I'd been staying on the nights that I didn't sleep in Gramma's room, and pulled open the big doors of the closet. I'd left behind all my formalwear in my haste to move to Trace's apartment, which served me well under the circumstances. I pulled out a smart and conservative green, camel, and white floral dress that complement-ed my wide-brimmed straw hat with horse figurines etched into a wooden "bow" on the brim. The hat had been Gramma Kay's, and I'd planned the entire outfit around it. As I got to putting on my makeup, I called Trace on speakerphone.

"Hello?" His deep rumble sent a shiver of excitement through me.

"Hi, Bear." I laid my foundation, squeezing my eyes shut as the powder flew across my face. "Today's a go."

Instead of the relief I expected, he drew a deep breath. "Okay. That's good."

I stopped applying my makeup and straightened my back, staring at the phone. "Just good?"

"What do you mean?"

"I don't know. We've been planning this for weeks. I'm pretty excited I can be there. Aren't you?"

In the background, an indistinct commotion was taking place. I couldn't tell if it was Willow-inspired or something else. Trace sighed. "Of course I'm excited. I'm just..." The silence of his pause felt immense. In my mind I supplied a thousand possible words in his absence of choosing one. *Scared. Stressed. Tired. Not in love with you. Second-guessing everything. Stop it, Mercedes.*

"Don't worry. I get it. We're going to have a great day. I promise you." I tried to sound as bright as I wanted to feel. Like I wasn't slightly hurt or doubting whether he even wanted me around. But that was just my pride speaking. My man was going through a rough time, which meant I needed to swallow all those hurts and *be there for him.* "You need this, Trace. You all do."

He sighed again. "Yeah. Mom's gonna stay here with Willow, and we'll head out in about an hour." He sounded exhausted. Resigned, somehow. "Where should I meet you?"

"Cell signal can be pretty spotty with the crowds. Maybe you could pick me up?"

He paused, as though the idea was hard to digest. "Uh...yeah. Let's do that."

I frowned at my reflection. I hated that he was struggling so hard since getting the news about the SEC investigation. But what else could I do other than remind him that we had time to enjoy *now*? I didn't want him to wallow in misery until the day they took him to jail—if that day even came. I held out hope that the trial would go their way.

I had to hold that hope, because I wasn't sure Trace could any-more.

We hung up, and I made quick work of finishing my makeup and slipping into my outfit. My mother intercepted me on the way out, praising my color palate.

"You look great, sweetie." She sent me a wink. "I'll see you there later."

Things with my Mom were looking up—and I was hesitant to ruin them again. We had a *Don't Ask, Don't Tell* policy in the house regarding Trace. My family never spoke of Trace or Willow. At all. It seemed like a compromise. I was helping the family with Gramma Kay, and they were helping me by ignoring my decision to stay with Trace.

But it wasn't sustainable.

When Trace arrived to pick me up, he parked in the same spot as always, beyond the sightline of my parents' house. Except Seven was behind the wheel. Trace was decked out in an impeccable camel-colored seersucker suit with a pink button-up beneath. It paired too well with his dark, perfectly glossed hair. My heart fluttered as I slipped into the backseat and leaned in for a kiss.

"How are you?" His voice was dull. The smile he offered lasted the briefest of moments before disappearing entirely.

"Good. Excited for the day." I grabbed his hand, not feeling any of the excitement or sparks that had sizzled between us for weeks.

"Seven will be joining us inside the Derby too," Trace informed me, his gaze sliding to the window. He squeezed my hand once before pulling it away. "Axel and Damian and everyone are on their way."

"Great." I studied him for a moment, trying to figure out what I could do or say that would help him most. I knew he was hurting.

No, more than that. Dissolving. Stressed beyond belief. I wanted to ease even an ounce of that for him if I could. "How are you feeling today?"

His laughter was devoid of humor. "New day, same misery." His gaze dropped to his hands, and he seemed like he was weighing his words. "Someone tried to deliver what we thought was a bomb today."

My mouth parted. "What?"

"Seven was tipped off by a suspicious delivery man attempting to come directly to the door. He intercepted it and noticed some strange powder residue, so he called the police, who in turn called the bomb squad." Trace made a fist, his jaw flexing. "It wasn't actually a bomb, but whoever sent it definitely wanted to spook us."

I wrapped my arms around him, squeezing him as tightly as I could. After a moment, I weaseled my way into his lap, where I cupped his face in my hands and stared into the dark swirl of his warm, brown eyes.

"We will figure out a way to make this stop," I whispered to him sternly so that he'd really believe me. Though I had no idea how to solve this. "You have hired all the right help, and more good help is on the way. This is not going to be forever."

"Only until I go to prison," he whispered back.

My nostrils flared. I didn't have the comeback ready for that yet. Too much time elapsed, which only made it seem like I agreed with him. "You're not going to prison," I started.

"That's a lie." He looked away. "I appreciate you trying to make me feel better, but I'm not stupid, Mercedes."

"Look at me Trace."

"Mercedes, you don't have to do this." He stared determinedly out the window, ignoring my attempts to cajole him into reason.

"Bear."

He slid his gaze my way. I cupped his face again and pressed a soft kiss to his lips. "There's the kiss we should have had the second I got inside the car. And when we get to Churchill Downs, we're going to have the time we planned for. The time we deserve. I know you are going through something devastating and unprecedented. But I want you to try to disconnect for just a couple hours. Because if you don't enjoy a little bit of life soon, you're going to kill yourself before you even go to trial."

His dark eyes searched my face, and then he nodded. "Yeah, Birdie. You're right."

"Thank you." I pressed another soft kiss to his lips, and this time, he returned it with passion. We kissed each other slowly, deeply, which I hoped would seal Trace's realization that he needed to disconnect and enjoy the here and now.

At least today.

While his family was gathered and the sun was shining and we had this brief window of normalcy until that, too, dissolved.

CHAPTER THIRTY-ONE
MERCEDES

Trace and his brothers had arranged for a private suite on the fifth floor, overlooking the racetrack. It was part security measure, part customary—after all, they were used to the VIP experience—but today they wanted to make extra sure none of the threats that had been stalking Trace would follow us to Churchill Downs. Seven posted himself outside our suite and brought along two extra bodyguards, who blended into the surrounding areas, keeping watch. That didn't include the bodyguard who'd stayed behind to watch over Willow and Trace's mom at the apartment.

I wandered the bright, window-filled room, pausing to inhale the bouquet of roses on the countertop of the private bar at the back. The brothers were inspecting the balcony, their conversation muffled by the shut door.

"This place is lovely," Cora murmured, pausing to inspect the horse-themed art on the feature wall.

"I just wish I knew more about betting on horses," Jessa said, sitting carefully in one of the gray armchairs. Her blue pinstriped dress ruffled around her as she sat—a creation she'd made specifically for Derby—and she touched the rim of her blue and white hat to make sure it was still in place. "I didn't mess up my hat, did I?"

"It's perfect," Cora said. She wore a black wide-brimmed hat with a pop of pink dahlias on the side. It complemented her black and dusty rose dress perfectly. "These hats take some getting used to, don't they, Mercedes?"

"After your first Derby, it gets much easier," I told them with a laugh. I joined them at the seats, easing into the chair that faced the television screen mounted on the opposite wall. It was already on, broadcasting the current race. Horses and their jockeys blurred past on the screen.

"How long have you been coming to the Derby?" Jessa asked me, still touching the rim of her hat. "I just feel like this thing is going to topple off at any second."

"I pinned it in there extra tight," Cora said.

"I know you did. I just don't have my hat legs yet," Jessa said. "That's like sea legs, but for hats. That's clever, right?"

Cora and I erupted into laughter. "The first of many clever things said today," Cora said. "And we haven't even opened the wine yet."

"No, ladies, today we drink mint juleps." I sent them mischievous grins just as a knock sounded on the front door. "Come in," I called out. The door swung open, and a server came in, pushing a metal cart.

"Lunch items for your group, ladies." The well-groomed server offered a quick smile and began laying out serving trays on a buffet table beneath the TV. Tantalizing aromas wafted through the air—cooked ham, smoked salmon, the tang of red onion from the salad bar options he laid out.

"Wow. Private lunch, too!" Jessa exclaimed. "This is the best."

The server wrapped up, and I hurried to hand over one of various hundred-dollar bills Trace had tucked away for gratuities.

"Have you ever come to the Kentucky Derby before?" I asked Jessa. "I know you and the brothers grew up, what, only about sixty miles east of here."

Jessa snorted. "We were way too poor for that. Coming to the city was rare for us, and Derby was definitely out of our price range. Same went for the brothers back in the day, too."

I nodded, a blush coming to my cheek. I sometimes forgot how hard it had been for the brothers growing up. I'd only ever known Trace as the confident, wealthy man that I'd first met six years ago. "I remember Trace told me once that sometimes the only way his parents could make rent was from all the accounting work he did on the side when he was in high school."

Cora shook her head. "When I met Axel, I didn't even know that working while going to school was a possibility. And Trace was working as an accountant at sixteen."

"Well, it was on the sly," Jessa clarified. "I don't think the guy he worked with wanted to admit he had a sixteen-year-old managing his books. But Trace *is* a financial genius, so he was probably just as good as the other accountants in Oakville at the time. All three of them worked their asses off from a young age. I remember running into Damian mucking horse shit in my uncle's barn. That's where I first fell in love with him," she admitted with a giggle.

"Then this is a fitting trip," Cora said with a grin. "Maybe you two can sneak off to the stables later, and he can put a pair of horse poop boots on."

The three of us erupted into laughter once more just as the brothers filed back into the suite. Axel and Damian similarly had pink shirts on, like Trace, though Damian had paired a baby blue bowtie with his while Axel had chosen a pink gingham print for his button-up. Together, they looked impeccable, handsome, and like the formidable trio they'd always been. The three of them exchanged looks, smiles tugging at their lips.

"What did we miss?" Axel asked.

Trace's brow was arched severely. "I think it had something to do with us."

"Damian and Jessa specifically," I clarified as each Fairchild brother beelined to his lady. Trace came behind my seat and pressed a kiss to the top of my head.

"Cora said you and I should have an intimate moment in the stables, since I first fell in love watching you clean stalls," Jessa said, grinning up at Damian.

"I think that's a great idea," Damian said before leaning in to plant a kiss on her lips. "I'll strip down to a wife beater and woo you all over again."

"You two are gonna get us kicked out of Churchill Downs on our first visit," Axel warned, "which normally I wouldn't be opposed to. Except for the fact that the SEC news leaked yesterday, so we should keep a low profile."

"No horse poop sex please," Trace added.

Laughter rippled through the group, but it was tempered by the dark cloud of the SEC news. We could forget about it only for small chunks of time. It always came barreling back, reminding us all.

"Is it time for mint juleps?" I asked suddenly, clapping my hands together. "This bar is fully stocked, y'all. I checked."

"I'd *love* a mint julep," Axel said.

"I know we could call the bartender to come in, but I want to make the first round myself. I make them a special way my dad taught me." I went behind the bar, pulling open drawers and checking for ingredients. "He taught me and my brother too young, actually. But mint juleps were such a thing in my family."

"We just drank moonshine in our family," Damian muttered.

"Also too young," Axel laughed.

"Which is one of the reasons we're the fun group of well-adjusted, successful men you've all come to know and love," Trace deadpanned.

"Yeah, we need those mint juleps *fast*," Axel said, sending a look to his brother.

"Coming right up!" I readied the bourbon and simple syrup, snagging the thin bottle of bitters to use as a garnish. I lined up six pewter cups—a relief to see, especially in this VIP bar—and added mint and simple syrup to each. I muddled the ingredients, added the bourbon, and filled the cups with crushed ice. Once they'd all been stirred gently, I topped off each cup with an extra mint sprig and added a touch of bitters as garnish. *Perfection.*

"Now start drinking this and go grab one of those devilled eggs over there," I told the group as I passed out the pewter cups. "Cheers."

Cora took a sip and sighed. "This is so delicious. Thank you, Mercedes."

"Tastes like we're about to have a fun evening," Jessa murmured.

I caught Trace watching me with a sad smile. I lifted my cup to his and we clinked them gently. "Drink it nice and slow," I told him. "It has a long shot, and I used the best bourbon."

The rest of the group had moved toward the windows, looking out toward the track as they nursed their drinks. My phone rang, and I reached for it on the bar. My mother was calling. I answered hesitantly, already feeling the conflict brewing as both the Hendricks and the Fairchilds were on the same property. "Hello?"

I could hear the commotion in the background first. "Mercedes, are you here?"

"Here as in...Churchill Downs?"

"Yes! I've just arrived, there are some family friends here dying to see you. Where are you?" A peal of cheers erupted from the background.

"I'll head your way," I told her. "Just hang tight. Are you on the Veranda?" Our family had always gone to the Veranda, a private area reserved for large groups with huge, open balconies overlooking the track. A group of local businessmen and executives, including my father, rented it every year. It was practically a Chamber of Commerce event, with everybody who was anybody rubbing elbows and getting drunk.

"Of course, dear." I could barely hear my mother's voice over the sudden round of shouts. "See you here!"

I set the phone down, looking up at Trace. "My mom wants me to go see some family friends."

Trace held my gaze. "Do you want me to come with you?"

I nodded without a moment's hesitation. "Yes."

"Don't you think it'll just piss everyone off?" Trace ran his thumb along my jawline.

I shrugged. "They need to start getting used to you."

Trace nodded, but I saw doubts swirling in his face. The same doubts I'd been sensing since surprising him in his bedroom a few days ago. It grated at me more than I could express, but I didn't want to say anything, because I knew he had enough to deal with.

"I'll have Seven tag along," he said. "Just in case."

I pushed up onto my toes to press a kiss to his lips. I tasted the tang of bourbon and mint, and I smiled up at him. "This will be fun."

"Yeah," he said, tilting his head as though he didn't entirely agree. "Fun."

Trace let his brothers know the plan, and I led him out of the VIP suite and down the long hallway. Seven radioed for backup and trailed behind us.

"I'm sure my dad and Jericho are here too," I told Trace as we walked hand-in-hand toward the grand entryway of the Stakes room, which led out to the Veranda. Inside, countless heads bobbed, glasses clinked, and the entire area was full of the sound of merriment. The entire far wall was glass windows overlooking the huge, covered balcony where even more tables were set up and filled with diners, gamblers, and more.

"Seems like everyone is here," Trace said, keeping my hand clasped tightly in his. People swarmed around us, and I spotted plenty of familiar faces in the crowd. I waved as the mayor drifted by. I spotted Aunt Rosie across the way, which meant my mother couldn't be too far off.

"I think I see them," I told Trace.

"Are you *sure* you want me coming with you?" Doubt filled his voice. "I don't want to make this harder than it needs to be."

"You aren't going to make this harder," I told him. "It's hard no matter what. And I want you at my side in hard times."

His throat bobbed as he scanned the crowd. When he looked down at me, real conflict strained at the edges of his composure. "Do you understand that adding me to your life is only going to make things *inexplicably* harder?"

His tone twisted with the dissonance I'd been feeling from him. I knew that whatever was beneath that comment was behind all the friction I'd been feeling. I needed to get to the bottom of it. "What do you mean?"

A hand grabbed my wrist. My mother was in front of me suddenly, wearing a mint green dress with a white fascinator. One of its spiraling adornments poked me in the face as I swung toward her.

"Ouch. Hi, Mom." I covered my cheek with my hand.

"I need you over here with me," she said in a low, firm voice, yanking me by the hand. Her gaze didn't waver from me.

I turned to look at Trace, tipping my head toward my mom. "Come with."

Trace dipped his chin, something hard sliding over his features. "Mercedes."

I recognized the plea behind my name. The disagreement. But I wanted him to begin bridging our worlds. It could happen—we just needed to take the plunge.

"*Alone,*" my mother added, as though responding to the intensity between me and Trace.

I opened my mouth to protest, but Caleb sidled up at that moment. He wore a jovial smile on his unnaturally tan face, which told me he'd been somewhere tropical recently. Not knowing about his trip—wherever it was—was a relief. It meant the disconnection was happening successfully. In fact, he didn't look at all like I'd dumped him and cancelled our wedding over a month ago.

"Mercedes. Good to see you." His gaze fastened on me for a brief moment before swinging to Trace. "And you, too, Trace."

My mouth hung open as I struggled to find a response. All words had flown out my brain the second Caleb showed up, and now I wasn't sure what to do. Follow Mom? Escape with Trace? Or just quietly disintegrate on the spot?

"Mercedes," my mother repeated. "Come. With. Me."

"I've been wanting to talk to you, actually," Caleb said, a tight smile stretching across his face as he clapped Trace's shoulder. "Maybe we could head to the bar?"

Trace's gaze was heavy on me. He jerked his chin in the direction of my mom. "Go on. I'll find you after."

I nodded and watched as he and Caleb slipped back into the crowd. I followed my mother to the balcony, weaving between people as my gut sank to the core of the Earth.

"Why did you bring him here?" she asked in a clipped tone over her shoulder as we arrived at the far edge of the Veranda. Family and friends occupied five separate tables. Jericho and my father, two of the taller men in the area, were at the farthest table from where we stood but I didn't catch their eyes. I doubted they'd even acknowledge me if they noticed me.

"I came with him," I told her. "He's my boyfriend."

My mother whipped around to face me, our noses inches away. "You will not call him that here," she hissed. "This is our one chance to have a good time as a family. I beg of you, do *not* ruin this day for me. You know we have limited time left with your grandmother."

I drew a deep breath. I didn't even know where to *begin*. But I didn't want to ruin this day either. I wanted to enjoy it with *my* people. So my plan was now to exit this area as quickly as possible and get back to the Fairchild crew. "Whatever you want."

"You should really think about your future for once," Mom said ominously. "I've done everything I can to make this plain to you. And I still try. Even when I shouldn't."

Her words left me puzzled, but it wasn't the time to unpack that now. Family friends approached us, all seersucker suits and huge, gorgeous hats. More than one person complemented me on the engagement, which I tried to diplomatically correct.

But it wasn't easy with my mother interrupting me each time saying, "Well, there's still time for a change of heart."

After the third time she'd said this, I turned to her sharply. "Why do you keep saying that?"

"Caleb misses you, honey." My mother sniffed, looking past me through the crowd. "Why don't you try reconciling with him? You know he'd take you back."

Her words didn't mesh well with the fact that Caleb had led Trace to who-knew-where. Anxiety formed a rancid stew in my gut, and I cleared my throat, preparing myself to be clearer than I'd ever been before.

"I don't want him to take me back," I said. There wasn't plainer language than that. "I don't want to be back with *him*."

My mother looked at me in a way that said *Are you serious?* "He'd be willing to give things another go. He told me so himself last week at dinner."

"You had dinner with him?"

"Of course we did! He's like a son to us."

I sighed, crossing my arms. They considered him more their child than their own daughter. "Okay. Well that's nice to hear, considering Dad and Jericho won't even speak to me."

"Well they would, if you'd start taking your future more seriously," she said with a sniff.

I huffed, throwing my hands out to my sides. "How am I not taking my future seriously?"

"By rejecting every measure of success we've set up for you?" She said it incredulously, topped off with a brittle, sarcastic laugh. "You know that man is going to prison. For *years*. We read the article in the newspaper this morning. Why would you attach yourself to a sinkhole like that? Think of your future, Mercedes."

I clamped my mouth shut. I'd forgotten to weigh this reality when trying to incorporate Trace into the fold. I suddenly felt very stupid. Very naïve. Very *exposed*.

"I don't care if he's going to prison—"

"Do you hear yourself?" My mother looked at me like I was insane. Like she didn't even recognize me. And seeing her assess me in that manner made me wonder if *I* was insane too. "Think of your future, Mercedes. Do you want to be writing letters to an inmate for the next twenty years? Or do you want to marry a man who loves you and raise children and have a relationship with your family?"

The question hung heavily in the air. The ultimatum was clear. *Do you want HIM or do you want YOUR FAMILY?* I caught Jericho's eye from across the way and he sneered at me, looking haughtier than ever. I barely recognized him, and suddenly, as I looked around at all these perfect individuals, with the right hairstyles, the right brand names, the right reputations, I realized I barely recognized anything about this entire life.

If this was what family was, why would I ever choose them over Trace?

Everything about Trace made sense, and I knew it down to my bone marrow. Even when everyone else thought it was wrong. He cared about me—my desires, my wellbeing, my needs, my preferences. He didn't make me feel like shit simply for wanting what I wanted. Trace was the only person in my life who had ever fought for *Mercedes*. And he'd done it since day one.

"I know things are going to work out on the legal front," I finally said, forcing myself to meet my mother's gaze. "They will."

Her incredulous laughter rose above the din of surrounding conversations. The sound of a bell signaled a new race on the racetrack below. "You are being delusional. You know that right? Delusional."

"You sound exactly like Jericho," I muttered, emotion beginning to claw its way up my throat.

"Because he has common sense," Mom retorted. "*Please*, Mercedes. I beg of you. Do not ruin what we have as a family, but more importantly, do not throw your entire life away for a felon."

Tears stung my eyes. I didn't want to break down in front of her, because I didn't want her to take it as evidence that she was right. But I couldn't take much more of being berated here—in broad daylight, no less. "We're done here. I'm leaving now."

She sighed, eyes fluttering shut as she pressed a hand to her forehead. "Whatever you say, dear."

My chest was like a rubber band on the brink of snapping. I weaved back through the crowd, looking ahead for Trace. I spotted him through the doors leading into the Stakes room. He was at the bar.

With Caleb at his side.

My heart leapt into my throat as I stilled, watching the two of them interact. Trace's face was stony as Caleb faced him, jabbing his finger vehemently as he spoke. Trace said something biting—I would have given anything to hear what it was—and then Caleb spun and stormed away, his face red.

This had been no casual meet-and-greet. But what had I expected?

I hardly knew how to react. Trace scowled as he picked up his tumbler and drained it. He flagged down a bartender, and finally I remembered how to move. I forced myself forward with heavy legs, beelining for him. He was at the far edge, away from most of the other patrons. So even though there were hundreds of people in the area, he was still somehow secluded.

I filled the empty space next to him, breathless from worry. "What did Caleb say to you? What just happened?"

He glanced at me but didn't react. If Trace had been building walls between us since earlier this week, he'd suddenly completed the construction.

"You know what? It really doesn't matter anymore."

The bartender approached, and Trace ordered a whiskey neat. I blinked rapidly, trying to parse this response.

"I think it does."

Trace studied his hand for a moment, then shook his head. "No. I really don't want to do this right here."

"Do what?" I felt like I was speaking in a different language, or at the very least shouting at a wall. Nothing made sense, and it was making me desperate. Hysterical, even.

Trace finally swung his gaze to me, his dark eyes hard and unfamiliar. He looked at me like he'd never seen me before. "End things with you."

My stomach plummeted to the core of the earth. My chin trembled before I could even hope to control my emotions. "Trace, what does that mean? You—you can't—"

"We need to end this now, Mercedes." The bartender came back with his drink, and Trace tipped him a fifty-dollar bill. "Before it's too late."

CHAPTER THIRTY-TWO
TRACE

My heart hammered against my ribs like an animal in its last, primal attempts to escape a cage. Raucous and loud, desperation propelled by the will to live.

The life I wanted to live was no longer possible. I'd been battling this truth since the lawyer had called earlier that week, but the fear had started gnawing at me back when we first got the news of being investigated by the SEC.

As time crawled by, the truth had settled into something firm and immutable.

I had nothing to offer Mercedes. The longer she stayed with me, the more she was at risk.

Caleb had just confirmed it. And though I sure as fuck didn't want Mercedes to be with Caleb, my calculations proved she shouldn't be with me, either.

"You are...a lovely person," I began, already suffering the immense weight of how ridiculous this sounded. I hadn't wanted to be the guy to break up with the love of my life in a bar. But things were getting out of hand. Some mornings, I asked myself if it was time to go into hiding.

Mercedes didn't deserve that. Neither did Willow. And I loved these women so much that I was going to spend every last dollar and resource I had to protect them.

Away from me.

"Don't say that to me," Mercedes spat, tears already spilling onto her cheeks. Her mouth turned downward as she stared at me through watery eyes. "Don't you even say those words."

"Mercedes, we knew it wasn't gonna work from the beginning," I said, studying the swirled marble pattern of the bar countertop. If I looked at her now, I'd crack. I'd take it back. I'd lose my resolve. "I've got too much going on. My family is a target. *I* am a target. I can't leave the house without armed bodyguards. Is that the life you envisioned for yourself?"

"I envisioned a life with *you*," she said, her voice cracking.

"And you'll never get it!" I slammed my fist against the bar. "Don't you understand that? I'm going to prison, Mercedes. For at least a decade. Why do you want to be with me when we literally will never be together?"

Mercedes reached for my hand, but I moved out of her reach. "But you'll get out someday, and I'll be there.... I can visit you when you're in there..."

I shook my head, dragging my hands down my face. "You're being naïve, and the worst part is that you don't even see it. I'm not going to let you waste your entire life on someone like me. You can go meet someone else. Fall in love. Have his babies. I know we wanted that, Mercedes, but I can't give it to you."

"But we can," she insisted, gripping the front of my coat. "We can make it work. I'll wait for you. I don't care how long it takes. I've waited six years for you, what's another decade?" She was talking so fast now, her words bloated from the tears in her throat. "I'll wait because I love you, because you're the only one I want."

"You're not getting it," I said succinctly. "I can't live with the guilt of you throwing your life away on me. I fucked up, Mercedes. I've ruined whatever might have existed. It's a non-option, now. This will be a lot easier if you just accept it. I know it's a hard pill to swallow, but...we're all gonna have to. Sooner or later."

"You're just depressed," she went on, shaking her head. "And feeling negative. I can help."

"You *can* help," I said, downing the rest of my whiskey. I wiped at the corners of my mouth as I stood, adjusting my coat. She looked up at me, tears streaming down her face as she clutched my lapels. "You can help by not following me when I leave. By getting used to the idea of me being in prison. I've already ruined my own life. I don't want to ruin yours too."

"You could never ruin my life, Bear," she said, resting her forehead against me. "Please don't do this."

People had started to notice now. We'd ruptured the privacy this area of the bar had afforded us now that Mercedes was openly weeping. Again, I'd caused this. I'd tried to do everything right in my life, yet somehow, still, I'd ended up here. Breaking a woman's heart because I couldn't give her what we both wanted so desperately.

You are the ultimate fuck-up.

But I had to make this right somehow. And the only way I knew how was in releasing her. Even if it broke my own heart too.

"You can't be in a relationship with me if I don't want to be in too," I told her. "And maybe someday you'll see it's for your own good. Stay away from Caleb...but stay away from me, too."

I tore myself away from her and strode out of the Stakes Room, my heart beating so quickly I thought I might collapse if I stopped or allowed myself to truly internalize what I'd just done.

When was it going to hurt more? Now or in a year, when we'd fallen even deeper into love and possibly had a kid on the way?

No, I was being smart. Rational. This truth had been weighing on me like a lead blanket since the SEC decision, and I was just being proactive. Broken hearts would heal. We knew this from direct experience already. What was the harm in a second round?

Seven trailed behind me as I took a circuitous path through the bars and lounges of Churchill Downs. I finally made it to the front of the property after too many wrong turns, drawing a big breath of air as I pushed through the main doors. I needed to get out of here. I didn't want to hear a single thing from my brothers. I knew they'd try to talk me out of it, to compare it to their own relationships. But our situations weren't the same. They hadn't had bomb threats coming in when they were falling in love. They hadn't been forced to figure out practical solutions to caring for a two-year-old or managing a squad of bodyguards.

I needed to become an island. People were better off away from me.

Seven drove me around Louisville aimlessly while I stewed in the backseat. It was times like these that I appreciated his stony, non-judgmental demeanor. I didn't want a single fucking person reminding me of what I'd walked away from, because I'd reverse it all in a heartbeat if I somehow ran into Mercedes again.

I was hanging on to this decision by a thread.

I'd been strong enough to enact it; I didn't trust that I was strong enough to uphold it.

Axel and Damian started blowing up my phone with calls and texts about fifteen minutes after I left Churchill Downs. I ignored everything. But after about an hour of aimless driving, I finally looked at the messages that had piled up.

AXEL: Um, care to explain why Mercedes came back to the suite a crying wreck???

DAMIAN: Where the fuck are you?

AXEL: OK, Mercedes disappeared again and the other bodyguard (let's call him Six) said she got into a big argument with her brother and punched him in the face. WTF happened when you guys left???

DAMIAN: Seriously. WHERE THE FUCK ARE YOU?

AXEL: Mercedes is back and she's crying again and you are still MIA according to Six. Did you fucking leave?

DAMIAN: Will you be at the apartment when we get back?? Answer me.

AXEL: The girls calmed her down and she's telling us that you broke up with her because you're going to prison. Kinda seems like you're setting the precedent for the whole family, which I find unfair. Should have consulted us on this first bro. Not cool. (No feud, though)

DAMIAN: I'm going to hack your phone in the next ten minutes if you don't fucking answer me. Douche canoe.

AXEL: But you're alive right? Send a thumbs up emoji at least. Even though I detest those.

DAMIAN: Hacking now.

I called Damian when I got to the last message. I trusted him to make good on his word. And to be honest, I was worried about what he could accomplish. He was, in my eyes, a little too good at what he did.

"I'm alive," I told him when he picked up.

"Yeah, I knew that much," Damian said wryly. "Care to explain?"

"Are you guys still at the racetrack?"

"Your stunt kind of killed the vibe," Damian said. "The girls called a car for Mercedes. I think she's going to coordinate with Cora to stop by and get her things from your apartment tomorrow or something. But I mean...you broke up with her. Why?"

I studied my knuckles. "I don't want to talk about it. I'll see you guys at the apartment."

"You know I tried to pull this shit when Jessa and I first—" Damian started.

"I do not need to hear your well-meaning bullshit right now," I snapped. "I love you. I'll see you later."

I instructed Seven to take another lap of the city. I needed more time to sit, ponder, and stew. I didn't like my decision any more than anyone else. But it had to be done. *Had* to.

When we finally got back to the apartment, it was almost dinner time. I'd only had bourbon since breakfast, but my heartbreak and anguish prevented me from having much of an appetite. My stomach twisted as we neared the building. I didn't know what else to expect. How much worse it could get. Seven cleared each threshold as we came to it.

This was life now.

Danger around every corner. Me skulking in the wake of my bodyguard.

Pathetic.

Upstairs in the apartment, Axel and Damian sat in the living room with my mom, deep in conversation, while Jessa and Cora were in the kitchen. Willow was in Cora's arms...happily. And when I opened the door and shut it behind me, she didn't even whine.

"Look who's home!" Jessa said, clapping her hands as she encouraged the same from Willow. Everyone was still in their Derby best, save my mom, who stuck out like a sore thumb in regular clothes. "Uncle Trace is here!"

Willow twiddled her fingertips, reaching toward me as I approached. An expectant silence filled the apartment. I waved at everyone before holding out my arms to take Willow from Jessa. "Hey, guys."

A rush of air whooshed past Axel's lips. "Man, that was awkward."

"Only because *you're* awkward," I shot back.

"Actually you are," he returned. "You're the one who broke up with your girlfriend at the Kentucky Derby and then just left everyone else to pick up the pieces."

I noticed Cora and Jessa grimacing beside me. Hell, he was right. It was a shit move.

"I'm sorry guys," I said with a sigh. "It wasn't ideal. But it had to happen. I lost my cool, but it was the right thing to do."

Axel exchanged a look with Damian. I knew some more of their well-meaning bullshit was about to come out, so I held up a palm. "Before you say anything else, can we just not talk about it?"

"I just need to know what Caleb said to you," Axel blurted. "Mercedes told us you were pissed after he talked to you at the bar in the Veranda."

"He didn't say anything I didn't already know." I hoisted Willow in my arms and headed to the great room to join my brothers and Mom. "He told me I'm a piece of shit going to prison where I deserved to rot. He reminded me that this city had never accepted us before, and now, after the news, not in a million years. And he reminded me that Mercedes was his, and that he'd be getting her back in short order."

Axel blinked. "Sounds like a fun guy."

"None of that shit is true, though," Damian said.

"Sorry, where's the lie?" I sank into the armchair facing the couch where Axel and Damian and my mom sat. Willow twisted in my lap and played with the lapels of my jacket. "We *are* going to prison.

This city has not and *will not* accept me. And Mercedes *will* likely go back to him once I remove myself from her life." As soon as the words left my mouth, I knew how wrong they were. Still, my pity party knew no limit.

Cora snorted, joining us in the great room. "I don't know about that last part."

"Yeah, she wasn't into that guy," Jessa added, plopping into the other armchair near me. "Like, at all."

"I said I didn't want to talk about this, guys." I rubbed my eyes with the hand that wasn't wrapped around Willow. "I'm sorry I made things weird. Let's just order dinner and forget about it."

If I wanted to keep my shit together, I needed to get busy pretending Mercedes had never happened.

It was the only shot I had at making it through the foreseeable future.

My brothers stayed on for a few more days as we'd planned, but without any of the joint Mercedes activities I'd been so excited for. There wasn't much in my life that excited me anymore, but I figured I just needed to get used to that.

Someday soon, I'd be going to prison. Excitement would become a thing of the past.

Honestly, I couldn't figure out how my brothers were able to forge ahead like life was normal. At every hour of the day, I wanted to crumble. I wanted to just give up. Willow and the strength of my family around me kept me going, even when nothing excited me and I'd stripped my life of the beautiful light that was Mercedes.

The day before my brothers were scheduled to leave, I got a tip from one of the few Fairchild-friendly contacts I'd made in the city. He'd heard of an office space that had cropped up and wanted to show me. Damian and Axel extended their trip so we could see it together. That same day I finally headed to Aurora's Nannies to wrap up the details there. I wasn't sure what Mercedes had told them—I wasn't even sure what *I'd* tell them. But I needed a new nanny for Willow, because apparently life *did* continue in the wake of the SEC telling you that you were a fraud.

So I bucked up and tried to carry on.

Without Mercedes.

Going back into Aurora's Nannies, months after my initial visit there, was surreal. I still remembered Mercedes stepping into Denise's office like it was yesterday, getting that first gut-punching glimpse of her after so many years. I'd known in that instant that everything would change. There was no way I could have her in my life and not be with her—even if I wanted to believe the opposite.

Which was yet another reason why I'd had to force her away.

I couldn't see her if I hoped to stay away from her. And she deserved more from life than I could offer her. She deserved happiness. I loved her too much to deny her a full life experience, complete with every last thing her heart desired. I didn't want to stain her life with my failures.

She didn't need to be dragged down by me too.

"Trace! Thank you for finally returning my calls. We were getting worried there for a bit," Denise said with a laugh as I stepped into her office. I sat in the chair facing her desk, wondering where to even begin.

"My apologies," I said slowly. "Things have been...complicated."

"Well I just hope that Mercedes's disappearance didn't leave you in the lurch." Denise sent me a meaningful look. "Truthfully, I was shocked when she quit. I know her mother made it seem like she was planning on getting married and leaving anyway, but Mercedes assured me she was here to stay. Except now she's gone." She shook her head, tutting to herself, as she clicked through screens on her computer.

I blinked a few times, trying to close the gaps on what Denise had said. "You called me because...she quit?"

"Yes, and I was worried that you didn't have any back-up care arranged for Willow. Have you been managing okay?"

Denise had no idea that I'd been looking after Willow with my mother's help while Mercedes went home to care for her grandmother. I'd never alerted Aurora's Nannies because it didn't bother me to keep paying her, or the agency, even though Mercedes had wanted to let them know she'd taken a leave of absence.

But now? I'd assumed Mercedes had applied for a change of position.

Not quit altogether.

"Do you know where she went?" I asked.

"Unfortunately no," Denise said, offering me a small smile. "Can I ask if things ended okay? Were there any issues we were unaware of?"

I shook my head, though on the inside, I was laughing hysterically at the ridiculousness of the question. *Issues? Only about three mil-*

lion. All my fault of course. "No, she was great. Willow and I loved her. I mean, well—" I cleared my throat, not exactly keen to out my romantic relationship with her employee "You know what I mean."

"Mercedes was certainly a favorite here," Denise said wistfully as she clicked her mouse. "Well, I'm sorry if there were any inconveniences. That is not our intention here at Aurora's, as you perhaps know by now. I've pulled up some alternate options. Let's look through the list and see if any of our other nannies strikes your fancy."

Denise and I combed through the options. None struck my fancy, because none were as striking as Mercedes. Not as gorgeous. Not as good a smile. Not as immediately refreshing. Not as fun to spend a morning with, reading quietly by a fire. But that was to be expected.

We landed on a lady named Addie. She had a warm smile, a proven track record with toddlers, and experience with high-security situations. Good enough for me. Denise set the schedule for her to make the first visit to my apartment, and I was released.

Exhausted. Lost. And missing Mercedes so much I thought I would die.

But as with all things in life, time went on. Wounds stopped throbbing. Well, that wasn't entirely true. My wounds continued to throb; I just learned how to look away from them better. Besides, once Axel and Damian and I scored the office in downtown Louisville, we had plenty to distract us.

And I needed it. Our new motto became *Just Shut Up and Try, Asshole.* It was the single most frequent thing Axel said to me, which meant it was now the official Fairchild phrase and the only way my brothers could combat my bouts of negativity. We said it amongst ourselves at least ten times a day as we renovated the ground floor office space from an art gallery to a wealth management firm.

The high-ceilinged, exposed brick space quickly became the newest outpost of Fairchild Enterprises. Complete with high-tech security systems, around-the-clock video surveillance, and a full team of bodyguards that would karate chop anyone's eyeballs out of their head if they tried anything suspicious.

In response to all the bad press about the SEC's decision about our practices, we called it TDA Solutions—Axel, Damian, Trace—only because T-A-D sounded like someone's nickname, and D-T-A sounded like a chemical one would be displeased to find in their cereal ingredients. So, TDA it was.

We weren't trying to be covert about it. We stated plainly on our website our affiliation with Fairchild Enterprises—that *we* were *them*. Just trying out a new business, in a new city, for new clients. I went into it expecting the tiniest trickle of new clients. I'd already built a small client base through my virtual-only approach, but I certainly didn't expect it to grow based on the welcome we'd received.

And something wild happened. Despite the SEC announcement, despite all the strife surrounding finding an office, despite the fact that I'd felt like the absolute lowest smear of shit for months on end...people flocked to us.

It turned out the Hendricks/Randolph circle was just one of many. And yes, many circles detested us. But plenty of other circles *loved* us, particularly our charitable activities. With a disclaimer on our website about the algorithm and a 100% transparency policy, our client roster grew so large and so quickly that Damian had to split his time between Louisville and New York. We had to hire a couple employees far sooner than we'd planned.

A full month of business-building in our new office showed me that life really *could* continue in the wake of the SEC announcement.

And that, though our future was uncertain, there was still a modicum of life to be lived in the interim.

I'd never felt so regretful. I wanted to punch myself in the face because I missed Mercedes so much and was furious with myself for handling things the way I had.

But it wasn't all tea lights and roses. Threats still filtered in. Slightly weaker than at their height during the spring, but they arrived nonetheless. One morning I showed up at our office to find the word SCUM spray painted in red across our front windows. It was a gut-punch. Deeply embarrassing. And *revealing*.

Damian's hi-def cameras caught the perpetrator in striking clarity. He'd paid us a visit around one a.m. on a Saturday morning. And although the idiot had hidden his face with a ski mask, he'd forgotten to hide one key detail. His UK class ring.

Fuck you very much, Caleb.

The police used the footage to track Caleb down and interview him, ultimately booking him for vandalism and destruction of property. It was a small victory, but important. We were finally getting answers to who was behind this months-long reign of annoyance—they weren't bold enough for a proper reign of terror. And if Caleb and his crew were the type of people to try to send a shitty bomb to my doorstep when I had a two-year-old in the house, then all bets were off.

Axel was visiting for a week about two months post-breakup when he forced me to confess that Mercedes was still haunting me. He placed his palms on my desk and zeroed in on me.

"Trace. Be real with me."

"Okay." I looked up at him, trying to figure out what he was getting at.

"Are you okay?"

I blinked, looking around the office. "...Yeah? Why do you ask?"

Axel gestured at me, as though this answered everything. "You look different. You look...gaunt. I don't know. Are you eating? I'm not around much, which I think helps me see it better. You look like you're wasting away."

I cleared my throat, shifting uncomfortably in my seat. My clothes *were* fitting looser these days. And I did forget to eat most days. But I knew that if I paused long enough to think about those things, the humiliation of losing Mercedes would eat me alive. Quickly followed by panic about the unknown, the future that awaited me on the other side of our SEC appeal.

"I forget to eat some days," I said with a shrug. "So sue me. We're busy. There's a lot to get done. There's a lot to...not think about."

Axel nodded, but he watched me suspiciously, as though he could hear between my words. I didn't want to vocalize how much I was still beating myself up for pushing Mercedes away. How much I still missed her. I knew my brothers relied on their better halves for support, comfort, love. I could have had that too.

But I didn't, because I was a fucking idiot who'd pushed away a beautiful woman who wanted to devote herself to me.

"Have you tried reaching out to Mercedes at all?" Axel sat on the corner of my desk, looking down at me intently.

I shook my head. "I think about it every day. I've never made the leap."

"Why not?"

I rubbed my face, sighing. "Because I feel like a complete failure. I pushed her away because of all the danger and the bleak outlook. Now the danger has lessened, but the outlook is still the same. Rationally, why would she take me back? If nothing has changed except it's slightly safer to be with me? I can't offer her anything better than I could before."

Axel sighed, rolling his eyes. "It's not about the offer, you numb-nut. It's because she's in love with you and you're in love with her."

"Yeah, well, love isn't enough to overcome some mistakes," I told him.

"Maybe not," Axel retorted. "But you guys have a lot more working for you than just love."

I hated how right he was. I thought about this nearly every moment of every day. Mercedes balanced me. She balanced the balancer. She gave me grace when the hardest critic of all—myself—wouldn't. I needed grace like I needed air, at least when it came to my own self-perception.

I needed *Mercedes* like I needed air.

Mercedes was the one place I could unwind and simply be. The only person in the world who I could sit comfortably with at six a.m. with a book and say nothing for hours, yet somehow feel like we'd been connecting deeper than we did with anyone else in the world.

She was the deepest, truest love of my life. And that fact was the reason I'd pushed her away.

Jesus Christ, Trace, you are truly stupid.

"I made a mistake," I whispered. "But I don't know how to fix it. We're living in an ongoing storm. I don't want to pull her into that again."

"But life isn't about avoiding storms," Axel insisted. "It's about finding the right person to weather the storm with."

"She can experience lesser storms," I told him, emotion clamping my throat. "They don't need to be this cataclysmic."

Axel laughed. "She's going to experience cataclysmic storms whether you're in her life or not. You can't protect her from that simply by removing yourself from her life. Sorry, bro. Besides, she *wanted* to be in your storm. And you built a wall around your tornado."

"My tornado?" I hefted with a laugh. "I'll allow it."

"Point is, she's a grown woman, and she made a decision about her own risks, but you wouldn't accept it."

I dropped my head, running my thumb along my eyebrow. "Maybe you're right. And maybe I'm ready to own up. But what am I supposed to do about it? It's been two months since I broke up with her. I was such an ass. I broke her heart."

"If Cora could break my heart and eight years could drag by, what makes you think you two can't find a way to make it work again?" Axel looked at me expectantly as his words sank in.

"But if she's moved on—" I started.

Axel scoffed. "Yeah, no. She loved you for years, and then immediately ditched her fiancé when you came back into the picture. I don't think she's moved on in two months. If it had been two decades, then I'd say maybe. But only maybe."

Axel's words stirred hope inside me. But it was hard to fully coax those embers into a flame. "I can't even fathom calling her up again after what happened. She'll hang up on me."

"Well then you should walk around the corner and—" Axel stopped talking suddenly, wincing. "Ah, shit. I wasn't supposed to say that."

"What?"

Axel waved me off, looking down at the ground. "Nothing."

"Axel? You can't pull that shit with me. What were you not supposed to say?"

He made a fist and tapped his mouth with it. "I'm really not supposed to say. I promised Cora I wouldn't."

I groaned as exaggeratedly as humanly possible. "You *cannot* do this to me after that intense and heartfelt conversation."

Axel pinched the bridge of his nose and looked like he might explode. When he straightened, he let out a gruff shout. "Ugh, fine! But you can't tell anyone I told you."

"I won't."

"This also means I love you the most." He jabbed his finger at me menacingly. "You got that? Forever more."

"Understood."

He seared me with this blue gaze. "Mercedes lives about two blocks from here."

I blinked about a million times. "Wh...h-...are you serious?"

"Cora told me."

"How does Cora know?" I asked slowly.

"They talk," Axel said with a look that said *duh*. "Often. Excessively, maybe. Like *sisters*."

"Wow." I leaned back in my chair, staring at the top of my desk as I processed this. "Just...wow."

"Listen. We're all in this together, right? As brothers. As a family. And if you really want to win back Mercedes," Axel said, leaning in closer to me, "I think you fucking will. In a way that only you can."

CHAPTER THIRTY-THREE
MERCEDES

I didn't see Trace again. At least not in real life.

I saw him on my phone almost every day, in the form of news updates I couldn't help myself from searching out, and by looking through pictures on my camera roll. Even though I couldn't be with Trace and Willow, I still needed to see them. Sometimes I woke up in the middle of the night thinking I forgot to check on Willow. Other times, I awoke soaked and needy, having dreamt of Trace's warm body covering mine.

But I'd made peace with the fact that I'd never get over him. I had all the proof I needed to know that Trace was just an indelible part of my heart. Even if he refused to allow me in, I'd spend the rest of my life in love with him.

I couldn't tell if that was pathetic or heartwarming. Maybe just insane. Or a fun combination of all three.

In a way, he was my anchor, even though he'd removed himself from my life. Even though my heart was still broken from the way he'd treated me, Trace still served as an inspiration to me.

Thanks to him, I finally moved out of my parents' house for good. Derby dresses included.

And sitting in the bedroom of the little room I rented downtown, my heart broken but my future finally solidifying, I found myself surrounded by acceptance letters from seven grad schools. Also thanks to Trace.

And I heard his voice in my head as I looked at the congratulatory letter from NYU. *But you love New York, Birdie.* I could imagine his warm smile as I decided that NYU was the school for me, practically hearing his accolades as I filled out the acceptance packet and returned it.

Even though he'd inspired me to do this, I was doing it under the assumption that I wouldn't see him again. I didn't plan on staying in his penthouse—even though it was directly above a bookstore. New York City was big enough for the both of us. I could follow my dreams while still respecting the space he so clearly wanted between us.

He wasn't the only one who wanted space from me though. My entire family wanted it on a permanent basis. After Trace dumped me in the Stakes Room, I'd marched my butt right back to my family to confront Caleb, which led to a confrontation with Jericho. I knew they had to be involved in Trace's about-face somehow. I pressured Caleb into sharing some of what he'd told Trace—I'd nearly gotten on my knees to beg before Caleb finally told me, *"I know it's been dangerous for Trace here in Louisville. He hasn't been welcomed. And I assured him that it would only get worse the longer he stayed here. With you."*

That had earned Caleb a slap across the face. Jericho had intervened, looking too amused by my outrage. Jericho had the gall to act surprised that I was upset by Caleb's comments. When I finally let Jericho know how done I was with his self-righteous superiority and his false moral compass, things had escalated in such a way that it still ran through my head on repeat:

"Don't act like you care about me at all," I told Jericho. "You can quit pretending now."

"Not sure how else you're supposed to care about a family," Jericho spat back.

"Try paying attention to your wife and daughter sometime?" My voice was nearly a shriek. I'd never felt this high on anger, on frustration. I no longer cared who was watching or what I said. I was ready to let it all hang out, consequences be damned. "That's a good place to start."

"Fuck you Sadie," Jericho snarled, stepping closer. "You're such a spoiled brat. I'm done trying to protect you. You think you know how shit works? You're wrong. You're fucking ignorant."

"I don't know how everything in life works," I shot back, the fierceness in my own voice surprising even me, "but I sure as fuck know that protecting family doesn't look like this." I gestured wildly to the family members in the area. "You guys have done nothing but try to control me, make my decisions for me."

"Because you're too goddamn stupid to make them on your own!" Jericho's shout rang out clearly over the din of voices.

"That's what you don't get, Jericho." This time, I stepped closer to him. Not away, as he was used to. "What you think about my intelligence doesn't matter. They're my decisions to make. Regardless of what you think of them, or me."

His gaze darkened. "Decision have consequences, you idiot. I made Trace disappear once. Don't make me do it a second time."

This time, I paused. He'd gotten me. The start of a sneer proved that he knew it. "What does that mean?"

"That you're fucking stupid. And I proved it. It was too easy to get rid of him. All I had to do was block him from your phone and all your socials—you never even fucking realized."

Rage simmered inside me, headed for a boil. "Were you behind the messages I apparently sent him back then, too?"

His cocky laughter was all I needed. The boiling anger inside me frothed over, scalding everything in its wake. Something primal unfurled. My fists clenched, my limbs moving of their own accord. I barely realized that I planned to punch him until my fist connected with his nose.

It was the first time I'd ever punched my brother, and I'd wager the last time, too. And it was in public, at the Kentucky Derby. Shock and outrage will do that to a lady, I supposed. My family, of course, was scandalized. They were more concerned about *Jericho's poor nose* than my lifetime of being gaslit, lied to, and controlled.

My father kicked me out. But I was already packing the rest of my things by the time he delivered the news. My mother didn't speak to me at all, instead just watched me coldly as I finished packing. Once my car was loaded, I elbowed my way back into the house and into Gramma Kay's room, where I hugged her and told her I loved her. She told me to "finally be happy." I wasn't sure if that was the last time I'd see her, but I took it as my cue to keep doing what I'd been doing. The internal churning, passion-related things, not the passive, wedding-chasing things. But as I drove away from the house that evening after the Derby, I knew it would be the last time I'd ever set foot in that house.

It hadn't taken long to find a place to land. I booked a cheap hotel for a couple nights until something cropped up. After an urgent social media post, I got a lead on a room for rent in a apartment—from none other than Renee, my old college friend who I'd run into with Trace at Willow's first psychologist appointment. She lived alone downtown and was more than happy to rent out her spare room to me, which took the edge off living on my own for the first time in my life. She rented to me at a below-market price, which I appreciated since I had very limited funds. I had money to get me through the summer and to New York to begin school, since every dollar I'd earned nannying for the past year and a half had gone into my savings. I also had a couple credit cards. But that was it.

But it was all I needed. I quit Aurora's Nannies because I had the money and wanted to start my next chapter. Even though it was also terrifying.

Renee's house was spacious. Bright. Well ventilated. Cute.

It was also located two blocks from Trace's new office, which felt like the biggest, cruelest *HA HA* from the heavens.

I spotted him once, accidentally, during my first month living with Renee. My favorite coffee shop was *on his block.* I watched him stride past the windows one morning, broad-shouldered and confident, while I shrank into the overstuffed armchair and prayed he didn't come inside. From then on, I began to skulk around my new neighborhood. I couldn't fathom the idea of running into him. I feared his reaction—or lack thereof. I feared finding out that he'd moved on or that he'd found some woman in the interim. I feared seeing Willow and not being able to hold her. I feared my heart being ripped apart all over again if we were ever to come face to face. Because it had to be something about me—that was the only thing that made sense. He must have been lying to me somewhere along the way. Because life had moved on for him. He could commit to business expansion, but not to me? It stung like salt in a fresh wound.

And I told all this to Cora and Jessa during our weekly video chats—which Renee eventually joined—when we all enjoyed the same wine and cheese and chocolates. Jessa selected the cheese and chocolate, Cora selected the wine and sent me a box of their selections, and I just sat back and enjoyed their curation. I loved these women who were practically my sisters now, even though the man who had brought us together was no longer part of the picture. We already were planning a Derby redo, where we'd go to the Kentucky Derby by ourselves and have the drunken, fun time we were meant to have. They also occasionally sent me pictures of Willow that Trace passed along, which were equal parts heartbreaking and beautiful.

These women were also there for me when Gramma Kay finally passed. Maddie had been the one to tell me, of course, along with the date and time of the funeral. I cried for a full day when I got the news. When the day of her funeral arrived, I went to the church to pay my respects and see her laid to rest. But Jericho wouldn't let me in. He'd hired some idiots to keep me away, and I wasn't strong enough to fight past them. They all but escorted me back to my car. The fact that he'd made me miss my grandmother's funeral and burial was still so raw for me—I'd never forgive him for it. Not in a million years. And when I told Maddie about his actions, she was similarly horrified.

To the point of beginning the process of filing for divorce. Jericho's actions around my grandmother's funeral were the final straw for her.

Even though this chapter of my life carried a lot of heartbreak, it was so freeing. There was a lot of growth tucked behind the pain. And I didn't plan on squandering any of the lessons or opportunities that came my way.

By the two-and-a-half-month mark, I'd finally begun to hit my groove. I spent my days preparing to go back to school in the form of researching information about the NYU campus, prepping for classes, doing suggested readings, and figuring out where the heck I was going to live. I worked part-time at a daycare center in the afternoons, helping with whatever needed done. And in the evenings, I usually spent some time in the park, watching people pass and reading my book of the day or walking in Cherokee Park, trying to not think about Trace and failing. Renee and I usually shared a glass of wine over dinner, which we took turns cooking.

And despite all the people no longer associating with me, despite all the love that had been unexpectedly lost, I was happy.

Because this life was mine. *Finally.*

Cora called one evening just as Renee and I were finishing up dinner. Renee had made a linguini with alfredo sauce and steamed broccoli, which we paired with a pinot noir from Oregon called Chateau L'Hiver. I didn't retain much from my college French classes, but I knew that translated to Winter Mansion. I took the last sip in my glass as I picked up Cora's call.

"Hello there, Cora," I said as I tucked the phone between my ear and shoulder. "What's up?"

"You got a minute?"

"For you? Always." I loved that this famous, powerful, and slightly contentious woman was part of my inner circle now. *Especially* since we shared the painful details of having broken up with our families. Cora had even turned me on to her therapist, who I was now calling once a week.

"I found out a detail that I think you need to know," she said with a sigh. "Trace is now aware you live nearby."

I blinked, looking at my empty wine glass. "O...kay."

"Axel swore he wouldn't mention it, but it slipped out, he says. According to Axel, Trace was having yet another sad-sack session about how much he misses you."

I blinked more rapidly this time. "He misses me?" It was a relief, since over two months had gone by without a single word from the man. In my darker moments, my brain tried to tell me that he'd never actually felt anything for me, that it had all been a convenient illusion.

"I'd say he more than misses you. According to Axel, Trace doesn't look good."

I squeezed my eyes shut. That hurt my heart to hear. "Thanks for telling me. I doubt I'll hear from him at this point. I'm about to leave for New York anyway—there's almost no point anymore."

This was what I *wanted* to believe. Truthfully, I knew that no amount of time or distance mattered when it came to Trace Fairchild. I needed to accept that we were done, because clearly Trace hadn't seen in me what I'd seen in him. Yes, he could go to prison, possibly for a long time. But Axel wasn't driving away Cora over it. Damian wasn't driving away Jessa over it. Why didn't Trace see any worth in the two of us staying together despite his rocky future? My deepest fears and insecurities told me it was because he didn't actually want to be with *me*.

I believed it so much that I was already trying to mentally prepare myself for the next few years without him while still being deeply in love with him.

Just like the first time.

Renee and I spent the next day, a Saturday, window shopping, and that evening as we were prepping dinner, a knock sounded on the apartment door. We exchanged a glance.

"Are you expecting anyone?" she asked.

"No, are you?"

She shook her head, jerking her chin toward the raw chicken she was dipping in batter. "You mind getting the door?"

"Of course." I left the lettuce I'd been chopping. As I headed for the door, my stomach wrenched violently. I peered through the peephole to see who was on the other side.

And suddenly everything ground to a halt inside me.

My organs paused. My lungs shriveled. My heart took a deep, wrenching gasp.

Trace Fairchild was on the other side of that door.

I swallowed hard, turning slowly to Renee. Her eyes widened when she noticed me. "Good God, Mercedes, are you okay?"

I shook my head and walked toward her on wobbly legs. "I can't open the door," I whispered. "Can you?"

She was already washing her hands. "Okay. Do I even want to? Who's out there?"

"Trace," I whispered.

"Aw, shit." She dried her hands, rolling her lips in.

"I can't see him," I told her. "But maybe you can talk to him and just see what he wants. I'm going to go hide in my room. I'm not here. Don't let him in. I-I-I can't." I bolted for my bedroom, locking the door behind me for good measure. I wanted to see him as much as I didn't want to see him. It was a confusing conflict, but maybe the undertones of his voice would satisfy me enough for now.

Trace knocked again. Renee pulled open the door, and I could practically see her cocky stance as she greeted him with, "Oh, look who it is."

Trace's reply was muffled by the door and the distance. But the rich baritone was enough to take my breath away.

"Please," I heard him say a moment later.

"She's not here. She doesn't want to see you. And that's all I can say. Goodbye." The door slammed a moment later. I didn't dare unlock my door until Renee finally called out, "It's safe to come out. I sent him away."

I clicked open the lock and drifted back out toward the kitchen in a daze. I looked at the door like he might knock again at any moment. "What did he say?"

Renee tipped her head toward a bouquet of flowers on the table near the front door. "He left those. And said he needs to talk to you. He asked where he could find you, and I told him you weren't here."

"Thank you." I headed for the flowers, tears coming to my eyes as soon as I spotted what was wrapped up in the delicate paper. "Oh my God," I whispered. Six still-unfurled peonies, with a tag around the stems that read *Command Performance*. There was a note tucked into the paper. Trace's chicken scratch read:

Pushing you away was the biggest mistake of my life. Please, can we talk?

Tears spilled out of my eyes as I carried the flowers into the kitchen. Renee's brows drew together. "He got you unripe flowers?"

I laughed softly. "Not unripe. They're my favorite flower. And as soon as I cut them and put them in water, they'll start to open."

I sliced the bottoms of the stems at an angle, filled a vase with water, and set them on the far edge of the island. "Now we wait," I told Renee.

"These better be good," she grumbled, stacking breaded chicken pieces on a plate.

"Oh, these are better than good." I returned to my lettuce washing, my gaze drifting back to the bouquet. "These are the best, and it's a show only we'll see."

The flowers were the first. Next came the texts, followed by more personal flower deliveries. My plan was to continue ignoring the calls and live in a sea of peonies. I was doing well until Trace called one evening the following week. I was walking in Cherokee Park in the heat of July dusk when the call came. As I looked at my phone, it slipped from my hand, and I accidentally swiped the call on.

I stared at it in shock as the sky blazed orange around me. I blinked a few times, unsure whether I should hang up or try talking to him.

"Uh, hello?" I said it without the speakerphone on and without holding it up to my face. Why did it feel like both the first time I'd ever used a phone *and* the first time I'd ever talked to Trace? I finally lifted the phone to my ear and repeated myself. "Hello?"

"Mercedes."

And there it was. That familiar baritone, winding its way through my veins like a drug and gliding over my skin like velvet. I squeezed my eyes shut, tears already waiting for me.

"Wh...What do you want?" My heart was pounding and I wiped a tear away. I looked out at the sparkling river. A tugboat moved past, slow and steady, while some late-evening runners jogged past me on the sidewalk.

"I just want to talk to you." A deep sigh rumbled out of him. "I fucked up so bad I can't stand it. I...I can't believe you answered. I didn't think you would. Shit. I'm not prepared."

I wiped away another tear. Hearing Trace stumble over his words was cute. But it didn't make up for the way he'd treated me. It didn't make up for him just disappearing for two and a half months without a single call or text. For ripping Willow out of my life, for casting me away.

"It's okay. Answering was a mistake. I'm not ready to talk to you either." I swiped off the call before I could think better of it, shoving it back into my purse with trembling hands. I took a moment to wipe the tears off my face and straighten my back before I started walking again.

Every part of me wanted Trace Fairchild back in my life.

But not at the expense of my dignity.

I'd given pieces of that away for so long that I needed to make damn sure Trace—or anyone else trying to come into my life—was vetted, certified, and vouched for.

Plus there was nothing wrong with making him grovel.

I hurried back to the apartment, wondering if I'd run into Trace there on the landing. But the hallway was quiet as I entered, and Renee was gone, off to visit her other friends that evening. I paced the apartment alone, too keyed up from my brief conversation with Trace to truly rest or unwind. And then a text came in.

TRACE: I get that you don't want to talk to me. But I'd like to show you something that might help explain things. It will be dropped off at your house tomorrow morning. Let me know what you think...if you want.

Tomorrow morning? Like this wasn't the most eternal cliffhanger of my life. I tried to distract myself with wine and a book, but my mind kept sliding back to Trace. *What will he send? What could possibly explain things? How much longer are you going to be able to resist him calling or texting or randomly bringing flowers?*

I couldn't resist him forever. Not when my soul craved Trace like the sun craved the sky.

Somehow, I fell asleep that night. And I was up at seven a.m. the next day, peeking out my door every ten minutes for the next couple of hours until a delivery worker finally knocked.

He consulted his delivery sheet. "Birdie Hendricks?"

A blush heated my cheek. "That's me."

He handed over a bubble wrap mailer. "Have a great day."

I slipped back inside the apartment and shut the door gently. Whatever Trace had sent, it was light. Much lighter than I had expected...though I hadn't known what to expect. Apologies and explanations seemed much heavier than whatever this was. I went to the couch and snuggled under a blanket, ready to dig into his explanation. I tore open the package and pulled out a very basic black notebook. As I opened to the first page, I realized Trace had sent me his journal.

Thumbing through the pages, which were soft and textured like they'd come from recycled fabric, I could tell this was essentially Trace's scratch pad. Dark ink musings stained every page, most of them business-related. Random numbers had been scrawled at the tops or bottoms of pages, some with question marks after them. But when I got to the back of the notebook, I discovered why he'd sent it.

Trace had drawn out full-page grids, filled in by hand. The left-hand page was titled "What Do I Want To Give Mercedes?"

And then he'd listed everything.

The life of her dreams

A winery named after her (Birdie Brews / Bird & Bear / You know what, we'll figure out the name later)

Wine trip to Chile

Cozy cabin getaway in Swiss Alps—solo if she wants

Babies, whenever she's ready

So many happy memories

A library magazines will interview her about

Rolling staircase for said library

Office in each residence for when she's studying for Master's degree

More of those green sweaters

New memorable Christmas vacation every single year

Peony farm in Alaska. Hand-picked peonies every June.

Girls' getaway just her and Willow every spring

The actual wedding of her dreams, every last detail approved by her, whenever she's ready, possibly in said cozy cabin or during wine getaway

The list went on for so long that I was laughing and crying by the end of it. But that didn't prepare me for what was on the opposite page. Trace had scrawled at the top "The Price Of My Infamy." And he broke down, line-by-line, the literal and figurative cost of every negative swirling in his life. Just like a true financial planner and investment genius would do.

I couldn't even follow some of the math. But he'd assigned a value to his prison term at varying lengths—whether it turned out to be five years, ten years, or fifteen years. He assigned a cost to prison commutes, unpredictable mail service and phone communication, he'd put numbers to the stress of being estranged from my family, from potentially bearing his children and raising them as a single mother while also having no familial support from my side.

The presentation was dizzying. A financial forecast as detailed and specific as anything Trace might draw up for a client. And glimpsing this insanely detailed spreadsheet of negative value stemming from what awaited him from the SEC decision and me if I threw my lot in with him was a heartbreaking look into how his brain operated throughout this mess.

At the bottom left-hand corner, he'd written in red ink: "Not a financially or emotionally sound decision for Mercedes to pursue a relationship with me at this time. Mercedes is better off finding someone else."

I swallowed a knot in my throat, looking back at the left-hand page. Looking back at everything he wanted to give to me. To do with me. To experience with me.

And that's where I knew the math was wrong.

He hadn't given enough weight to the value of being in love with him. He'd only calculated what he was taking away from me, not what his mere existence was giving me.

One cabin trip to the Swiss Alps, in his arms, was worth whatever cost he'd assigned to his infamy.

I turned the page. More awaited me.

Trace had written a financial assessment and recommendation.

Based on the financial breakdown and accompanying projections, Mercedes's investment in Trace is ill-advised at this time. Trace's investment in a 25-year-old with a full life ahead of her is ill-advised at this time.

But an advisement cannot account for future market fluctuations or unexpected changes of heart. Mercedes is a grown woman who has had too many people telling her what to do with her life. Trace made a decision for her, and he would like to retract this decision and let Mercedes speak for herself. Because despite all the evidence and projections, Trace's final recommendation is that being together makes more sense than being apart. Love has a value that cannot be calculated.

204 Clay Street. 6PM tonight.

CHAPTER THIRTY-FOUR
TRACE

I FELT LIKE I was going to puke.

I hadn't been this nervous in ages. It was five thirty, and I'd been checking my wristwatch compulsively for the past ten minutes.

"You still have a half hour," Axel told me, squeezing my shoulders from behind. I sat in a chair, my knee bouncing wildly, as time crept toward six o'clock. "There's nothing you can do but hurry up and wait."

"She could be early," I told him.

"Well if she is, your punctual ass has everything and everyone assembled. So it will still go off without a hitch," Axel reminded me. "Though I guess I should say *almost* everyone. You didn't invite Ferdinand?"

I smirked. "If only it wouldn't kill him. No matter how humid it gets in here with all the drinking, it will never be enough for my Ferdinand."

Axel laughed as he strolled away. He and Damian were here, along with Cora, Jessa, my mom, Willow, Seven, two other guards, and Renee. I'd invited Mercedes's sister-in-law, Maddie, who Renee said I should reach out to as the one Fairchild-friendly person on the Hendricks side. I'd also printed out a photo of Mercedes's Gramma Kay and framed it, setting it on the bar facing the door.

I'd rented out a private room in a wine bar for the evening, a hip place near downtown that had impressive walls of wine bottles and a cute gravel-and-wood patio filled with fairy lights and picnic tables. I'd also chosen this place because they had petit Verdot from Chile *and* they had lobster bisque on the small plates menu. Mercedes was going to love it. As long as she didn't turn right around and walk away.

The sound of conversation floating from other parts of the wine bar lulled me into contemplation. I'd sent her my breakdown, the driving force behind my decision to push her out of my life, because I felt like it would help illuminate why I'd made that decision.

But not knowing exactly how she'd responded to it was *killing me*.

I stopped Cora as she walked by. "You think she'll come, right?"

"For sure." Cora nodded, rolling in her red-painted lips. "I think, at least."

I sighed, my gaze swinging back to the main door, visible outside the private room. "This is going to kill me."

"I talked to her this afternoon," Renee said, drifting up to the table to pop a cheese cube in her mouth. "She said she was planning on coming."

"Okay. That's good." My gaze didn't move from the door. My adrenaline response was at the level of preparing to jump off a cliff. Or asking her to marry me. Or both at the same time.

I surged to my feet, needing to expend this nervous energy somehow. I paced the room, looking at the decorations we'd hung. We'd all created banners with different personal phrases on them. For example, mine said, "I'm smart but sometimes I can be so dumb. Love, Trace."

Cora's said, "Join our family now please!"

Axel's said, "The Fairchilds are more than fair. They're the best!"

Jessa's said, "We love you so much. Automatic Sister Wife."

Maddie hung toward the back with her daughter Grace, where Willow curiously poked at Grace's cheeks while my Mom laughed and snapped pictures.

"Somebody tell me the plan again if she just tells me to fuck off and leaves?" I cracked my knuckles as Damian came up to my side, patting my back.

"That's when you hunt her down. Wherever she goes."

"God, that sounds ominous," Axel said, joining us as he popped a shrimp into his mouth. "Are you a sociopath, Damian? Because that sounded like some sociopathic shit."

Damian sent him a flat look. "Not serial killer style hunting, you oversized lugnut. Like, romantic hunting."

"Like when you followed Jessa back to our hometown?" I asked with a wry grin.

"Exactly. And then we had a very lovely make-out session in the playground down the street from her brother's house and all was well." He offered me a smile and a shrug. "Though I don't think you'll have to do so much chasing. She's right here in Louisville, and she loves you. Despite the fact that you were a jackass."

"I appreciate the vote of confidence."

"We're all jackasses, for clarification," Damian added.

"Speak for yourself." Axel winked as he squeezed my shoulders, jostling me before wandering away. I kept vigil on the front door, terrified that I'd miscalculated something along the way. I'd done so many calculations on this I didn't think there was any mathematical stone I'd left unturned. Willow toddled up to me, lifting her hands so that I'd pick her up. I'd put her in a pink dress with tulle at the bottom and white buckle shoes. Mom had helped me get her hair pulled back with a little pink bow. She smiled up at me and patted my shoulder. "Dada."

"Are you comforting me in my time of stress?" I smiled down at her, suddenly overcome with tenderness. I kissed the top of her head. "You are the sweetest. Thank you. Uncle Trace feels better."

Seven came up to me, tipping his head toward the main doors. "She's a half block away."

All my anxiety came barreling back, this time with a few of its friends. I drew a deep breath. "She's almost here, guys," I told the rest of our party. Jessa pumped her fists, which Willow tried to imitate, much to the delight of our guests. Jessa and Willow did that a few times together until I noticed the front door opening.

A flash of glittering blonde hair.

High-waisted camel shorts and an off-the-shoulder, mint green T-shirt.

Mercedes.

I stood rooted to my spot as I watched her confer with the host near the front door. Then she was pointed this way. I froze. All I could do was watch and repeat to myself *I love you I love you please don't go.*

Time slowed to a stop as she crossed the threshold of the private room. Shock rippled across her face as her gaze found me and Willow. Her lips parted, a hand coming up to cover her mouth. Around me, everyone shouted "Surprise!", which I was thankful for, because my voice had disappeared entirely, along with my ability to function, move, or breathe.

Willow shrieked with delight, wriggling out of my arms. "Mama!" She bolted for Mercedes, who bent down and welcomed Willow into her arms with a big, extended hug. Mercedes buried her face in Willow's hair, but I could tell she was crying. No, sobbing.

I drifted their way, though I wasn't sure how, since my legs had been replaced with stone pillars. I knelt down beside them, pressing a hand to Mercedes's back.

"Birdie," I whispered, unsure what else I was supposed to say other than *I love you.* "I love you."

Her shoulders shook with more sobs and when she looked up at me, her eyes were shimmering with tears. Shock and delight mingled on her beautiful face, and it was all I could do not to kiss her and bring her into my arms.

"What is going on here?" she asked, sniffing. She looked past me and waved with her free hand not clutching Willow. "Hi, guys."

Everyone cheered.

"We're here because I love you. Because we all love you. Because I'm sorry. Because I fucked up and I desperately need to make it right. And, well, because you're part of our family." We stayed crouched on the floor, our heads drifting together until our foreheads touched. I was lost in her green gaze and I couldn't pull myself out. Didn't *want* to pull myself out. "Did you read my analysis?"

She nodded gently, the seal of our foreheads unbroken. "Yeah, I did. It was a fun journey through your brain."

I smiled. "Well, now you're aware of all the risks. You saw the way I tried to make the best decision for both of us. But sometimes the best decisions on paper aren't the best decisions in real life. I was letting fear rule me. Fear speaks my language—logic and reason. And it spoke a lot louder than love."

Mercedes's chin wobbled as she watched me. I grabbed her chin between my thumb and forefinger, searching her shimmering green gaze. "I don't work right without you, Birdie. I lost you the first time, but I pushed you away the second time. I thought losing you a third time, if I go to prison, would be the end of me."

"But you won't ever lose me," she whispered, her voice thick through tears. "Because even when you push me away, I'm still yours. There's no other man for me but you, Bear."

"Please take him back, Mercedes," Axel called out. "He's insufferable when he's moping."

"Also we really, really, really want you to be our sister-in-spirit," Jessa added with a hopeful smile.

I laughed and ran my thumb along her cheek, wiping away a few spilt tears. "You heard it from them. Now let me formally make my request." I shifted so that I was down on one knee in front of her. She watched me, her shoulders shaking with laughter, face beaming with joy. "This bear needs his bird. You are the fuel for my rocket. Mercedes Hendricks, will you give me a second—I mean, third chance?"

"Third time's the charm," she said, and then she pressed her lips to mine in a long, tender kiss.

When our kiss broke, I stood and helped Mercedes up with Willow in her arms. "All right, guys, I've got one more chance. She said yes. Not gonna fuck this one up."

Everyone around us cheered again. Mercedes laughed and dabbed at her eyes as our friends and family filtered toward us to hug us both in turn. It was a blur of happy tears and sweet words. Willow didn't leave Mercedes's arms, and I didn't leave Mercedes's side. Someone uncorked champagne, and then suddenly we were all lifting glasses toward the ceiling.

"To the next chapter," Axel said.

"To turning the page and creating an even better story," Cora added.

"To third chances and finding your true family," I finished up. "Because the trials and tribulations of life can only be endured with less logic and more love." It was the truest thing I'd ever said. And it was the one thing I couldn't have properly accounted for in any of my analyses. There was no value that encompassed this woman. The way she loved me. All the ways we were meant for each other.

Mercedes looked up at me with a wobbly chin. We all clinked glasses. Before I drank, I swooped down and captured her lips in a kiss.

"I love you, Birdie," I whispered against her pretty pout. "I have since you were nineteen. And I'll love you till you're a thousand and nine."

"Which would make you a thousand and fifteen," she added with a laugh. "*Quite* the distinguished older man." She pushed up onto her tiptoes and pressed a kiss to my lips. "I love you, Bear. I loved you when it didn't make sense and I'll love you until I forget who you are."

Willow clapped her hands as she watched us, her eyes wide. "Mama n' Dada."

"Our sweet girl," I said, pulling them both into a hug, pressing kisses to the tops of both their heads. It was moments like these when the doubts tried to creep in and tell me how much I'd be missing if I went to prison. How hard it would be not to be able to hold these two each day, to wake up to their smiling faces.

But I wouldn't cut the joy of today short just because of the unknowns of tomorrow.

"Let's eat some lobster bisque with our family," I told her.

She gasped, excitement shining in her face. "There's bisque here?"

"Of course. It was the first requirement. Well, that and the petit Verdot, which is coming later. And the ability to use a private room in order to beg my woman for forgiveness. And, of course, free rein to hang these custom banners." I gestured toward them behind us.

She twisted to read them, a big smile pulling at her pretty lips. When she faced me, joy poured from her and so much tenderness filled her eyes that I thought I might choke on my own happiness.

"I know we've been reconciled for approximately ten minutes, but just know, I am now unhinged. If you aren't careful, I'll ask you to marry me by the end of the evening," I told her.

Laughter poured out of her. My smile was so big my cheeks hurt.

"Well, you are my rocket, after all," she said with a wink.

"Also what you'll come like later," I murmured into her ear.

She laughed and swatted at my chest just as Axel came up to us. "Okay, listen, I love that you two are being all lovey-dovey over here, but we need to chat up this wonderful woman you so rudely pushed away from us, mm-kay?"

"Fine. Fine." I held my palms up in submission. "She's yours."

Mercedes sent me a toothy grin as she danced away with Willow in her arms, following Axel into the group conversation happening with the rest of our guests. Mercedes and Maddie hugged, followed by my mom, while I stood off to the side and took it all in like the teary-eyed sap that I was.

This. Right here.

Laughter and warmth—with bisque and Verdot around the corner. Sunny evenings. Axel giving me shit. A happy, adjusted Willow and so many quips and conversations and funny exchanges.

These were the moments I needed to hang onto.

Not just for whatever scary future awaited me, but because this was the only thing that mattered.

EPILOGUE
MERCEDES

"Hey, Bear." I lodged the phone between my ear and my neck as I glided out of the grand double doors of the psychology building on the NYU campus. I'd just finished my morning seminar, and I was headed for my favorite coffee shop a couple blocks away to get caught up on reading and homework. "Where are you?"

"Heading wherever *you* are." His sexy chuckle through the phone sent my core clenching, like it always did. It seemed that no amount of sex with this man would ever truly sate me. We'd been living in honeymooners' bliss for the past three months with no signs of it slowing down.

Trace was commuting between Louisville and NYC every so often so that he could attend the requisite custodial hearings for Willow. Ian had received a five year prison sentence, which meant Trace would secure permanent custody without issue. He'd procured a new nanny for Willow here in NYC, a wonderful woman named Harietta, who also happened to be the wife of Damian's driver, Legs. How he got *that* name, I'd never know. Apparently it was a well-kept secret in the Fairchild inner circle and I needed to complete a certain number of rides with Legs in order to get the full story. But their couple nickname was Hari-Legs, which made me giggle every time I heard it come up.

"Meet me at the coffee shop I've been telling you about. Then you can finally check it out," I told him, weaving through throngs of pedestrians as I walked along E. 8th. *Black & Brewtiful* was my new favorite place, as much for the chill ambiance and book-worm-friendly chairs as the wide range of strong drinks I now need-ed as a graduate student in psychology. "I've been hanging out with that new barista each time I go in and she's so cool, Trace. There's something about her. I think she might be my first real friend in New York."

"Oh yeah? What's her name? Will I meet her today?"

"I'll see if she's working," I told him. "Her name is Jordan. She's like...my opposite. But I feel so called to her. I can't wait for you to meet her."

"Sounds great. Hey, Axel and Damian are joining me today. We went out to meet a client this morning so they're with me. We can all check out your favorite coffee shop together. We'll be there in a half hour, Birdie." His smooth baritone sent shivers up my spine. "Love you."

I told him I loved him and hung up, smiling to myself as I con-tinued my trek to the coffee shop. It was an exceptionally warm September day, but the hints of the upcoming fall were beginning to flourish. Leaves had started to turn on our visits to Central Park. Nights were chilly, some of them even requiring sweaters and leg-gings. My Basic Girl Autumn was almost here—which was just a prelude to my favorite time of year, Cozy Bookworm Winter.

I sighed happily as I spotted *Black & Brewtiful's* boldly lettered sign and the tall, tinted windows. The scent of espresso washed over me as I entered, the chill murmur of conversation a welcome respite from the chaos and noise of Manhattan streets. I loved living in New York City—the fascinating characters on every street corner, the isolated togetherness, the towering buildings that seemed to cradle you as much as they challenged you. But as a bookworm introvert, I loved the quiet spaces tucked away where I least expected. The garden nooks on the roofs of skyscrapers. The calm corners deep inside architectural behemoths, where you could still hear a pin drop and the freeway seemed like it was on another planet. The way the view from Trace's penthouse—where I lived now, because it was only a few blocks from NYU, and I loved the man so much it made my heart ache—made it seem like the rest of New York was caught inside the snow globe, and we were the observers causing the storm.

"Mercedes! There you are!" Jordan's voice was the first to reach me as I approached the glossy black coffee bar. She was a punk rock angel—at least that's how I saw her. She was everything edgy my conservative southern upbringing had lacked. She had striking blue eyes that seemed to pierce my soul. Her dark blonde hair was swept back into a low bun, the most conservative thing about her. Her bare arms showcased tattoos I would have stared at if we'd been anywhere else. Shiny jewelry dotted her face—her septum was pierced, along with her nose, and a whole array of earrings lined the cartilage in her ear. We couldn't look more different, yet we'd found out during a previous visit that she and I were the same age. She smiled warmly at me, the expression at odds with the hard edges of her appearance. "I was wondering when you'd come in today."

"Class ran a little long," I told her, rummaging in my crossbody bag for my wallet. "I know I'm usually here earlier on a Wednesday."

"What's it gonna be today, sugar?" she asked, assuming her stance behind the register.

I smirked. "That sounds like what people say where I'm from. Are you from New York City originally?"

She scoffed. "Definitely not. I'm from Kentucky."

"No way!" I slapped the countertop. "Me too! What part?"

"The tiniest town you've probably never heard of," she assured me.

"My boyfriend is from Kentucky too," I told her. "He'll be stopping by later with his brothers—who are *also* from Kentucky. What a small world. We should start a Kentucky group here."

"Maybe a Kentucky recovery group," she said with a smirk.

"Yeah, I could use one of those." I laughed, pulling my credit card out. The Fairchild credit card, with my name on it and everything. "I'll take my usual. An oat milk latte made better by your prowess and attention behind the espresso machine."

Her grin was ear-to-ear. "See, this is why you're my favorite customer."

"That, and now we know it's also because we're both secretly from Kentucky." I inserted my card in the reader as she started my drink. Nobody was behind me in line so I lingered near the espresso machine. "How long have you lived here? I just moved here about a month ago and I'm still not used to it."

"It takes most people about a year to get used to it," she said. "If they stick it out that long. This city can really chew you up and spit you out. You need to be a certain type of masochist to really enjoy it. I've been here going on four years now. Came here after getting my undergraduate and never left."

I nodded, thinking about her words. "I never really considered myself a masochist, but...I guess there's a first time for everything."

"Everyone's a masochist in New York." Jordan nodded as she pulled the shot of espresso for my latte. "Just give it time." She finished off my drink and handed it to me in an oversized clay mug at the end of the coffee bar.

"I'm not sure if that's a threat or a promise," I murmured, taking the big cup into my hands.

Jordan's laugh was sharp and genuine. "Maybe a little of both?"

I took my drink and wandered to the nearest comfortable seat, which was right near the coffee bar and Jordan. I settled into the oversized armchair, set my latte down, and rummaged through my backpack for my class materials.

Trace showed up less than ten minutes later. He and his brothers walked in, the formidable trio they'd always been, commanding the attention of everyone inside the coffee shop. Dressed in their typical designer duds, business casual to the extreme, they didn't necessarily look any different than anyone else on Wall Street or working in finance in Manhattan. It was just that special *je ne se qua*. The air of men who'd started from nothing, built their empire from scratch, only have it threatened.

As Trace would say, his garden of fucks was barren.

And *that* was the Fairchild special sauce.

"There you are, Birdie." Trace took his sunglasses off as he headed my way. I popped up from my seat to wrap my arms around his neck. The familiar scent of him—spice and leather—wrapped around me, soothing any stress I'd accumulated so far today. A low, happy hum rumbled out of him.

"God, I've missed you in these three and a half hours we've been apart," he murmured.

"I miss you even when I'm next to you," I returned.

He pressed a kiss to my lips through the laughter. "That one wins."

Damian and Axel stood behind Trace, waiting for their chance to say hello.

"Hi, boys," I said with a little giggle. Damian saluted. Axel just smiled and shook his head. "How was the meeting today?"

"Boring," Axel said. "I'm ready to over-caffeinate myself."

"I can help with that. Let me get it. I've been wanting you guys to meet Jordan." I led the brothers to the coffee bar, where someone was currently placing an order. "I just found out today she's from Kentucky too."

Trace squinted at the menu, his hands propped on his hips. "Small world."

Damian squinted at Jordan, seemingly studying her. "Huh."

Axel's gaze, too, had landed on Jordan. "What was her name?

"Jordan." I laughed, swatting Trace's arm. "Wouldn't it be funny if she was from the same town as y'all? I asked her where she was from, but she just said it was a tiny town."

"Yeah. Funny." Damian's gaze hadn't moved from Jordan, and I was beginning to sense that something was...amiss.

"Do you know her last name?" Axel asked, similarly staring.

I shook my head. "Haven't gotten that far, I'm afraid."

By now, Trace had caught on to the strange energy emanating from Axel and Damian. His gaze followed their line of sight, landing on Jordan. "You guys..."

Damian cleared his throat, as if he was breaking a spell. "It can't be," he said in a low voice, more to Axel than anyone else. "Even though she looks like..."

The person in front of us moved to the far end of the coffee bar, which meant it was our turn at the register. I stepped up, smiling brightly at Jordan. "I'm baaack."

Her gaze moved to me, a smile curling her lips, until her gaze hit the men around me. The bright smile on her face sank away slowly, bit by bit.

I had no idea what was going on, but there was no way out of this but *through*. "Jordan, I'd like you to meet Trace, my boyfriend, and his two brothers, Axel and Damian."

Jordan went pale, her gaze jerking away.

Now something was seriously wrong. Something uneasy tightened the air, made my stomach feel like an elastic band.

Damian placed a hand on the countertop, leaning toward her. "What's your last name?"

Jordan shook her head, gaze fastened to something unknown behind the countertop. "It doesn't matter. What can I get for you guys?" Her normal verve was gone.

Axel looked over at Damian. An impossibly awkward silence filled the air. Trace cleared his throat. "I'll have an espresso. I hear you make them really well. Mercedes talks about how great you are."

Jordan nodded, punching the order into the register, emotionless. "Okay. Anything else?"

Axel stared at Jordan so hard it made *me* embarrassed. "You look so familiar."

"Anything else?" Jordan asked, just as a male co-worker came up to her with an envelope in his hands.

"Haynes, this is for you," he grunted, handing her the envelope. Jordan's cheeks flushed and her gaze fell to the envelope in her hands. Understanding boomed through me just as Axel leaned forward.

"It *is* you," he said. But it wasn't accusatory. It was revelatory. Shocked. Maybe even elated. Damian rubbed at a temple, his eyes shimmering with tears. Axel went on, "Jordan. It's us. Your *brothers*."

THE END

Find out more about Jordan and the bodyguard she falls for in the final installment of the series, THE PRICE OF FOREVER.

Have you read the FREE prequel to the Bad Boys series? Check out The Price of a Promise to see the brothers before they became wealthy (and to get Axel and Cora's backstory!)

Need more brothers? Check out my Winter Harbor series and get to know the alpha Winters brothers as they settle their father's estate and confront a fractured family dynamic. Start with book 1, The Bastard Heir.

ACKNOWLEDGEMENTS

A thousand THANK YOUs go out to the following incredible people:

Angela Howard-Seely, for always giving me beta reads on an excruciatingly tight turnaround;

Whitley, Becca, and the rest of my author/beta/brainstorming crew — thank you for always being there to hash out plot details;

My editor Elisabeth Nelson, who puts up with my weird repetitive words and bizarre Easter eggs (not to mention my consistent tardiness despite my best attempts to not always be four weeks behind);

My husband, for countless evenings taking the children somewhere else so I could focus on writing or editing;

All my readers and fans who have spared a kind word or shared their excitement with me. Those things are fuel for me. THANK YOU.

LET'S STAY CONNECTED!

Stay connected with me via my newsletter (http://bit.ly/EL-newsletter), where I share teasers, sales, and other exciting news.

Or join my Facebook reader group, EMBER LEIGH'S BLOSSOMS, to hang out up-close and personal! Early looks at new covers, exclusive access to ARC sign-ups, and more.

FACEBOOK
INSTAGRAM
GOODREADS
BOOKBUB
http://www.emberleighromance.com/

And before you go...

Please consider leaving an honest review about this book! Even just
a few words or a line mean so much to us authors.

ALSO BY EMBER LEIGH

THE BAD BOYS OF WALL STREET
The Price of Revenge
The Price of Passion
The Price of Infamy
The Price of Forever

WINTER HARBOR
(co-written with Whitley Cox)
The Bastard Heir
The Asshole Heir
The Rebel Heir
The Matchmaking Heirs

THE BAYSHORE SERIES
Make Me Lose
Make Me Fall
Make Me Yours
Make Me Choose
Make Me Hot
Make Me Smile

THE BREAKING SERIES

Breaking the Rules

Changing the Game

Breaking the Sinner

Breaking the Habit

Breaking the Fall